W9-AZT-780

PEACHTREE CITY
PLAN TO STAY™

THE FALLEN

Also by Jassy Mackenzie

Random Violence
Stolen Lives

THE FALLEN

JASSY MACKENZIE

SOHO
CRIME

Published by
Soho Press, Inc.
853 Broadway
New York, NY 10003

Library of Congress Cataloging-in-Publication Data

Mackenzie, Jassy.
The fallen / Jassy Mackenzie.
p. cm.
ISBN 978-1-61695-065-1
eISBN 978-1-61695-066-8
1. De Jong, Jade (Fictitious character)—Fiction. 2. Women
private investigators—Fiction. 3. Murder—Investigation—
Fiction. 4. Saint Lucia—Fiction. I. Title.
PR9369.4.M335F35 2012
823'.92—dc23
2011042050

Printed in the United States of America

10 9 8 7 6 5 4 3 2 1

In memory of Bree O'Mara

I

Themba Msamaya didn't suspect a thing on the morning he
opened his door to death.

He was halfway through his first cup of tea when the knock
came. Over the past few months, he'd developed something of a
ritual. He'd get up early, boil the kettle and dunk a bag of cheap,
Shoprite own-brand tea into a chipped South African Airways
mug. He'd learned to do without milk, but a teaspoon of sugar
was an essential. Black tea didn't have to be so strong—it tasted
better weak, in fact—and he had discovered one teabag could
easily stretch to two mugs.

He would drink the steaming, reddish brew while sitting at
the desk in his tiny Yeoville bedsit, yesterday's papers open at
the Classifieds, his elderly laptop ready to browse the Jobsearch
websites.

Over the last few days, his searching had become more stressful, because his useless Internet connection, slow at best and
unreliable at worst, was close to reaching its cap. He'd nearly
got through the five hundred megabytes that his low-spec package allowed him, God knew how, seeing it was only the twenty-
second of the month, and all he'd been using it for was trying to
find work. But once the threshold was reached, he would be cut
off. Rudely, instantly and without any warning. It had happened
a couple of times recently, once while he was right in the middle
of sending off his CV.

Today, JobSA was slow to load and Workopolis had no new
listings, but his favourite site, NATS Careers, was advertising a
position that looked promising.

Email us your application and cv, the advert read. All companies required candidates to do that these days. Phone calls appeared to have become redundant.

A quick read through the well-worded cv that he'd paid a specialist company to put together for him five months ago. Now he wished he hadn't wasted the money on it.

Did he need to change anything in the accompanying letter?

He scanned the document once more, slowly, even though he knew the damn thing by heart. He thought it sounded fine. As fine as was possible, at any rate. He attached it and pressed 'Send', willing the email to go through the first time, praying that the connection would not drop, as it often did, forcing him to repeat the task and gobbling up even more of his precious bandwidth allocation.

A series of clanging sounds and shouts from outside disturbed his concentration, and he looked up, frowning. Was this his neighbour causing trouble again? Themba didn't know him by name, but he was convinced the guy was a drug dealer. People were in and out of that room at all hours, talking, partying, banging on his door late into the night, and occasionally on Themba's door by mistake; and just last week he had overheard an argument that had ended in a gunshot.

No, it couldn't have been his drug-dealing neighbour. The morning after the gunshot, he'd been on his way to the shops when he'd seen the man hurrying down to the garage, carrying what looked like a hastily packed gym bag, half zipped up, in one hand, and his firearm in the other. A few minutes later, Themba had heard the unmistakable roar of his black, souped-up, spoiler-decorated BMW. The man had left and, as far as he knew, he hadn't been back since.

Then Themba realised what the sound was. It was the dustbins being emptied. There had been a municipal strike for weeks, and the bins lined up on the uneven paving outside the building had quickly gone from full to overflowing. Black bags had split open and vomited their contents onto the pavement and into the road. Those that hadn't split had been torn apart—by stray dogs or vagrants or both, he guessed. Crumpled plastic now littered the sidewalks, mushy piles of leftover food had swiftly started stinking in the heat, and dirty nappies disgorged their foul contents, which were soon blanketed by flies.

Now he could hear the loud drone of the garbage truck and the clanking of its crushing mechanism. Above this, the shouts of the workers, more clanging as empty metal dustbins were flung on their sides, and the clatter of the plastic wheelie bins being upended.

And then a second, closer sound, only just audible above the racket. A quick, polite-sounding rat-tat-tat on his door.

Themba glanced at the email. It looked like it was going through. Then he got up from his wooden chair and squeezed past his bed. As he wasn't expecting anyone, he was sure that whoever was outside the door was yet another customer looking for his drug-dealer neighbour.

He twisted the Yale latch open with his right hand, pulled the door handle down with his left, and opened the door a crack, snapping out a rather irritated 'Yes?' before squinting out into the shady corridor.

That one word was all he had time for. The door exploded open, its handle wrenched out of his hand, its edge smashing against his temple as he staggered backwards and a sharp, stabbing pain lanced through his gut.

Themba slammed against the rickety desk and sprawled down onto the floor, blinking as hot rivulets of spilled tea splashed down onto his face.

And then a black-clad figure wearing a dark mask was inside, standing over him. The pain in his stomach was dreadful; he could taste blood in his mouth, but in his shock he hadn't begun to associate any of this with the slim black handle that now jutted from his midriff.

Until his assailant leaned forward, grasped the handle with a gloved hand, and pulled.

The pain was sickening. Themba screamed, a shrill, breathy sound, and clamped his hands over the deep gash, now pouring blood. He glanced up, only to see the knife coming at him again.

'Don't . . .' he begged, but his voice had reduced to a whisper. He mouthed the words, 'Please don't.'

He wanted to plead for his life, to explain that this wasn't fair, that this was the wrong room, that he was not the right man. That he didn't deal in drugs and never had. That this was all a terrible mistake.

But there was no time.

He tried to stop the blade, tried to grab it with his right hand, but it sliced cleanly through his palm and buried itself in his chest.

And then his attacker was gone.

Themba found he couldn't move. He wanted to cough, but he couldn't do that either. All he could do was lie in his own blood, watching as a dark mist rushed to cover the smeary ceiling.

Outside, the clanging of the garbage truck faded into silence.

2

Jade de Jong was fighting to convince herself she wasn't going to drown.

She was six and a half metres under the surface of the sea and sinking, with tons upon tons of water forcing her downwards. She was burying herself in a pale-blue grave, every movement of her fins taking her closer to the ocean's sandy floor and further from the sky and sun above.

She reached out in front of her, striking forward, pushing just a tiny fraction of all that water aside, noticing that her cupped hand looked sickly white in the dim light. Like a sea spectre. Or perhaps more like a corpse.

The thought paralysed her with fear—she was unable to keep going down, unable now even to breathe. Just as she had been on the dive before. And the dive before that.

God, get me out of here, she thought frantically. She knew how easy it would be to escape. A few kicks with her flippers and she could be hurtling up out of the depths, shooting to the surface, ripping the mask off her face. The next big breath she took could be real air. Proper air, not the dry-tasting canned stuff in the tanks on her back.

With her heart banging so hard she was sure it must be sending a subsonic message of panic to all sea life within a two-kilometre radius, Jade forced herself to stay put. She did what Amanda Bolton, her personal scuba-diving trainer, had told her to do. Gently exhale and send a rush of bubbles upwards. Then breathe in again. Slowly and easily. She had to force herself to relax, a command that Jade had realised on her first dive was physically impossible. This time, though, she managed to keep her fear at bay. She took a long, relieved gulp of air and then signalled to the wet-suited figure who was a few metres in front of her and looking at her enquiringly, waiting for her to communicate what she wanted to do next.

Closing her fist with her thumb towards the surface, Jade gestured upwards.

Get me out of here.

Amanda signalled back 'OK'. Escaping locks of her dark hair swirled, mermaid-like, around her face. Then she made another sign that Jade knew meant: slow. Take it slow going up. No panicking.

As Jade kicked towards the surface, she saw a shoal of fish swimming past. Small silvery-looking fish that seemed almost impossibly bright in the clear water—a scattering of marquise-cut diamonds on an aquamarine backdrop. They swam fast and purposefully, as if they were late for an important appointment.

Pretty, yes. But worth the dive? Jade didn't think so. And as for the rest of the sea life she'd heard so much about but hadn't seen yet, like the huge leatherback and loggerhead turtles that the St Lucia estuary was famous for—well, she was sure there'd be some in a glass tank, ready for viewing, at uShaka Marine World in Durban.

Jade had thought learning to scuba dive would be easy, but it was proving to be the opposite. She'd managed her training dives—eventually—but open water terrified her, and she had never thought it would.

She'd expected that she'd take after her mother in this regard, as she did in so many other ways. Her late father had been a reluctant swimmer, a man much more comfortable out of the sea than in it. Although he'd never spoken much about her mother, Jade was certain that she remembered him saying once how much she had loved scuba diving.

Now she realised she must have inherited her father's dislike of the ocean.

At last she broke the surface and pulled off her claustrophobic mask. Treading water, she looked up gratefully at the cloudless sky and felt the coolness of the air against her face. It wouldn't have this effect for long—not in this heat, with the humidity smothering the estuary like a pillow, but the first few minutes out of the water always felt refreshing.

Miles of sea all around her in every direction, stretching all the way to the horizon on the seaward side, and the faraway rolling outline of the forested dunes on the shoreward side. The vastness of that distance didn't worry Jade too much. It was the depths below her that gave her the shivers.

Then Amanda surfaced beside her.

'Short break?' she suggested.

Jade nodded and they swam over to the dive boat waiting nearby and clambered on board.

'Well, that seemed to go better,' Amanda said in an accent that Jade had originally thought was from southern England, but which she had laughingly confessed was pure East End. 'Fifteen minutes under, this time. That's two minutes longer than on the last dive, and you went further, too. Quite an improvement, I think. How do you feel?'

Jade frowned.

'It still doesn't feel like my environment. I'm just not comfortable going so deep, although I know by scuba standards six metres is barely under water.' Bending over, she eased her fins off, then unzipped the wetsuit, which was already feeling too warm, and pulled it down off her shoulders.

'You'll get there, don't you worry. Most people take to it like a fish to water, 'scuse the pun, but some never get the hang of it. Others learn how to do it, but just don't like it.'

'Does that ever change?' Jade asked, glancing longingly at her T-shirt and shorts that were folded up on the bench.

'Oh, it often does.'

Amanda sounded so chirpy that Jade had no idea whether she was humouring her or not.

'Just you wait. In a couple more days, we'll have you out on the big boat, diving in a group with your boyfriend. That's where you really want to be, isn't it?'

Jade didn't miss the sympathy in her voice. But she couldn't argue with her, because the scuba instructor was spot on. One hundred per cent correct. She didn't want to be here, taking private lessons that were being offered at no extra charge, thanks to Amanda's kind-heartedness. She did want to be out on the big boat with police Superintendent David Patel, who might or might not be her boyfriend, but who was most definitely going to be her partner on this trip.

David already knew how to scuba dive, so Jade's plan had been for her to complete the diving course with a couple of other beginners at the resort, which rejoiced in the name of Scuba Sands, and then to join David in exploring the rich coral reefs that lined the estuary in the iSimangaliso Wetland Park—reefs that Jade had been interested to learn were the southernmost in the world.

But nothing had gone as planned.

Jade's own fear of open water had held her back. The other beginners had completed the course without trouble and had left that morning for a full-day's diving out on the reef with Monique du Preez, the other instructor.

And David wasn't even at the resort yet. He'd been supposed to drive down with Jade at the start of the week, but he had been delayed in Jo'burg after a drug-smuggling case he was working on had, in his own words, 'hit the bloody fan harder than a shit-bomb'.

He'd messaged her last night to say that he was getting an afternoon flight from Jo'burg today and would be landing at King Shaka International Airport in Durban at four-thirty. As soon as she and Amanda got back to shore, Jade would set off to fetch him. But before that, she had one more dive still to get through.

She stepped over to the prow of the boat and grasped the metal railing. Just a few minutes out of the water and she was already starting to feel sweaty in the oppressive humidity. The sea was as flat and still as a pond, and the sun burned down from a metallic sky.

'I'm not used to failing,' she admitted. It was easier to say the words when she wasn't looking at the other woman. 'Up till now,

I've always managed to do everything I've wanted to do. Some things have been easy, like . . .'

She stopped herself. She'd been going to say: like shooting. That had come naturally to Jade. The first gun she had fired at the age of twelve had been a rifle almost as tall as she was, and she'd hit her target—a Coke can—at a distance of more than a hundred metres.

Admittedly, that gun had had telescopic sights. But the hand-guns she'd fired since then had not. Guns felt like an extension of her own body; shooting was almost as instinctive as breathing.

She had made a promise, though, that she wasn't going to talk about her work activities on this holiday. Not with David there. Her ability to shoot, and what she had used it for, had caused problems between them that, at one stage, Jade had feared were permanent and would never be resolved.

Amanda laughed, obviously misinterpreting Jade's sudden silence. 'Yeah, I know. You can never remember all the things you can do easily when you're thinking about the one thing you can't.'

'Cycling,' Jade said, picking a safer subject. 'I love to cycle. I bought a mountain bike a while ago and I try to get out on it at least three times a week. I'm good with uphills. They don't bother me at all. Not when I'm cycling or when I'm running. I do that as well, and I've been training myself to run barefoot.'

'Well, that's incredible. Hills just about kill me, whether I'm on a bike or my own two feet. But I can see you keep yourself fit.'

'I'd like to do the long cycle races one day. The 94.7 kilometre one up in Jo'burg and the Cape Argus.'

'Ah,' Amanda said. 'And have you done the L'Eroica Chianti cycling race in Italy? I was wondering when I saw your shirt.'

Jade glanced across at her faded T-shirt that had, indeed, been a free gift to all entrants from the race organisers a few years back. She hadn't completed the ride, though. She'd been assigned as security detail to a wealthy British businessman's wife who'd gone there hoping to cycle the medium-distance route. But the woman hadn't put in nearly enough training for the tough, 135-kilometre course over rough, hilly terrain, and she'd been forced to retire before she'd even reached the halfway point.

That meant that, as her bodyguard, Jade had had to swallow her disappointment and put her own bicycle in the back of the pick-up van together with her client's when it came round to collect the stragglers.

'I didn't finish it,' she said. 'I was there with a client who pulled out before the halfway mark. I was disappointed, but there was nothing I could do. It felt like a failure, too, even though it wasn't my fault.'

Amanda gave a small nod and a shadow crossed her face.

'Failure's never easy to cope with,' she said in a soft voice. 'Especially when it's not your fault.'

Her hand strayed to the small gold airplane pendant that she wore on a chain around her neck, and she slid it from side to side; an instinctive gesture that Jade had seen her make before, but thought Amanda herself was unaware of.

Taking comfort from the familiar action, perhaps.

Jade wondered what failure Amanda had experienced. What-ever it was, she clearly didn't want to talk about it, and Jade wasn't going to ask.

Changing the topic, she said, 'That's a pretty piece of jewellery.'

The dark-haired woman smiled.

'My mother gave it to me when I started work at Heathrow.'

'Flight attendant?'

Now Amanda's smile widened. 'No. Actually, I'm an air-traf-fic controller. I started out in England and then travelled around the world. That's what I'm qualified to do; what I've always done. The scuba diving is just a hobby, really.'

Jade nodded, hoping her surprise didn't show on her face. She'd never have imagined that the woman who had been so patiently teaching her to dive had held down one of the toughest and most responsible jobs in the world—co-ordinating the approach and departure of airplanes at what must be one of the world's busiest commercial airports.

'I see,' she said. 'Sorry.'

'For what?'

'Underestimating your abilities.'

'You wouldn't be the first one to do that. People see a dive instructor in her thirties, working in a little resort like this, and they assume she's a drifter who never had any ambitions in life. At least you asked.'

Jade smiled.

'That was my old life,' Amanda continued. 'Up until last year. I've been here almost six months now.'

'Are you enjoying the change? It must be far less stressful.'

Jade had thought Amanda would agree, but instead she looked away.

'Not really,' she said.

Her words struck a chord with Jade. Made her reflect on her own situation. She was qualified as a bodyguard and had years of experience as a private investigator, working on her own and with big firms. But that might well have to change now.

She knew David didn't approve of the work she did, because of the danger to which it exposed her. Not to mention the fact that in solving her cases she often chose to go beyond the law, or that some of the cases she handled were not legal at all.

Could she do what Amanda had done? Turn her back on her previous life and start afresh doing something else? And if so, what on earth would that new career involve? Would it be too late to finish the law degree she'd started long ago, before she had decided that her heart and her talent lay elsewhere?

One thing was for sure—becoming a scuba-diving instructor was definitely out of the question.

'Shall we go under again? Aim for sixteen minutes this time?' Amanda asked.

Jade dug her fingernails into the palms of her hands. One more dive. Another visit to the depths. The time stretched ahead of her, endless as a prison sentence, but she had to do it. The only thing she feared more than being under the water was giving up on trying.

'OK. Let's give it a go,' she said.

3

The tin roof of the small meeting room amplified the heat a thousand times over. Bradley felt as if the corrugated metal was a magnifying glass, and he was the bug trapped underneath.

Sweat poured through the close-cropped hair at the back of his neck. It had long since drenched the armpits of his starched shirt, sluicing straight through the thick layer of antiperspirant he'd applied earlier that morning and causing him to stink like a pig.

His chest was also slick with sweat, but his tie was still dry. More importantly, so was the large and heavy cellphone that hung on a lanyard around his neck.

He was sitting on a plastic chair in a room with a closed door, a sealed window and a broken air-con unit that seemed to be actively taunting him.

Bradley had been used to air conditioning that worked. Plush meeting rooms with upholstered furniture, audio-visual equipment, jugs of iced water and bowls of perfectly ripe fruit. There, in those cool and airy spaces, he would impress the chairman of the board, the directors, the committee members. Always aiming to be under budget and ahead of schedule, whatever marine engineering project he tackled.

He'd never found himself dripping with sweat in those meetings. And he'd never had to go into them with the kind of bad news that he had to break now. He'd always reported on successes, not problems, not that he could remember, anyway. And particularly not problems that he himself had caused.

Across the table from him, Chetty, his current employer, lifted a stubby-fingered hand and scratched his balding head. Chetty wasn't wearing a suit and tie, only a shabby golf shirt and a pair of chinos. And Chetty wasn't sweating. Chetty was the kind of man who looked like he never broke a sweat. 'So everything's on track?' he asked.

'Ahead of schedule,' Bradley said, starting with the positives. 'All ready for action. You have a full team of workers now, ready for the final assignment.'

'The work on the *Karachi*'s hull?'

'Finished. And all the—er—special equipment you requested is in place.'

'Any other issues?'

And there it was. Should he tell them or not? Bradley had no idea. His employers had said they needed to know about everything and anything that could possibly affect the outcome of this project. But this problem was personal, something that involved him. Did they really need to be informed?

Not if he could handle it, and make it go away. But what would happen if he couldn't?

Chetty rocked back on his chair, a small smile on his pudgy face, looking for all the world like he was out relaxing on the deck of an international cruise liner and not stuck inside this suffocating little room.

'Are we good?'

In that instant, Bradley decided he wouldn't mention what was worrying him. He would sort it out by himself, in his spare time. It would be better if he kept his employers in the dark, he thought.

'There is something, isn't there?' a voice said softly.

The words came from the third person in the room. A muscular giant of a man whose tight black T-shirt and jeans blended so well with his body that Bradley could hardly tell where skin ended and fabric began.

Bradley knew him only as Zulu. A code name or a surname— he didn't know which, and he wasn't going to ask. Even on this sweltering day, the man still gave him the shivers.

Zulu looked directly at him, as if he could see right into Bradley's guilt-stained core.

'What aren't you telling us?' he asked.

Chetty rocked forward on his chair. Its legs hit the floor with a thud.

'Well? Is there a problem?' His voice sounded suddenly sharp.

Bradley's stomach churned with sick dread. He snatched a breath and started speaking, aware that his voice was now fast and panicky.

'OK, I had a text message yesterday.' He glanced down at his knees. 'Not on this work phone. On one of my old numbers. It's nothing to do with the job—almost certainly—but it seems that an old friend, well actually an old acquaintance, is attempting to blackmail me.'

'What?'

Chetty shouted so loudly that he earned a glance from Zulu.

The black man raised an eyebrow. 'Given your history, I am assuming this acquaintance is a she, not a he.'

Bradley nodded miserably. 'It is a woman.'

'And how do you know her?'

'We were—er—involved for a short time, a while ago.'

'What does she want?' Chetty leaned forward, his elbows on the table.

'Well, money, of course....'

'What she wants is irrelevant,' Zulu said. 'What is important is this: why does she want it? What does this woman know?'

'She doesn't know about this operation. It's personal,' Bradley muttered. 'Personal stuff. An amateur attempt at getting money out of me.' He felt his face burning with shame.

'Shit,' Chetty said.

Zulu nodded, his face giving nothing away.

'How did you know who it is?' he asked. 'Blackmail, by its very nature, is supposed to be anonymous, is it not?'

'I picked up on some clues. It wasn't difficult. In one of the texts, she told me where she was working.'

Chetty let out an explosive guffaw.

'She gave away her location?'

'Yes.'

'You're right. That is amateur.'

'Amateur, perhaps, but I would still prefer that the amount

not be paid and that the problem . . . is simply disposed of.' Zulu cast a meaningful glance at Bradley, who felt a fresh wave of sweat flood down his back—this one prompted by fear.

His left leg had started to tremble, too. What was wrong with him?

Bradley tried hard to suppress the thought that in his past life he had never received assignments like the one he was working on now. Be tough, he told himself. You can deal with this. You know you can.

He clamped his knees together to stop his leg from shaking, and folded his arms.

'Her details, please, just for the record,' Zulu added.

Stammering slightly, Bradley told him the woman's name, and the name of the beachside resort where she lived and worked. He knew that Zulu would memorise the address, rather than write it down. Nothing had ever been written down during their meetings, and his employers had told him that the phone he'd been instructed to wear around his neck at all times had an in-built anti-bugging mechanism that would beep if any recording devices were in the area.

Or on Bradley himself.

'I think it's best you stay out of it. You shouldn't be seen in the area at all,' Chetty advised.

'I understand.'

'Get Kobus to do it.'

'I will.'

'That's all for now, then. You can go.'

Bradley got up so fast he almost knocked over his chair. He wrenched open the door and stumbled outside.

Chetty groaned as the door banged shut behind the departing project manager.

'What a bloody screw-up,' he said, although whether he was commenting on the situation or on Bradley himself was unclear. 'How'd you know he was hiding something?'

Zulu smiled lazily. 'The room is hot, but not that hot. He was sweating like a guilty man. Like somebody with a secret.'

'You think we've been wrong to trust him?'

Zulu considered the words in silence for a while.

'No,' he said. 'He is trustworthy.'

'I worry he's planning on selling us out to the cops.'

'He won't sell us out to the cops.'

'How do you know?'

'Because he is greedy and because he is scared. He is waiting for his money, and is frightened about going back to prison.'

Chetty didn't look convinced.

'Getting him paroled early might not have been enough incentive. Or is there something you're not telling me? Have you got something else on him?'

Zulu didn't reply, but his smile widened.

4

Jade had never been more relieved to feel solid ground under her feet. Calling out a hasty thanks to Amanda, she jogged back along the jetty, her footsteps sounding hollow on the boards. She crossed the wide strip of blindingly white sand and headed up the grassy hillside towards the row of wooden chalets beyond. Her chalet was on the far left, next door to the more modest staff quarters.

After a quick shower, she was ready to go.

David's flight would be landing in three hours' time, and the airport was only two and a half hours away. But Jade wasn't going straight to the airport. First she was going to drive to the nearby town of Richards Bay and visit the local graveyard.

Jade had never known her mother—Elise de Jong had died when her only child was less than a year old—and she had only recently learned the truth about who, or rather what, she had really been. Now she wanted to see her grave; to stand at the final resting place of the woman who had passed on her deadly talents, as well as her slim build, brown hair and green eyes.

What was she going to say to her at her graveside?

Jade didn't know. Perhaps it would be something simple like, 'Why couldn't you have been good at needlework instead?'

She started her car and turned on the air conditioning full-blast, an exercise she had discovered reduced the little rented Fiat's engine power by about fifty per cent and doubled its fuel consumption. Then she set off up the concrete driveway flanked by palm trees on one side and bushy forest on the other, and through the low wooden gate that stood wide open between battered-looking white pillars and a rickety wooden fence. The gate and the fence were the only barriers separating the private resort from the outside world—a fact Jade found rather troubling. She hadn't realised how accustomed she had become to the high walls and electrified wires that protected almost every property in Johannesburg.

Like so many other places in South Africa, Richards Bay had grown dramatically in the past thirty years. The expansion had been accelerated by the end of apartheid in 1994. The once-sleepy little seaside village was now a major hub of industrial activity. It was the place where many of the motor vehicles produced in South Africa were assembled, and it was also home to two aluminium processing plants, as well as a number of mining operations that took place near, but not inside, the iSimangaliso Wetland Park.

As Jade turned off the highway and onto the main road that led into the centre of the sprawling town, she tried to imagine what might have been there when her father had been posted here, long ago, as a police detective. Her father had never talked much about his life before Jade—he hadn't been a great one for talking in general, and had only occasionally opened up to his only child.

The main road had been in existence back then. She knew that from an old map of the area she'd found in the box of her father's possessions that David had given to her when she'd returned to South Africa more than ten years after his death. So Commissioner De Jong, or whatever rank he'd held in those days, must have driven along it many times, just as she was doing now.

The buildings on her right wouldn't have been there, though. They were far too new—a walled Mediterranean-style residential complex built on what must have been vacant land. But the houses on the left looked older. Perhaps he would have seen them too, when their roofs were in better repair, their paintwork fresher and brighter.

And there, ahead of her, was the town cemetery.

She saw rows and rows of gravestones behind the high wrought-iron fence, their shadows sharp in the afternoon sun. Some graves untended, some well cared for, a few with colourful bunches of flowers at the foot of their headstones.

'How did my mother die?' she'd asked her father once.

'There was a very wet summer in Richards Bay, where we lived at the time,' her father had told her, his voice sad. 'There was an outbreak of malaria in the town.'

'Did that kill her?'

'Malaria on its own doesn't often kill. But the complications often do. Cerebral malaria is nearly always fatal.' He'd turned away from Jade in a manner that made it clear that any further questions would be unwelcome.

The cerebral malaria that her mother had contracted had indeed been fatal. It had swiftly led to the kidney failure that had been the eventual cause of her death.

Jade drove through the cemetery's main gateway and stopped under a tree in the otherwise deserted parking lot. Not far from her, an elderly black man wearing shabby trousers and a ragged cast-off T-shirt bearing the faded legend 'Richards Mining Triathlon Team' was sitting on a rock under another, smaller tree. Next to him, in a blue plastic bucket, were a few bunches of lilies. When he saw her, he heaved himself to his feet, lifted the bucket, and made his way slowly towards her.

'How much are the flowers?' Jade asked. She realised she was feeling nervous, butterflies fluttering in her stomach the same way they might do if she'd been on her way to meet a stranger that she had heard about for a long time, but never known.

'Fifty rands a bunch,' the old man replied. His 's' sounded thick and sibilant. He smiled, showing a gummy gap where his front teeth should have been.

'I'll take one, thanks.'

Clutching the flowers, she made her way towards the cemetery gate, then stopped. She realised she had no idea where her mother's grave was and she hadn't expected the cemetery to be so large. In fact, it was probably a few acres in size. She turned around.

'Do you know where I can find the caretaker?' she called.

The old man hunched his shoulders in an expressive shrug. 'He's not here.'

'Oh.' Jade paused. 'Is there a list, or a plan of the graves inside; some way of finding out where somebody is buried? This is the first time I've been here.'

The man didn't answer immediately. He made his way back to his rock and carefully put down his bucket. Then he straightened up again. From twenty paces, Jade heard his back pop.

He started shuffling towards the gate.

'This way,' he said, making an impatient gesture with his hand, as if she were the one lagging behind.

Walking at a snail's pace and keeping a respectful distance behind the elderly man, Jade followed him through the cemetery gates and down a paved pathway in the direction of a small brick building.

The paving was lifting in places and thick dark-green shoots of grass had pushed their way up through the cracks. More grass lined the path, the overgrown blades whipping in the strong wind that had started to blow.

When the old man reached the building, he felt in his pocket. To Jade's surprise, he produced a key that, after a short struggle, opened the rusty padlock on the door.

'In there,' he said gruffly. 'There's a list on the wall.'

Jade walked inside. The little room was chokingly hot, a mini-sauna. With the old man watching her, she stepped over to the notice board on the wall. On it, a yellowed plan of the cemetery was held in place by four blobs of rust that may once have been drawing pins. Next to it, a few milky plastic folders held papers with a list of names and plot numbers.

The list was arranged alphabetically, by surname.

Eagerly, Jade scanned the list, looking for the letter D.

But there were only two De Jongs on it—Mildred and Kenneth, who from the looks of it must have been married, because their graves were right next to each other. Jade blinked, peering more closely at the oddly spaced names that had been typed out long ago on an old-fashioned typewriter.

Why wasn't her mother listed here? Was the grave in her maiden name, for some unfathomable reason?

Jade didn't have to look far—just a little further down the Ds. She swiftly established that there was no Delacourt buried in this graveyard either.

Just in case the name had been mistakenly listed under J for Jong, she looked in that section as well, but it wasn't there.

She stepped away, shaking her head, then read through the entire list, just in case she was missing something obvious. It was impossible that her mother's name was not here. Thirty years ago this was the only graveyard in town. She'd checked up on that before booking her trip.

Her mother had died in Richards Bay. The death certificate had stated this clearly. But she was not buried here.

She turned back to the elderly man.

'Are you sure this has all the names? Is it totally up to date?' A silly question, she knew, since her mother had died so long ago.

'That's the list,' he said, the sibilant hissing through the gap in his teeth.

Jade bit her lip, trying to make sense of this. Could her mother have been cremated and her ashes scattered? But if so, why had her father told her that the jade engagement ring he had bought her, the ring whose stone she had been named after, had been buried with her?

Those had been his exact words. She would never forget them. Her father had said 'buried'.

Back outside, the wind snatched at her hair. It cooled the sweat that had dampened her hairline and rustled the cellophane wrapper on the bunch of flowers. Now that the flowers could not be used for their intended purpose, Jade found herself carrying the bouquet self-consciously, blossoms pointing down, the way that a teenage boy might hold a floral arrangement after being informed at the front door that his new girlfriend was out of town.

She gave the old man another ten rands for his trouble. While he refastened the padlock on the office door, Jade walked back towards the car park.

Before she left the cemetery, she turned right and made her way down one of the gravel paths, past the ranks of tombstones.

The name on one of them caught her eye. A small and simple granite gravestone that had no flowers. She stopped beside it and read the inscription.

'Elizma Pienaar. 1929–1983. Sadly missed.'

The name was close enough to Elise. As close as Jade was going to get today, at any rate.

She gently placed her flowers on the grass covering Elizma's grave. Then, still frowning, she left the windswept graveyard and headed for her car.

5

'I need your help, babe.'

Those words, more than anything else, had prompted Jade to book a holiday and get away from Jo'burg for a while.

Robbie had been waiting for her a week ago, when she arrived home late one night after finishing up a surveillance job. He had stepped out of the shadows, directly into the path of her car, as she'd made the slow turn off the narrow dirt road and into her cottage's driveway. Even though her headlights were dipped, she'd recognised him immediately, but still she had not been able to stop the instinctive, frightened stamp of her foot on the brake pedal.

It had caused the wheels to lock and to skid on the sandy soil. Only for a moment and only for a few inches, but when he had heard that noise Robbie's lips had parted and he had grinned briefly, a shark-like expression that told Jade just how accurately he had sensed her fright.

Her heart had pounded.

She hadn't seen Robbie for over a year. She'd assumed he had left Jo'burg and started doing business somewhere else.

Occasionally, she had wondered whether he was dead and found herself ashamed to be hoping that this was so.

He was as lean and wiry as she remembered. But his hair was shorter, the peppercorn curls now cropped close to his head. He also had a new scar on the left side of his jaw, slashing its way down towards his throat, the brown skin puckered and ridged.

He held out a hand to stop her, rings flashing gold on his long, bony fingers, even though her car was already at a standstill. And then he strolled over to the driver's door and rested his elbows on the edge of the window that Jade had just wound down.

'Babe,' he said. 'Good to see you. It's been a long time.'

She looked into his eyes and saw a new hardness there; a coldness that she didn't remember from before. Then she glanced down and saw the large SIG Sauer pistol holstered on his hip. She didn't remember that from before, either.

She took a deep breath. 'What do you want?'

Robbie smiled again. 'What makes you think I want anything?'

'Where's your car?'

He jerked a thumb in the opposite direction. 'Parked back that way. Out of sight. You can't be too careful at night in Jo'burg, you know.'

Jade knew that all right.

'So, what do you want?' she asked again, although she already knew the answer, because his arrival at her house in this way and at this time could mean that Robbie wanted only one thing.

His next words confirmed her suspicions.

'I need your help, babe.'

Jade stared at him somewhat disbelievingly.

'I can't help you,' she said. 'I don't do those jobs anymore.'

Robbie's lips tightened and he leaned towards her. 'I thought you might say that. That's why I came here to ask you in person.'

'The answer's the same.'

'Bullshit.'

Jade had a sudden strong feeling he was going to grab her, hurt her, try to use force to make her change her mind. If so, she'd rather be out in the open than trapped inside her car. Outside, there were more options available. She could run. Or she could draw her own gun.

But he didn't touch her. When she started to open the car door to get out, he just took his elbows off the window frame and moved aside to give her some room.

She stood facing him, her weight poised on the balls of her feet, aware that the night was very quiet. Only the soft hum of her car's idling engine and the faraway chirp of a cricket disturbed the silence.

'I'm not taking no for an answer,' he said. 'You owe me a favour. I saved your arse last year. Have you forgotten already?'

'I haven't forgotten. I will return the favour. But not now, and not this.'

His face had darkened. 'You don't get to pick and choose. That's not the way it works. Not according to my code of honour.'

Jade bit her lip and refrained from passing comment on the hypocrisy of a code of honour that embraced murder for money.

'I'm not letting this go,' Robbie said. 'I need you, Jade. There's nobody else I can rely on, a professional, who can do things the way you do them. Slick.'

Jade suddenly felt sick. Robbie's perception of her was not inaccurate. It was based on experience, on jobs that the two of them had done together. She couldn't erase the past, or her memory of it. She couldn't remove her ability to aim a gun at another human being and to hold it there unflinching, without hesitation and without remorse, while she pulled the trigger.

Her mother had killed for money. But Jade wasn't going to do that. Not ever, and certainly not for Robbie.

'No,' she said again.

For just a moment, she saw Robbie's confident façade dissolve. He stared back at her, and on his face she picked up an expression she had never believed she would see; had never associated with Robbie at all.

Fear.

'I'm in deep with this one,' he told her softly. 'I'm way over my head. I'm asking you a favour, as a friend. It's . . . I can only say this job's too big for me to handle alone. And if I fuck up, I'm history. These people are connected. There's nowhere in the world it'd be safe to hide.'

Now Jade's heart threatened to hammer its way straight through her ribcage.

'Why'd you take it on?'

Robbie shrugged. 'The cash. This one's the big one. The one to retire on. Babe, if you help me, we'll split it. Fifty-fifty. You'll be set up for life, I promise you. And I'm sure I don't need to tell you, the people they want taken out are scum. Evil beyond belief. I wouldn't have said yes to it otherwise. You know me.'

Jade hesitated. Her mind was spinning with possible scenarios.

She could help Robbie with this one last job and become rich. Wealthy enough to retire; to spend her days reading and running, cycling and cooking for herself and David.

Or she could help him with the job and things could go wrong. She could be hunted down by the people who'd put out the contract. She could end up on the SAPS Wanted list, with sufficient evidence against her to send her to prison for life.

'When do you have to do it?' she found herself asking.

'I don't know. They said it might have to happen in a week—there's a strong possibility of that. Or it could be in another month or two. It all depends, but I don't know on what.'

She'd given another small, hopeless headshake.

'I really can't,' she had told him. 'No matter what the situation is, I can't help you.'

To her surprise, Robbie hadn't tried to argue with her any further.

'Later, babe,' he'd said, and then turned and walked quickly away. Within moments he'd vanished into the darkness.

Getting back in her car, Jade had spun her wheels again as she'd driven hastily through her gateway. Once inside, she had double-locked her security gate and set the alarm.

Early the next day, she'd booked the holiday and invited David along. In a week's time, when Robbie came calling again, Jade had decided she was going to be somewhere he couldn't possibly reach her.

6

Jade arrived at King Shaka International Airport just as David's flight touched down. She had to wait less than ten minutes before he strode through the arrival gates, carrying an oversized gym bag that presumably held his diving kit. She couldn't wait to see him wearing it. The tall police superintendent had a good physique, although she had recently observed a couple of love-handles developing above his hips. But in the tight embrace of a scuba suit, she was sure he would be transformed into Jason Statham.

A brown-skinned, half-Indian version of Statham, at least, with pale-blue eyes as cold and clear as ice.

She couldn't stop a delighted smile from spreading across her face when she saw him. He was here at last. They'd had the occasional weekend away in the past, but this was the first time that they would be on a proper holiday together.

For a couple of months now, things had been better between them. Good, in fact. And then, the day before she left for holiday, Jade had driven past David's house in the southern Jo'burg suburb of Turffontein, and had seen the sign that had made her heart leap into her mouth.

For Sale.

She'd slammed on brakes so suddenly that her car had slalomed to a standstill. And then she'd backed up and looked again, just to check that what she was seeing was true.

David was selling his house.

Up until a few months ago, David had lived in a rented apartment above a garage next to the cottage where Jade stayed. But when his wife, from whom he was separated, had gone to live in Pretoria with their young son, he had moved back into his Turffontein home.

Jade had left for St Lucia without getting the chance to ask him about the real estate sign. But she hoped that this meant he was going to move closer to her again.

Perhaps she could even suggest to him that he moved in with her. Even if it was a temporary measure. She'd have to free up some cupboard space; find another place to stash the innumerable lacy scatter cushions that she'd packed away soon after taking occupation of the furnished cottage. But it could easily be done. On holiday in a place like this, while they were sharing a bedroom, it seemed like a good opportunity to suggest such a move.

David, however, didn't return her smile. He nodded when he saw her and hefted his bag onto his shoulder as he walked over to her. She was expecting a kiss. She could already anticipate how his stubble would scrape against her cheek, the softness of his lips on hers. But David didn't put his bag down. In fact, he barely slowed down when he reached her and, instead of the kiss she was expecting, all she got was an awkward hug.

'Good flight?' she asked, hurrying to keep up with him as he strode across the terminal building.

'Plane was just about empty,' he said.

He didn't elaborate further. As they headed towards the airport exit gate, Jade glanced at him again, but he was staring straight ahead, stony-faced.

What on earth was bothering him? Work pressure? He'd said that the shit had hit the fan on one of the cases he was working on, but that was nothing unusual. She sometimes thought that 'hitting the fan' basically defined his job description.

With a twinge of guilt, she remembered Robbie's night-time visit. Had David somehow found out that the gangster had contacted her again? Surely not. In any case, there was nothing she could have done to stop him and she had, after all, said no to his offer.

Jade forced herself to stop being paranoid. Whatever was bothering David, she was sure he would open up about it after a few drinks and a good dinner. Earlier that morning, she'd put a bottle of Villiera Brut Natural sparkling wine in their chalet's fridge and marinated two large free-range fillet steaks in red wine and rosemary. If that didn't improve David's mood, then nothing would.

The journey back to Scuba Sands passed in heavy silence. A full two and a half hours of it. Jade concentrated on her driving and tried to suppress the growing suspicion that David's mood had something to do with her.

David didn't comment on the amazing aquamarine-blue of the ocean that had taken Jade's breath away the first time she'd seen it. He didn't say anything about the vast tracts of coastal forest that hemmed the white-gold beach, or the sign at the lake that warned people against swimming because of the hundreds of crocodiles that lurked in its innocent-looking waters. He didn't even comment on the lack of security when they drove through the resort's wooden gate and headed down the driveway towards the chalets.

Two narrow brick tracks branched off the driveway just before Jade's chalet, forming a makeshift parking bay under a tall and leafy tree. Reading the brochure on the living room table, Jade had discovered the tree was a hardwood, one of many that flourished in the area and that were more commonly found on the leeward side of the enormous dunes that fringed the coastline.

She stopped the car in the shade and climbed out. 'We're in the Huberta room,' she told him.

He cleared his throat. 'What's that?'

Jade hoped the room's history would cheer him up, or at any rate distract him from whatever was bothering him.

'When I checked in, Neil—the resort owner—told me that Huberta was a very famous hippo. Probably the most famous hippo in the entire history of South Africa. She lived here, in St Lucia, but one day in 1928 she decided to start roaming for some reason. And she just went. Across rivers, across roads, through fields . . . For miles and miles, all the way down the Natal coastline. She wasn't scared of people, so she munched her way through parks, gardens, farms and even golf courses as she went, followed by larger and larger numbers of interested people who watched her and photographed her, and tossed her fruit and sugarcane.'

'Hmmph,' David grunted.

'The authorities decided to try and capture her for the Johannesburg Zoo, but she evaded pursuit and just kept going, pursued by hordes of journalists and photographers. When she was in a playful mood, she'd chase the photographers up trees. She actually walked right across the verandah during a big function at the Durban Country Club. Then she spent time in one of the Zulus' sacred pools, which convinced them that she had a connection with King Shaka, and she became a godlike animal in their eyes. And Neil also told me the Xhosa believed that she was the spirit of a great chief who'd returned to seek justice for his people.'

'Interesting,' David muttered.

'Then she was declared royal game and it became illegal to try to catch or hunt her. Three years after she'd started roaming, she eventually reached East London. On her journey, she'd crossed 122 rivers. Isn't that amazing?'

She glanced sideways at David.

His face had softened slightly, but he said nothing. He just took the last bag of gear out of the car and slammed the boot.

Looking towards the shoreline, she saw that the boat that had taken the group out for the all-day excursion had now returned to shore. Monique du Preez, the other dive instructor, was strolling towards her room with a bag of equipment slung over her shoulder. Her faded denim shorts showed off her deeply tanned legs and her pale-blonde hair shimmered in the sunlight.

Velcro for men. That had been Jade's first impression of Monique. She was Velcro—the side with the hooks, not the loops. On their first night at Scuba Sands, they'd built a campfire down at the beach. Jade had sat quietly on a rock, sipping her wine and watching Monique chat to the group of people, all the while flirting openly with each of the men in turn.

She had occupied herself pleasantly that evening by guessti-mating what Monique's life expectancy might be, should she try the same trick with David when he arrived?

'Who are they?' David asked.

Jade turned her head towards him sharply, but David wasn't looking in Monique's direction. He was staring at the couple who were walking up the path behind them and had now caught up. The well-built man with a ponytail and a short, blond beard was digging in his shorts pocket for the key to their chalet. The slim, red-headed woman beside him walked with her head bowed and her back slightly hunched. With her arms crossed over her chest and her large, dark sunglasses, this was clearly a woman trying to hide from the world.

'They're our next-door neighbours,' she said. 'Craig and Elsabe. That's Craig's Land Rover parked over there.'

David nodded glumly, as if Jade's answer had somehow disap-pointed him.

Jade walked over to the chalet entrance, which had a doormat with a picture of a smiling hippo on it. Craig was busy unlocking the door of the neighbouring chalet, the old-fashioned key rattling in the lock. Elsabe stood behind him, arms still folded. She was looking at Jade, but made no attempt to acknowledge her, and her actions reinforced Jade's initial impression of her as being somebody who she instinctively disliked, and who disliked her in turn, with no real reason being necessary.

Craig didn't look in Jade's direction at all. He just opened the door and stood aside for Elsabe to go through, before following her in and locking it behind him.

Nothing like having a good relationship with the neighbours. It was just like being back in Johannesburg, Jade decided. Home sweet home.

She'd actually exchanged a few words with Craig on the night of the campfire. He'd walked over to her after he'd unhooked himself from Monique's clutches. Elsabe hadn't joined him. Instead, the petite woman had sat near Monique, glancing over at Jade from time to time with an expression on her face that suggested she could smell something unpleasant.

Jade wasn't good at small talk at the best of times, especially with strangers. Their conversation had been short and punctuated by a number of silences.

She remembered that he'd referred to Elsabe as 'my friend'. She'd wondered what that had implied. And she'd sensed something about him; something that she couldn't quite put her finger on, but had nonetheless given her an uneasy twinge in the pit of her stomach. She was relieved when he'd said goodbye, turned away, and walked towards the sea. The last she had seen of him that night had been him striding purposefully along the beach on his own.

Inside, the chalet was pleasantly cool thanks to the small air-conditioning unit chugging valiantly away under the lounge window. David put his bag down next to the coffee table and lowered his six-foot-five frame down onto the couch, landing with a bump.

'Christ in a bucket,' he muttered, a statement that made no sense, yet was perfectly logical. He covered his face with his elegant, long-fingered hands and leaned back, stretching his legs out in front of him. Then he let out a sigh so deep it seemed to come all the way from the soles of his feet.

'Beer?' she offered. 'Water? Or there's some bubbly in the fridge if you'd like to break it open now.'

She'd been hoping to break open more than champagne. If Jade had had her way, she'd have undone David's shirt and had his trousers off almost before the door had closed behind them. But since that was clearly not about to happen, bubbly was the next best option.

His hands still covering his face, David shook his head as violently as if he was trying to rid himself of an entire colony of sandflies.

Then he dropped his hands and looked straight at Jade. It was then that she noticed the whites of his ice-blue eyes were red, as if he was short on sleep.

And then he uttered the words that filled her with dread.

'We need to talk,' he said.

7

'Talk?' Jade's voice sounded hoarse, and she took a large gulp of water from the bottle on the counter. 'What about?'

'Take a seat,' David told her, as if he were the original occupant of the chalet and Jade the new arrival.

Jade didn't feel like sitting down. Right then, she would have preferred to pace the room, the way that David himself did when he was stressed.

She perched reluctantly on the edge of the chair opposite him.

She'd expected that David would want to talk to her, now that the Turffontein house was being sold. This meant he was making life changes, and she had assumed that she would be part of those changes. That they involved her. But maybe she'd been wrong.

She waited for David to speak again, but he stared at the floor in silence, his elbows propped on his knees and his fists bunched under his chin.

The knot in her stomach was growing bigger and tighter. She wished he would just get on with it and tell her, because nothing could be more unbearable than this waiting, here in this silent room.

Or so she thought at the time.

'Speak up, Patel,' she said encouragingly.

Eventually David lifted his head and took a deep breath. He still wouldn't look at her; he just kept on staring at the wooden wall unit that was home to the television, a giant seashell and one flickering lamp.

Then, at last, he dropped his bombshell.

'Naisha's pregnant,' he said.

His words hit Jade like a fist in the face. She recoiled—she couldn't help it. Even though she'd steeled herself to take David's news without showing emotion, she hadn't been expecting this. Not in a million years.

Her mind raced as she took in the implications of his words.

Naisha, David's wife, was pregnant. But as far as Jade knew, the woman was determinedly single and had been that way for a long time. She'd had her heart set on David moving back in with her. She'd told him on numerous occasions that she wanted to give the marriage another chance.

So how . . . ?

The answer was as big and obvious as an open gateway leading straight to hell.

'Is it . . .' She found herself choking on the words; having to force them out of a mouth that was suddenly dry again in spite of the water she'd just had. 'Is it yours?'

He didn't answer. Didn't meet her eyes, just gave a small nod.

Jade bit into her bottom lip so hard she tasted blood.

So this was why the Turffontein house had been sold. Not to give David the freedom to choose where he wanted to live, but because he was going to Pretoria. Going to move in again with his wife, who was now expecting their baby.

'When did this happen?' she asked in a small, tight voice.

'She's four months along, but she only told me about it last weekend.'

'So four months ago, you slept with her.'

David gave a small nod.

'Do you know how that makes me feel right now?'

'I—look, Jade, I can't even say I'm sorry. Sorry doesn't begin to describe how I feel. I can't even say I made a mistake, because what I did goes beyond that. All I can say is you and I were going through a rough patch, and I . . .'

'So is this what I have to live with now? The knowledge that every time I've ever pissed you off or done something you've disapproved of, you've run off and jumped into bed with your supposedly separated partner? Why? If you'd slept with Naisha every time you and I had had a rough patch, you could have fathered a whole bloody soccer team by now.'

David buried his face in his hands.

'Jadey, it was just that once. Just that one damn time. I thought it was over between us. I regretted it as soon as it had happened, and I've felt bad about it ever since. And when Naisha told me she was pregnant . . .' His voice sounded very small.

'And there's nobody else in her life? She hasn't been screwing you around again? It's happened before, in case you've forgotten. You told me that was why you originally separated.'

A shake of the head.

'There's nobody else. That I do know.'

'Well, you're an idiot.'

'I am, Jadey.' The way David said her pet name made her feel as if her heart had been ripped from her chest. Finally he looked at her. 'Whatever you want to tell me now, whatever you call me, it can't be worse than what I've been telling myself and calling myself. I've screwed up more badly than I ever thought would be possible. I made a crap decision that night. The worst mistake I could ever have made. I betrayed you, and that's something I'll feel guilty about forever. I've had sleepless nights deciding what I should do. But I can't walk away from this. I've tried to convince myself that I can, but it's impossible. I cannot let Naisha bring up two children as a single mother. I won't abdicate my responsibility like that.'

'So this is the end for us, then?'

He stared at her, his pale eyes gleaming in the dimming light.

'I don't want to lose you forever.'

'Why did you come along on this holiday? Why didn't you cancel before you left Jo'burg, and tell me all this over the phone?'

'Because I only found out after you'd already booked the trip. Dammit, Jade, I didn't want to disappoint you. And perhaps it's good that we're both here now, to have some time and space to think this through. I'll sleep on the couch. Please, I know it's hard for you now, but I'm hoping that you can try to forgive me. That you can offer me your friendship.'

Friendship?

Jade sprang to her feet, a white-hot surge of fury goading her into physical action. With a supreme effort, she restrained herself from smashing her fist straight into David's eye-socket.

His eyes were closed now, in any case, as if he couldn't bear to witness her anger.

If she'd known this would happen, she would never have organised the damn holiday. What had she gained from it, apart from a lasting fear of deep water and having to suffer the humiliation of David's news? For Christ's sake, here she was, faced with an issue that she'd never even dreamed could happen. 'I got my wife pregnant while I was having an affair with you....'

She wanted to shout her feelings to the rooftops, but she couldn't find the words to express the immensity of her rage, the bitterness of her disappointment.

Instead, Jade opened the fridge and grabbed the bottle of champagne. Her first impulse was to lift it above her head and hurl it to the floor as hard as she could and watch as it shattered in a deafening explosion of glass and gas.

But at the last moment she stopped herself. Still holding the bottle, she yanked open the door and marched outside, slamming it so hard behind her that the bang could probably have been heard in Port Elizabeth.

8

Bradley's second-floor flat was in a crummy area in the poorer part of Richards Bay that was sandwiched between the railway tracks and Bayview Aluminium, the biggest of the operational aluminium processing plants. It was small, cramped and shoddy, and was losing the battle against the foul smell of the outside drains. To Bradley, it seemed to smell worse every day he lived there.

But this was where Zulu and Chetty had told him he would need to be based until the operation was over. The flat was close to the harbour and, more importantly, it was just a short walk away from the labourers' accommodation. This allowed him to go back and forth quickly and discreetly. Later tonight, when it was dark, he'd take them supper. Four loaves of brown bread and a jar of peanut butter.

They should be grateful. When he'd been in prison, supper had been plain bread, six slices per man, to be eaten in the cells after lockdown.

His hands had stopped shaking by the time he got home, although his left leg was still twitching so badly he'd stalled the car twice on the way. He glanced into the rear-view mirror, ran his fingers through his neatly trimmed blond hair and straightened his tie. One of the many mantras his domineering father had spent endless years drilling into his head was that one should always leave home, and arrive home, looking respectable.

One of the first things he'd done with the advance salary he'd been paid was to have two separate air conditioners installed. One in the main bedroom and one in the tiny open-plan area that comprised the lounge and kitchen. Both chugged away around the clock, on their coldest setting, sending his electricity bill into the stratosphere, but keeping the apartment at a liveable temperature.

Once inside, Bradley resisted the temptation to tear his drenched and stinking shirt off his body right then and there. Instead, he turned round and locked the Trellidor, closed the front door and slid the bolt into place.

Then he went straight to the bedroom, which he'd sound-proofed with heavy foam immediately after he'd moved in.

Opening the door quietly, he greeted his woman with a soft 'Hey, hon.'

Her eyes were wide open and she was propped up on the pillows he'd arranged so comfortably around her that morning. A glass of water, half full, stood within easy reach of her head on the bedside table, with a straw inside.

Bradley walked over and knelt down beside her. Gently, he took one of her hands in his and squeezed it.

She didn't squeeze back. Instead, she screamed.

Her entire body shuddered and her back arched as she convulsed, writhing and struggling against the soft ties that he'd attached to her wrists and ankles, for her own safety.

'Shit,' Bradley muttered. He grabbed one of the many pairs of neatly balled socks he kept in the bedside drawer and stuffed it into her open mouth, keeping his fingers well away from her teeth.

'Damn it all, I thought you were over this. Do you want to stay gagged all day while I'm gone? Because you will, if you carry on.'

He turned away and rooted through the drawer of pharma-ceutical drugs that his new employer had obtained for him at his special request. Grabbing a fresh syringe, he drew up two ccs of Dormicum, a potent sedative. When he grabbed her arm at the elbow, she did her best to pull away from him, her face turning crimson with the effort and her eyes bulging.

Last night, after kneeling on her upper arm and subduing her by sheer brute force, he'd managed to plunge the needle into a vein. With hands that were trembling slightly—*don't get this wrong, now, or you'll kill her, too*—he'd pulled back on the plunger, sucking a trail of bright blood into the colourless liquid, before pressing down and sending the drug into her bloodstream.

Tonight, she was struggling harder and he knew he just couldn't risk it. Instead he pulled the needle off the syringe and stuck it as far up her nose as he could get it before depressing the plunger.

She coughed and snorted, tears streaming down her cheeks, but a few minutes later all the tension had left her body. Her arms were limp and the fear was gone from her half-closed eyes. Looking down at her, Bradley felt a surge of desire so powerful it was frightening. His helpless sweetheart. He would do anything to protect her. Anything. He wouldn't falter in his care of her. He would never make the same mistake again—the one that had ended up causing the accidental death of his wife.

Bradley could still remember exactly how he'd felt when he had been summoned from his prison cell and into the visitors' room where, for the first time, he had seen Chetty and Zulu on the other side of the thick, soundproof glass.

To Bradley's surprise, all the other booths were empty. And instead of standing in front of the exit door as he usually did, the guard had stepped outside and locked the door behind him.

Frowning, he had sat down in the chair. Chetty had gestured to the phone by his right hand, and Bradley had picked up the receiver. He had listened with growing hope to the proposal that the two men had for him—a proposal as audacious as it was lucrative.

They'd get him out of prison early, shortening the ten-year sentence that he'd begun after the lawyers had cross-examined him, the witnesses had said what they had to say, and the doctors and psychiatrists, the men in the white coats, had analysed it all. He would get out of prison immediately, but in return they wanted his help. They wanted him to run a repair project, one as important and involved as the high-budget undertakings he'd managed in the past.

For a few months, he would be theirs.

In return, he would be a free man. And, when the project was finished, a rich one.

'Are you agreeable?' Chetty had asked. His voice had sounded tinny. The men had been passing the receiver back and forth between them as they outlined the proposal to him, and Chetty had smiled knowingly when he said the words, as if he already knew what Bradley's answer would be.

'Yes. Yes, of course. But I want a woman with me,' he'd said, clutching the receiver tightly. 'If you can bring a woman to live with me, then we have a deal.'

Now, staring at the soft, drowsy blonde in his bed, Bradley felt another overpowering surge of lust for his sweet, helpless little prisoner. He was tempted to rip off his trousers and screw her immediately. He knew he must wait, though. Cleanliness, as his father had forcibly reminded him on many occasions, was next to godliness. He would use her later, after he'd had a shower and given her supper—he hoped force-feeding would not be necessary tonight—adding some crushed Rohypnol to the food to ensure her compliance through the night.

Right now, he had urgent work to do.

Bradley went back to the kitchen where he made himself a cup of instant coffee. Three spoons of coffee, four sugars. Lifting the heavy phone that hung around his neck, he scrolled through the list of contacts and dialled the number for the contact he'd made in prison and who was now assisting them with this job—Kobus.

It is night. Pitch-black night, the kind you can only get in Africa, where those towns big enough, or First World enough, to have electricity are so far apart they seem to have no connection to each other at all. They may not even appear to be in the same country. Just tiny oases of light scattered among an endless desert of darkness.

You look down on them. Your vantage point gives you an excellent view. Do you wonder who lives inside those small towns and what their lives are like? How many of them ever leave, ever venture out on one of those endless, straight and dusty roads that slice across the continent like knife strokes, looking for change, to end up in a better place or a worse one?

Do you ever consider whether they might be passing the night in houses or in shacks with rickety tin roofs or, for the poorest and most despairing residents, perhaps wrapped in blankets, shivering under the stars, but grateful that, tonight at least, they are not being battered by the freezing, lightning-laced force of one of Africa's violent storms?

Perhaps you don't. Perhaps you turn your eyes away, get back to work. Even at this early hour of the morning, you have a lot to do. You tip back the plastic mug and swallow the dregs from your last small cup of bland-tasting coffee—everything tastes bland in your rarefied and roaring environment—and think about the morning and what it will bring.

9

The sea mirrored Jade's mood. It gave her some small comfort to feel her own emotions expressed in the force of the crashing breakers and the wind that whipped her face with spray.

That must be why her eyes were so wet.

At least the wind had cooled things down and blown away that muggy, oppressive heat.

The sand felt firm under her feet as she strode along. If she could walk fast enough, perhaps she could break free of the pain that clutched at her every time she thought about Naisha, now four months pregnant with the child that would bind David to her forever.

Naisha, with her body growing plumper and her breasts swelling. Accepting the minor discomforts—heartburn, constipation, aching joints—as part of the natural process of pregnancy. Wearing newly bought maternity clothes, because the ones she had owned when expecting the now nine-year-old Kevin would surely have been donated to charity long ago.

Thinking about what to name her new baby.

Marriage and children had never featured in Jade's life plans, so she couldn't say she felt jealous of her in any way. But it was the thought of David, coming home to Naisha in the evenings, dumping his briefcase down in the hallway as she knew he liked to do, bending his long legs to get them under her dining room table, that made her grind her teeth so hard her jaw began to ache.

The end at last. She'd never imagined this could happen. She and David had somehow kept things going ever since Jade had returned to South Africa, through good times and bad—the good being very good and the bad disastrous. In the back of her mind, though, she had often worried that David had seen their relationship as time out from his troubled marriage. That, try as she might, she would never have all of his heart.

She'd occasionally toyed with giving him an ultimatum, but had always decided against it, telling herself that in the end, he had to make up his own mind.

But in the end, he hadn't. His own idiotic actions had decided his future for him.

Jade picked up her pace, her feet sinking deeper into the sand as she stomped angrily along.

Friends.

As for that, well, how clichéd could you get? And how unlikely. There was more chance of President Jacob Zuma embracing Zen Buddhism.

She should drive back to Johannesburg tomorrow. This holiday was proving to be nothing but a heart-breaking waste of time. David could spend the rest of the week down here alone.

In fact, perhaps she should pack up the car and leave as soon as she got back to the chalet, rather than spending a night alone in the double bed, with David sleeping on the couch, like a 'friend' would do.

The thought of the steaks she'd lovingly prepared for him made her clench her fists. What *had* she been thinking? With the benefit of hindsight, she should have filled the car with bags of lentils and salad ingredients.

And Tabasco sauce, which David frequently complained turned his guts to napalm.

Eyes narrowed against the spray, Jade marched on into the growing darkness.

As she neared the jetty, she heard a loud flapping sound coming from the water. Frowning into the gloom, she saw that the tarpaulin covering the larger dive boat was loose. It was catching the wind like a sail, then slamming down onto the unsteady deck.

A slim figure was struggling with the tarp, trying to secure it back into place, but as Jade watched, the wind snatched the heavy, blue plastic away. It billowed up into the air again, the force rocking the boat so violently that the figure slipped and almost fell overboard.

Jade turned and jogged down towards the jetty. As she drew closer, she realised it was the denim-shorted form of Monique, the Velcro-for-men dive instructor, battling with the wind.

Jade also realised she was still carrying the champagne bottle. She bent down and placed it carefully onto the sand before attracting Monique's attention.

'Need a hand?' she shouted.

She saw the blonde woman's head turn sharply in her direction, but Monique made no reply.

Jade was tempted to leave her to her struggles. Instead, grasping the edge of the jetty rail, she lowered herself carefully down into the boat, which felt like a bucking horse, and grabbed hold of one edge of the tarp. The deck was slick with spray and Jade found it was just about impossible to keep her footing when every tug of the tarp almost yanked her off her feet. She fell twice; the second time bashing her hip painfully on the front seat.

Even with their combined efforts, what they were attempting was seemingly impossible.

But then Jade managed to get two of the hooks into place, subduing the thick plastic long enough to allow Monique to get a firm grasp on her side. From there, it was easier. A few more minutes and they were done.

Jade scrambled up onto the slippery jetty with Monique close behind. Jade saw she was holding a small black object in her hand, but before she could get a good look at it, the dive instructor pushed it into the back pocket of her shorts.

'Thanks,' she muttered to Jade.

A gust of wind blew her blonde hair over her face and she lifted an arm to tuck it behind her ear.

'Is everything . . . ?' But before Jade could even complete her question, the instructor turned and hurried away. As soon as she'd crossed the beach, she broke into a run and headed up towards her room.

Left on the jetty, Jade found herself frowning, and not because of the dive instructor's rudeness and lack of gratitude.

When Monique had pushed her hair back, Jade hadn't been able to help but notice that the woman's face had been sheet-white, frozen-looking and tense with what could only have been overwhelming fear.

A wave crashed against the edge of the jetty, the coolness of the spray shocking, but invigorating. In the distance, lightning illuminated enormous, bulky clouds.

She wondered what David was doing. He'd probably gone to bed without even a bite of food. He did that sometimes when he was tired, and he'd looked exhausted. Jade let out a sharp breath, frustrated by her seeming inability to stop her thoughts from returning to him.

What to do? Drive back to Jo'burg now, or stay here for the night?

Her car keys were in her pocket. But her gun and cellphone were in the chalet, and after storming out so dramatically she was reluctant to go back inside for them.

Jade leaned on the metal railing, temporarily indecisive.

Lightning flashed once more, reflecting off the clouds with an eerie, but surprisingly bright glow. In the distance, Jade noticed a skinny, ragged-looking man heading in her direction along the sand.

A vagrant or a beach bum in this area? Surprised, and rather taken aback by the sighting, she realised the idea of drowning her sorrows alone on the beach had started to lose its appeal. But when the next lightning flash came, the vagrant was no longer right on the beach. Instead, he was heading up towards the chalets, his stride decidedly more purposeful.

Jade frowned.

Picking up the champagne bottle from its resting place in the sand, she walked back, more slowly now, along the beach towards the chalets.

It was now pitch black. Jade could still make out the white, foamy crests of the waves and the thick clouds overhead, but not much else. And then, suddenly, she saw there was somebody ahead, somebody walking swiftly towards her.

Jade's heart sped up and she gripped the heavy bottle more tightly.

The vagrant?

No, too tall.

He slowed down when he saw her and they approached each other cautiously. When she saw the tell-tale ponytail, Jade felt herself relax.

'Craig.'

'Jade?' He came closer, studying her carefully. And then, perhaps sensing her mood, 'You OK?'

A lock of blond hair had escaped from his ponytail and curled over his shoulders.

In her industry—police, private investigation, bodyguarding—close crops or clean-shaven scalps were the norm. Those types of men didn't have long hair. Perhaps because it was too easy to grab it in a fight. Or maybe because it was a sign of weakness; of femininity. The shorter the hair, the tougher the guy underneath it.

'I'm just heading back to the resort.' She almost had to shout to make herself heard over the noise of the ocean. Even so, the wind threatened to snatch her voice away.

'I'm going down to the dive boat. I think I left something there.'

'The boat's covered with a tarp. I helped Monique with it just now. I don't rate your chances of getting it off and back on again.'

'Damn,' Craig raised a hand and rubbed his beard.

'What did you leave behind?'

'My wallet.'

Jade was going to tell Craig that he'd do better to come down again first thing in the morning. She didn't think that anyone would be willing to do battle with that tarpaulin, in that swell, on the off-chance there'd be something of value underneath it.

But then she remembered what she'd seen when she climbed out of the boat.

Monique, avoiding Jade's gaze as she shoved something small and black into her back pocket. And doing it furtively, not in a way that somebody would handle a legitimate personal possession.

'A black one?' Jade asked.

'Yes. Did you see it?'

'I think Monique might have found it and taken it up to the resort with her,' Jade said carefully.

'Oh.' Craig glanced down the beach to the jetty, where waves were pounding the dive boat against the dock bumpers, and then looked back at Jade again. 'Did she say she'd found it?'

'No. But you could ask her anyway.'

'I suppose I could. Are you heading back that way?' Now Jade saw Craig look down, with some curiosity, at the champagne bottle she held.

Jade began to wish she had smashed the damn thing on the floor after all.

'Yes,' she snapped. She didn't offer any further explanation. Just turned, bracing herself against the wind, and walked up towards the resort with Craig, keeping a sharp eye out for any signs of the scrawny man she thought she'd seen a short while ago.

She wasn't really paying any attention to Craig as he headed across to the staff quarters and, after some hesitation, stepped up onto the covered paving and gave a gentle knock on the nearest door.

But when she heard his startled cry and saw him frozen in the doorway of the room he had just opened, Jade came running.

10

Jade hurried up the shallow wooden steps and along the corridor that led to the open door where Craig was standing, stock-still, staring into the room in disbelief.

Looking over his shoulder, Jade saw the small bedsit was splattered with crimson.

Red gouts were trickling down the peeling back wall of the kitchenette, where the dirty-brown curtain was twisting and flapping in the wind, and more of them streaked the tiled floor. It half covered the unmade double bed, thick-looking streaks that were deep red in colour, a stark contrast to the crumpled, off-white sheet.

The gruesome sight was bathed in bright light under the uncompromising glare of the bare electric bulb that hung from the wooden ceiling.

There was nobody inside the room.

Jade felt her heart start pounding, fast and hard.

She put a hand on Craig's arm, aware of a smell in the air, incongruous and yet familiar. A strong, spicy odour. That smell . . . and the fact the room was empty . . .

And what was that gleaming on the tiles? It looked like a jagged shard of clear glass.

Jade let out a deep breath that turned into a small, relieved laugh.

'It's ketchup,' she said.

Jade moved her hand as Craig lowered his arms. Her palm felt warm from where it had touched his skin. He turned and looked at her, then stared more closely at the scene in front of him again.

'Tomato sauce? Are you sure?' He sniffed the air, then started to laugh. 'So it is. It's a glass bottle of All Gold. That caught me by surprise. I thought it was . . .'

'I know. So did I.' Jade pointed to the windowsill above the hot plate, where the curtain was still twisting and writhing in the wind as if possessed.

That sill was where the room's occupant obviously kept the condiments. The curtain's movement had also knocked over a plastic tub of mayonnaise, which was lying in between the hot plates on the little cooker, and a Perspex salt grinder that was rolling to and fro, perilously close to the sill's edge.

The large bottle of tomato sauce must have hit the corner of the cooker when it tumbled off the narrow shelf, shattering into pieces and splattering its contents all over the floor and the bed.

Jade put the bottle of champagne down again. Picking her way delicately over the messy tiles, she squeezed round the edge of the bed, grabbed the flapping curtain, then leaned over and closed the window. She picked up the salt and the mayonnaise and put them both on the small wooden table next to the hot plate.

Then, turning round, she took another look at the bed.

Lying on the pillow was a slim black wallet.

Craig had seen it too.

'Is that yours?' she asked him.

'Looks like mine.'

Stepping carefully, just as Jade had done, he walked over to the bed and picked it up. He opened it and checked the contents with fingers that Jade noticed were tanned and calloused. Whatever Craig did for a living, she was willing to bet it wasn't a desk job.

Frowning, he pocketed the wallet.

'Everything there?' she asked him.

'All my cards are there. And my driver's licence.'

'But?'

'There's cash missing.'

'How much?'

Craig shook his head, clearly frustrated. 'All of it. There must have been a few hundred inside.'

Jade shook her head. 'You should report it to the police. Report Monique.'

'How can I prove she took it? The wallet was left in the boat.'

'Not for that long.'

'Anybody could have come past and stolen it.'

'True. It was her, though. I saw how she looked when she put it in her pocket.'

Jade moved back towards the door. She was starting to feel uneasy, standing in this cluttered, messy little room. Over the strong smell of the spilled ketchup, she began to recognise other odours. Deodorant. Perfume. The smell of Monique herself, emanating from the unwashed sheets on the bed.

And just where was she now?

Jade found herself thinking back to their encounter on the boat, and the way she had looked. Jade knew fear when she saw it, and Monique had been terrified. Now she'd taken money from a customer's wallet, left her room unlocked . . .

Glancing inside the wardrobe as she passed it, Jade noticed a selection of shorts and T-shirts in disorderly piles. An ancient-looking wetsuit was folded on top of a backpack on the floor. Clearly, Monique hadn't packed up and left. Her possessions, such as they were, were still there, but she had gone.

'She was frightened when I saw her earlier,' Jade said.

'Why?'

'I don't know why. When we were down by the boat, I asked her, but she didn't answer. Just ran off.'

Craig shook his head again as he walked out of the room.

'I guess we'll have to wait till we see her again,' he said.

'I suppose so.'

Jade closed the door gently behind her. Monique might not have gone far, but until she returned her room would just have to remain unlocked.

'Does she have a car?' she asked.

'Yes. She parks it round the corner, behind these rooms.'

'Let's go and see if it's there.'

'Good idea.'

The elderly white vehicle parked on the grass reminded Jade of the cars she drove. She got her rides from a Jo'burg company called Rent a Runner, and every month she switched the car for a different one. Monique's vehicle was even older than the worst of the Rent a Runners that Jade drove. It seemed to be more rust than metal. The rear windscreen was cracked and the front number plate was missing.

The memory of the beach vagrant returned to Jade as she headed back down the wooden corridor with Craig. As she rounded the corner, stepping out of the lit area and into the darkness, she thought she saw something.

A flash of movement, further up the driveway close to the trees.

Jade stopped and squinted into the gloom, aware that a misty rain had started to fall and was growing heavier by the minute.

The wind was still whipping the trees, their canopies rustling and swaying, but it wasn't that movement that Jade had seen. She was sure of it. It had been a swift, furtive motion, as if somebody had seen them and wanted to hide.

'Anything wrong?'

Craig's voice, softly, behind her.

'I saw something. Could have been someone. Up there.'

'Monique?' Craig sounded surprised.

'I doubt it. But when I was down on the beach, I noticed a man heading towards the resort—he looked like a vagrant or a tramp. He came up this way.'

'You want to go check?'

'Do you have a torch?'

'In my chalet.'

As they walked back past Monique's room, Craig glanced down at the champagne bottle that Jade had left outside the door. 'Could I . . . would you like me to put that inside for you?'

'Thanks.' Jade picked it up and handed it over. She was glad to be rid of it.

Craig walked the short distance to his chalet, unlocked the door and stepped inside. He returned a minute later holding a torch, with a yellow waterproof jacket slung over his shoulders.

In his hand, he held another jacket, this one leather, which he handed to Jade.

'You want to put this on? It'll help keep out the worst of the rain.'

'Thanks.'

Jade had expected that the jacket would be Elsabe's—a woman's size—but when she slid her arms into it, the sleeves were far too long, and she realised that this garment must also belong to Craig.

'Where exactly did you see it?'

'Right there.' Jade pointed.

Craig shone the torch onto the shadowy foliage that lined the two brick-paved lanes of the driveway leading up the hill. The beam lit up nothing out of the ordinary.

Jade wrapped the jacket tightly round her shoulders, glad for the protection from the worsening rain, especially since her legs were bare. Craig was also unsuitably clad for the weather in his khaki shorts and Teva leather hiking sandals.

The leather jacket smelled spicy and smoky, making her think of red wine and log fires.

They walked up the driveway, Craig shining the torch to and fro.

'You know, there are no fences here,' Jade said. 'This place is not well secured. It bothers me that anybody can walk off the road or off the beach, right up to the resort.'

Craig nodded. 'A lot of the smaller resorts here are pretty laid-back about security, especially compared to the big cities. There isn't the same level of crime here. You get petty theft, the occasional burglary. Maybe, if you're unlucky, a smashed car window.'

'Are you from around here?'

He shook his head. 'From Cape Town, originally. I've spent some time doing fieldwork here, though.' Prompted by Jade's questioning glance, he continued. 'There have been some large-scale ecological studies commissioned here, and that's my field of expertise. Marine ecology.'

'Sounds interesting,' Jade said. 'So was there an oil spill here recently, then?'

'An oil spill? No, heaven forbid. Absolutely not. Why?'

'I've noticed black streaks in the sand around here. I thought they might be oil. I didn't know if I should try to avoid them when I walk on the beach.'

'No, those are mineral deposits, mostly titanium ore. They occur naturally in the sand around here. The ore originated in the Drakensberg mountains. It was eroded over time, transported to the sea by the rivers, and then washed north by the current to end up in these dunes.'

'Oh, OK then. That makes sense.'

'That's why the leatherback turtles come here to breed.'

'How do you mean? Because of the dunes?'

'Because the sand is so incredibly mineral-rich. They swim thousands of miles every year to lay their eggs here.'

'I haven't seen any of those yet. They sound like amazing . . . er . . . animals.'

Was it correct to call a turtle an animal? Or should she have referred to them as reptiles? Jade wasn't sure.

'There should be some loggerheads around now, although it is early in the season. They are incredible. The world's fourth-largest reptile. But sadly, they're an endangered species.'

So she'd been wrong. They were reptiles. Oh well. Turning her attention back to their surroundings, Jade watched as the torch beam swept over the dark tree trunks, brightening the foliage from shadowy grey to deep green. She kept her gaze fixed on the trees, listening to raindrops spattering on leaves, scanning the narrow strip of forest for any signs that somebody might be hiding there. There would be giveaways. A flash of colour from clothing. Sudden movement that was not caused by the wind.

'The mineral wealth in the sands is a mixed blessing, because it has historically made this area an endangered one,' Craig continued. 'Back in King Shaka's time, we know that limited mining took place here, because there are remains of metal weapons in the old Zulu settlements—weapons made from minerals mined from these dunes.'

'And what about more recently?'

'In the mid-1990s, there was a massive outcry when a company wanted to strip-mine the dunes.'

'I'm sure I remember hearing about that in the news,' Jade said.

'It made headlines all over the country. All over the world, in fact, because it would have been an ecological disaster. One of my very first projects was working to oppose that strip-mining operation. It was successful.'

'What was the outcome?'

'The St Lucia wetlands area, or iSimangaliso, as it's now known, was proclaimed a world heritage site, the first one in South Africa. That put a stop to all such operations within the park, although a couple of areas were mined nearby. And now the dunes are under threat again.'

'Why's that?'

'There's increasing pressure from developers to have the 1996 legislation overturned, to allow mining to take place in the park, and to open up the area to industrial development.'

The forest area was jungle-like in its density, the area under the trees thick and matted with ferns, lichens and other plants that Jade didn't recognise. She supposed Craig would know their names. And she assumed that if anybody had tried to hide in here, they would have left an obvious path behind them as they battled their way through the overgrowth.

Craig was still chatting casually about the local ecosystem. It was fine for him to do that, because that was his work. But Jade's work was different. She knew only too well that locating a hiding fugitive could literally mean the difference between life and death. She couldn't allow herself to relax, or get too distracted by a conversation that she had to admit was beginning to pique her interest.

'What's the justification for scrapping the old laws?' she asked, despite herself.

'Well, the argument for declaring the area a national park was that ecotourism could bring as much benefit to the area as mining. But that hasn't ended up happening as fast as it should have done, for a variety of reasons.'

'What are those?' Jade paused to wipe the rain from her face.

'Practically, the lack of roads is the biggest problem. And, of course, you can't even build an ecolodge in an area that has sensitive vegetation or problematic soils.'

'That would be pointless,' Jade agreed. Even she could see that would be a non-starter.

'Meanwhile, the local communities have their own problems. They're among the poorest in the country and they rely on natural resources to survive. With the park a protected area, it means that the forests outside its boundaries are starting to become depleted. They're pressurising the authorities to open up the areas within the park, because they need more space and materials for subsistence farming.'

'That's depressing.'

'Not as depressing as the fact that the developers have now managed to get a review on the titanium-mining ban. They have requested an ecological reassessment of the area to be done, which will be starting next month. It's a real worry that the results of that report could tip the balance and see industry winning over the environment again.'

'I can see how that could happen.'

Craig sighed heavily. 'It's a beautiful, peaceful part of the world. But under the surface, it's a simmering pressure cooker of conflicting interests, and we're all hoping we can keep the lid from blowing off.'

Ahead, Jade could see the wooden gateposts that marked the boundary of Scuba Sands. They'd walked the length of the driveway. No sign of the person she'd seen earlier. Perhaps he'd simply been using the resort as a shortcut and had gone on to take shelter from the rain somewhere else.

Then Jade recalled how she'd noticed the change in the man's demeanour; from his aimless wandering along the beach to the focused purposefulness with which he'd then headed up towards the chalets.

And then she caught her breath. She'd seen movement, illuminated for just a moment in one of the passes that the torch had made.

'Over there,' she said. 'Something's there.'

II

'You've seen something? Where?' Craig swung the torch back in the opposite direction.

'Over that way.' Jade pointed to a clump of trees. 'More to the right. Yes, there. Look.'

The beam picked up the gleam of two eyes amid a brown-grey wall of skin. Its shape and size were unmistakable. Out of the water, it looked almost comically porcine—very different in real life from the smiling, cartoon-like animal on the doormat outside the Huberta room.

Jade's legs felt suddenly unsteady. She knew only too well that these mammals were responsible for more human deaths than any other.

'It's a hippo,' she whispered. 'And it's moving.'

Craig slowly arced the torch back across the trees. 'It's OK—it's heading away from us, I think, into that thick bank of bushes.'

They strained to hear it making its way through the under-growth, but above the clamour of the wind and rain Jade wasn't sure if the tearing sounds she thought she could hear were real or her imagination playing tricks on her.

'Still, we'd better get out of here,' Craig said softly. 'We certainly don't want to get between it and its intended destination.'

'The brochure in the chalet did say to be careful about going out at night. Now I can see why,' she whispered.

They turned and headed swiftly back down the road, Jade still feeling lightheaded from adrenaline and wondering if it would be possible to outrun three tons of angry hippo moving at more than forty kilometres an hour, should the beast decide to charge them. Thinking about it more logically, though, surely all she would have to do would be to outrun Craig?

One thing was for sure—with hippos on the loose, she didn't think that many vagrants would be choosing to bed down for the night anywhere near their chalets.

They walked along for a while in companionable silence and, as she saw the lights of their resort ahead, she felt herself start to relax.

'You've got good eyesight, Jade,' Craig said. 'At that distance, in that light, I'd never have spotted it on my own.'

Jade nodded. 'I'm lucky that way. Twenty-twenty vision. And I can see well at night.'

'Just like my father. I didn't inherit his eyesight, unfortunately. I wear contact lenses.'

'What does your dad do?'

There was an awkward silence and then an abrupt response from Craig. 'Not much. He's dead.'

'I'm sorry.'

'It still . . . it's still shocking when I think about it. It's barely been six months.'

'What happened?' Jade felt a coldness inside her. She didn't want to ask the question, but she knew that now it would be expected of her. That Craig was already preparing himself for the pain of answering it.

'A crash up in northern Africa, in a town called Freedom. The stuff nightmares are made of. I went to go and identify his body, but it was so badly damaged that I couldn't.... They had to do a DNA comparison. That was how I met Elsabe—at the crash site. She also lost family there, including a child. Half a year on and I'm still trying to deal with it. It's even worse for her.'

Jade didn't reply immediately. She had also lost her father in a horrific crash. Emotion overwhelmed her as she remembered seeing the smashed and buckled car in which he had been a passenger. He'd been trapped inside the stalled vehicle, unable to undo his jammed seatbelt, as a huge truck had come hurtling down a side road and smashed into it.

Only later did Jade realise that his death was no accident, that it was murder, an organised hit hastily arranged to protect the criminal whose identity her father had uncovered as he investigated a sensitive case.

The driver of that car had been the first man she had ever killed.

Had her father suffered? Had he died in terror, watching the truck's large, angry grille thundering towards him?

Jade had prayed that his death had been quick, that he had been distracted by the deliberately jammed belt, unaware of the approaching vehicle. That it had happened in an instant. One moment alive, dead the next.

She wondered if Craig had prayed for the same.

'I'm sorry to hear that.' Her voice was shaky. 'I'm so sorry, Craig.'

He sighed deeply. 'Time heals, apparently, but I'm still waiting.'

Jade didn't think it was possible for the rain to get any harder, but suddenly it was as if the floodgates to the Gariep Dam had been opened. Icy water fell in torrents from the sky. Hailstones stung her bare legs and ricocheted off the back of the leather jacket.

'Inside!' Craig shouted.

They raced to his chalet. A brief fumble with the padlock and they were inside, standing in the middle of the lounge, water dripping off them and down onto the tiles. As the door slammed behind them, Jade found herself waiting for Elsabe to call out from one of the bedrooms or appear in the passage, asking what all the noise was about.

She eased the jacket off her shoulders and hung it on the back of a dining-room chair. It had provided some protection against the rain, but her T-shirt was now sporting huge damp patches and her shorts were soaked. Luckily the heat that the storm had chased away outside was still lingering inside, so she wasn't cold.

Looking round, she realised that both the doors in this bigger, two-bedroom chalet were open.

'Where's Elsabe?' she asked.

Craig shrugged. 'She went into town to visit a friend. Said she wouldn't be back tonight.'

The reluctant way in which he said it made Jade think that the person Elsabe had gone to visit might be more than a friend, and that Craig himself was upset by this.

'Well, thanks for lending me the jacket,' she said. 'I'd better be going.'

'Wait. Your champagne.'

He'd put it in the fridge. Now he took it out and handed it to her. Strong, tanned fingers clasped the neck of the bottle. Water trickled down from his sodden blond hair.

Jade shook her head. 'You might as well keep it,' she said.

Now his eyes met hers and she saw concern in them.

Hazel eyes. Brown, with flecks of green and yellow.

Again, she noticed the twinge in the pit of her stomach she'd felt the first time she'd spoken to him. Not unease . . . something else.

'Don't you . . . ?' he said, then stopped himself as if he'd been going to ask her something personal but had decided against it.

And then, after a pause, he continued. 'Don't you want to drink it?'

'What, now?'

'Yes. Now.'

Jade could feel the tension in the air, like the way everything had felt before the thunderstorm, as he waited for her to answer.

She hadn't looked away from him. She found that at that moment she couldn't.

'OK.'

Craig moved over to the door. The key rattled as he locked it.

The pop of the champagne cork sounded very loud in the otherwise silent room.

12

Jade dreamed about drowning that night. She was far under the water, which was warm but pitch black. She had no scuba gear on, no diving apparatus at all, and, in the gloomy depths, she couldn't tell which way was up. She knew she had no more air left, that the next breath she would take in would send water rushing into her lungs, but somehow the knowledge wasn't frightening.

'Follow the bubbles,' a woman's voice whispered.

'But it's too dark,' Jade responded, although how she spoke the words she had no idea. 'I can't see any bubbles. Can't I just stay here with you?'

'No. You can't do that.' Suddenly a slender, pale arm appeared in front of her. Its hand opened and the index finger flicked out. 'There they are.'

A stream of silvery bubbles flooded upwards and Jade followed them, speeding through the blackness like a shooting star. She broke the surface and she was out, into the clear, beautiful air. She was blinking water out of her eyes, and in her ears she could hear the scream of seagulls.

The birds' loud, intrusive calls continued as they wheeled above her. They grew shriller and shriller until the irritating noise pulled her right out of the dream.

It was fully light on a grey, rainy morning.

Her hair was tangled and her mouth felt dry. She could taste stale champagne and fresh guilt.

And the shrill ululations were still coming from somewhere nearby, audible even above the splashing of rain and the more distant booming of the sea. Rubbing her eyes, Jade sat up, trying not to wake the sleeping man lying next to her, and listened.

She was sure that somebody, probably the cleaner, had opened Monique's door and been startled by the devastation inside.

Jade swung her legs over the side of the bed, stood up, and pulled on her clothes. In the bathroom, she ran her hands through her shoulder-length hair, splashed some water on her face and drank some from the tap, then unlocked the front door as quietly as she could.

As soon as she opened it, the spray-soaked wind snatched her hair away from her face. Ahead of her was the restless ocean, which, if Craig's facts were correct, was flanked not by a beautiful national park, but by a war zone. A territory where developers and miners, the indigenous population and ecologists, fought for the upper hand every day.

Above the sound of the rain, she could still hear the cries. They were, if anything, louder than they had been. Jade started to feel uneasy.

She was starting to fear that her first guess might have been wrong.

Ducking her head against the hard, driving rain, she ran towards the staff quarters, following the direction of the sound. A few seconds later she burst into the narrow corridor, under cover at last.

Right in front of her was the cleaner. She was a few feet away from an open door, crouched down against the railings, her head buried in her hands. Sobs racked her body and the loud cries burst from her lips, harsh and agonised, as if she had no control over them at all.

'Hi there,' Jade called. 'What's the matter?'

She could hear the uncertainty in her own voice, too. She walked forward and, although her feet made a loud noise on the hollow-sounding board flooring, the cleaner gave no sign she had heard her.

Looking more closely at the door, Jade now saw the wood surrounding the lock was splintered, as if it had been forced.

Inside . . . Jade's breath quickened and she blinked rapidly as she took in the gruesome scene.

The body of a young woman was sprawled face up on the floor in front of the bed, her arms outstretched, her head half covered by the duvet. The floorboards were stained dark with blood and the pale bed linen was covered with deep-red splashes and streaks.

And the corpse . . . Jade steeled herself for a closer look, realising her hands were cold and her heart was hammering.

The wounds must have been made by a knife. One long, deep cut had slashed right through her pink T-shirt and sliced her stomach wide open, the wound exposing a bloody mess of innards. A smaller stain on her left breast showed Jade where the only other visible cut had been inflicted.

Looking around the tidy room, Jade could see no sign of the weapon that had been used to kill her.

Then she heard herself give a small, involuntary moan as the awful truth hit her.

This little bedsit was neat. The covers might be blood-stained, but there were no half-empty bottles of mayonnaise on the windowsill and the window itself was shaded by a new-looking bamboo blind, not by curtains.

This was not Monique's room, as she had first assumed. Looking further down the corridor she could see that Monique's wooden door was shut tight, the way they had left it last night. In fact, since Monique clearly hadn't been alerted by the Zulu woman's screaming, Jade doubted whether she had even come home.

This was the room next door.

Stepping forward carefully to avoid a dark, sticky-looking pool of blood, she took hold of the top of the duvet and carefully teased it away from the corpse. To her dismay, she found herself staring into the lifeless eyes of the woman she had last seen alive the day before; the scuba-diving instructor she now realised she had come to regard as a friend.

Amanda Bolton.

13

Detective Inspector Pillay from the Richards Bay investigation unit reminded Jade of a startled fawn. She had no idea they made detectives so young these days, so wide-eyed, or indeed so slim. He barely looked out of his teens, although she knew he must be in his mid-twenties at least.

At any rate, she didn't place a whole lot of confidence in the slender, olive-skinned, smooth-jawed man who, after having instructed his even younger-looking black assistant to cordon off the corridor on both sides of the door with a brand-new roll of yellow crime-scene tape, was now approaching Amanda's corpse as cautiously as if it might bite.

Although inexperienced, the crime-investigation unit had certainly been prompt. They had arrived within a few minutes of Jade dialling 10111, and an ambulance had arrived shortly afterwards.

The first thing Jade had done was to run back to the chalet and wake David. He had been fast asleep on the couch in an uncomfortable-looking position that she was sure his back would start telling him all about later in the day.

He'd frowned when he saw her, struggling into a sitting position, and she knew he was going to ask where on earth she had been.

She'd pre-empted his questions by telling him, rather breathlessly, to call the emergency services and then get his arse over to the staff quarters as fast as he could, because there had been a murder.

Then she'd run straight back to the scene of the crime, where she had helped the cleaner to her feet and led her gently back to her own room at the end of the passage. There, Jade sat her down on her bed and made her a big mug of strong, sweet tea.

The woman, whose name Jade learnt was Nosipho, was still trembling from head to toe. She held the mug of tea in both hands and sipped it carefully, staring at the wall with the blank gaze of somebody who had seen too much.

At the sound of approaching sirens, she'd hurried outside again to find David standing by Pillay's car. Once introductions had been made and David's assistance been offered and accepted, the detectives had splashed over to the crime scene, leaving Jade waiting near the police car, staring across at the splintered door.

The news had already begun to spread throughout the resort, as fast and nasty as a bad smell driven by the wind. And, just like a bad smell, the closer people were to it the sooner they reacted.

Her immediate neighbour was the first to appear.

'Is there something wrong?' She heard Craig's voice, softly, from behind her.

She turned to see him standing a few feet away and staring through the rain at the crime-scene tape, his waterproof jacket slung over his shoulders. His hair was still rumpled from sleep.

'Yes, there is,' Jade replied, her voice equally hushed. 'Amanda's been murdered.'

Craig stared at her, shocked into silence. His eyes widened and his jaw slackened as the horror of the words sank in.

'Jesus,' he said eventually. 'You mean, here?'

'Yes. In her room.'

Jade had to speak loudly, because another set of sirens was signalling the arrival of an ambulance.

'She was stabbed,' she added.

'Holy shit.'

They were silent for a minute. Then, 'Where's Monique?' Craig asked.

Jade shrugged. 'I don't know. The detective knocked on her door a few minutes ago and there was no answer. Her car's still parked round the back.'

Craig's lips tightened and he shook his head.

Then wheels splashed through water as Elsabe's Corsa drove slowly towards the chalet. Elsabe braked hard when she saw the ambulance, then inched her car forward and into its parking bay. Craig turned away and went to meet her.

The policemen went slowly about their work. Jade watched Inspector Pillay dusting the outside of the door for prints. He did it carefully, methodically, with narrowed eyes and rather unsteady hands. He looked like he was doing it the way that a person did it when they'd only ever read about it in books, or perhaps done it a few times at training college.

It took a few minutes for the news to reach the last chalet in the row; the one occupied by a married couple called Larry and Roxanne. They were from Gauteng as well, according to the number plate on their oversized, bright-orange Hummer.

Roxanne's hair was almost exactly the same colour as the car. When Jade had first seen that, she couldn't help wondering which of them Larry had acquired first.

Jade was still on the balcony when she heard the distinctive growl of the Hummer's gas-guzzling engine. Larry and Roxanne weren't walking the short distance to the crime scene. They were driving. Definitely from Gauteng, then.

The ridiculously large vehicle skidded to a stop on the verge, its thick tyres digging deep gouges into the wet sand. Roxanne didn't get out. She stayed in the car, dark glasses covering her eyes.

Larry got out, but he left the engine running. Jade was sure the environment would be pleased about that.

The squat, dark-haired man marched over to Jade and glared at her as if she was responsible for the disruption. His shirt collar was open and Jade noticed a number of gold chains nestling in his abundant chest hair.

'I was told there's been a murder.'

'Yes,' Jade said. 'Amanda was stabbed. The scuba instructor.'

'Hell,' Larry muttered. Then, louder, 'What is the resort doing to take care of our security? I mean, it could have happened to any of us. I heard her door was broken down.'

'Not exactly. The lock was splintered.'

Once again, Jade glanced across at the damaged door.

Larry stared at her as if she was mad. 'Same thing, isn't it? So, what precautions are they going to take?'

'I'm sorry,' Jade said. 'I'm not the right person to ask.'

Looking through the Hummer's passenger window, she saw that Roxanne was combing out her orange hair, peering into the little vanity mirror while she did so.

Priorities.

With an exasperated sigh, Larry strode over towards the taped-off crime scene.

David came to the door when he saw Larry arrive, and the two men exchanged words. David's voice remained calm, but Larry's grew louder and more aggressive as the conversation played out.

Eventually, Larry threw his arms in the air, turned around and marched back to his Hummer. He climbed in, slammed the door and stomped on the accelerator hard, turning the car around so fast that Jade was surprised Roxanne didn't stab herself in the eye with her comb.

He stopped when he drew level with Jade and buzzed the window down.

'Are they going to be finished before ten?'

Jade shook her head. 'No way. They'll be here longer than that, probably most of the day.'

He turned and spoke briefly to Roxanne. Jade heard the word 'brunch' mentioned. Then he stuck his head out of the window again and addressed Jade.

'When they're done, can you come and tell us?'

'No, I can't.'

Larry glowered at her. 'Why not?'

'Because I'm not going to be here.'

He blinked. 'Oh.'

Then he buzzed his window up again and the orange vehicle roared back down the bumpy driveway, belching exhaust fumes in its wake.

Behind the crime-scene tape, Jade saw Inspector Pillay tap diffidently on Monique's door once again before opening it. He stood stock still for a moment, frozen when he saw the mess inside, until he too realised what he was looking at.

The ketchup was still there. Jade could see the splashes. They were darker, now. Congealed, just like spilled blood.

Monique was nowhere to be seen.

14

Richards Bay had grown to such a size that it now boasted two hospitals—a large and relatively new clinic to the north of town, and the old hospital that had been built more than fifty years ago.

Jade's GPS had become confused when she'd asked it to locate the old hospital. It had wanted to send her to the new clinic. Then, on the second try, it had directed her into an area full of dilapidated houses near the railway lines. So she'd done what any sensible South African in her situation would do—backtracked and pulled over at a petrol station to ask for help.

One of the pump attendants gave her detailed directions. Drive along this main road. Go through four robots. Turn right at number five, then left at the second stop street, then right at the next robot. Keep going through one more robot, and look for the hospital on your right-hand side.

Distances did not enter into the explanation, but Jade knew from experience that the numbers of robots and stop streets that the man had told her to look out for would be both exact and reliable. All she had to do was keep driving and keep counting.

This she did, and in due course the signpost for the hospital appeared on her right.

As Jade drove closer, she saw that the hospital was showing its age. The tarmac in the car park was cracked and broken. The security guard's booth looked as if it might well fall to pieces in the next strong wind. The guard himself, a young black man, didn't even do a proper check on her or her vehicle; he just walked out of his cubicle and pressed a forearm down on the handle of the peeling red and white boom.

It lifted, and Jade drove inside and parked in the half-empty lot.

This was Richards Bay General Hospital, where she had been born.

There were no other visitors arriving on this dull, drizzly morning. The main reception desk was unoccupied, but barely a minute passed before Jade heard the increasingly loud slapping of shoes on the linoleum floor. A black woman who looked as if she could have been the security guard's grandmother came hurrying in through the doors leading to the wards.

'Good morning,' the woman said somewhat breathlessly. She sat down heavily on the squeaky chair, propped her elbows on the ward register and looked enquiringly at Jade.

'I'm here to find out about a patient.'

'Visiting hours are from twelve to one, *intombazane*.' Her use of the Zulu word surprised Jade. She'd thought she was too old to be referred to as 'girl'. 'I can try and phone the ward for you, if you want. What is the patient's name?

Jade shook her head.

'Do you know the ward number?'

Jade stared at the lady in silence. She wasn't used to finding herself so tongue-tied.

'Sorry,' she said eventually. 'I'm not talking about one of your current patients. This lady was a former patient. She was here a long time ago.'

The woman's face wrinkled into a puzzled frown. 'A long time ago?'

'Yes. I don't think you'll have any records, but I'm hoping that you might know of somebody who worked at the hospital at that time.' Seeing the woman's frown deepen, Jade added, 'The patient's name was Elise de Jong. My mother. She died here.'

Watching the woman give a small, understanding nod, Jade allowed herself to acknowledge the impossibility of the task she had set herself. Elise de Jong had been admitted to this hospital long before computers were in general use.

Her mother had not passed away recently either, as she was sure this grey-haired receptionist assumed. How could Jade hope to obtain any information on a woman who had been dead for almost thirty-five years?

To Jade's surprise, however, when she'd explained the situation to the grey-haired receptionist, she hadn't been told that it would be impossible. Instead, the lady had asked her to take a seat while she made a couple of phone calls. She'd pointed to a row of cracked plastic-covered chairs against the opposite wall, and Jade had obeyed.

Now, perched on the edge of the nearest chair, she realised this was decision time.

Should she go back to Jo'burg or not?

She'd packed up before leaving the resort and her bag was in the boot of the car. If the police wanted to get a statement from her regarding the murder, she reasoned, they could damn well talk to her over the phone. She wasn't a key witness, and she had little information that would be of value to the investigation team.

Going home was by far the most appealing option. And yet, she knew that David could use her help. That there were many ways in which she could assist with the investigation.

Jade resolved to put her fate in the hands of the hospital receptionist. If the lady didn't come up with anyone who may have known her mother, then she would get on the highway and drive straight back to Jo'burg.

If she did locate somebody who'd known Elise de Jong—well, then, Jade would stay a little longer, just until she'd spoken to them. Assuming that the person was still living in Richards Bay.

She had tried to persuade herself that she didn't care either way.

But when the grey-haired lady called out to her, '*Intombazane*, you can come to the desk now,' Jade felt a thrill of the same nervous expectation she'd felt when she'd arrived at the grave-yard the day before.

A few minutes later, she was climbing back into her car, her decision made. The receptionist had given her two names, written on a small white notelet bearing the logo of a pain-relief product she'd never heard of.

Martha Koekemoer, who had been the matron of the maternity ward at the time when Jade was born, and Doctor Abrahams, who had worked at the hospital for many years and was now on the board of directors.

Much to Jade's disappointment, the receptionist had not given her their contact numbers. Perhaps she hadn't trusted her. Instead, she had taken Jade's number and promised to pass it on to the two of them.

Slamming the car door, Jade reversed out of the parking space.

She would go back to the resort and stay there until she'd spoken to one or both of them.

15

Jade changed the channel on the radio as she drove, hoping to find a station that was playing hard rock or heavy metal. She felt like listening to something nihilistic, that would match her mood. Enrique Iglesias crooning 'Tonight I'm Loving You' just wasn't doing it for her. She didn't want to think about tonight—especially not as far as loving was concerned.

She slowed down as she approached the intersection with the winding access road that led to the chalets, and prepared to make the turn across the double-lane road. A glance in her rearview mirror showed the snarling grille of a large truck with a big steel bull-bar coming up behind her.

It was going way too fast. What the hell was the driver thinking—or hadn't he noticed that her brake lights and indicator were on? She didn't think the truck would be able to stop in time to avoid hitting her. In which case, making the right-hand turn would be suicidal, because the driver would almost definitely swerve right, trying to overtake her when he realised he couldn't stop in time.

Jade jammed her car into gear, stamped on the accelerator and swung hard left, off the road and onto the bumpy, sandy verge. The pint-sized Fiat bounced and rattled.

A horn blared behind her and the screech of brakes seemed to slice right through her eardrums. With tyres smoking, the truck swerved past her. As she'd thought he would do, the driver had swerved right, into her turning lane.

As he passed, he turned and looked her straight in the eye. His face was drawn and weather-beaten, so lean and deeply lined that the skin appeared to be hanging from the bones.

Like his truck, he seemed to be snarling at her.

And then he was gone, roaring off into the distance.

Glancing ahead, reflexively, Jade made a mental note of the rear number plate of the accelerating truck. ZN300-420.

She let out a deep, shaky breath. What the hell had he been thinking? She was supposed to be on holiday here, safely out of the big city and away from stress-fuelled maniacs who drove as if the devil was after them.

Checking her mirrors carefully, she pulled off the uneven verge, crossed the now-quiet road and headed down the hill towards the resort.

By the time she'd got back, the rain had stopped. Its continuous pattering was now replaced by a harsher sound—the whine of a drill and the splintering groan of thick nails being driven into wood.

Vusi, the elderly handyman who did most of the maintenance and repair work at Scuba Sands, was now busy installing two big steel bolts on the inside of her chalet door. One roughly thirty centimetres above the handle and the other the same distance below.

Neil Cronje, the owner of Scuba Sands and the person who'd told her about Huberta the wandering hippo, was supervising this important task. On the day she'd arrived, she'd gone up to the front porch of his small house that was situated just beyond the furthermost chalet to sign in. As he'd welcomed her, she had noticed, much to her amusement, that he'd paired his short-sleeved collared shirt with yellow swimming trunks sporting large green frogs, and thonged sandals. On the wall behind the reception desk she'd seen several photos of him, looking about twenty years younger and as many kilos slimmer, riding his surf-board on enormous waves.

She hadn't seen him much since then—he'd kept to himself—but now she noticed that the sandals and brightly patterned shorts appeared to be a permanent fixture in his wardrobe.

'I'm sorry about this,' he told her now, rubbing his forehead. 'I'm just so sorry. We're putting extra security precautions in place for everybody today. I've spent most of my life in this area and nothing like this has ever happened here before. And I mean nothing.'

'I understand,' Jade said. She put her travel bag down next to the coffee table. 'Thank you for organising the extra security.'

She couldn't help but feel sympathy for him. When he reached Larry's chalet, she was sure he was going to become the target of all the wealthy man's pent-up frustration. He'd probably end up feeling like Larry's Hummer had ridden over him.

After Neil left, the handyman finished his job by kneeling down and carefully sweeping the tiny piles of wood shavings and dust into a dustpan, which he tipped out of the front door. Then he picked up his toolbox and walked outside, heading for the neighbouring chalet.

A minute later, her stomach tightened as she heard David's familiar footsteps approaching.

He walked in, scowling and rubbing his hands together as if he was washing them in air. Suddenly, she remembered her father doing exactly the same when he'd peeled off his rubber gloves after investigating a crime scene.

When he saw her, he stopped in his tracks, and his frown deepened.

'Jade. Where the hell did you go?' he snapped.

If tension could be bottled and sold, Jade would have become an instant millionaire, because the air between her and David suddenly felt as if it was about to split right open.

She shrugged. 'You were busy helping the detectives, so I went out. You're not my boss. I don't have to report to you.'

'I don't mean just now.' He gesticulated angrily with an open hand. 'I mean last night. Where did you disappear to? I was worried sick.'

Jade dropped her gaze. For a moment she didn't know what to say, because she didn't want David to know where she'd been.

'You'd better stop doing that,' she told him icily. 'Or at any rate, save it for your wife and your new baby. Don't keep fretting about me.'

'For Christ's sake, Jade . . .' David barked out the words before cutting himself short.

He banged his weight down onto the couch and jammed his chin down onto his clenched left fist. She saw his jaw tighten.

An uncomfortable silence descended. David didn't move. Chin on his bunched hand, he was a passable impression of Rodin's *Thinker*.

Jade, by contrast, realised she felt sick. With hunger, probably, although the idea of food wasn't exactly appealing to her right now. But supper had been half a bottle of champagne and she'd had no breakfast.

She walked over to the fridge and took out the first thing that came to hand—a jar of chilli-stuffed olives. She got a spoon and a plate from the drying rack, spooned out several olives, sat down on one of the bar stools and forced herself to eat them one by one.

'How's the investigation going?' she asked in a more casual voice, after the third olive.

David grunted.

'I didn't want to get involved, but those detectives are green as grass, and they're not going to get any help from other precincts, because there isn't anybody else available to assist. They were going to ask Durban Central to send a couple of officers, but that idea bit the dust when Durban Central came back and said they couldn't spare anybody; that they've had six violent crimes, two fatal shootings and an accidental drowning in the last twenty-four hours. They said there must be something causing it, but I'm damned if I know what.'

'Can't be the full moon,' Jade said, trying to keep the conversation light.

'Nope. It's new moon. Spring tide's tomorrow night, apparently. I was told to be careful if I go swimming, because the undertow will be very strong.'

Jade nodded. 'It's national Drive Like a Maniac day on the roads as well. I was nearly wiped out by some poor-white type in a bakkie on my way back.'

'There you go, then.'

Jade sensed that he was also choosing his words carefully, aware that they represented fragile strands that stretched across an abyss. Amanda's murder was more than a topical news subject. It also provided—somewhat perversely—a safe subject for conversation.

'What's your next step with the investigation?' Jade asked.

'Pillay's going to interview everybody this afternoon.' He sighed. 'There's no sign of the murder weapon, which, as you can tell, was obviously a large, sharp knife. Bugger all trace evidence either. A few hairs, which they're sending off to the lab, but that's about it.'

'Any other clues?'

David shrugged. 'Nothing, really. She had a shell collection. Beautiful stuff. And a very good waterproof digital camera.'

'Which was still there?'

'Which was, as you point out, still in her room. I saw an album full of photos on her bookshelf. Some stunning images. Close-ups of coral reefs, fish, the most incredible underwater shots.' He let out a deep breath. 'Amanda obviously loved the sea, given the way she captured it on camera. I don't know if I'll get a chance to go out on the boat at all, with all this going on, but this really is an amazing part of the world. Probably one of the last great, unspoilt diving places in existence. But those photos were just about the only personal stuff we found. A couple of postcards, but apart from that, nothing much. Minimal personal possessions.'

Jade found herself looking away. Right now, she'd be happy never going underwater again. That mystical ocean world could stay right where it was. Or perhaps she could view it through a glass-bottomed boat instead.

'No cellphone?' she asked.

'No. No computer, either. Don't know if she even owned one. I found a card for an Internet café in Richards Bay.'

David raised his head and, for the first time, noticed the shiny metal bolts on the inside of their door.

'Security precautions,' he observed flatly.

Jade nodded. 'Not that I think they're worth much.'

'Because the door's so flimsy?'

'No.' David's questioning glance prompted her to continue. 'Because Amanda's room wasn't broken into.'

'How do you mean?' he asked slowly.

'While I was standing outside her rocm this morning, I noticed that although the wood around the lock was splintered, the lock itself wasn't broken out. I think it must have been damaged after the murder, to make it look like a forced entry.'

David's forbidding expression softened and he nodded wearily.

'Jadey,' he said. 'You're right, and you were fast. It took us two hours to figure that out. Admittedly, we had a lot else on our plate.' His face darkened again. 'Amanda let her killer in. Which means that, in all probability, it was somebody she knew.'

16

Pillay interviewed Jade on the small verandah outside her chalet, both of them sitting on the plastic chairs that the resort had provided. The sun was still battling to break through the clouds, but at least the wind had dropped. Most of the other guests were inside, perhaps hiding away from the horror the morning had brought. At any rate, Jade had yet to see anyone other than Larry and his flame-haired partner, who were walking up towards their chalet from the thatched lapa near the reception area that doubled as a bar. Roxanne was wearing a filmy sarong over a black diamanté bikini. Larry was in an electric-blue Speedo with his towel slung over his shoulders. He held a glass filled with amber liquid that splashed over onto his hand as he walked. Raised voices wafted over to her as Pillay opened his notebook, and she realised the couple must be having an argument. Neither of them acknowledged Jade, nor even glanced in her direction, and a short while later their chalet door slammed behind them.

Pillay cleared his throat self-consciously and glanced down at his spiral pad. In response to his polite questioning, Jade told him about her movements the previous evening. About her walk down to the beach, how she had helped Monique secure the tarpaulin. How she had noticed the fear in the young woman's eyes, and seen her stuff Craig's wallet into her pocket.

She gave Pillay a sketchy description of the unknown man she'd noticed weaving his way along the beach shortly afterwards. How he had headed up towards the resort with purpose, but had then disappeared. She explained how she and Craig had looked inside Monique's room and discovered the missing wallet.

'At that stage, did you see or hear anything from Amanda Bolton's room?'

'No,' Jade said. 'Amanda's door was closed. I don't know if she was there or not. Even if she'd had somebody in there with her, we didn't hear anything and I doubt she would have heard us outside, because the sound of the rain on the roof was so loud.' She risked a question of her own. 'Has the pathologist estimated a time of death yet?'

Pillay nodded, 'The estimated time of death was early this morning. At around dawn. I . . .' He stopped speaking abruptly and jumped as if an electric current had been run through his chair. Watching his reaction, Jade realised he'd made a novice detective's mistake by unwittingly disclosing privileged information.

Bowing his head to cover his confusion, Pillay jotted down his final notes.

'Thank you,' he said. 'I may need to speak to you again at a later stage.'

'I'll be here if you do. For the next day or two, anyway.'

Pillay closed his pad, which Jade couldn't help noticing was brand new. His interview with her had taken up the first page.

'Is this your first murder investigation?' she asked him.

The young detective hesitated, but then nodded. 'Yes. I was promoted a month ago, but the murder rate in this precinct is not very high.'

'What department were you in before?'

Pillay checked his watch and placed his notebook and pen in a briefcase that also didn't seem to be suffering much wear and tear.

'Missing Persons,' he said proudly..

Jade fought to suppress a smile.

'And do you get many of those in this part of the world?'

'Oh, yes.' Pillay spoke with quiet confidence. 'Quite a number of people were reported missing during the past few months. The job kept me busy, I can tell you.'

'You find any of them?'

Now the Indian detective's face fell. 'Not one, despite my best efforts. There was a promising lead recently on one man who worked at the harbour, but it didn't come to anything.'

'Well, I hope you get luckier this time,' Jade said. 'Where are you going now?'

'I'm going to speak to your neighbours next.' He pointed in the direction of Craig and Elsabe's chalet. 'I'm hoping that they'll be able to give me some more background on Monique.'

Jade had turned her phone off during the interview. As Pillay headed for the next-door chalet, she turned it back on. It started to ring almost immediately.

She recognised the area code as Richards Bay, but the number was unfamiliar and so was the voice of the lady on the other end of the line.

'Is that Miss Jade de Jong?'

'It is.'

'Good afternoon, dear.' It was the voice of a frail, older woman, soft and quavery, and it seemed to have a smile in it, as if it really was a good afternoon for her. 'It's Mrs Koekemoer speaking. I used to work at the Richards Bay General Hospital. I got a message that I should call you. Apparently you would like to talk to somebody who knew your mother.'

'That's right. I do.'

'She was Mrs Elise de Jong?'

'Yes.'

'Well, I knew her. And I'd be glad to tell you what I remember.'

'Thank you so much for getting in touch with me.' Jade found herself speaking more slowly and clearly than usual. Assuming, perhaps, that because the lady was old, she might also be deaf.

'I don't know how useful I'll be, but I'll do my best. Would you like to come here for a chat? I don't get out much anymore, I'm afraid.'

'When would be convenient for you?'

'Well . . .' The lady paused and sighed, as if wondering how she could fit a visit into an already busy schedule. 'Tomorrow morning isn't good, but at lunchtime I'll have some time. Shall we say . . . twelve-thirty?'

'Twelve-thirty it is. And where are you?'

'Oh.' Mrs Koekemoer sounded taken aback for a moment, and then laughed. 'I'm sorry. I'm so used to people knowing where I live. I'm at the Rose Village retirement home, dear. In End Lane, Harbour View.'

'I'll see you then,' Jade said, and thanked the old lady again before disconnecting.

She found herself looking forward to the meeting. Mrs Koekemoer sounded like a chatty soul. Jade had no idea what she might learn, if anything, or even what questions she should or could ask. Still, it was a start, and she was sure it would lead somewhere.

Lost in thought, Jade nearly jumped out of her skin when she heard a chalet door slam, the sound of wood hitting wood as loud as a gunshot. Swivelling in the direction of the noise, she saw Larry marching out of his chalet, hefting two very large travel bags with him. Given that his hands were full, Jade guessed he must have kicked the door shut behind him.

He dumped the bags on the ground, opened the Hummer's boot and then hefted them both inside. Jade noticed that the boot was already three-quarters full of other luggage. She wasn't sure how many clothes the two had thought they would need for a short stay at a scuba resort, but they had obviously decided to err on the side of plenty.

And now, it seemed, they were packing up and leaving.

'Hey! 'Scuse me, folks!'

Neil was standing outside the front door of his house, staring in consternation at the departing guests.

Larry glanced briefly in his direction before climbing into his Hummer and slamming the door. From where she was sitting, Jade couldn't see through the mirrored window, but she assumed that Roxanne was already in the passenger seat.

Combing her orange hair, probably.

'Hey! Wait a minute!' Neil waved an arm. Then, sandals slapping and his smart shirt working loose from his baggy shorts, he began running towards the Hummer.

'Sir, please. If you're leaving, we still need a payment from you.'

The driver's window buzzed down and Larry's face appeared.

'You must be shitting me. Is this some kind of a joke?' he yelled at the manager.

'Sir . . .' Neil sounded breathless, and Jade only caught snatches of his voice. '. . . so sorry . . . only a fifty per cent accommodation deposit received . . . four nights' stay . . . the scuba-diving course . . . a substantial bar tab . . . two sets of dive equipment hired . . .'

She had no problem making out Larry's response.

'Someone got murdered because your bloody resort isn't secure. Then you get your guy to come in and screw two bolts into the door. Two bolts! That's supposed to keep us safe? It's a farce. This place is a joke. You can forget about your payment.'

'But the police want to talk to you!' Neil's voice rose even higher.

'They can talk to my lawyer!'

'At least . . .'

Before Neil had time to complete his sentence, the Hummer's engine roared and it sped away, spinning giant slashes of sand from under its thick black tyres.

17

The aftermath of murder. David knew he should be used to it by now, but every time it saddened him. Sorting through the personal possessions of the deceased, trawling through papers and diaries, photograph albums and cellphone data, looking for information and possible clues, was so damn depressing.

Strictly speaking, there wasn't much more he could do at the crime scene. Surfaces had been examined, brushed and vacuumed. Forensic specimens had been collected, fingerprints taken. The bloodied sheets were long gone; only the stains on the floor remained.

David could have locked up the room and left an hour ago. Left this sad and empty scene, and headed back to his chalet.

But he was still here. Rereading his notes. Going through the two cardboard boxes of Amanda's possessions that he, Pillay and his assistant had neatly assembled earlier in the day.

The murder was so unexpected, so incongruous, here in this beautiful, peaceful little resort. As terrible as the incident was, however, David couldn't help feeling grateful that it had provided him with something of overriding importance to focus on.

It had pretty much stopped him from thinking about Jade; the way she'd looked yesterday when he'd dropped the bombshell of Naisha's pregnancy. David realised that he must have looked pretty much the same after Naisha had sat him down in the lounge of the Turffontein house last Tuesday, and calmly and quietly told him the news that was going to change his future.

The minute she'd said the words he'd known it was his child—that this was the result of the one regrettable night he'd spent with her since they'd been separated. There was nobody else in Naisha's life. Up till now he'd been glad about that, in a way, because a new partner for Naisha would have meant disruption in Kevin's life, with the promise of even more disruption if the relationship didn't work out. Children complicated things in that regard.

On the other hand, David had wished that Naisha would settle down with somebody else, because it would have meant that she would no longer be pressurising him to give their relationship another chance.

He remembered her look of quiet satisfaction as she'd broken the news. She'd been watching him carefully too, which meant David had had to struggle to control his own expression, and not make a difficult situation worse by gaping at her in dismay, his face reflecting the utter, dismal shock he'd felt.

Of course, there had been some discussion about timing, days of the month. But he'd known with a sinking feeling that this was simply observing the formalities.

He'd screwed up, and now he was paying for it.

David groaned, slamming down the folder of papers he'd been examining.

These papers were from one of the boxes containing Amanda Bolton's personal items. There weren't many of them. The dive instructor had lived alone. It seemed she hadn't socialised with many people during her months in Richards Bay, or had a boyfriend. There was no evidence of one, at any rate. Not according to the resort owner or the cleaner, and not according to the belongings the detectives had gone through that morning.

These days, computers and phones provided a wealth of information. People shared everything via email or their mobile. David learned from the cleaner that Amanda Bolton had possessed a BlackBerry, but to his frustration it was nowhere to be found. It must have been stolen, presumably by her killer, although in South Africa that was never a certainty. Equipment and valuables frequently disappeared from crime scenes.

With the cellphone missing, there was a delay in contacting Amanda's next of kin. Neil had a phone number on record for her mother in the UK, but no address and David didn't want to break such bad news over the phone. After obtaining the address from international directory enquiries, David had phoned the local police in Tooting Bec, where she lived, and requested that they go and give Mrs Bolton the news in person.

Amanda's passport revealed she'd done some travelling on it in the last few years and all of it in warm climates. Six-to-twelve-month stays in the United Arab Emirates, Egypt, and a few other countries in the Middle East and north Africa. From the stamps, he noticed that she had permission to work in those countries, too. He wondered if she'd worked as a scuba-diving instructor, or as an air-traffic controller, which, he'd learned from Neil, was her former occupation.

When he'd removed it from the top drawer of her desk, he'd discovered an old-fashioned postcard. It had caught David's eye, because it was just about the only personal item he'd seen, apart from the collection of shells and an airplane pendant.

The postcard was of the new Calabash soccer stadium in Johannesburg. The message on the reverse was short:

'Hi Amanda! When are you coming to Jozi? Let me know— we must meet up for a drink. I'm staying at 10 Harwood Court in Dunbar Street, in Yeoville. It's a dump, but there are some cool bars nearby on Rocky Street! Hope things are good down there with you and that you're OK after 813. We need to stick together! Chat soon, Themba.'

This time, David's brow furrowed as he reread the card's cryptic message.

Hearing a soft knock, he looked up to see Jade standing in the doorway.

'It's almost seven o'clock,' she said.

David blinked in surprise as he realised it was almost fully dark outside.

'Guess I'm finished here.' He stood up and, feeling his back click, tensed in anticipation of the shooting pain he knew would follow. God, he was turning into a middle-aged wreck. A middle-aged wreck who had recently made a teenager's mistake.

'I'm making supper. Thought you might like some.'

'Thanks.' The word sounded as heartfelt as he'd intended it to be. He followed her out of the room, grateful not only for the supper, but for the peace offering that it implied.

Jade was halfway through making a tomato and lentil curry, and garlic naan breads were ready to warm in a large frying pan. David was usually a committed carnivore, but Jade knew only too well that after a day spent in the close confines of a bloodied room, the thought of meat would make him nauseous.

That wasn't why she was making the curry, of course. If she'd felt like eating steak, she would have cooked up rare fillets regardless. Her days of worrying about what David wanted were over. He was damn lucky he was getting any supper at all.

As he'd walked behind her to the chalet, David's phone had rung. From the one-sided conversation that ensued, Jade had deduced that the police officers somewhere in London were phoning him back to let him know they'd notified Amanda's mother about her death.

He didn't follow her inside, but stood on the patio while he finished his call.

The television was on in the chalet, although Jade couldn't have said what programme was playing. She'd been too preoccupied with her own confused thoughts and, when her attention hadn't been focused on her cooking, she'd found herself checking the window. Moving back the blinds to peer into the growing darkness outside, scanning the trees for any sign of the tall, lean male she'd seen the previous night.

Now, glancing at the screen again, she saw that the evening news was on. It didn't take long for her to deduce that most of it was bad. ANC Youth League leader, Julius Malema, had managed to piss off just about everyone again with another of his inflammatory statements. Jade wondered if he'd been specially briefed to do this, to create a distraction that would grab the media's attention so completely that it wouldn't look too closely at anything else that might be going on.

Or perhaps he was just one of those people who only opened his mouth to change feet. She didn't know. The picture flicked away from him and on to international news. A forest fire was raging out of control in Australia, decimating thousands of acres of indigenous forest, and the Pakistani government was coming under increasing international pressure to start recycling the millions of litres of engine oil that were well on their way to creating a major pollution problem in the densely populated country.

'We are putting steps in place to recycle the oil,' a worried-looking government official was telling Sky News.

'And what steps are those?' the reporter shot back.

'Two recycling plants are being set up on the outskirts of Karachi.'

'But those will take time to build, won't they? The problem is there now.'

'Well, what we are doing in the meantime is collecting up the oil at special recycling points and shipping it to Kolkata.'

'No, you aren't. You have not done that successfully as yet. The last lot of dirty engine oil that you tried to get rid of ended up being shipped in a damaged tanker.' As the reporter spoke, footage flashed onto the screen, with last year's date posted above it. A massive oil tanker, half submerged in blackened water, followed by more footage of oil-soaked sand littered with poisoned fish and dead birds.

'This tanker set off from Karachi, ran into bad weather soon afterwards, and sank just off the coast of Sri Lanka last August, discharging its load of filthy oil onto the beach there. By the time it went down, the crew had all abandoned ship, which wasn't surprising since the vessel was subsequently found to be totally unseaworthy.'

'I . . . er . . .'

'That beach is still contaminated and will be for years to come.'

Staring at the screen, Jade could see why somebody with Craig's qualifications would be kept busy. It seemed as if people all over the world were on a mission to destroy their environment.

She muted the sound when David walked inside. He was looking ahead of him with the thousand-yard stare that Jade had come to realise meant he was absorbing difficult news.

'That can't have been easy,' he said eventually. 'Amanda was an only daughter. Only child, I should say. Anyway, they said Mrs Bolton doesn't want to come out here. Just wants the body repatriated to England. I'll have to call her tomorrow to find out what she wants done with Amanda's clothes and personal possessions.'

'Are they going to do a post-mortem?'

David shook his head. 'No point. The pathologist's already confirmed the stab wounds were made by a large, sharp-pointed blade and that from the angle of the cuts the killer was right-handed. As I don't think we're going to get more than that, the body might as well be sent straight home.'

The knives in the chalets were not sharp. Knives in self-catering units seldom were, having been blunted from years of continuous use. Expecting that this would be the case, Jade had brought her own sharp knife with her. It was a Wusthof, one of the five-piece block set that David had bought her last Christmas, a present that she'd been delighted with, in spite of—or perhaps because of—the fact it had obviously cost him a fortune.

She remembered how the blade had sliced so cleanly through the large piece of fillet she'd prepared the previous morning, and which was now still in its marinade in the fridge. She'd cut it effortlessly into three smaller, but still thick and substantial, chunks. When you prepared meat, you focused on finishing the job and getting it done efficiently. It was all too easy to forget that you were handling something that had once been a living animal.

Jade wondered whether she could stab her chef's knife into somebody's stomach, just like Amanda's killer had done. Feel it cut through skin, slice its way through muscle and connective tissue. She wondered how much effort it would require. Physically, she was sure she could do it, because the blade would do the work. All she would really need would be resolve.

She'd like to think that she could never bring herself to do that to another human being. But she suspected that if that person was threatening her, if it was a life or death situation, a question of survival, she would be more than able to.

Without cause, though, she couldn't ever have done it.

The question was: how could Amanda's killer?

Tonight, her knife lay innocently on the chopping board, its blade still half buried in a crimson mound of chopped tomatoes. These Jade now added to the simmering lentils. Spices were next on the list. She'd brought a basic selection—black mustard seeds, ground cumin and ground coriander. She added a generous teaspoon of each to the pot.

On the other side of the chopping board lay a much smaller mound of sliced chillies. She liked her food much hotter than David did, despite his Indian heritage, so in a few minutes she would pour half the contents of the pot into another, smaller saucepan. Then she would add the chillies—just a few pieces for him, the rest for her.

Apartheid may be over in South Africa, but a culinary equivalent was still practised regularly in the De Jong kitchen.

'What does 813 mean to you?' David asked suddenly.

Jade gave the pot a stir and turned around to face him.

'In what context?' she asked.

'It was on a postcard in Amanda's room. The card was sent to her by a guy called Themba, from an address in Yeoville, Johannesburg. He wrote that he hoped she was OK after 813.'

'Why don't you send someone round to ask him, if you know where he lives?'

'I'm going to get Moloi onto it tomorrow. It could be nothing, but it struck me as worth following up. She didn't have much personal stuff in her room at all, but she kept that postcard for some reason. And I'm curious to know what 813 means.'

'When you first said it, I thought it was a date. Like 9/11. It sounds similar, doesn't it? Could it be the thirteenth of August? Something to do with something that happened on that day?' Jade hazarded.

'It isn't written like a date. Just three numbers, one after the other.'

Jade shrugged. 'Maybe they're old friends and it's a personal code of some kind.'

David nodded. 'I'd like an explanation, just to stop those damn numbers bugging me. It's not urgent, though. At the moment we have other, more important issues to pursue. Like where Monique's disappeared to. And finding your unknown man.'

Turning back to the cooker, Jade deftly transferred half the curry into another pan, added the chillies and breathed in their eye-watering aroma.

'If the vagrant's got any sense, he's probably far away from here,' she observed.

At that point, David got up and walked over to the front door. He locked it and fastened the bolts that had been screwed onto the wood earlier that day. Then he drew the curtains, shutting out the dark.

18

In the neighbouring chalet, Elsabe and Craig weren't doing anything about supper. Elsabe had told Craig she was too upset to eat, and Craig, although he could have done with some food, was also upset, and in any case was feeling too tired to cook.

He was making do with a pack of peanuts that he had bought some time ago while filling up with petrol on a journey through Zimbabwe, and which had remained, ignored and then forgotten, in his glove compartment ever since.

He sat beside her on the couch, eating the peanuts slowly, one by one. Elsabe, her face half hidden by her long hair, was reading a historical novel, but he didn't think she was focused on the story at all. Normally a fast reader, she hadn't turned a page for minutes.

What a thing to happen, he thought, wondering if he should turn on the television.

Suddenly, Elsabe raised her head, sat up straight and glanced nervously at their tightly bolted door.

'Did you hear that?' she asked.

'Hear what?' The plastic crumpled as he dug inside the bag's small opening, searching for another nut.

'There was a noise outside. I'm sure of it. Would you please stop rooting around in that bag?'

Craig put the bag on the table as carefully as possible. Now he too stared at the door, and for a while there was a tense silence.

As hard as he tried, Craig couldn't hear a thing. Not that that meant there was nothing to be heard, though. He knew from experience that Elsabe's hearing was far more sensitive than his own.

'What did it sound like?' he asked quietly.

'I don't know. I'd need to hear it again. A sort of rustling noise. That's why I noticed it—because there's no reason for it. It's very still tonight.'

Craig moved over to the window and pushed the curtain back just far enough for him to be able to see outside. He'd spent some time in Johannesburg a few years ago, and one of the security tips he'd been given by a friend during his stay was that opening the curtains wide and staring outside would present a potential assailant with a large and obvious target.

As he had expected, there was nothing to be seen in the darkness. But he could hear the tremor in Elsabe's voice and he couldn't stop himself from looking once again at the two new steel bolts on the front door.

'I could go and . . .'

'No!' she hissed, clenching her small hands tightly. 'Don't go out. That's how people get killed. Somebody could be waiting there.'

Exasperated, Craig found himself wanting to snap at her, 'Well, what do you want me to do then?', but thought better of it. Then he had an idea. The powerful LCD torch that he'd used so often on his field trips, and again the night before, was in the chalet, in the box with the towrope, the orange traffic cone and the reflective vests that he always took along as a precaution, but had never needed to use. In fact, a couple of months ago, he'd had to give one of the vests to a customs official in a central African country who, for some reason, had taken a liking to it and refused to let him through without a 'donation.'

Grabbing the torch from the box and turning it on, he hurried back to the window. The beam of white light looked dazzlingly bright, even in the well-lit chalet.

In one swift movement, Craig pulled back the curtain and shone the flashlight through the glass, scrutinising the sudden pool of brightness.

'There's . . .' He was going to say, 'There's nothing there.'

But then, suddenly, he saw there was. The beam had picked out a faint shape near the tree-line above the beach.

Breathing more rapidly now, he stared at what he saw. Bracketed between the pinpoint glows of two newly installed outdoor lamps, and now caught in the strong gleam of his torch, there was something that looked very much like a man. He could see the faint smudge of greyish-looking trousers and, above that, what might be tanned arms. Tall and thin, standing stock still, as if he knew that if he moved now he would give his presence away completely.

'I think I can see something . . .' he said in a voice that, even to him, sounded strained.

'What?' Her response was high, tense, panicked. 'What can you see?'

Hurrying over to the window, she grabbed at his arm. His right arm; the one holding the light.

'Wait! Careful . . .' he told her.

His warning came too late. Her anxious grasp jerked his elbow down, and the beam of light swung away from the intruder and went arcing up into the sky, where it was swallowed by the darkness.

Jaw clenched in annoyance, Craig redirected the beam and scanned the tree-line, trying to find the greyish form he'd just seen.

But however hard he gazed at the boundary, no matter where he aimed the beam, there was nothing to be seen. The man—if there had been one there at all—had vanished.

The call came just as David was digging his fork—with some trepidation—into the steaming bowl of lentil curry that Jade had dished up for him.

'Oh, dammit,' he said, in a voice that Jade thought didn't sound altogether sincere. Putting his fork down, he pushed his chair back and went to find his phone.

A minute later he was back, his face serious.

'Problem, Jadey.'

'What?'

She lowered the piece of naan bread she'd been holding. Her mouth was burning from the spicy food, but she didn't find the feeling uncomfortable. In fact, she found it enjoyable. Who was it who had told her once that chillies were addictive? Her father, most probably. The stern Commissioner De Jong had routinely eaten dinner—whatever it might be—with a small bowl of chopped raw chillies by his plate. He would add one or two chunks to every mouthful, nodding with pleasure as he chewed, and it wasn't long before she had asked to try them too.

'Guys next door think they've seen an intruder.'

'Whereabouts?' she asked, already on her feet.

'I'm not sure. Somewhere close, though, because they saw him from their window. They've already phoned the police and they're getting hold of Neil. I'll go over there via the staff quarters and ask the domestic workers to come along too. Safer that way, I think. We're going to do a search.' He stopped, looked again at Jade, this time seeming to notice that she was no longer eating her dinner. He let out an impatient sigh. 'You want to come along, I suppose?' he asked in a tone that suggested she would be wiser to do the opposite.

'Of course I'm coming,' Jade responded, with some irritation. 'What else am I going to do—sit here and wait for you? You do realise if this is the same intruder that was around last night, I'm the only one who'll be able to ID him.'

Jade hurried into the bedroom and took her holster from the top shelf of the cupboard. David was already opening the safe and removing their guns. He held out the Glock to her, but when she tried to take it from him, he held onto the barrel, causing a brief tug-of-war. Looking at his face, Jade guessed he wanted to say something. A warning, perhaps? But he didn't. Just gave another of his annoying sighs, let go of her gun, and strapped his own service pistol around his waist.

Then he collected his Maglite from the kitchen counter.

'Let's get going,' he said. 'See if we find anything out there.'

They stepped out into the night.

19

Elsabe looked terrified. She was huddled on the couch, hugging her knees with her slender arms. Craig had his arm around her, obviously trying to offer her some comfort. When he saw Jade walk in, he quickly removed his hand from her shoulder.

They were soon joined by David, who brought Nosipho and Vusi the handyman with him. Nosipho looked exhausted and scared, ill at ease among the people whose rooms she cleaned. Despite Craig's offer, she didn't sit down, but stood near the door, rubbing her eyes and adjusting her headscarf.

'Where's Neil?' David asked.

'I called him,' Craig said. 'He said he wasn't going to come along.'

'Not coming?' David frowned. 'Did he say why?'

'Nope.'

David's frown deepened. 'Oh well. It's his damn resort. We'll go out in pairs, then. Nosipho, will you stay here with Elsabe? Vusi, if you'd like to come along on the search, you can pair up with me. Craig, you can go with Jade.'

It was a sensible way to split their available resources, Jade thought. One light for each group and one gun for each, because neither Vusi nor Craig had a firearm.

'Lock the door and bolt it as soon as we're outside, and if you hear or see anything suspicious, phone one of us immediately. Understood?'

Elsabe craned her neck to look up at the tall police superintendent. Under her mane of hair, her face looked very pale.

'Understood,' she said in a small voice.

■

'Let's all head over to the place where you thought you saw him,' David said. 'We can split up from there.'

Before she left Craig and Elsabe's chalet, Jade walked over to the kitchen sink, squeezed some Sunlight washing-up liquid onto her hands, and carefully washed away every trace of grease that was left on her skin from handling the buttery naans. Slippery fingers wouldn't help her if she needed to use her gun fast.

As she moved towards the door, Elsabe muttered something she couldn't make out.

'Sorry.' Jade turned around, wondering if the comment had even been directed at her. 'What was that?'

'Huberta.'

The red-haired woman was staring at the wooden key ring carved in the shape of a smiling hippo that dangled from the hook on Jade's belt.

'What about her?'

'She died.'

Jade blinked. 'How do you mean?'

Now Elsabe looked up, straight at her. Her freckled face was as narrow as a rat's and deep rings formed purple smudges under her eyes.

'She was shot. Did you know that?'

'What are you talking about?'

'I overheard you telling the story to your boyfriend yesterday.' She emphasised the word 'boyfriend' slightly and Jade wondered with a guilty pang if she somehow knew, or if Craig had told her, that they'd slept together. 'But you didn't tell him the end of the story.'

'I didn't know what the end was.'

'Well, she was shot dead by three hunters a month after she arrived in King William's Town. Someone saw her bloated body floating down the river. The hunters were found and fined twenty-five pounds each for destroying royal game.'

'Oh.'

'Later, she was stuffed and put on display in a museum. But it couldn't bring her back, of course. Nothing could. That's the tragedy of murder, isn't it?'

Jade didn't know what to say in response to that, so she said nothing. She simply walked outside and set off towards the tangle of shrubs and bushes where the men were heading, moving as quietly as she could.

Recalling what Craig had told her about the horrific crash that had brought them together, she thought it quite likely that Elsabe's odd behaviour was shaped by grief.

All the same, why did she have to tell her about the damn hippo being killed? Jade would much rather not have known. She'd thought the story had had a happy ending, but she'd been wrong.

Behind her, she heard the rattle of bolts as Elsabe locked the door.

She hurried past the first of the two new outside lights that Vusi had installed near the chalets.

Then she jogged over the uneven grass to catch up with the others.

Craig was standing near the back wall of the staff quarters, roughly halfway between the two lights and a good twenty paces from the perimeter.

'He was standing somewhere around here,' he said. 'In this area.'

Jade watched the torch beams criss-cross the ground as the two men scanned the area for any sign that an intruder had been nearby. But although they walked right to the perimeter, the coarse green grass offered up no discernible footprints, only sharp black shadows.

'Neil really should consider getting this place fenced off,' David suggested, echoing what Jade had been thinking ever since she arrived. 'Palisades, chicken wire, electric wire, whatever. Just something to prevent every man and his dog from roaming inside the resort. He'd need to run it all the way round the property. Put a gate at the top and another leading down to the beach.'

Vusi nodded solemnly. 'I will tell him what you said, but I do not know if he will listen to me. There has never been a problem until now. This is a peaceful place.'

'Well, he should listen, because you've got a problem now.' He paused, scanning the area with his torch beam once more. 'No sign of him here, so let's widen the search. We'll go right, you go left.'

Taking the right-hand route would lead David down to the beach. Jade guessed he had opted to go this way because it was darker, more deserted and potentially more dangerous.

Turning left, she and Craig headed up the long, winding driveway. He shone the light a couple of metres in front of them, but every few paces he raised the torch and swung it slowly from right to left and back again. As he did this, Jade was suddenly reminded of their walk last night, which had followed almost exactly the same route; what had happened before they left, and what had happened between them afterwards.

Neither of them had spoken since they set off together, and this time the silence felt uncomfortable. Jade wondered if Craig felt guilty, too. She'd seen the way he looked at Elsabe. She was sure that if he'd had the choice, he would have opted to spend the night with his 'friend', not with her.

As they headed towards the entrance gate, they passed Neil's house, where Jade noticed that a couple of lights were on but all the curtains were tightly drawn. Neil was hiding away from the world.

Along the access road, the torch beam lit up the nearest palm trees, their fronds spiky-pale in the glare, and banana trees, slender-stemmed but with leaves so broad a man could have hidden behind them. Their shadows stretched darkly away from them before being swallowed by the forest.

Jade had no idea what else was growing in this bushy jungle. She didn't have green fingers. She didn't understand plants and, like her father, she had no interest in identifying them

She followed the beam. Looking for anything—a footprint, the compact cylinder of a cigarette butt.

There was a strong likelihood that this search, like the previous one, would be a waste of time. There was only a slim chance that they might find evidence of the intruder, if he even existed. There was virtually no chance they would locate the stranger himself.

Even so, despite Neil's protests that everything had been safe until now, the grim reality was that they were no longer secure.

In Jo'burg, nobody felt secure. That was why everyone lived in impenetrable fortresses, behind high walls topped with ten-thousand-volt electric fences. There, people were prepared for the war against crime, but here they were not. Ironically, it was sometimes only in the most dangerous places that you were the best protected.

Perhaps the unlikeable Larry and Roxanne had made the right decision by leaving.

'Just like yesterday, isn't it?' Craig's whispered words broke the silence.

'Let's hope it doesn't have the same outcome as yesterday,' she whispered back. She'd been thinking of the murder, but felt the blood rush to her face as she remembered how the night had ended for her and Craig.

Jade was glad Craig couldn't see her blush. He didn't reply. In silence, they continued walking along the forest-lined access road.

A movement in the bushes ahead jerked Jade away from her distracting thoughts. She looked towards it and froze, her hand automatically closing round the grip of her gun.

'Something there,' she whispered. 'In front of us and to the right.'

A moment later, the flashlight found its source and lit up the area to reveal nothing more than a sleek ginger cat with a still-struggling rat in its jaws. Seemingly unfazed by the beam of light, it gave them a baleful look, its eyes flashing bright green.

'Phew,' Craig whispered. 'I expected the worst there for a moment.'

And then the cat tensed and darted off to the left, fleeing deep into the undergrowth. Before Jade could even begin to wonder what had caused the animal to panic, she heard another, much louder, noise coming from roughly the same area. The sound was massive—half roar, half scream, accompanied by the gunshot-like reports of cracking branches. It was so huge and so entirely unexpected that, for just a moment, Jade was certain the source of the noise was a charging hippo.

A heartbeat later, she realised how wrong she was when she saw the gleaming metal body of a large, dark truck burst from its hiding place. Its engine howled, and branches snapped as the vehicle gouged a path through the undergrowth.

The thick metal bull-bar on the truck's bonnet swung in her direction. At first she thought the vehicle was heading for the entry gate, but then she realised it was showing no signs of turning to the right. It continued to surge straight forwards, straight at her. Jade knew if she didn't move within the next few seconds she would be crushed by a two-ton piece of machinery as deadly as any wild animal due to the intent of the person behind the wheel.

'Craig! Get out of the way!' Jade screamed, as she flung herself desperately to the side of the road. She landed hard on her left shoulder and rolled through the wet undergrowth, twigs clawing at her face. The truck passed so close to her that its front wheel caught her left elbow, ramming it with such force that her shoulder was almost jolted out of its socket.

Arm on fire, Jade struggled to her feet and stared at the truck's retreating taillights. It was moving so fast over the uneven road it was impossible for her to read the whole number plate, but she did manage to get the last two digits.

'Jade? You OK?'

Craig's voice sounded shaky. A moment later, the torch beam—also rather unsteady—found her. Jade cupped her right hand over her eyes and turned her head away from its light.

'I'm not hurt. Are you?'

'I'm fine. But that truck was going straight for you.'

'It didn't knock me over. Just grazed my elbow. No lasting damage. It'll probably just bruise.'

Craig shone the torch on Jade's muddied arm and they both examined the large, red-stained weal. She flexed her arm and opened and closed her fingers. Then, using her right hand, she took her cellphone out of her pocket and dialled the number for the flying squad.

20

The meeting was an emergency one this time. Bradley was in the same tiny shed with the same plastic table and rickety chairs. There were three differences, though. One, it was night, so the place was less of a furnace than it had been during the day, although it was still stuffy, filled with suffocating humidity after the rain. Two, he had screwed up a second time, so he was sweating even worse than he'd done the day before. Three, Chetty didn't look as if he'd come from a relaxing day on his yacht. This time, his pants were crumpled and his face was drawn and anxious.

Zulu, however, looked exactly the same; expressionless.

Somehow, Bradley found that the worst of all.

He was rubbing his thumbs and forefingers together in a non-stop back and forth rhythm. He couldn't stop this action, so he'd put his hands under the table. At least his two bosses wouldn't see him doing it, and hopefully they couldn't hear the tiny whispering sound of flesh against sweaty flesh.

'How could you let this happen?' Chetty asked him in a voice that made Bradley think of knives.

Until he'd walked into the shed five minutes ago and Chetty had briefed him on the latest shocking developments, Bradley hadn't had the faintest clue that anything was wrong.

He hadn't known about the latest screw-up; his screw-up.

Bradley shook his head helplessly. 'I don't know how it happened. Kobus was properly briefed. I made sure of it. Everything was under control.'

'No. It wasn't.'

Bradley blinked rapidly, feeling his face start to twitch.

'He didn't tell you about it?'

'Not a word. I didn't know until you told me.'

'Why?' Chetty barked out the word, furious. He slammed his fist down on the table so hard that Bradley thought the flimsy plastic might crack. 'Why would he do such a thing? It's so bloody stupid. He was supposed to stay out of sight. Find the girl, grab her and go. Now we've got the wrong person dead and the local police force swarming round the area. If they find her before we do . . .'

'He was well briefed,' Bradley muttered. The heavy phone hanging around his neck seemed to be pulling his head down, keeping him from being able to look the Indian in the eye.

'Do you realise how this could jeopardise the operation?'

Now Bradley found the strength to raise his head, to look into Chetty's narrowed eyes and Zulu's dark ones.

He'd sat in countless boardrooms before now, and looked at innumerable faces. He'd always been able to read them well. He'd had excellent instincts in the past and, in spite of his recent troubles, he'd thought they were still good. And that made his stomach curdle, because what he was seeing now in the eyes of both men was doubt. Serious doubt.

A screw-up this bad in his previous days may have been a career-damaging move, but not a life-threatening one. But this was different. If these guys were starting to mistrust him, well . . . he was finished.

Taking a deep breath, Bradley fought hard to hide the panic he felt.

'They won't trace anything back to the harbour. How could they?'

There was a pause. Neither of the other two replied, so he continued. 'It may even be a good thing, having an unexpected distraction like this. It'll occupy the investigators' attention. Focus them on what's happening at the resort.'

More silence. His confidence growing, Bradley continued.

'I understand that this isn't the main issue. The main issue is that Kobus did something he was not ordered to do, and I can't have anyone working on my project who doesn't follow orders to the letter. So I'm going to fire him, as of now. He's off the team. We can manage without him now. There's so little time left to go in any case.'

Chetty nodded.

'A good idea,' Zulu said gently. 'But please, leave the firing to me.'

He said it in such a manner that Bradley was left in no doubt about the intent behind his words. He would have liked nothing better than to let the black man have his way, but he daren't.

'No,' he said.

Zulu raised an eyebrow. At least, Bradley thought he saw it twitch. 'Why not?'

Bradley wiped his sweaty forehead with the back of his hand.

'Because the guy's an old-school racist. I spent time with him—lots of time, in fact—back when we were inside. He doesn't trust either of you. If you call a meeting with him, he'll automatically suspect something is up, because he's always taken orders from me.' Bradley swallowed, burned by the knowledge that his ex-prison buddy had let him down in the worst way possible. That he had not, in fact, followed Bradley's orders, despite all his promises. 'Kobus is a dangerous man and he has a gun. This is my job. It has to be.'

The other two men exchanged a glance. For a minute, neither one spoke. Then, finally, he got a reply.

'Do it properly,' Zulu said.

Did this mean they were giving him another chance?

If so, Bradley knew only too well it was the last one he would have to prove his loyalty to his bosses. To make things right again and help limit the damage that Kobus had done.

'I will.' He let out a deep breath. 'Trust me, I will.'

21

Now that the truck had gone, so had the feeling of uneasiness that had been prickling at the back of Jade's neck ever since they'd left the resort. She listened hard, but could hear nothing else in the still, quiet night.

Quickly, she made two calls, speaking first to the flying squad and then to the local detectives.

'Pillay said he'd alert the local Metro Police,' she told Craig, putting her phone away. 'And he's coming back now. He'll be here in ten minutes.'

'Something I wanted to ask you,' Craig said carefully, as they turned and made their way back down the road towards the little cluster of lights.

'Go right ahead.'

'How the hell did you get that truck's number plate? I tried to, but it was too fast. And I wasn't even in its path.'

'I saw the same vehicle earlier this afternoon, speeding on the main road. He almost wiped me out. I took his number plate because . . . well, because that's what you do, isn't it?'

'Is it?' Craig shook his head. 'I don't think so. Not everybody would have the presence of mind to do that in an emergency.'

'You would have.'

'I would have tried, yes.'

'Well, then.'

Jade would have liked to leave it there, but she sensed Craig was waiting for her to say something more.

'I'm a trained private investigator,' she confessed somewhat reluctantly. 'And a bodyguard.'

'You are? That's incredible. Why didn't you tell us that on the campfire night?'

'Because people always end up asking too many questions.'

'I suppose they do,' Craig said ruefully, as if he'd been about to ask them too.

'I knew a woman in the States who worked in the same field as me, and at parties she used to tell strangers that she ran a nail bar.'

'A nail bar?'

'Manicures, acrylics, you know? Then it was a two-minute conversation. Oh, how lovely. Having your own business must be such a challenge! What are the new season's colours? And that was it. Over and out. Much easier that way.'

Craig started to say something else. Then he stopped himself and gave a small laugh. 'Jade,' he said. 'You know . . . hell . . . if I'd met you before . . .'

'Craig,' Jade said. 'It's OK.'

'It's not. I feel . . .'

'Don't.'

'I feel as if I'm making mess-up after mess-up. Digging myself deeper into trouble all the time. Getting further away from where I'm trying to be, and hurting people in the process.'

'I understand. But I'm not hurt. What happened last night was good for both of us, I think. It doesn't matter that it won't happen again.' Jade spoke the words with conviction, but, as she said them, she wondered how true they were.

'It was more than good,' Craig said softly, and she felt her face getting hot.

She said nothing in response, just walked beside him in the darkness, listening to the distant sound of the sea. If she looked to the left, she could see the faraway headlights of the cars on the main road. Traffic was light. No flying-squad vehicles in evidence yet. And the man who had tried to run her down was on that road, getting further and further away with every moment that passed.

'Elsabe and I had a fight last night, before she went out,' Craig added. 'I started getting pushy. Wanting to know where she was going. Like I owned her; like we were lovers instead of just friends. Like she wasn't fully entitled to spend a night some-where else. It isn't even any of my business who she went to see.'

'It isn't, but it is,' Jade said.

'Sometimes I think she hates me,' Craig said. 'That it'll never work out between us.'

'There are times when I think I hate David, too. Lots of them,' Jade said, privately acknowledging the fact that it hadn't stopped her from loving him. Nothing could do that, not even the fact that he and his wife were now expecting another child. As for Craig, well, Elsabe was here with him now. Didn't that count for something?

'This holiday was Elsabe's idea,' Craig said, as if reading Jade's mind. 'She invited me along. I get here, and then she basically ignores me. Spends time with everybody except me.'

'Have you spoken to her about it?'

Craig shrugged. 'I've tried to a couple of times, but she just shuts down.'

'You need to explain to her how you feel. Then you'll find out the truth. Either she feels the same way, but can't express it, or she isn't interested in you, or she's playing mind games.'

He sighed heavily. 'I know.'

Pillay passed them, driving fast, just before they reached the chalets.

Nosipho was peering nervously out of Craig's kitchen window. Seeing the police officer arriving, the cleaner unlocked the door and scurried back to her own room. Through the open door, Jade could see that Elsabe hadn't moved from her awkward position on the couch. Craig headed inside and sat down next to her and, once again, Jade noticed Elsabe tense up and edge away from him.

Pillay hauled himself out of the car. He looked exhausted and skinnier than ever. Although it was late in the evening, no trace of stubble darkened his smooth brown cheeks and, yet again, Jade couldn't help thinking how ridiculously young he looked.

Notebook at the ready, Pillay trotted up the stairs and onto the verandah.

'Are you all right?' he asked, giving Jade a worried look.

'Yes. The truck didn't actually hit me.' She glanced down at her muddied clothes. Her elbow had stopped bleeding, but it was stiff and sore, and her whole body felt bruised.

'Are you sure? I could call an ambulance or a paramedic if you'd like . . .'

'Not necessary.' A morning on the beach tomorrow would do her all the good in the world, she thought, if the sun actually managed to burn off the thin grey haze. That was what she wanted to do. She didn't want to have to struggle with wetsuits and goggles and air canisters, to fight her fear of the depths. She needed to stretch out, cat-like, on the warm sand and feel the hot air soothe her body. And her mind.

Ideally, she would like to be naked, although on a public beach she supposed that this would be inadvisable.

And, in a perfect world, a willing partner would be lying beside her. After all, somebody would need to rub sunscreen onto her back. David would do the job perfectly—he had done it before now—but, with a twinge of guilt, Jade found herself thinking of Craig's strong, capable hands applying the lotion.

Pillay cleared his throat and glanced down at his notebook. Looking at his hands, Jade noticed he had a slim golden band on his ring finger. She hoped the young detective was happily married, because right now, in her personal opinion, there was more than enough relationship angst circulating in the greater St Lucia area.

'Now, Ms De Jong . . .'

'Call me Jade, please.'

'Er . . .' Pillay shifted from foot to foot in a way that made her think he was uncomfortable with being on a first-name basis. 'Was the driver the same man you saw on the beach last night?'

'I'm not one hundred per cent sure. It was too dark on the beach to be able to see him clearly. But I am sure that it was the same man who nearly crashed into me on the main road earlier today. That's how I managed to get his licence plate.'

Pillay gave a satisfied nod.

'Yes. Well done. And that's why I'm here now.'

'Because of the car?'

'Yes.'

'Is it stolen?'

'Not exactly.'

'How do you mean?'

'The vehicle is registered in the name of Vishnu Padayachee.' Pillay spoke the words with quiet pride, although they meant nothing at all to Jade.

'Who's he?' she asked.

'He is one of the missing people that I have been trying to trace.'

'Oh, is he?' Jade felt her heart quicken at the news.

'Yes. He works at the harbour, or did until he disappeared a month ago, along with his vehicle. Neither have been seen since. I don't think the driver you saw was Padayachee, but the car is definitely his, so if you could sit down with me for a few minutes, I'm going to ask you for a full description of the man behind the wheel.'

'Happy to help. I hope this leads somewhere,' Jade said.

'I hope so too.'

Pillay pulled out one of the verandah chairs for her and then sat down on the other.

'What does Padayachee do?' Jade asked. 'What's his job at the harbour?'

The detective hesitated, as if wondering whether he should disclose this information. For a moment, Jade thought he had decided against it, but then he gave a thoughtful nod and spoke again.

'Padayachee works with explosives. He's a blasting technician. He was apparently involved in a building project at the harbour when he went missing.'

22

Jade and David arrived at the Richards Bay port just after dawn. The last few stragglers of yesterday's clouds seemed to be regrouping for another offensive. It made for a dramatic sunrise. Bulky grey clouds with bright-pink and deep-crimson edges clinging to a dark and forbidding-looking horizon.

'Pretty,' David said rather dismissively, glancing to the east as he drove through the main gates.

The harbour was larger than Jade had expected, with large signposts pointing the way to a dizzying number of different ports and terminals. However, when they'd asked for the main offices, they'd been directed away from the shoreline towards a secure-looking area surrounded by a high chain-link fence. The access road led up to a steel-barred gate, which was firmly locked from the inside by a solid-looking chain and padlock. Near the gate, and also on the inside, Jade saw a small, rather weather-beaten room that she supposed must be a guardhouse.

'So what's this, then? Alcatraz?' David said.

He brought the car to an abrupt stop, yanked the handbrake up and climbed out. He walked over to the gate and rattled the chain.

Jade opened her own door. The wind coming off the sea was strong, buffeting the door back against her body. Somewhere above her a seagull cried and, in the distance, she thought she heard the sound of a train. At this early hour, the small car park inside the secure area was already more than half full. Beyond it, she could see what must be a construction area, although she had no idea what they could be building, because a towering screen of sheet metal hid everything from view.

David's phone rang and, with a brief apology to Jade, he climbed back into the car and out of the wind, to take the call.

As he did so, the door of the small outbuilding opened and a weary-looking guard in a creased uniform stepped out and made his way over to the gate.

The man seemed to be in his fifties, and years of exposure to the sun had weathered and permanently darkened his skin to a deep mahogany, blurring the boundaries of his race.

The guard didn't greet her, just glanced down at the clipboard he was carrying.

'Your name?' he asked.

'I'm Jade de Jong. That's David Patel,' she replied.

Jade assumed that the guard had asked for the information in order to write it down on the clipboard, but she was wrong. Instead, he took a longer look at what must have been a list of approved names. Then he looked up again and shook his head.

'You're not on here,' he said. 'I can't allow you in.'

Jade blinked, taken aback by this unexpected response.

'It's police business,' she said.

'You're police?' From the guy's expression, it was clear to Jade he wouldn't have believed her if she'd said she was.

'No. But he is.' Jade pointed to David, who had finished his call and strolled over to see what was going on.

'Superintendent David Patel,' he said conversationally, while snapping open his leather wallet to display his police ID. 'Is there a problem here?'

Moving right up to the chain-link fence, the guard took a careful look at the wallet's contents. Then he turned and walked back to his little office. Inside, Jade saw him picking up a radio-communication handset, close the door, and turn his back to the window.

Nothing happened for a few minutes except that the morning got brighter, the crimson clouds fading slowly into pinkish yellow, and a train left one of the harbour sidings. Jade heard it before she saw it. An old-looking engine with a few identical carriages chugged out of the harbour from beyond the tall sheet-metal walls and then swung left.

Then a figure emerged at a run from one of the offices and scrambled into a white Golf. Jade could hear the squeal of rubber as he spun his wheels and drove out of the car park, heading towards the gate.

23

The new arrival was Indian. Short and stocky, and dressed in a smart suit and tie with a business-like attitude to match. Calling out a hurried greeting to them, he waved the guard impatiently back into his little office. Jade was glad to see the back of him.

Moving swiftly to the gate, he unlocked it and rolled it open.

'Please,' he said, extending an open palm towards the access road. 'Come in, Superintendent. Good morning. And a very good morning to you too,' he said, turning to Jade. 'I'm the harbour master, and I'm sorry about the inconvenience. We've had big security problems recently and have just implemented a whole new access system here. We're still experiencing some teething problems, as you can see.'

Jade revised her initial impression of him. He didn't look business-like so much as deeply stressed.

She and David got back into their car and followed the white Golf down the surprisingly potholed access road and into the car park. Looking over her shoulder, Jade saw the guard reappear and swiftly close and lock the gate behind them. He'd find himself having to open it again in a couple of minutes, because two other men, who, judging by their tired expressions, were night-shift workers, were starting up their own vehicles.

The harbour master hovered by their car as she and David got out again, shifting from foot to foot as if he were cold.

'We've got a backlog,' he said, as if to explain the departing night-shift workers. 'We've had a high . . . er . . . turnover in staff these last few weeks.'

'That's what I'm here to speak to you about,' David said. 'I understand one of your employees, a Mr Padayachee, went missing a while ago.'

The Indian man started speaking again, the words spilling from his mouth like water from a wide-open tap.

'That's right. It's all been chaotic, I'm afraid. I've been run off my feet trying to sort out the irregularities we've found. There's more to Padayachee's disappearance than we first thought. Would you like . . . can I ask you to come back next week? I'll have more time for you then.' His plea fell on stony ground. David simply shook his head and Jade watched the harbour master's expression change from hopeful to resigned.

'Irregularities?' David asked.

The other man chewed his lip for a moment, his small white teeth pressing deeply into the soft flesh.

'Unfortunately so. We're being advised by our lawyers at present on how best to put a case together. Currently there are a couple of workers on suspension, and of course the one who's disappeared.'

The harbour looked busy. One ship was docking; another was being towed in by a tugboat. Two cranes were in operation, winching large, dull-coloured containers from a third ship and lowering them into a cordoned-off area that Jade supposed was where goods were inspected by Customs.

She wondered how much one of those containers weighed and what its contents might be. Different ports must handle different shipments, she thought, although from what she could see, most of the offloaded cargo here was coal, transported loose in the ship's hold.

'Where can we go to discuss this?' David said.

The harbour master chewed his lip again.

'We can talk in my office. I don't mind giving the details to a police detective, of course, but I'd prefer our conversation to be in private, if you don't mind.' He glanced apologetically at Jade.

'Go right ahead,' she said. 'I'll wait in the car.'

She watched David follow the shorter man along the roughly

paved path that led to the offices and enter a low doorway. David had to duck his head to go through and, even so, she thought she heard the distinctive thunk of his forehead hitting the lintel as he disappeared from sight.

Jade suppressed a laugh. Cruel, she knew, but what could you do?

The offices weren't very grand-looking. In fact, the squat, beige, oblong buildings with their small windows and flat roofs distinctly reminded her of the containers that were being offloaded from the ship.

Surely the offices weren't made from old containers? From here, she couldn't see the walls clearly enough to tell what they were.

Jade had heard of old shipping containers being used to provide everything from housing and offices to shops and hair salons in third-world countries. But in a major South African harbour?

Perhaps the architect had just had a sense of humour. That, or a very small budget for design.

The wind was growing stronger now, gusting onshore, doing its damnedest to blow all the clouds on the horizon overhead.

It was making her cold. She went to open the car door to get her jacket out, but found to her irritation that David had locked it before setting off.

In that case, Jade decided, she might as well go for a brisk walk before she froze to death.

She followed the path down towards the office buildings. As she drew closer, she discovered that the buildings were, in fact, made of badly painted brick.

Slightly disappointed by this, she walked on. Past the offices and in the direction of the harbour itself. She didn't want to go too near the offloading area, so she turned away from the cranes and the activity, following a route that took her towards the massive sheet-metal barrier.

The steel towered so high above her head that even with the tallest ladder she doubted whether she would have been able to see over its top. Was there a gate anywhere, she wondered, or was access only possible from the water itself? Surely there must be a gate or a door somewhere along its length. Curious to find out, Jade set out along the perimeter.

The sheets were solid, but above head-height she saw small ventilation holes had been drilled into them. The wind shrieked and moaned as it passed through. The breeze caught the edges of the tarpaulins covering the piles of bricks and wood stacked nearby, and they flapped loudly in accompaniment.

But even above this racket, Jade could hear a loud voice behind her; the angry shout of another uniformed guard.

Turning round, she saw the man heading down the access road towards her at a shambling run. He waved his arm in a big, sweeping gesture that said, more clearly than words, 'Get back.'

Jade took one last look at the barrier. There was definitely a doorway in the metal wall, although the door itself looked firmly shut.

'Lady, that's a construction site. It's off limits,' the guard called to her. 'Go back to your vehicle, please.'

'All right.'

She started walking away from the barrier and the guard fell into step beside her.

'What's behind the screen?' she asked. Given his officious attitude, she hadn't expected an answer, but to her surprise she got one.

'It's a dry dock, for repairing tankers and other large vessels. They're busy rebuilding it.'

'Oh.'

'The wind is causing problems. One person has already been injured.'

'Shouldn't you put a notice up warning the public away, then?'

'Lady, the public is not actually allowed to enter this area.'

'Fair enough.'

Back at her car, Jade leaned against the door. It felt chilly to the touch. Hugging her arms around her body, she was about to resign herself to a long, cold wait when, to her relief, she saw the door of the office open and David emerge, with the harbour master close behind him.

This time, David had made sure to bend way down before

going through the doorway, as if he was bowing, leaving a size-able gap between himself and the lintel.

'What did he say?' she asked David as he reversed out of the parking bay. He'd taken the wheel again without asking, a habit that was beginning to annoy Jade. After all, it was her car.

Seeing them approach, the deeply tanned guard unlocked the heavy padlock and pulled the gate open to allow them to leave. Jade fastened her seatbelt tightly in anticipation of the speedy drive back to Scuba Sands, and twisted the heater's dial as far over into the red as it would go.

'He said there have been huge problems with theft. Stuff going missing from containers, equipment going missing from the harbour, and a whole lot of materials disappearing from a construction project they're busy with.'

As David drove out of the compound, Jade turned and watched the deeply tanned guard pulling the gate closed again.

'Apparently they're rebuilding one of the dry docks,' she said, pointing over her shoulder at the tall barrier. 'Another guard told me.'

'Oh, OK. Anyway, when all this came out, they think Paday-achee must have done a runner. He isn't a permanent employee, by the way—they hired him specifically for this project. After he'd been absent from work and uncontactable for a couple of days, they phoned his nearest relative, a brother, who subse-quently reported him missing. I have the brother's phone number here.'

'And are the police investigating the theft?'

David nodded as he turned onto the main road and acceler-ated. 'He gave me the case number and the name of his lawyer. I'll follow up when I have time, but it doesn't sound like a prior-ity. I think it'll end up being a dead end myself.'

'So can he explain how Padayachee's truck ended up being driven by a man who looks like a poor white and who's now wanted by the police for questioning?'

David took his hands off the steering wheel and spread them, palms up, in the air. 'He had no idea. He said that for all he knew, Padayachee might have sold the truck, or lent it to somebody.'

Jade told herself she wasn't going to grab the wheel. She wasn't. In a moment, David would take hold of it again. He must have noticed the vehicle was already starting to veer to the left.

'But wouldn't he . . .' Jade couldn't help it. She reached over for the steering wheel, but before she could touch it, David took hold of it again. The car swerved noticeably as he corrected his course.

'I keep on calling him "he", because you haven't told me who he is,' she continued. 'What's his name?'

'Whose name?' David frowned, obviously not following Jade's train of thought.

'The harbour master. The man you've just been speaking to.'

'Oh. Sorry. He only introduced himself to me when we were in the office. His name is Chetty. Sanjay Chetty.'

24

Back at the resort, Jade saw Neil, the owner, outside his house unpacking a bootful of grocery bags from his yellow Beetle. It looked like he'd been shopping for a small army. Perhaps he was anticipating a siege.

'Be careful if you go down to the beach this evening,' he called to her. 'There's a spring tide late tonight and the sea will get very high.'

'I will. Thanks for the warning,' she responded.

Craig was nowhere to be seen, but Elsabe was sitting outside her chalet, sewing. A yellow felt workbag lay open at her feet, and on the wooden table in front of her, scissors, pins, needles and thread were neatly arranged.

Jade climbed out of the car and walked up onto her own verandah. She called out 'good morning' to the other woman. She hadn't expected a response, but to her surprise, Elsabe looked up and greeted her with a nod.

Jade moved over to the verandah's edge.

'What are you busy with there?' she asked.

Elsabe smoothed a hand over the white ruched fabric on her lap. 'A skirt. I'm taking in the waistband,' she said. 'It's too loose. I can't wear it anymore.'

'Wouldn't a sewing machine make it easier?'

'It would. But I don't have my machine with me and, to be honest, I find this therapeutic.'

She looked down again and deftly moved the needle in and out of the material.

'Working with one's hands is soothing,' Jade agreed.

'Do you like needlework?'

Jade gave a rueful shake of her head. 'I'm barely capable of sewing on a button, I'm afraid.' Cleaning her gun was her form of manual therapy, but she didn't think that now was the time to mention that.

'There's something about sewing,' Elsabe said. 'One little thread. On its own, you can snap it so easily. But stitch it into fabric, and it's strong enough to hold a whole garment together.'

'I suppose the opposite applies too,' Jade said. 'Cut one little thread . . .'

'And everything falls apart,' Elsabe tightened her lips.

The two women were silent for a moment. Behind her, Jade heard David unlock the front door and walk into the chalet while speaking yet again on his cellphone.

'Are you all right?' she asked Elsabe.

The redhead nodded. Looking more closely, Jade noticed the circles under her eyes looked even darker. Her skin was porcelain-pale, as if she had never been exposed to the sun.

'Yes,' she said. 'I'm frightened, though. I had to cope with a personal tragedy in my life quite recently, and it's left me feeling vulnerable.'

'What happened?' Jade asked softly. Craig had spoken to her about it, but she thought it only polite to ask.

'I'd really rather not share my problems with a stranger.'

Jade took a step back, temporarily silenced by the snub.

Elsabe turned her attention back to her needlework for a while. Then she looked up, as if surprised to find Jade still there. 'I'm only staying here for as long as the police need me. Then I'm driving back to Johannesburg.'

'You live in Jo'burg?'

'In Emmarentia, near Zoo Lake.'

The old part of the northern suburbs. Big trees, beautiful old houses, quaint roadside stores. More character and history than the 'new north,' where cluster-home complexes and shopping malls had been rudely hacked out of the veld, the bush and indigencus grasses replaced by acres of paving, matchbox squares of instant lawn, spindly looking palm trees and endless ranks of tiled roofs.

Jade paused, then asked, 'You've spent a lot of time out on the boat on those all-day dives. Did you get to know Monique well?'

Elsabe peered down at her sewing. 'I spent time with her, yes. But knowing her well, no. I found her . . . superficial, I suppose.'

That was a good way of putting it, Jade thought.

'Sometimes even superficial conversation can hold valuable clues.'

Elsabe gave a small shrug. 'I've told the police what I know. I can't do more than that.' Then she turned away from Jade and began rummaging in her workbag.

Conversation over, Jade guessed. The short exchange hadn't made her like Elsabe any better. She'd feel sorrier for her, she decided, if she wasn't so damn prissy.

Inside her pocket, her cellphone made a bleeping noise, telling her its battery was low. She went into the chalet to charge it up, but found to her annoyance that the only available two-prong plug adaptor, which she had brought along, was being used by David to charge his phone.

Jade suppressed the urge to yank it from the socket, put hers in instead, and shout angrily at the closed bathroom door behind which he now was. Something about respecting people's property and asking first. If they'd been in a relationship, it wouldn't have mattered. Now it did matter. The boundaries had changed.

She bit back the words and stuffed the phone back in her pocket. She wasn't going to scream at him like a fishwife. After all, from what he'd told her, that was what his wife often did. So he'd surely be getting more than enough of it in the years to come.

The thought barely out of her head, the bathroom door opened and David walked out.

'Pillay's just phoned. He wants to meet at the police station. Any chance you could give me a lift? I won't be long.'

Jade wasn't going all the way into town. Only as far as the retirement home where she was going to meet Mrs Koekemoer and ask about her mother, a fact that she would rather not have shared with David. Too late now, she supposed.

'I need to go to Harbour View. You can take the car from there and pick me up on your way back.'

'Thanks.'

David took his service pistol out of the holster and put it back in the safe. Before he could lock it, Jade took her Glock out. She shoved the compact weapon deep into the pocket of her cargo pants and pulled her T-shirt over it to hide its shape. After all, she didn't want to frighten the old lady; but, at the same time, she was nervous about going out without a weapon. At least one of them should be armed, she reasoned.

To her surprise, David didn't ask why she was going to Harbour View. He was too preoccupied, immersed in his own personal problems and in the complexities of the unwelcome new case he'd taken on.

This murder should never have happened, Jade thought. Not here, in this small and peaceful community. It was incongruous—a big-city crime in a seaside village.

'Right. Let's go, then.' David picked up her car keys and jingled them in his hand, an action that forced Jade, yet again, to bite her tongue.

Harbour View, despite its appealing name, was a suburb of small criss-crossed streets that appeared to be wedged in between a disused railway station and the eastern boundary of the harbour, where the only available view was of rows of blank-walled warehouses.

This was the bad side of town—or as bad as Jade supposed it got in Richards Bay. Overall, the place had none of the energy of Johannesburg. She'd never thought that she would miss the traffic-clogged roads, the queues of roadside hawkers, the brilliance of the high-altitude electric storms that sent bolts of lightning through the thin, dry air—but she did. And, of course, there could never be any shortage of work for a private investigator in a city that had come into being as a result of gold and greed.

In contrast, Richards Bay had started out as a tiny beachside community. When, in the late sixties, an aluminium smelter was built, the industrial area expanded massively and the town had followed suit.

At about the same time, Jade's father, at that stage a young police captain, had been posted there, to head up the brand-new Richards Bay precinct. He'd spent a few years here—Jade wasn't sure exactly how many, and she'd been too young to know her exact address. The words 'police village' sounded vaguely familiar, so she thought her father must have lived in specially assigned accommodation. Jade wasn't sure where that would have been. Not in an expensive area, certainly, although the house had had a well-treed, but otherwise neglected, garden that had seemed enormous to a small child.

She must have been three or four when her father had been promoted to lead a national investigation unit. His work had taken him all over the country, sometimes for months at a time, but he had been officially based at Jo'burg Central police station, which in those days had been known as John Vorster Square. She remembered sitting on a row of cardboard boxes in the Richards Bay house, watching her father help the removal men load their simple furniture into a van. Then they had embarked on the seven-hour drive to Johannesburg. It didn't take that long today—the highways that had been built since then had taken a good hour off the journey.

By the time they had reached Johannesburg, it had been almost completely dark and, even now, Jade could still remember the sense of utter wonderment she had felt as their car crested a hill and there, in front of them, had been the last orange smudge of the setting sun . . . and the lights.

Twinkling lights in every direction, as far as she could see, stretching right to the horizon. Some bright, others so dim they were only a faint shimmer. Some clustered thickly together, some marching away from her in an orderly sequence, following the straight lines of the roads.

Jade had had no idea that a city could be so big. It had seemed to her like another planet. Foreign, mysterious and exciting.

'Wow,' she had breathed, turning her head from side to side to take in the dazzling view.

She remembered how her father had laughed, stretched out his hand and ruffled her hair.

Rose Village Retirement Home looked more like a prison camp. A series of stark buildings surrounded by a scruffy garden and a low brick wall, with not a rose in sight.

She'd asked David to drop her off at a shopping centre on the way, so that he wouldn't know exactly where she was headed. Her quest to find out more about Elise de Jong was a private matter. She didn't want David knowing—and most probably disapproving, since he knew who her mother had been. Jade had told him soon after she had found out, although in retrospect she wished she hadn't.

At the shops, she had bought a big tin of biscuits as a gift for the old lady, and taken a close look at a street map of the area before embarking on the fifteen-minute walk to the retirement home.

Inside, the place smelled institutional, as if decades of bland meals and cheap disinfectant had seeped into its very pores. Jade asked for Mrs Koekemoer at reception and, after a short wait, was escorted down the corridor by a smiling coloured nurse.

'Is she your granny?' the nurse asked her, and Jade shook her head.

'She knew my mother,' she replied.

The nurse gave a soft knock on a door that already stood ajar, before walking inside. Jade followed her. The small room was warm—stuffy, even. Cream-coloured blinds were pulled up, revealing a rather grubby window that looked out onto the rear garden. Still no roses to be seen, but other flowers and shrubs filled the untidy-looking beds.

A portly, white-haired lady was sitting in a wheelchair by the window, staring out at the garden.

'Mrs K?' the nurse called. 'You have a visitor.'

The elderly lady looked round. Her eyes were confused and somehow opaque-looking.

'Mrs Koekemoer? I spoke to you yesterday on the phone. I'm Jade de Jong. You knew my mother, Elise, when you worked at the Richards Bay hospital.'

The lady stared at Jade, her expression blank.

'Elise de Jong?' she asked.

'Yes.' Jade said gently.

The old lady looked away.

'She has some good days, and some days that are bad. Yesterday was a very good day for her. Today is not so good, I think,' the nurse whispered.

Jade was beginning to wish she'd asked the questions over the phone the previous day.

'What should I do?' she whispered back.

The nurse shrugged. 'Stay for a while. Perhaps she will remember just now.'

Jade stepped forward and put the Spar shopping bag down on the table next to the narrow bed.

'I brought you a present,' she said, taking out the tin.

The old lady's face lit up.

'Biscuits!' she exclaimed.

'Would you like one?'

'No, no thank you. Later, with my tea. Who are you?'

'Jade de Jong. You knew my mother, Elise. You looked after her in hospital. I'm her daughter.'

The old lady whispered something so softly Jade could hardly hear it. She stepped closer and sat down on the plastic chair that was obviously for guests. In her pocket, she heard her phone beep its low-battery warning and she pushed her hand against it to muffle the noise.

The old lady whispered the words again, and this time Jade heard them exactly.

'She died. Buried in the gardens.'

Despite the warmth of the room, Jade shivered.

'Yes, I know. That's why I've come to visit. To find out . . .'

But Mrs Koekemoer interrupted her, again with words so soft Jade had to lean right forward to make them out.

'Car accident, right here in town.'

Jade felt as if a bucket of icy water had just been tipped over her back. The skin on her arms turned to gooseflesh.

'No . . . it can't be.'

'She was speeding,' the old lady mumbled, nodding her head so that her white curls bobbed. 'Going far too fast. She and her baby daughter, both. They're with the angels now.'

A gentle touch on Jade's shoulder made her jump.

The nurse was back, holding a glass of water on a saucer.

'She's talking about her own daughter,' she said in a low voice, handing the water to Jade. 'She's the one who died in the crash with her baby. It was many years ago, but she still speaks about it as if it was yesterday. Sometimes she forgets it happened and asks us where Daphne is and why she does not visit.'

Jade nodded. 'Thank you,' she whispered. Then, turning back to Mrs Koekemoer, she said, 'That must have been terrible for you.'

'Yes, yes. A terrible loss.' Lacing her knotted fingers together, she bowed her head. 'I pray for them every day. Pray they did not suffer.' She glanced up at Jade again. 'Who are you?' she asked.

Jade was beginning to think that this visit was a waste of time—that she should simply sit here and offer the elderly lady some company for a while, and come back another day.

One last try, then.

'I'm Elise de Jong's daughter. You looked after her at the hospital.'

When Mrs Koekemoer turned to stare at Jade, it was like a light had suddenly gone on behind her eyes.

'You are so like your mother, my dear. I'd forgotten how she looked, but seeing you brings it all back.'

Jade took a deep breath. She realised her hands were clenched so hard her nails were just about piercing her palms. 'You remember her well?' she asked.

'Oh, ja, of course. She had the very first c-section we ever did in the new maternity ward. A beautiful lady?'

Jade nodded encouragingly. 'Yes.'

'Her glass of red wine,' she said thoughtfully. 'I remember that. Her husband would visit every evening, and he'd bring along a bottle of red wine and pour a glass for each of them. Just one glass each, every night. It wasn't really allowed, but we turned a blind eye.'

Jade smiled. She could imagine her father's pleasure in this evening ritual. He'd enjoyed red wine, although he'd only ever had a glass on special occasions. Perhaps her birth had been special enough for him and his wife to celebrate every night.

'My father didn't speak much about my mother,' Jade offered. 'There's a lot I don't know.'

Mrs Koekemoer nodded sympathetically. 'I see.'

'I don't even know where she's buried.'

The old woman's eyes widened.

'That's a secret, my dear. I'm not allowed to tell. You must speak to the doctor in charge. What's his name? Let me think now . . . Abrahams, that's it. Ask him.'

This odd reply made Jade start to worry that Mrs Koekemoer's window of lucidity was narrowing. Changing the subject, she continued.

'My dad said she loved to dive. Loved the ocean.'

'Oh, yes. She was a diver, wasn't she? Until the accident, of course.'

The accident?

Jade sat forward, propping herself right on the edge of her chair. 'What accident? I've never heard anything about that.' For a moment, she thought that Mrs Koekemoer must be thinking of her own daughter's car accident again.

'She'd been out at sea. Not diving, of course, because she was pregnant. She was snorkelling. A boat ran right over her. Her arms were all cut up from the propeller—it looked like somebody had taken a carving knife to her.'

With those words, the vivid image of Amanda's bloodied body flooded back into Jade's head. She gave an involuntary shudder.

'Elise was knocked out—she almost drowned. Luckily someone managed to get her back to shore before the sharks came along.'

Jade's breath caught in her throat.

'For a while, we were worried she might miscarry, but she didn't. She made a full recovery, but I remember her saying that as it happened, all she'd been able to think about was her baby . . . about you. Elise told me in hospital that she didn't know if she could ever enjoy diving again. Having so nearly died had made her feel differently about it,' the old lady whispered in a conspiratorial tone. 'She said she was terrified to go back underwater, that she thought she had developed a fear of drowning.'

25

As Jade walked out of the retirement home, ready to make her way back to the shopping centre where she had said she'd meet David, her phone started ringing. The incoming number was unfamiliar.

She cast a glance up and down the narrow road before answering, but there was nobody to be seen except for a young black man in shorts and a ragged T-shirt walking ahead of her.

Jade punched the answer button.

'Hello?'

The voice on the other side stopped her in her tracks.

It was sharp, confident, horribly familiar.

'Babe. Thought I'd better give you a call, because I see you've skipped town.'

Jade snatched the phone away from her ear as if it were a red-hot coal.

Robbie. As soon as he spoke, she couldn't help remember the way he'd looked when she'd last seen him, just a week ago, waiting for her in the darkness outside her cottage.

The new scar on his jaw, the gold rings on his fingers, the hardness in his eyes.

His expression when he told her he wanted her 'help' with a job.

Heart banging in her throat, she stared at the instrument, bitterly regretting having answered the call. How bloody ironic. She'd refused to help because of David, because she knew it was what he would have wanted. And now that David was getting back together with his wife permanently, her noble decision had been in vain.

She still wasn't going to help Robbie, though. This was her chance—the opportunity to step out of his world and break ties with him forever. It would mean she'd just have to be more cautious when arriving home alone.

She raised the phone again, to find he was still speaking.

'. . . haven't heard from them for a few days now, and it looks like the assignment's changed profile, so I thought I'd better keep you in the loop . . .'

'Robbie,' Jade interrupted him, speaking loudly.

'Yes, babe?'

'This job. I'm . . .'

And then, with the words she needed on the tip of her tongue, Jade heard her phone play the cheery little tune that meant the battery was drained.

She stared down at the blank screen of the instrument in exasperation.

'Damn you to hell!' she shouted, so loudly that the black man turned, noticing her for the first time, and stared at her for a long, assessing moment.

Jade raised her head and met his gaze until he looked away. Then she pocketed the useless phone and stomped back up the street.

Immersed in her own frustrated thoughts, it was a while before she noticed that the yellow car parked up ahead by the side of the road outside the entrance to one of the dilapidated blocks of flats looked oddly familiar.

She slowed down and took a better look.

The car stood out from its surroundings, by virtue of its colour as well as its shape. The number plate looked familiar, and the unusual sticker on the rear window advertising a Durban surf shop confirmed her first thoughts.

This car belonged to Neil Pienaar, the owner of Scuba Sands. She'd last seen it less than two hours ago, parked outside his house while he unloaded shopping bags from it.

What on earth was it doing here?

Jade's first and immediate thought was that Neil was visiting a prostitute. After all, he was a single man and she'd seen no evidence that he had a partner or lover of either gender. So perhaps this was how he preferred to conduct his intimate relationships.

But in this ramshackle part of town?

Jade frowned up at the apartment building, noticing the crumbling plaster, the rusty balcony railings, the two broken windows on the first floor.

And then she saw Neil.

Hurrying along the corridor of the third and top floor in the direction of the external stairwell. As she watched, he headed down the first flight of stairs and disappeared from sight.

He would soon reappear, though, and when he did he would see her. And until Jade knew why Neil had been on the top floor of a dodgy-looking building in an unsavoury part of Richards Bay, she wanted to keep her presence here a secret.

Jade sprinted to the opposite side of the road and crouched down behind the only available cover on that side of the street— another parked car, this one an old beige Toyota. If the car's owner appeared, she'd be exposed and have some explaining to do. But Jade didn't think the owner would be heading this way any time soon, because the car's tyres were so soft that it was basically listing sideways on its heavily rusted rims.

Lifting her head, Jade peered through the car's dirty windows and looked across the road. She heard the thud of Neil's shoes before she saw him. He emerged from the ground-floor entrance and marched towards his car with shoulders squared, fists clenched and arms swinging by his side. He looked very different from the inoffensive and rather timid man that Jade remembered. Was he angry now? And if so, what had caused his rage?

The Volkswagen started with a roar and a moment later its rounded yellow backside shot off down the street.

Jade got up from her hiding place and crossed the road. Standing outside the flat's entrance, she looked up.

The building was designed in an L-shape, with the longer leg of the 'L' running parallel to the road. Since Neil had come round the corner, from the shorter side of the building, there were only one or two apartments that he could have been visiting.

On the left-hand side of the main doorway there was an inter-com system with eighteen buttons. Jade could have pressed all of them if she'd needed to, and the chances were good that one of the residents would have let her in. However, the security system, such as it was, was rendered null and void by the fact that the steel access gate at the building's entrance, the one which Neil had so recently pushed open, was unlatched. In fact, looking more closely, Jade saw that the latch was broken.

She walked in and headed up the gloomy stairs.

Jade didn't go straight to the third floor, but walked along the second-floor corridor to get an idea of the layout. On her right was the railing, and on her left the wooden doors to the flats themselves. The entrances to flats seven to ten looked onto the road, and when she rounded the corner she saw that those of numbers eleven and twelve faced the bare wall of the next-door building.

So, assuming the third-floor numbering system mirrored this pattern, Neil could only have been visiting someone in flat seven-teen or eighteen.

Returning to the main entrance, Jade pressed the buzzers for both these numbers. The intercom was working—she could hear the loud ringing noise it made. After a pause, number seventeen answered.

'Yebo?'

A woman's voice. Jade couldn't tell more than that, because the voice was just about drowned out by the yelling of babies in the background. The sound burst out of the cheap intercom, accompanied by a series of distorted crackles. More than two infants, certainly. Perhaps three or four, each trying to gain ascendancy over the other in terms of the pitch, volume and duration of screams. Gritting her teeth, Jade took a deep breath.

'Did a man come and visit you just now?' she shouted.

'Angizwakahle.'

Huh?

Jade's Zulu was too sketchy to understand the response, so she pushed open the security door and walked all the way up to flat number seventeen. This time the cries of the children were audible even before she turned the corner of the 'L'. With some trepidation, she knocked on the cheap plywood door.

It was opened a short while later by a plump, twenty-something woman. She had a white headscarf wrapped around her braided hair, a baby on her hip and a half-full bottle of milk in her right hand. The infant was screaming so loudly that the sound waves actually battered Jade.

The woman looked out at her, her manner suspicious, but not entirely unfriendly.

Behind her, Jade could see that the apartment was well lit, clean and, apart from a number of toys and blankets strewn on the living room carpet, relatively tidy. Another child was wailing from the confines of a push-chair in the passage and two toddlers were on all fours on the carpet, bellowing as they struggled for possession of what looked like a stuffed zebra.

'Hello,' Jade said. The baby drew breath for another scream and into the silence she said quickly, 'Did a man just come here? A white person, name of Neil?'

The woman's smooth forehead furrowed into a small, confused frown and she shook her head.

'No white man comes here,' she said in halting English.

'Sorry to disturb you,' Jade said, taking a step back as, once again, she was bludgeoned by a wall of noise. 'Thank you,' she called, as the door to the flat closed. 'Er . . . *Ngiyabonga*.'

Jade's eardrums were still ringing as she turned away from number seventeen. She really did need to learn better Zulu, she decided. It just didn't make sense that she was less capable of communicating effectively with the woman than the baby in her arms had been.

Even though Jade hadn't been able to speak the black woman's native tongue, her body language had told Jade that she was genuinely confused by her presence. That ruled out this apartment, which meant that Neil had definitely been in the flat next door.

Jade walked the short distance down the corridor to number eighteen. To her surprise, when she reached it, she found the flat was extremely well secured, even by Jo'burg's high standards. The door—not plywood, but solid timber—was guarded by a heavy steel security gate, which had two separate locks. Unlike the flat next door, the burglar bars on the window overlooking the corridor were thick and solid—no doubt custom-made. Jade also noticed there were alarm sensors on the window frame.

Whoever lived in number eighteen took safety very seriously. And they clearly weren't home; no one came to the door when she knocked and there was no sign of life inside.

So whoever Neil had come here to see, he'd been disappointed. Not an arranged meeting, then.

Walking back down the corridor, Jade thought again about the way he'd looked as he'd strode out of the building. For some reason, his demeanour had reminded her of a sight she'd seen more than a decade ago in a private game park, when a zebra stallion had spotted a rival male entering his territory. The way the dominant zebra had held himself as he faced his competition had been similar to the way that Neil had looked.

She had no idea why he'd looked that way, though.

Just as she reached the top of the last flight of stairs, she heard the access gate slam.

A few seconds later, a blond man with a pair of sunglasses pushed back on his head started up the stairs towards her. He had several bulky shopping bags in each hand and she had to press herself against the wall to allow him to pass.

The man didn't look as if he belonged in the building. Wearing a mid-grey suit, pale Oxford shirt and dark tie, he was far too expensively dressed for this part of town. The effect was rather spoiled, however, by the large cellphone hanging from a lanyard around his neck, which swung wildly with each step he took.

He glanced briefly at Jade as he passed.

Curious as to why he was living here, she stopped and turned to take another look at him.

She was taken aback to see that the blond man had stopped for a second look at her too.

Jade hurried down the last few stairs and out into the fresh air.

She'd already had a suspicion about where the blond man was going, and it was confirmed when she saw him striding along the third-floor corridor, obviously heading for flat number eighteen.

So this was the man that Neil had hoped to see. But why?

Jade turned away and carried on down the road to the place where she was meeting David, her mind spinning.

If she'd looked up over her shoulder, she would have seen the blond man leaning out over the parapet, watching her.

She would also have seen him lift his heavy phone to his ear and start speaking urgently into it.

26

After the amount of time she'd spent with Mrs Koekemoer and the lengthy detour she'd taken on the way back to the dilapidated flats where she'd seen Neil's car, Jade was sure that David must have been waiting for her for ages. Rather than walking back around the wide loop of road, she decided to take what looked like a quick and convenient shortcut back to the main street. At any rate, it was a well-trodden, if somewhat muddy, grass-lined path that led directly away from the road, down the hill and over the railway track towards some old-looking buildings. Surely after that there would be a road up the hill towards the shopping centre. It would be worth checking out, at any rate, as it would save her time.

Jade set off at a run, jumping over the muddier sections and puddles in the boggy ground near the bottom of the hill. She noticed that, apart from mud, the narrow strip of beaten dirt was surprisingly free of the litter that normally collected on the edges of a well-used shortcut.

After barely a minute, the black-stained bricks of the buildings she'd seen came clearly into view. Much to Jade's relief, the path led to a gap in the chain-link fence that surrounded them, which she climbed easily through.

The main building was actually part of an old railway station that looked as if it had been disused for years. Tall shoots of straggly, yellowish grass had pushed up through the bricks alongside the graffiti-covered outside walls. One train, with its engine, was permanently halted in a siding outside the building. The train itself looked ancient, although the tracks it was stopped on looked oddly shiny and free from weeds, and the railway cars smelled strongly of old, dirty engine oil.

The harsh stink of it caught in her throat, and she found herself coughing as she hurried past. And then she stopped as, from somewhere inside the building, she heard another cough.

Unlike hers, this one was deep, heavy, rattling. An old man's cough—or a sick one's. It was soon joined by another.

The old station was obviously a refuge for homeless people or squatters.

More disturbingly, though, the path didn't lead where she'd thought it would. Instead of going past the building and up towards the main road, it ran along the side of the station, then down to the tracks and into the main entrance, where the railway tracks themselves led.

Following the path anyway, Jade discovered that the station was locked. A pair of enormous doors prevented all access to the building itself.

Above her, the clouds were starting to thicken. It wasn't exactly raining, but the air felt damp, as if rain was just a click of the fingers away.

She retraced her steps back to the road and set off at a run to go the long way round. By the time she arrived at the little shopping centre, David was already parked outside, tapping his fingers on the dashboard. His head was turned away from her, watching the shops, and when she yanked open the passenger door he jumped so hard he smacked his head against the driver's window. He must have been deep in thought.

Lunch, Patel-style, was laid out on the car's dashboard. Coke, bottled water, a brown paper bag of biltong and a large packet of salt and vinegar crisps.

'Where were you?' he asked. 'I was about to start driving round the area looking for you.'

'I went for a walk,' Jade said.

David grabbed a handful of the biltong and crammed it into his mouth before starting the car.

'Go on, take some,' he said with difficulty around his large mouthful, handing her the bag. 'It's good stuff.'

Jade tried a piece. She didn't agree with David's assessment. It was tough and tasteless; quite possibly the worst biltong she'd ever had in her life. But David often forgot to eat when he was stressed or upset and, as her father had always used to say, hunger was the best sauce.

David joined the main road and sped up, his attention divided equally between the road in front of him and the brown paper bag on his left. Jade hastily fastened her seatbelt. David, of course, wasn't wearing his.

'Do me a favour and please don't speed,' she said, pressing herself back into her seat.

David gave her a pained look as he reached for another fistful of the dried meat.

'Jadey, I never speed.'

'I don't want to get a bunch of fines.'

'But it's a rented car.'

'Rent a Runner keeps records of all their regular clients. Speeding fines get passed on to them as part of their monthly bill. They're a small operation and they can't afford to subsidise bad drivers. At least, that's what they told me a while back, when I queried the extra thousand rands added to my invoice.'

'And that was me?'

'Yes. They emailed me the tickets and I had a look. Three fines. I checked the dates. Three hundred rands for doing ninety in a sixty zone when you drove us to the Local Grill in Hurlingham. Another three hundred for doing one hundred and forty on the highway when you were driving us back from the weekend in the Pilanesberg. And four hundred rands for doing one hundred and twenty-five in an eighty zone on a day when you borrowed my car. You were on your way to Pretoria, I think,' Jade said, emphasising the city's name meaningfully since that was where Naisha lived.

There was a short, embarrassed silence.

'I'm sorry, Jadey.'

If he called her by her pet name once more, Jade decided she was going to slap him. 'Don't be sorry. Be careful.'

'You should have said something before now.'

'Things were different before now.'

David gave another deep sigh.

'I guess so,' he said.

Glancing down at the speedometer, David eased off the accelerator.

They didn't speak again. Wrapped in her own suddenly gloomy thoughts, Jade stared blankly out of the window at the lush foliage lining the quiet main road.

After a while, hoping to distract herself from her relationship difficulties, she turned her mind to Pillay's missing persons portfolio.

One man had been reported missing and his truck had been found at a crime scene, having been driven by somebody else. But what had the detective told her so proudly when she'd asked him during their interview? He'd said that there were a number of missing persons in his files. Quite a few, from the sound of things. He'd been kept busy.

That didn't make sense. In a small town like Richards Bay, why would the number of missing people be so high? And if one missing person had been loosely connected to a crime through his vehicle, what about the others?

She was about to share these thoughts with David, when he braked hard and swore.

'Oh, crap. I don't bloody believe it.'

Jade's seatbelt tightened hard across her chest. Ahead, she saw a tall police officer standing authoritatively in the road and waving their car over. His policeman's cap was perched on the top of his head, as if it were a size too small.

'This is KwaZulu-Natal,' she reminded him. 'Zero tolerance for speeding.'

'But I wasn't exceeding the damn limit. We just had that conversation, remember?'

'Don't tell me. Tell the cop. Perhaps he'll let you look at the camera and you can see how fast you were going.'

'I was not speeding,' David muttered, changing down a gear. 'The limit's eighty here, isn't it? The one time I'm actually keeping my speed down, I get pulled over.'

'Maybe he just wants to see your licence.' Jade said, even though she thought it unlikely. This didn't look like a routine roadblock. Roadblocks had traffic cones and backup vehicles and groups of policemen on duty.

This was a typical speed trap. Just one police car on duty, half hidden from view.

David indicated left and carefully pulled onto the verge. Every bit the upstanding citizen, although it was surely a case of too little too late. Checking the wing mirror, Jade noticed a car some distance behind them. A black truck, which seemed to be driving very slowly. What irony it would be if this was the truck Pillay was looking for and the Metro policeman allowed the man they were hunting to go free, because he was busy writing out a speeding ticket.

David stopped the car and turned off the engine. The police car was parked with its bonnet deep in the bushes, a big white BMW that looked more than capable of giving chase to even the speediest offender.

'I'd get out and speak to him face to face, if I were you,' Jade advised.

David nodded. 'Good idea. I'll show him my ID and explain I'm busy with an important investigation. Hopefully that'll get any fine waived.'

Shifting onto his right buttock, he dug in his left back pocket for his wallet.

Jade watched the Metro policeman stroll over towards their car. Big, dark wraparound glasses covered his eyes. His Metro Police uniform was ill-fitting; the collared shirt was too tight across his shoulders and the trousers too short. They showed off his beige socks and his shiny black shoes.

And something else was unusual. What was that around his . . . ?

Alarm bells started to ring in Jade's head.

She glanced again at the BMW. It was difficult to see from this angle, but the car didn't appear to have any Metro Police signage on its sides. It definitely didn't have any on its back and it didn't have a rear number plate, either.

The alarm bells were ringing louder and faster now. She should have realised something was wrong earlier. Would have, if she hadn't been so preoccupied and out of sorts.

David opened the car door, but, as he was about to swing his legs out, she grabbed his arm.

'David, wait. Don't get out. I think . . .'

She was going to say—I think this might be a hijack attempt, but she didn't have time. As David hesitated, she heard the roar of a powerful engine. She looked round to find the solid bull-bar and grinning steel grille of the black truck rapidly filling her view. It was speeding straight towards their vehicle, but at the last minute it braked hard and swerved to the right. The truck passed so close that its thick bull-bar caught the edge of the driver's door and ripped it right off its hinges. Jade's little car slewed to the left, rocking violently. Tyres screamed as the driver forced his truck into a tight handbrake turn and stopped just in front of their car. The driver's window was wide open and through it, Jade could see a deeply tanned man aiming a gun.

A neat, effective trap, and they'd driven unsuspectingly into it.

'Down!' Jade screamed. She tried to duck down, away from the pistol's steel muzzle, but her seatbelt had jammed, holding her in a mercilessly upright position. For a moment, all she could think was that this was the way her father had died, trapped by his seatbelt and unable to escape his fate.

And then she realised that David wasn't ducking down either, and it wasn't because he had a belt holding him back. In fact, he was leaning over towards her side.

Leaning in front of her, offering a human shield.

'Get down!' Jade shouted again. When the clasp magically released its hold and the belt slid up and out of the way, she dived down at exactly the same time the gun went off.

The sound of the shot was gigantic. It exploded in her ears; the force of it splitting the air, but it was followed by a blood-chilling noise—David's shout of pain.

Oh Christ, he'd been hit.

In her doubled-over position, it was hard to wrestle the Glock out of her deep pocket, but she managed to wrench it free as another shot went off.

It took a huge effort to suppress her panic, to sit up in one smooth, easy movement and aim her weapon unflinchingly at the place she'd last seen her attacker. There he was—stopped just a few metres away, leaning out through the window of the truck and frowning with concentration as he moved the muzzle of his gun towards her. In her peripheral vision, she could see blood. Blood on the soft fabric of his short-sleeved checked shirt, seeping through his tightly clenched fingers.

Don't think about it, don't look at it. Focus.

Jade squeezed the trigger.

With a short cry, the deeply tanned gunman dropped his weapon. She fired again immediately, but his reactions were cat-quick. He ducked out of harm's way and her bullet sped through empty air. The truck's engine roared and, with a belch of exhaust smoke, the injured man sped away down the road.

The other man—the fake cop—where was he?

Gone. The white BMW was no longer half hidden in the bushes. Only two shallow tyre tracks remained.

Jade put her gun down and turned her attention to David.

He was slumped in his seat, eyes half closed and a river of blood welling from between his fingers. His breathing was fast, but shallow.

'They've gone. We're safe for now. Move your hands so I can see what's going on,' she told him, but he wouldn't and she had to prise his slippery fingers away.

'Jesus, Jade,' he whispered. 'My chest. I'm not . . .'

He tried to press his hand back onto the wound, but his arm just slid back into his lap.

'Shhhh. Don't talk,' she implored him. 'Try to keep still.'

When David tried to say something else, he coughed, and a splatter of bright blood landed on Jade's sleeve.

Oh shit, the bullet had pierced his lung. She needed to plug the wound with something, and fast. But what was there to be had, in this poxy hired car? All she could see was the biltong packet, and that wouldn't do.

After a frantic search, she found an old chamois leather under the back seat. She folded it lengthways, then widthways, and pressed the wadded fabric hard against David's chest. Then she gently tipped him forward. She didn't want to look, but she knew she had to. When she saw the fist-sized exit wound in his back, she couldn't stop herself from gasping in dismay.

The shooter had used a hollow-point bullet.

The back of the seat was soaked with blood, and she could see the gash in the fabric where the slug had pierced straight through.

She didn't want to think about the damage that had been done to David's lung as the bullet had flattened and mushroomed and tumbled its way through his body, ripping and tearing an ever-widening path until it shattered his shoulder blade on its way out.

A sucking chest wound. And there was little else she could use as a plug. Except the clothes on her own back.

Jade pulled off the T-shirt she was wearing. With difficulty, working one-handedly, she balled it up and then, with her right hand, packed it into the exit wound.

'Is it . . . bad?' David's whisper was punctuated by shallow, gurgling breaths.

'A good vet should be able to save it,' Jade said, using a phrase that David occasionally used when telling a waiter how rare she liked her steak. He gave a weak smile, acknowledging the joke.

'You should have ducked. Got away from him,' she said.

'Couldn't . . . or he . . . would have . . . shot you.'

Suddenly, Jade felt as if she couldn't breathe.

'Tell Kevin . . .' David mouthed the words. 'Tell Kevin I . . .'

'You can tell him yourself,' Jade snapped, but David's words had left her cold with fear. She lowered him gently back onto the seat again, keeping firm pressure on both the entrance and the exit wounds. Her muscles were beginning to ache and she was so hot she felt like she was in a sauna. Her face was dripping with sweat, and the warmth of the air flowing in through the gap where the driver's door had been wasn't helping. In contrast, David's skin was alarmingly clammy and cool.

Her major worry was that in order to phone for an ambulance she'd have to take her hand off the chamois plugging the entry wound. She'd have to press her knee into the front of his chest while she did this, because maintaining pressure on his chest wall was all that was preventing David from suffocating as his lung collapsed, or from bleeding to death.

Jade shifted herself round, ready to make the switch.

And then, as hard and shocking as a bull-bar crashing into a car door, she realised the truth. Her phone's battery was dead and David's was charging back at the chalet. She had no way of calling the ambulance.

This was checkmate. She couldn't leave David; couldn't take her hands away from his wounds for even a moment. All she could do was wait to see which arrived first—help, or death.

27

'Take your hand off the wound and let me see,' Bradley said.

Kobus had his left hand clamped around his right forearm and his injured hand in his lap. His pants were rusty-dark with blood.

'I was a fool,' he hissed. 'Should have put the girl down first. But how was I to know she was a goddamn shooter? I thought the man was more dangerous.'

'You did right to take out the man first.'

They'd both driven straight to Bradley's flat—it was the nearest safe place—and were now parked in the building's dank underground garage. The smell of the urine-stained concrete wasn't as bad as the strong, metallic stink of Kobus's blood. Leaning into the passenger side of the black truck, Bradley tried hard to breathe through his mouth and wondered how long he could keep himself from throwing up. He had never been good with blood.

He reached up and turned on the car light. As gently as he could, he prised Kobus's hand off the bullet wound. Now he had blood on his own fingers, too. The stuff was everywhere.

'Got him, square in the chest.' Kobus's eyes squeezed shut. 'Good goddamn shooting for someone who hasn't handled a gun in twenty years.'

Bradley didn't know if he was telling the truth about handling the gun, but if so he suspected that the shot had been more blind luck than anything else. Squinting in the yellowish light, he examined the injury.

From what he could deduce, the bullet had entered the outside of his arm just above the wrist and ploughed its way through his flesh, before lodging at a point on the inside a couple of inches further up where Bradley could actually see its shape through the bruised and reddened skin.

Kobus had managed to drive the black truck this far, one-handed, but Bradley suspected he'd been on an adrenaline high. Now, the man was bent over in agony.

Bradley couldn't help thinking that if the bullet had hit Kobus in the head instead of the wrist, it would have saved him from having to do an unpleasant job later on.

A job that he should already have done.

Why was he delaying it? Any minute the heavy phone around his neck could start to ring, and Zulu or Chetty would be demanding to know if he had carried out their most recent orders.

By deliberately knifing the wrong girl at the resort, Kobus had let him down in the worst possible way. And yet, back inside, he had been the most loyal of cellmates. He had saved Bradley from serious injury a number of times. From rape as well. When the weather-beaten Afrikaans man had taken him under his wing, protecting him from the violent lifers in the maximum-security wing, Bradley had known that this debt could never be fully repaid.

Tonight, he told himself. I'll do it tonight. For now, I must wait. I still need him.

'We need to get you to a hospital,' he said. 'The bullet must have hit bone. It could have splintered inside you.'

'Can't.' Kobus stared down at the still-bleeding wound. 'The doctors will call the cops. Besides, nothing's broken. Look, I can move my fingers.' With an effort, biting his lip so hard Bradley thought his teeth would rip right through it, Kobus slowly closed and opened his hand.

'You could tell the doctors it was an accident. That you were cleaning your gun.'

'No. Too dangerous. They might already have a description of me, thanks to that bitch. We need to go and finish her off now. Get this bullet out of me and give me some painkillers. I know a GP who will give me antibiotics later, no questions asked.'

Bradley shook his head, unhappy with the situation.

'Go on,' Kobus urged.

'All right.' He didn't want to let Kobus inside his flat, because that was his private world. But he had no choice now. This was urgent. How the hell had the woman from the resort discovered who he was and arrived at the flats where he lived, barely an hour after Chetty had told him that she and Patel, the Jo'burg police detective, had been snooping around at the harbour? He wanted to ask her, to get the truth out of her, but finishing the job efficiently took priority. Failure was not an option that Bradley wanted to entertain.

And Bradley had some strong painkillers in his place, because he suffered from terrible, blinding headaches. Dilaudid, Fentanyl, Dolophine. One or more of those might just be able to keep the agony at bay.

'Come on, let's sort this out upstairs,' he said. 'The stuff I've got will have to do. Here. Put this jacket over your arm. Try to walk normally, and don't let anyone see you're bleeding.'

'David,' Jade said.

She sat in the passenger seat, half turned towards him, pressing as hard as she could on the makeshift plugs that covered his wounds.

Sweat beaded David's upper lip and trickled down his temple. As she spoke, he gave a shallow cough, and another bright spatter of blood landed on his chin and dripped down onto the front of his shirt.

'We don't have a phone. I'm going to have to drive us to the hospital. I'll need you to help. Do you think you will be able to work the accelerator and the clutch?'

'Can . . . try.'

This was going to be an impossible task, but she had to try, because the only alternative was to sit here and watch him slowly dying.

It would be far better to die trying. She knew David would agree with that.

The hospital was a ten-minute drive away. Fifteen minutes if they limped along at a slow speed. Hopefully she'd be able to jam the car into second gear, keep it there, and somehow manage to steer while maintaining the pressure on David's wound with her hands.

Jade leaned across the central console, preparing to relinquish her grip on the bloodied chamois on David's chest in order to start the car. One . . . two . . . now. A quick twist of the key and the engine grumbled into life.

'Clutch,' she called, shoving the gearstick into second. Then, 'Accelerator, hard.'

The car lurched forward. Her plan had worked. David had managed to get his foot on the accelerator and they were on the move.

But to Jade's horror, instead of following a relatively steady path in the middle of their lane, the car kept veering right. The steering felt impossibly heavy and mushy, and she found herself having to fight it every metre of the way. She could hear an ominous bumping noise coming from the right front wheel.

Her heart sank.

The right front tyre must have punctured in the collision with the truck, effectively crippling the car. Her plan was impossible. Driving on one rim would mean she'd need both hands on the wheel, and it would take three times as long to reach their destination.

David grunted in pain and the car slowed abruptly to a crawl and then stalled as his foot slipped off the accelerator.

'Sorry,' he whispered. 'Try . . . again.'

And then his head slumped sideways and his body toppled towards her as he lost consciousness.

'Shit! Shit! Shit!' Jade shouted, because the movement had prompted a fresh surge of blood from the exit wound in his back. Damn it to hell, he was going to die, and there was nothing more she could do.

And then, glancing across the road, she saw the sight she had been praying for.

Another car, a modest white Toyota, was pulling slowly over onto the verge opposite.

Relief flooded through her as she realised help had arrived. Two Zulu youths leapt out and jogged across the road. Lithe, strong-looking young men in shorts and T-shirts who, judging from the carefully applied white paint they had on their faces, must have been taking part in a tribal dance display.

One of them had a cellphone in his hand.

'Accident?' he asked as he approached. 'Are you hurt, *sisi?*'

'The driver is,' Jade said. 'Attempted hijacking. We need an ambulance— he's been shot in the chest and is bleeding to death.'

'Eish!' the young man exclaimed. He dialled the number and a moment later Jade heard him speaking to the emergency services.

He gave the location, listened, and then said, 'Yes. She's already doing that. She's pressing on the wound.' And to Jade, 'They are on their way right now.'

Then he spoke swiftly in Zulu to his friend.

The other man ran back to the car and returned carrying a smart-looking leather waistcoat. He held it shyly out to Jade.

'Do you want to put this on?'

Jade glanced down. She'd forgotten she was shirtless, clad only in her bra, and had gouts of David's blood splattered across her torso like a bad body-painting job.

'No,' she said. 'I can't wear that. It's a nice garment. It'll be ruined.'

But the young man kept holding it out, his face anxious.

'I'll tell you what,' Jade said. 'When the paramedics arrive, give me your t-shirt and you put on the waistcoat.'

She spoke half jokingly, the humour a desperate attempt at concealing her worry. The makeshift fabric plugs in David's wounds were saturated and each breath David took seemed shallower. She could feel his heart beating valiantly, but he was losing too much blood. Soon, his heartbeat would weaken and start to fibrillate before giving up completely.

She had no idea how long he had left, or whether his failing respiration would outlast his heart. She felt air bubbling from out of the folds of the shirt and tightened her grasp. Her arms were burning, but she couldn't let go now. She must hold on. Firmly enough to control the escape of air, but not so tight that he couldn't breathe.

More people were arriving now. Glancing up, Jade noticed

another car stopping, this one with a Free State number plate. A seemingly infinite number of noisy, sun-bronzed children were leaning out of the windows and goggling at the scene. They were pulled back into the vehicle and their windows were swiftly closed when their mother saw all the blood.

Finally she heard the sound she'd been waiting for—the urgent wailing of the ambulance siren. Within a minute, a paramedic was by her side. Gently, he moved her hands away from David's torso.

Blessed relief. With an effort, Jade lowered her arms, which were now so stiff and sore that she could hardly move them. Her fingers were coated with congealed blood and felt as if they were permanently rusted into their clamped position. She wriggled backwards out of the car through the passenger door and was helped to her feet by one of the tow-truck drivers who had arrived on the scene. A stretcher and spinal board were standing at the ready, and the paramedics were now busy attaching life-support equipment to David.

Someone handed her a plastic bottle of mineral water, and Jade used it to rinse most of David's blood off her hands, arms and chest. As her adrenaline ebbed, she felt cold all over. Gratefully, she accepted the threadbare shirt that the Zulu dancer handed to her.

With the action over, the finality of the situation had started to sink in. She could lose him now. Not lose him to his wife, the scenario she'd always dreaded the most, but lose him forever.

It couldn't happen that way. It just couldn't. David was too contrary to die, too much of a fighter.

But looking at the paramedic's grim face as he turned to confer with his colleague, she realised that it might have already happened.

28

Just five minutes after the ambulance left, taking David to the same hospital that Jade had so recently visited to ask about her mother, Inspector Pillay arrived at the crime scene in his unmarked Ford. He climbed out, nervously clutching the holster of his gun, looking as if he'd just walked back into his worst nightmare.

'Was this an attempted hijacking?' he asked Jade.

'No,' she told him. 'I recognised the gunman. I've seen him before, twice. The second time was last night, at the resort, when he tried to run me down with his truck.'

After taking down a full account of the shooting, Pillay loaned Jade his cellphone so that she could contact the car-hire company and arrange for the tow-truck driver to remove her damaged vehicle. He then offered Jade a lift back to the resort. Carefully, she got into his clean car. There were stiff, blotchy stains on her borrowed shirt where the last of the blood had soaked through, but hopefully it wouldn't stain the sedan's grey fabric seats.

She found her mind kept flashing back to the instant of the shooting. The explosion of the gun, the way David's face had looked as he'd attempted to stem the bleeding with his own hands. What could she have done differently? How could she have saved the situation?

Irritably, she shook her head, trying to banish the thoughts. There was no point in hashing it over. She couldn't rewrite what had happened. All she could do now was to hope against hope that he would make it through surgery. Assuming he was still alive.

'How are you doing?' Pillay glanced at her, looking concerned. 'If you need trauma counselling or any . . .'

'I'm fine,' Jade interrupted him, aware of how snappy she sounded, but equally aware that she could do nothing about it.

They drove in silence for a while. Then Pillay cleared his throat somewhat nervously, as if anticipating another sharp response from his passenger.

'The paramedics told me that if you hadn't done what you did, Superintendent Patel would have died before they'd arrived,' he said. 'If he makes it, it will be thanks to you.'

Jade suddenly felt a huge lump rise in her throat. 'I did what I needed to do,' she said, but her voice sounded wobbly and not like her at all.

'Are you trained in first aid?'

Damn it, he was being deliberately nice to her. Trying to chat, to take her mind off the horror she'd left behind. Jade didn't know whether it was his kindness, or her reaction to the shock, that was making her want to lay her head in her arms and bawl her eyes out.

'Only a basic first-aid course,' she replied. Her voice was still unsteady, and it was in an effort to say something without seeming to be on the verge of hysteria that prompted Jade to share a piece of her past that, until now, she'd never spoken about. 'But I've dealt with that particular incident before. I've worked a number of assignments as a bodyguard. There was a security breach on one of my jobs and a man was shot in the chest at close range. I helped keep him breathing until the ambulance came.'

'They must have been glad to have you there,' Pillay said, sounding impressed.

Jade didn't add that she had also been the one who had shot the man.

She had been part of a security team guarding a rock band while they toured Europe. A British heavy-metal group from Birmingham, infamous for what many considered to be their Satanist lyrics. It had been an attempted assassination in Cologne,

Germany, as they were leaving a concert venue. Two-thirty A.M. on a rainy morning and they had all been tired. Among the mass of fans waiting outside huddled in raincoats, but cheering and singing, had been one man who she had noticed immediately, because of his stony expression and the fact that his eyes were fixed on one person only—the lead singer.

His two personal bodyguards were too far behind him and, for just a few seconds, the wild-haired star had been left unprotected. She had seen the would-be killer raise his gun. He hadn't looked at her; hadn't noticed her at all. She was deliberately low profile, unobtrusive, dressed to blend in. Most people had thought she was a backstage coordinator or a wardrobe assistant.

At any rate, she had her own weapon unholstered as his finger touched the trigger, and her bullet slammed into his chest as he pulled it. Her shot punched him backwards and his own bullet went harmlessly high, over the heads of the singer and his entourage.

There had been momentary silence after the man went down. Then pandemonium had ensued. Screaming, shouting, hundreds of people all trying to flee in different directions. The police and bouncers had their hands full trying to control the panicking crowd. She had knelt down beside the dying man and packed a shirt into the entry wound in exactly the same way she did for David.

Ironically, the shirt she used had had a death's head logo on it, and had been ripped off the back of the singer the man had been trying to kill.

'Will 'e be OK?' the metal-head had asked her, over and over again in his Brummie accent, and she'd heard the guilt in his voice, as if he was worried that all of this had somehow been his fault. 'D'you think 'e'll make it?'

She'd given him the only answer she could. She just didn't know.

But the man had died while in surgery. During the investigation that followed, it had emerged that his gun had been fully loaded with hollow-point bullets and that the would-be killer had spent months practising his marksmanship. Without a doubt, the bullet would have hit his target had she not intervened.

As a result, she'd been cleared of all blame. She'd been twenty-six years old then, and it had been the third time she had killed someone.

'Pillay,' she said.

'Yes?'

'Have you interviewed Neil yet? You know, the resort owner.'

A slight frown creased Pillay's smooth brow. 'Not yet, actually. We've spoken to him, of course, and he has been very helpful in providing us with all Amanda's details, but we haven't been able to schedule an official interview yet. He's a very busy man, it seems. I'll probably try and speak to him this afternoon.'

'Have you been into his house?'

'No. Only as far as the reception area in the small front room. Why do you want to know?'

'No reason,' Jade said. 'Just curious.'

'Well, you're welcome to ask anything you like. If I can answer it, I will. But I would like to know why.'

'All right then. I do have another question or two.'

'Fire away.'

'The cases of the missing people you've been dealing with.'

'What about them?'

'You said there were a number of them.'

'Yes. That's right.'

'You don't think that's odd, here in a small town like Richards Bay?'

'Definitely. To have nine individuals reported missing in the space of six months is most unusual. But it's not unheard of.'

'Do they have anything in common?'

'Well, all are male, apart from one missing female. That's unusual, statistically. And all the men are in their twenties or thirties. The woman too. She's twenty-six, and a waitress at a seafood restaurant in town.'

'Backgrounds? Do they come from the same area?'

'Various areas, and there doesn't seem to be any connection between them, apart from the fact that most of them disappeared while on the way to or from work. I did look at the possibility that

a serial killer might be targeting a certain profile of person, but . . .'
Pillay shrugged expressively, 'no bodies have been found.'

He turned off the main road and made his way down the
winding lane that led to the resort.

'Isn't that unusual too?' Jade asked.

'Come to think of it, yes it is,' Pillay said, looking suddenly
thoughtful.

Bradley's flat was small and badly lit. Kobus choked on the
stench of blocked drains as he followed the tall blond man past a
closed door and into the small living room.

He was bent over his injured arm, cradling it in the crook of
his left, gasping with the pain. Sweat was trickling down his
temples and he couldn't wipe it away; couldn't make any move
that might jar his injured limb.

Carefully, moving as slowly as he could, he laid the arm on
the coffee table and rested one of his knees on a wooden chair.

'Those pills,' he gasped.

'Yes?' Bradley was rummaging through a bag emblazoned with
a pharmacy logo on the tattered-looking Formica counter, from
which he produced disinfectant, gauze and Elastoplast. Kobus
blinked. Had the guy been shopping specially for him, or what?

'I need them. Now.'

'Hang on a minute. I'll get them for you now.'

Bradley opened a drawer and pulled out a big white box of
prescription painkillers. Kobus could read the label, but in his
haze of pain the words made no sense to him. All he could see
were the tablets themselves. A foil package containing two rows
of pills.

Bradley snapped two of them out of the foil and poured a glass
of water. He gulped them down.

'How long do they take to work?'

'Not long.'

'Wait a sec. I can't deal with this. I don't want you to touch it
until they've . . . Hey! What the hell's that?'

Bradley had produced a medical syringe, which he was filling
from a small brown bottle.

'Local anaesthetic. This will numb the area fast.' He peered down at Kobus's arm; at the shape of the bullet pushing up against the skin. Then he looked back up at Kobus, his face serious.

'Are you sure you want me to take that out for you?'

Kobus didn't want the slug left inside him, that was for sure. And surely he couldn't be in worse pain than he was already?

'Do it,' he said, forcing the words out through clenched teeth. 'Then let's go and get the bitch.'

29

When Jade arrived back at the resort with Inspector Pillay in the late afternoon, the first thing she noticed was the smart security boom that had been erected at the bottom entrance gate. Nearby, four uniformed security personnel were offloading a mobile guard booth from a short, flat-bed truck. Before Jade and Pillay were allowed through the boom, one of the guards hurried over and asked to see their identification.

Pillay stopped outside the chalets and, before Jade climbed out, offered her a brief warning.

'Please think carefully about leaving the resort,' he said. 'I would prefer it if you stayed in the chalet area. If you want to go and visit Patel in hospital later, let me know and I'll try to get one of my officers to accompany you.'

Then he executed a neat three-point turn and drove back the way he had come.

Looking around, Jade noted that Neil's Beetle was nowhere to be seen.

Craig came out of his chalet and hurried over just as she was unlocking her door. From the worry she saw on his face, Jade knew that the news of the shooting had preceded her arrival.

'I heard what happened,' Craig said. 'Inspector Pillay phoned me on the way to the scene. I'm so sorry. Is there any news on David?'

'Nothing yet. It'll be an hour or two before he's out of theatre.'

'Do you need transport? You can use my Land Rover if you like. Or Elsabe's car. I've got her keys here and she says it's fine for you to borrow it.'

'Thanks,' she said, forcing a smile. 'If you don't mind giving me Elsabe's keys, I'll take you up on that offer as soon as I've had a shower.'

'You're going to go and see David at the hospital, I guess?'

'No.'

She took the keys and turned away, leaving Craig open-mouthed in surprise.

The right choice.

It's not always the obvious choice, or the easy one, or the one you want to do. That was what her father had told her many times. Choices are difficult. And sometimes the only way to know whether you are making the right choice or not, is to think about what would happen if you did the opposite.

Jade went into the chalet and closed the door, locking it behind her and sliding both of the newly attached bolts firmly across.

If she went to the hospital now, she'd be doing what she wanted to do. She'd be as close to David as she could get, pacing the room anxiously, waiting for news of him. If he survived the surgery, she might even be allowed into ICU to see him, if she could convince the nursing sister on duty that she was his common-law wife and, therefore, close family.

What good would it do?

David would live—or die—whether she was there to watch him or not. If her face was the first thing he saw when he opened his eyes, it wouldn't make any difference in the long run.

But right now, it would make a difference to her.

Staying in the hospital with David would make her feel better. It would also waste valuable time—time she didn't have. The men that had ambushed her and David were still out there. They had shot David and now they would be after her.

Jade stepped into the shower and turned the water on full, letting the cool needles of water lash her skin.

She remembered how the blond man with the phone around his neck had glanced back at her on his way up the stairs of the run-down apartment building, heading for flat number eighteen. Less than half an hour later, a tall man had flagged them down, wearing a badly fitting Metro Police uniform, stopping Jade's car for long enough to allow his accomplice to start shooting.

The Metro cop had also had a phone around his neck.

It was the same man. Jade was convinced of it.

The question was why.

Jade towelled herself dry and pulled on some clean clothes. Dark clothing. Black pants, charcoal top. She buckled her gun's holster around her waist and clipped the Glock inside before knotting a sweatshirt over the top.

She picked up her sunglasses from the table and put them on. Then she pulled David's phone out of the charger. She wasn't going to risk being caught without a working cellphone again, which meant she'd have to use his, because her battery was still flat.

Jade locked the door behind her and walked over to Elsabe's car. The interior of the compact sedan was impeccably clean, with a box of tissues on the passenger seat and a white cotton jacket on a coat hanger in the back.

The jacket partially obscured Jade's view out of the rear passenger window behind her, so she took it off the coat hanger and laid it carefully on the back seat.

Then she climbed in, reclining the seat to make herself more comfortable behind the wheel.

Jade turned onto the main road, keeping a sharp eye out for anyone who might be following her. She'd expected that the criminals might have a vehicle patrolling the area. What she hadn't expected was to be stopped by the police just before she reached the main highway into town.

30

This time, Jade wasn't pulled over by a lone traffic cop. She was directed into the emergency lane at what looked like an official roadblock.

Even so, she couldn't help it. When she saw the orange traffic cones and the white cars parked up ahead where the two-lane road narrowed into one, she started to sweat.

She slowed right down, straining to see whether she could make out any official signage on the vehicles. Whether these were real Metro Police, or whether this was another trap.

There were more police vehicles here, which was reassuring. She counted three cars and one large van parked on the same side of the road as her, and another car, this one with a clearly visible official logo on the door, on the opposite side.

Jade breathed deeply and tried to reassure herself that this was a normal roadblock. Especially in view of the fact that there were two drivers already at the barricades ahead of her and another slowing down behind her. Safety in numbers, or so she hoped.

Even if it was a routine police operation, that didn't mean she was out of danger. The blond man had been wearing a genuine, if ill-fitting, uniform. That meant officials in the Richards Bay Metro Police force could be taking bribes in exchange for assisting criminals, and that any one of the officers manning the roadblock could also be informers.

Swallowing her anxiety, Jade pulled over and wound down her window in response to the urgent waving of a harassed-looking woman officer.

'Driver's licence, please.'

Jade eased the card out of her wallet sleeve and handed it over. The woman read it carefully, but did not hand it back immediately. Instead she walked round to the front of the car and examined the licence disk. Jade found herself praying that Elsabe had kept her car's registration up to date; that she wouldn't end up being delayed by factors that were out of her control.

To Jade's disappointment, the policewoman walked over to a large police van that seemed to be doubling as a mobile office, still holding her driver's licence. After a short wait, another cop, a fit-looking black man, appeared in the doorway.

He spoke in Zulu to the lady cop, who then marched back to Jade's car.

'Lady, you have outstanding traffic fines,' she said.

Jade stared up at her. Impossible, surely. She'd paid all the ones that Rent a Runner had notified her about and it had been a month since David had last borrowed her car.

'Fines in my name?' she asked.

The lady cop shook her head. 'They have put your car's number plate into the system. This vehicle has outstanding fines.'

'It's not my car,' Jade replied, as politely as she could manage under the stressful circumstances. 'I borrowed it from my next-door neighbour at the resort where I'm staying.'

The woman officer shouted this information to the large black cop. After giving it a moment's thought, he strolled down the steps that had been set up at the van's back entrance and across to her car.

'This vehicle has got outstanding fines totalling two thousand rands,' he said.

Two thousand rands' worth of traffic offences committed by a woman who hung her cotton jacket on a coat hanger and did needlework in her spare time? Surely impossible.

Jade spread her hands in a gesture of appeal. 'Officer, it's not my car.'

'Wait here.'

Holding her driver's licence, he walked back to the mobile office.

Inwardly seething with frustration, Jade turned off the car's engine, silencing the irritating chatter of the DJ on the local radio station. This delay was exactly what she hadn't wanted. If anyone had paid a local cop to be on the lookout for her, they'd now know what vehicle she was driving and in what direction she was headed.

After what seemed like an interminable wait, the cop returned.

'You are clear,' he said. 'You yourself have no outstanding fines. But this vehicle does, and they go back five months.'

He folded his arms in a gesture that made it clear he was not willing to forgive this breach of the law.

Jade didn't believe for one minute that the borrowed car had outstanding fines. No doubt, if she were to insist on seeing all the documentation, the black cop would discover that an administrative 'error' had occurred in the system.

But that would take time, and it would be time she didn't have. The quickest and easiest way out of this was also going to be the most expensive. 'Can I pay them now on behalf of the owner?'

'You may do that. We have a credit-card machine in the office if you need it.'

Jade cursed silently as she climbed out of the car. She hurried over to the office, which was manned by a total of three cops and had two people waiting to pay fines. The black cop stood at the door for a while and then walked away. Jade wasn't sure, but she thought she could hear him speaking into his cellphone.

The man in the queue in front of Jade was clearly there to argue, rather than pay. She started to wonder whether kicking his ankles would speed up the process. Or perhaps she should offer to pay for his fines too. Anything to get out of the cramped office that reeked of sweat and was uncomfortably warm despite the overcast evening.

She was worried that the black cop was on the criminals' payroll. The roadblock was clearly a routine operation, but they'd got lucky and that meant her luck was running out.

Eventually it was her turn to pay. The lady at the desk allowed her to get a discount on the more recent fines, but even so it cost her fifteen hundred rands to pay the amount that, according to the system, had in fact been incurred by the car's legal owner, Ms Elsabe Marais of 64 Mowbray Road, Emmarentia.

She was about to leave the office when the black cop returned. He was pocketing his cellphone and, from the way he glanced immediately at her right hip, Jade knew that he'd been speaking to one of the people who had organised the earlier shooting.

'You are carrying a firearm,' he said.

'Yes, I am.' Jade's stomach was clenched so tight it hurt.

'Is it licensed?'

'Of course.'

'Please show me your documentation.'

'It's right here in . . .' And then, to her dismay, Jade realised it wasn't.

The original of her gun licence was in the cubbyhole of her hired car, where she'd put it after showing it at a roadblock when she was on her way down to the coast.

Her hired car—the one that had been towed away after the crash. In the chaos that had followed David's shooting, she'd forgotten to take the licence out of it.

'I was the victim of an attempted hijacking a couple of hours ago,' she said. 'I was with a police detective from Jo'burg. He was shot and is now fighting for his life in hospital. My car was badly damaged and it was towed to a panel beater. My original licence is in the glove compartment. I do have a certified copy here, in my wallet . . .'

The cop remained unmoved by her hijacking story. Probably because he'd just heard about it from another source.

'We do not accept copies,' he said. 'I must see the original.'

'I'll be able to bring the original to a police station within the required seven days,' Jade said. 'Please correct me if I'm wrong, but I understand that according to Section 106 of the Firearms Control Act, I'm permitted to do that.'

She didn't think quoting the law to a police officer was a good idea, but she was out of options.

The cop shook his head, looking smug, as if she'd started a game he knew only he could win.

'Section 107 of the Firearms Control Act allows a weapon to be seized without a warrant and held in police custody until the correct documentation is produced. Hand me your gun now and wait here while I fill out the receipt.' He turned to the lady officer who was waiting outside the van. 'And in the meantime, search her car thoroughly for any other unlicensed firearms.'

31

Ten minutes later, relieved of her weapon and certain that her pursuers now knew exactly where she was, Jade climbed back into Elsabe's car.

She was furious, with herself and with the policeman. The black cop had taken her gun and told her she was lucky not to be arrested. Then he'd asked her to wait again, and he'd just disappeared.

For all Jade knew, he was only going to let her drive off once he was certain he was delivering her directly into the hands of her hunters. She wasn't prepared to stick around for that. Not when the lady cop had finished searching her car, found nothing, and was now busy checking another motorist's licence.

And not when it was starting to get dark. She didn't have much time left before rush hour, such as it was, was over, and the roads became quieter.

Jade started the engine and pulled out into the road. As she passed the mobile office, she half expected the black cop to jump out of the doorway, hand held out, and stop her again. Or to hear the sirens of one of the backup vehicles as they pulled onto the road in pursuit.

But nothing happened. She drove until the orange cones and lights marking the roadblock had disappeared into the distance.

Her sense of relief was interrupted by the ringing of David's cellphone. Looking at the screen, Jade saw the caller was Captain Moloi, who had been in David's team when he had worked for the serious and violent crimes division.

Moloi did not like Jade. Jade didn't know whether this was because she had been romantically involved with David, a married man, or whether it was because he knew about some of the criminal acts she had committed. Or whether it was a mixture of both, with a dash of personal feeling thrown into the mix as well.

When she answered, it was clear Moloi's negative opinion hadn't changed.

'Jade? Where's David?' he barked.

She could hear the subtext, or thought she could. Why are you answering David's phone? Why are you interfering in his life when his wife is pregnant?

Perhaps she was being over-sensitive. Moloi might not even know Naisha was pregnant. Perhaps David had waited and told her first.

'David's been rushed to hospital. If he made it there alive, he's either in the operating theatre or ICU,' she said quietly.

Now Moloi sounded concerned. 'Why? How?'

'He was shot in the chest while driving. I was with him. He was pulled over by a criminal impersonating a policeman.'

'My God. Do you know what the prognosis is?'

Jade was surprised to find her own voice unsteady. 'I don't know yet.'

'Was it an attempted hijacking?'

'No. Trust me, it wasn't. It was an attempted hit.'

'But—but he's not even in Johannesburg at the moment. He told me he was going down to the coast somewhere. St Lucia, I think.'

'Richards Bay.'

'So how . . . ?'

'There was a murder at the resort where we are staying. He's helping with the investigation.'

'Oh.' Moloi paused. Then, clearly assuming that Jade was also up to speed on the investigation, he continued. 'Has this got anything to do with that address in Yeoville he asked me to check out?'

'It might, although I think the Yeoville angle is a long shot.'

'Well, I haven't had a chance to go out that way yet. I was phoning to tell him I'll be able to get there later on.' He paused, then said in a softer tone, 'Does his wife know this has happened?'

'I don't think anyone's contacted her yet.'

'Where is he?'

'Richards Bay General Hospital.'

'I'll phone Naisha now.'

'Thanks.'

Moloi disconnected and Jade drove on, regularly glancing in her rear-view mirror to check and recheck the line of headlights behind her and wondering who, if anybody, was following.

Jade had been a hunter herself more than once in the past. Empty roads and darkness were a killer's friend. Fortunately, the highway heading into town was fairly busy. The lights of the cars nearest her were clear and bright, the others blurred into smudges in the mist that had started to form.

If the mist got any thicker, it would present a new danger, especially later on. Richards Bay was a small town and it would get quieter as the evening progressed.

She had two choices.

The first was to flee. To leave this humid town behind. Just drive off, turn her back on whatever was going on here.

If it had been her decision alone, she'd have no problem doing it.

But she couldn't, because David was involved and she had to protect him.

If she was fast and cunning enough, her would-be killers wouldn't have a clue where she had gone, but they would know exactly where to look for him. If he survived the surgery, he'd be in danger as soon as he came out of the operating theatre. She had no idea what security measures were in place in an ICU, but a hospital was one of the hardest places to keep people safe. That much she did know.

By staying in the area, she'd be the one commanding the criminals' attention and resources, reducing the threat to David.

In fact, she could go one better.

She could make herself an obvious quarry and lead them into a trap of her own design.

32

'I've got her!' Leaning forward in the passenger seat of the souped-up Mazda that they were now using, because Bradley had said putting the truck on the road again would be unwise, Kobus frowned at the worsening fog.

He didn't know whether visibility was worse on the inside of the car or the outside. The windscreen demister was fighting a losing battle with the mist that kept creeping over both sides of the glass. The interior certainly smelled as if a previous owner might have had a bad incontinence problem. Perhaps that would explain it.

'Where?' Johan, the gate guard from the harbour, was in the driver's seat. He hadn't yet spotted the number plate that one of the Metro cops from the roadblock had called in just a half-hour ago.

'There.' Kobus pointed. 'Keep her in sight, OK? And watch out for that robot up ahead. It's about to turn red.'

'Can't jump it,' the weathered-looking man replied. 'I'll have to stop. Watch if she turns.'

Waiting at the red light, the car filled with tense silence. Then, with a squeal of rubber, the Mazda shot forward as soon as the light turned green.

'She's up ahead somewhere. Go slow now. We don't want to . . . hey, wait. Look at that. It's her. The car's pulling off the road. She's goddamn parking it.'

'That's lucky.'

'Slow down.'

'We can't get her now. Not while she's stopped at a shopping centre. We'll have to wait till she gets going again.'

'You think she's seen us?'

168 • Jassy Mackenzie

'No way. Look—she's getting out. She's going into the Internet café.'

'Well, she can't stay in there for long. It closes at eight.'

'And by then this traffic will be gone. Hey, are we lucky fish or what?'

'Huh?' The Mazda's indicator ticked loudly as Johan pulled over and parked further down the road.

'Lucky fish. Don't know why I said that. It's an old saying. The last time anyone called me that was in school.' Kobus laughed. He suddenly felt high on adrenaline. Perhaps it was the painkillers. At any rate, he liked the feeling. It took his mind off the dull throbbing in his arm and the brownish-looking blood that had already oozed through the bandage.

'In school, hey?'

'Haven't heard it since. Might be because I don't stay in touch with my school friends.' He was the only one who'd ended up in prison. The only one that he knew of, anyway.

'Might be because you stopped being lucky,' Johan said.

Kobus laughed again. 'Not this time.'

Using his left hand, he pulled his phone out of his pocket and called Bradley.

Bradley answered after four rings. He sounded distracted and his voice thrummed with tension. He was busy now—too busy to help with the hunt, which was why Kobus had enlisted Johan's help. The operation was going ahead. The deadline, Kobus knew, was looming. Only a few hours left to go.

He relayed the good news and hung up.

'So now we wait,' he said.

'Ja,' Johan said. 'Let's sit tight here.'

The car following Jade was a clapped-out, white, bottom-of-the-range Mazda. A generation older than the cars supplied by the company that Jade used.

It was an unlikely looking tail, and the driver was good, staying a few cars behind her when there was traffic around. The only reason she picked him up was that she was expecting to be followed. The car never got close enough to allow her to see who was driving, or how many people were inside.

She could put her plan into action now. But first she needed to stop for water. Where would be safe?

She drove past a bar, but it looked just about empty and the parking area outside was shadowy and unfenced. She suspected that her pursuers wouldn't think twice about following her inside and doing the job there.

She was nearly out of town and she certainly didn't want to start driving in circles, because that would alert her tail to the fact she'd spotted him.

And then Jade saw where she could go.

The small shopping centre where David had picked her up that very morning was brightly lit and the street outside was lined with parked cars. The fast-food outlet looked busy and the Internet café was swarming with teenagers.

It was the ideal place for a quick stop.

She parked as close as she could to the Internet café and made her way into the takeaway next door. Trying to look as casual as possible, she ordered a can of Coke and a toasted cheese sandwich. The fizzy drink provided a welcome sugar hit, but her stomach was too knotted for her to take more than a few bites of her sandwich. Still, knowing she would need the energy later, she forced the food down.

She drained the last of her Coke and tossed the remains of her meal into the dustbin. Then she wiped her hands with a paper napkin and walked over to the Internet café, where a sternly worded notice on the inter-leading glass door informed her that no food or drink was welcome inside.

The machines were occupied by a number of teenage boys, each immersed in their own online world. The air was thick with testosterone. Jade paid the goateed man at the desk for half an hour's Internet usage and took a seat at the only available computer. Her neighbour was playing an online game that involved butchering a monster with an axe. Sheets of virtual blood flew through the air and Jade found herself turning away from the sight.

Focusing her attention on the screen in front of her, she clicked on Google, hoping that in this limited time she'd be able to find answers there.

Something was going on at the harbour. Jade was convinced of it. She and David had arrived there early that morning to ask questions, and the attempted hit had taken place on their way back.

She remembered the way the uniformed guard had called her away from the screened-off area. What *was* behind it?

An Internet search informed Jade that the Richards Bay harbour, today the country's biggest and northernmost port, had got off to an inauspicious start when Commissioner Henry Cloete, surveying the estuary in 1843, declared that it had little or no potential as a future harbour.

Despite this discouraging verdict, the harbour had been built in 1976 for the purpose of exporting coal, and had since expanded to deal with other bulk cargo, mainly exports. Twenty-one berths were currently in service, and an additional coal berth was under construction. Jade couldn't find any information on the tanker berth that the gate guard had mentioned.

She did, however, learn that the port was a popular stopping point for international cruise ships, because of its proximity to the local game parks and the St Lucia World Heritage Site.

The article on the harbour linked to a news report on the environmental assessment that Craig had mentioned. According to its author, there was a strong possibility that dune mining in the park would go ahead. It was only the ongoing protests of the environmentalists that were keeping the bull-dozers and drills at bay.

'If it pays, it stays. That is our motto,' the CEO of a company called Richards Mining had told the journalist. 'It is untrue that the coastal environment north of the park is being adversely affected by our current mining operations. Expansion of our operations into the park itself will create 150 additional jobs, which are sorely needed by the local population and which ecotourism, despite its promises, has failed to deliver.'

Smoke and mirrors, or the truth?

Reading on, her heart skipped a beat as she found the writer had sourced a comment from none other than Craig Hitchens himself, local ecologist and a member of the conservation team that was now in the process of reassessing the park's environment.

'The Richards Mining operation has already exceeded the northernmost limits that were agreed on prior to the start of the dunes being strip mined. They are also re-mining previously mined dunes that were supposed to have been fully rehabilitated by now. While we believe that any mining that takes place in the park will have disastrous consequences for the ecosystem surrounding the dunes, and we will oppose all such activities, we also believe that Richards Mining has acted in breach of contract and should have their existing licence revoked.'

Below the quote, which ended the article, were head shots of the two men, taken separately but pictured side by side, as if they were having their argument in person.

Looking down at the bottom right-hand corner of the computer screen, Jade checked the time. It was still a little early, but she could try.

Mustering some courage, she called the Richards Bay General Hospital and asked to be put through to ICU.

'I'm phoning to find out about David Patel,' she said, having introduced herself as his wife.

'We don't have a Patel in this ward.' The nurse who answered sounded confused and, for a dreadful moment, Jade thought David hadn't made it as far as the hospital; that he had died in the ambulance. Then the woman said, 'Hold on.' Jade could hear her speaking to somebody else in muffled tones, as if she'd covered the phone's mouthpiece with her hand.

Then she came back on the line.

'I'm sorry. We do have a Mr Patel who was admitted earlier this evening, but he's still in theatre. I don't know when he'll be out.'

Jade felt a huge, crushing relief. Premature, she knew, but at least David was still alive, and safely out of harm's way.

She quit the Internet browser and stood up, car keys in hand. Engrossed in their online world, the other occupants of the café didn't give her a second glance. For a disconcerting moment, she wondered whether they would show any surprise if the people following her burst into the shop and gunned her down at the door.

She walked back into the fast-food outlet. Aware that someone had followed her out, she turned to look, only to see a spotty youth whose attention was firmly fixed on a dark-haired teenage girl on a bar stool near the counter. His testosterone-fuelled swagger made Jade think yet again of the zebra stallion.

She bought two plastic half-litre bottles of water and, declining the offer of a carrier bag, strolled as calmly as she could out into the car park.

Elsabe's car was a familiar brand. Jade had driven a Corsa many times before. In her experience, the older models tended to overheat easily. One of the hired cars she'd had a few months ago had developed a water leak, forcing Jade to pull over every few kilometres to top up the radiator. It had been a fiddly experience, and she still had the scar from where her forearm had brushed against the scaldingly hot engine block.

Better to take some water along just in case, and to check the radiator level before she set off. She was about to attempt some evasive driving, and an overheating engine would present a deadly risk.

33

As soon as the target left the Internet café, Kobus got going again.

The Mazda might be old, but it didn't lack power. Recently overhauled, the original engine had been replaced by a three-litre monster from a newer model.

The result was a car that looked like an old skedonk, but could keep up with just about any vehicle on the road. The perfect vehicle for a tail.

'She took her time in there,' Kobus observed, gently rubbing his fingers over the blood-stained bandage on his arm. It hurt like hell, but, thanks to the cocktail of medication that Bradley had given him, it was as if he was a watcher, rather than a participant, in the pain. Weird, but he wasn't complaining.

Johan shrugged. 'She was having supper.'

Kobus laughed. 'Meat is meat and a girl must eat. Think she's seen us?'

'No.' Johan spoke the word slowly, thoughtfully. 'Not yet. But I think she will see us. Or at any rate, she'll expect somebody to be following.'

Kobus nodded. 'My guess is she'll make a run for it. She'll try and lose us when she's out of town.'

'She looked under the bonnet before she got going. Did you notice that?'

'I did. Wonder if she's been having engine problems.'

Up ahead, the brake lights of the Corsa lit up and Johan slowed his own vehicle, keeping as wide a distance between them as he dared.

'So we get her when she's on the main road?'

'Yes. If she takes the main road back to the resort, we'll wait till it's quiet. Just her and us. Then force her off it. The harder she crashes, the better. That might do it. If she's still alive afterwards, we'll go in and finish the job.'

'Right.' Johan stared ahead, into the thickening mist. 'And if she goes another way?'

'Then we make another plan.' Kobus tapped a dirty-nailed finger against the holster of his gun.

They knew the girl didn't have a gun. It had been taken from her at the roadblock, thanks to the swift thinking of the Metro Police sergeant who'd also supplied them with the uniform. She wasn't carrying, she didn't have another weapon stashed in her car. All the dice were loaded in their favour.

'Orange light ahead,' Kobus warned. 'Slow the hell down, man.'

'Sorry, but I have to jump this one. Otherwise we won't be able to see if she takes the highway turn-off or the main road.'

The Mazda surged forward. Hooters blared as they roared through the light a couple of seconds after it had turned red.

'Look. She's spotted us.'

The girl was turning on the main road, accelerating back towards the resort, and at a frantic pace. Driving too fast, braking hard when a light turned red and pulling away like a drag-racer when it turned green again. It made her easy to follow. They could have tailed her by the whine of her engine alone.

Kobus could feel himself grinning as they pursued her towards the main road. The girl was panicking and the girl was running.

Now it was just a case of playing the waiting game, letting the right moment present itself—which it would do soon, because the roads out that way were quiet and traffic wouldn't be a problem for much longer.

Then he saw the flash of her emergency lights.

Johan slowed immediately, hitting the brakes hard and pulling over onto the verge. The Mazda juddered and bounced on the uneven ground. The two cars following them swished past. In the distance, Kobus saw a few sets of headlights approaching.

'Kill your lights,' Kobus ordered, and Johan complied. He didn't want her to see them waiting.

'You think we should do it now?' Johan asked. He was whispering now, as if she might be able to hear them, even though they had stopped well back.

'Not right now. Too many people around. We need to wait. If she's got engine trouble, she'll be calling the AA, won't she? They'll take at least twenty, twenty-five minutes to get here. Gives us plenty of time.'

'She's opened the bonnet again.'

Luckily for them, the girl had stopped right under a street lamp. If Kobus squinted, he could see her fiddling with something. He wondered whether they should try and take her now.

But then Johan spoke again.

'She's closed it. She's getting back inside.'

A second later, the emergency lights were turned off. The brake lights flashed red, then disappeared. The Corsa was pulling away.

Johan turned his own lights back on and followed. As the Mazda passed the spot where she'd stopped, Kobus glanced down and saw, discarded on the verge, the distinctive blue-labelled shape of an empty plastic water bottle.

Now he was grinning again.

'Looks like she's been overheating. Shame.'

'That could make things easy for us,' Johan agreed.

A few minutes passed, Johan keeping his distance, staying patiently back as they left the last of suburbia behind.

And then they were out of town, with only the ocean and the forest to keep them company. She was in the danger zone now. In the killing zone. And they had an empty highway up ahead. Not even the glow of oncoming headlights in the distance.

'Let's do it,' Kobus said.

He'd never killed a white woman before. Only black ones, a few of them, up north in the old days.

Kobus wondered if it would feel any different.

Johan flattened his foot on the accelerator and Kobus watched the red taillights ahead of him get bigger and sharper as they drew ever closer to the fleeing Corsa.

Suddenly, Kobus realised she was going more slowly than he'd expected. She'd dropped her speed right down and, when he saw the reason for it, he couldn't help but laugh.

Swathes of steam were erupting from the Corsa's bonnet. He even thought he could hear the loud hissing as the overheated engine boiled away all the water it had left in its cooling system. The vehicle was crippled. This was a gift—the best bit of luck they could have possibly hoped for.

And she wasn't stopping. She was pressing on, which meant that even if she was lucky, she only had a couple more minutes before the last of the water was gone and the engine reached an unsustainable temperature. Then it would seize. The pistons would fry, jamming themselves together, welded by heat into an immovable mass.

When that car stopped, it would be stopped for good.

A thought occurred to Kobus.

Could she have called for help earlier? He hadn't seen her use a phone when she'd pulled over, but perhaps she had made the call before that. Was she hoping she could keep going until backup arrived?

They would have to make it quick, he decided.

'What's wrong?' Johan asked.

And then Kobus saw it.

The moment he'd been waiting for. The sudden, wobbly deceleration. She tried to move her crippled car over to the side of the road, but barely managed to get halfway before it finally juddered to a halt.

Once again, the emergency lights began to flash.

Johan hit the brakes as another car came past them, headlights on full beam. Kobus had no need to worry about whether this was help arriving, because the driver was clearly no Samaritan. Without so much as touching the brakes, he—or she—swerved into the oncoming lane to avoid hitting the disabled vehicle and disappeared into the distance.

'Nothing,' he said. 'Nothing's wrong.'

He would have liked to stop beside her car, to open his passenger window and pump her full of bullets without worrying about collecting up the casings afterwards. But they weren't going to play it that way. Bradley had said that one shooting on the main road out of town could be regarded as a freak incident, but two would be more closely investigated—and by police who weren't on their payroll.

In any case, the car had stopped at the wrong angle to allow him to do that.

They were going to grab her. Do the job by hand and, when it was done, send her and her car over the cliff at the top of the coastal road. That made more sense, Bradley had said, and Kobus agreed. Driving badly because she's worried about her boyfriend and scared of being out on the road alone, such a thing could easily happen.

As they pulled off the road behind her, Kobus found himself grinning like a wolf. It had been twenty years since he'd done a job this way, and he'd forgotten how good the excitement felt.

Man, he was flying.

Or perhaps that was the painkillers, too.

He wrenched his door open and jumped out. Beside him, Johan mirrored his movements.

Now to overpower the girl.

'You take . . .' He was going to say to Johan, you take the passenger door.

But then two white pinpoints winked into life in front of him, and before he could think—*reversing lights?*—he heard the rough spin of wheels and the howl of an engine racing. The next moment something dealt him a hammer-blow and hurled him backwards. He slammed into the ground and the world exploded into blackness.

34

The law of thermodynamics.

Jade was no scientist, but her father had explained a part of that law to her long ago, when they'd gone camping in the Magaliesberg.

They'd taken along what her father had called 'padkos' or food for the journey; a brown paper bag filled with tender chunks of biltong, two bars of chocolate and about eight bottles of fizzy drink. They'd eaten over half the biltong before they were even halfway there, washing it down with mouthfuls of orange Fanta. They'd shared the rest the following afternoon, at the top of the steep hill that had wonderful views of the area. Then, without saying why, her father had taken the brown bag and, instead of crumpling it up and shoving it in his backpack with the chocolate wrappers, he'd folded it carefully and put it into his pocket.

That evening, Commissioner De Jong had set about making a beef stew inside the small, heavy, cast-iron potjie that they'd brought along with them. After adding a pinch of salt and a heaped tablespoon of chilli powder to the chunks of meat and sliced vegetables, he had held his hand over the top of the campfire, testing its heat. Clearly satisfied with the temperature, he placed the steel grill over the fire, balancing it on two wide brick supports.

Then he'd reached into his pocket and taken out the paper bag. He'd shaken the last crumbs of biltong out of it and asked Jade to pass him one of their water containers.

Mystified, Jade had handed the bottle over to him and Commissioner De Jong had carefully proceeded to fill the sturdy paper bag half full with cool water.

'What do you think will happen if I put this on the grill?' he'd asked her.

Jade frowned. Was this a trick question? It couldn't be. She could see the flames licking the steel. The answer was obvious. Or so she'd thought.

'The bag will start burning,' she'd said. 'But don't do it, Dad. The water might spill onto the fire and put it out.'

Her father had smiled at her words. 'Think so?'

'Of course.'

Then he had torn a piece off the top of the bag and put it onto the grill. In a second, the brown paper had crisped and charred, flaming briefly before falling through the diamond-shaped gaps.

'Now look,' he'd said.

Jade had watched expectantly as he'd placed the water-filled bag in exactly the same spot. She hoped they'd be able to light the fire again when the water put it out, or what would they do for supper? To her amazement, though, the brown paper hadn't ignited.

'The water inside the bag is keeping the outside cool. It won't burn through. Not even when the water's boiling. That's part of the law of thermodynamics, Jadey,' he'd told her.

He'd gone on to explain in more detail—she remembered him talking about entropy, the exchange of energy and temperatures—but what Jade remembered best was her shock at seeing the top of the bag, above the water level, catch fire when a high-leaping flame caught it, creating a charred, u-shaped gap that ended just where the water began. But the bottom didn't burn. Instead, the water inside the bag had started to produce little wisps of steam. Then a bigger plume of steam. Finally, she had heard it start to bubble.

At that point, Commissioner De Jong had wrapped a tea towel around his hand and lifted the paper bag carefully off the grill, tilting it so that the water didn't slosh out of the burnt section. Then he'd poured the water into two enamel mugs and made them each a coffee.

That was what Jade remembered best about that camping trip. That law of thermodynamics. The bubbling water inside the brown paper bag, seemingly impervious to the leaping flames.

And the fact that her coffee had tasted, not unpleasantly, of biltong.

Jade had used the same principle to mislead the men into thinking her car had overheated. Knowing they would make their move on the empty road outside town, she had stopped in a reasonably safe place, under a street light where they could see her, but where they wouldn't risk attacking.

She'd taken the two water bottles with her when she got out. The first she had thrown onto the verge after pouring the contents away. Then she'd loosened the lid of the second bottle and wedged it between the blisteringly hot engine block and the exhaust manifold. She'd tried to be careful, but even so she'd earned another red burn on her wrist as she struggled to push the bottle firmly in place. Then she'd slammed the bonnet, got back into her car and driven like hell.

Driven like a woman who had known she was unarmed and outnumbered, but was hoping to make it back to safety before her pursuers caught up.

She'd timed it just right. She'd guessed the water would take between five and fifteen minutes to reach boiling point. In fact, it had been closer to fifteen, because the bottle had only just come out of the fridge.

When it had started to boil, she'd driven on carefully, squinting at the road through the billowing steam, as if she were attempting to eke the last possible mileage from her damaged car. She'd stopped a minute later, half off the road near the top of a hill. She didn't want the driver on her tail to be able to see oncoming traffic, and she wanted gravity on her side. Even with these in her favour, she still hadn't dared turn off the engine in case she wasn't able to restart it fast enough. Thankfully the Corsa idled quietly, as they wouldn't have expected to hear her car still running.

Then she'd waited, checking her mirrors, her hand poised over the gear stick.

And there they were. Pulling up confidently behind her. The doors of the Mazda flew open and Jade recognised both men who leapt out; one was the security guard from the harbour and other the gunman who'd shot David that afternoon, the blood-ied bandage on his right arm evidence of her bullet having almost struck home.

They started running the ten-metre distance up the hill towards her. They were sharp silhouettes now, backlit by the dazzling bright beams of their own vehicle.

Now!

Jade shoved the car into reverse and rammed her foot onto the accelerator. The Corsa shot backwards down the hill and her reversing lights lit up the face of the nearer man, his expression one of total shock.

There was a horrible, meaty thud as the Corsa hit him square on. He was knocked backwards and she almost felt the massive thud of his skull connect with the ground. Then Jade felt the car tilt sideways and the chassis bounce violently, as her left wheels ran over him.

Sorry, Elsabe.

Jade braced herself as her rear bumper collided with the Mazda's bonnet. Metal screamed, and the impact slammed her head into the car's headrest.

Wrenching the clutch into first, she put her foot down and shot forward. There was a crunch as the Corsa disengaged itself from the Mazda's front bumper. It was still driveable, although the suspension felt wallowy and it rattled and shook as she eased it back onto the road.

She knew she'd left the shooter unconscious and, if his ribs had pierced his lungs, he'd probably be dead before long. As for the security guard, well, his car had serious front-end damage, which hopefully meant it was no longer driveable.

Breathless, Jade headed towards the resort. She'd done all she could for now.

35

People very seldom changed their ways. That was one of the axioms that Jade's father had repeated to her, over and over again. They followed their nature. Over and over again they did what they were programmed, by heredity or environment, to do. Like animals, they were creatures of habit.

When they behaved abnormally, what did it mean? In an animal, it was a warning sign that something was wrong, that it was sick, injured or scared.

Were people the same?

When Jade had first met Neil, the resort owner, he'd struck her as a diligent man. An ex-surfer. A loner who kept to himself, but worked hard to make sure that everything in his domain ran smoothly.

After Amanda's murder, Neil's demeanour changed immediately. His behaviour pattern had altered. He hadn't volunteered for the search party. He'd avoided speaking to the police. She hadn't seen him out and about at all, apart from the one occasion when he'd been striding out of the tumbledown apartments near the old station, after his fruitless visit to flat eighteen.

Jade had wondered whether Neil was somehow involved with the criminals, although she'd had no evidence to prove it. His behaviour was worrying her. It was like a piece of a puzzle that hadn't fitted anywhere on the board.

But sometimes, in order to make a piece fit, you had to look at things from a different angle. Take a step back. A good way to solve the problem, in her experience, was to pay more attention to the other pieces, checking where they were placed and whether they really fitted.

And suddenly, in the investigator's part of Jade's brain, the part that had been obsessing over the reasons for this behaviour ever since she'd noticed it, the solution had finally slotted into place.

She drove into the resort, glad to see that the security boom was being manned by a guard who waved her through.

Jade didn't drive directly to her chalet. Instead, she parked on the grass in front of the reception area that led into Neil's house. His car was parked round the back. She could see its yellow bonnet, so he was definitely around.

With relief, she got out of the Corsa, noticing that on this cool, damp night the croaking of the frogs was already at its fullest—a non-stop chorus that was all but deafening when it started up, but faded into the background after a few minutes.

She walked up to the front door and knocked loudly.

When Neil answered, she was going to insist that she be allowed inside, because she was sure she knew what she would find there.

Or rather, who she would find.

Jade was certain now that Monique the scuba instructor had not in fact left the area voluntarily; nor had she been snatched. She'd done exactly what a frightened animal would do. She hadn't made a run for it. Instead, she had chosen to hide close to home, in a place of safety.

With Neil, the resort owner, her boss, and now—Jade believed—her lover, too.

She had no idea what Monique's predicament was, but she suspected that she was somehow connected with the man whose scruffy flat Neil had visited. And Jade was going to find out why.

She heard a noise from inside, the sound of somebody coming to the door. A key turned in the lock and the door opened to reveal Neil, dressed in his usual attire of short-sleeved shirt, swimming trunks and sandals. But he didn't have to open his mouth for Jade to know that something was wrong. His body language spoke volumes and his eyes were full of fear. He looked at her pleadingly.

Then he stepped aside and she saw Monique.

To Jade's disbelief, she had her hands tied behind her back and was being held in a headlock by the blond man, who was still wearing his Metro Police uniform. He had a pistol jammed against her temple. Looking at the uniform, Jade now realised how he had got past the security guard at the boom.

The fake cop had been too quick for her. She had arrived too late and in too much of a hurry. Two small, but crucial mistakes. She should have asked the guard at the boom if anybody else had come through. And she should have checked the chalet area to see if there were any unfamiliar vehicles parked there.

This was a hostage situation and, whatever the outcome for Monique and Neil, the best thing she could do right now was to run.

But before she could do that, Jade heard a voice come from behind her. A deep, smooth voice, calm and full of confidence.

'Put your hands above your head and turn around slowly. I am holding a silenced weapon and, if you hesitate, I will pull the trigger.'

36

The sky is completely dark when the utility van leaves the building and heads out along the long, straight road.

It's a plain economy vehicle. Cheap, but relatively new. The one luxury that it does have, which the driver is very glad about, is a radio. Crackly, but functional.

The driver is listening to music that would sound totally unfamiliar to me, fascinating and somehow unsettling in its strangeness, although you must have heard it before in your comings and goings.

On either side of the road is a landscape as bleak and barren as the surface of the moon. Smothered by darkness, only its edges are visible to the man. The van's headlights shine over reddish-brown soil and withered shrubs.

They aren't the only lights on this road.

Spaced at regular intervals, the fixed lights at ground level on either side of this narrow strip of road each have a special significance. So too do the newish steel signs whose paint is swiftly becoming weathered by the sun.

The man reaches his destination. He gets out of the van and does what he has to do.

The early morning air is uncontaminated by the smoke, pollution and petrol fumes that are the curse of densely populated places. But something is there. He can smell it. He sniffs it in.

Dust.

Last night, the winds blew strongly, churning up the fine sand—because that is all the groundcover there is in most of this drought-ridden, desertified and eroded city—and whipping it into a low-lying storm that whirled in on itself for hours, before subsiding. If you had been out in that, you would have covered your face and your eyes to get away from the incessant blasting of millions of tiny, sharp-edged grains of sand.

A few miniature dust-devils still scud over this landscape, churning up plumes of dust into an air that is already thick with its residue. He glances up at the sky, but from his standpoint the stars are only just visible—dim pinpoints in the hazy air.

The man pays no attention to them, though. He shivers, more from tiredness than from the cold. He climbs back inside and turns on the heater in his van, which doesn't work as well as the radio. He executes a three-point turn and heads back the way he came.

He is driving directly east and he can see the faintest lightening of the sky ahead of him.

The buildings are silhouetted against it; large, low, black-edged outlines against the faint, yellow-grey glow. It's a desolate, but strangely beautiful picture.

The start of another perfect day in Africa.

But he doesn't think that, of course—why would he? For him, it is just another working day in Africa, like all the others. Filled with small, routine acts that are part of his job, but are critical to the bigger picture.

Although this day, as it turns out, will be different.

He lets out an enormous yawn, without covering his mouth, as the song ends and the announcer on the radio starts speaking in a language that I don't understand at all.

And I don't think you do, either.

Jade felt a terrible coldness in the pit of her stomach. She raised her hands in the air and turned slowly around.

The speaker—a tall black man in dark clothing—had told the truth. He was aiming a silenced weapon directly at Jade's chest.

Even in the soft glow of the porch light, she could see him clearly. He had distinctive, square-looking features that, though handsome, seemed to be set in a permanent frown. Full lips curving down at the corners, a wide forehead, well-defined cheekbones and a clean-shaven head.

Familiar features. But where had she seen him before?

'Cooperate and we'll let you go unharmed,' he said, a promise that Jade found difficult to believe. 'Bradley, bind her arms. Quickly.'

'Yes, Zulu.'

The next moment, her hands were yanked behind her back and she felt a tugging motion as the blond man, whose name she now knew was Bradley, secured her wrists together with what felt like a thin length of wire.

Then, holding her arms tightly, Zulu hustled her and Monique round the back of Neil's house and over to a black Land Cruiser that was parked out of sight of the access road. He forced her into the back seat. Monique was shoved in next to her. Jade could hear her breathing, fast and panicky, each exhalation a whimper.

Bradley bundled Neil unceremoniously into the driver's seat as Zulu wrenched open the passenger door. A moment later Bradley was in the back with them. He grabbed hold of Monique's hair and forced her head down onto his lap.

'Drive,' Zulu told Neil, holding his weapon low. 'And go carefully. If you try to warn the guard, I will shoot your girlfriend first, and then you.'

'Can you tell me . . .' Jade began, but Zulu turned in his seat and pointed the long barrel of the silencer straight at her.

'No talking,' he warned.

The car started up. Neil's driving felt jerky, but the guard at the boom noticed nothing wrong. He lifted the barrier and waved them through.

Twenty minutes later they were at the harbour. Zulu directed Neil straight to the barriered-off section, where another uniformed guard opened the gate for them. The parking lot was almost empty.

The black man swiftly climbed out of the passenger seat. Then he pulled Jade's door open, dragged her out and held her by her wrists.

'Bring your girlfriend here,' he told Neil, as he pushed Jade face-first against the side of the Land Cruiser.

Frustration surged through Jade. Damn it, she needed to get out of here, and fast—in fact, she should have tried to escape as soon as she realised that Neil's security had been compromised. That was what she'd been trained to do. There will never be a better opportunity than the first one—and once the bad guys have got you where they want you, there will usually be no chance at all.

But Jade hadn't had a chance. There hadn't been one moment where escape would not have equalled potential suicide.

And there wasn't going to be. The next thing she felt were thin, strong fingers wrapping another length of wire around her wrists and then the soft touch of another woman's skin.

Her wrists had been fastened to Monique's, back-to-back. An effective way of restraining both of them.

'Where's the closest boat?' Zulu's voice. He was still behind her, so she could hear him, but not see him.

'Down this way,' Bradley replied.

Fastened back-to-back, Jade and Monique stumbled forward, each struggling to keep their balance as Zulu pulled them roughly along. She trod on Monique's heel with her right foot, and felt the back of her head bash against the dive instructor's and the gasp of pain that followed. She couldn't see where they were going; she could only see Neil's terrified face as he was herded along behind her, arms also tied, by the gun-wielding Bradley and the uniformed guard.

The lights of the car park grew more distant and the tall metal barriers grew closer. They didn't go into the barriered-off area, though, but continued straight down towards the water's edge.

Then the tarmac under her feet changed to wooden boards.

They were on a jetty. The boards sounded hollow under Jade's feet and were warped and uneven.

Monique stumbled, dragging Jade's wrists back, and a sharp end of wire dug into her wrist so painfully that she thought it might have drawn blood.

She twisted her fingers upwards, hoping to find it. Her middle finger brushed against the needle-like point and, with some difficulty, she managed to bend it away from her.

And then Monique stopped suddenly and Jade cannoned into her, feeling the other woman stagger and almost pull them over.

They had reached the end of the jetty and Jade could hear the soft thudding of a boat bumping against the barrier.

'In,' she heard Zulu say.

'But I . . .' Monique's voice, terrified. She felt the other woman push back against her and realised that Zulu was asking her to do the impossible, because there was no way that two of them tied together would be able to get down into the boat without risking injury to at least one.

But then, Jade didn't think at this stage that avoiding injury to their prisoners was a priority for either of the men.

'Get in, bitch!'

Bradley's voice. And then Jade was yanked backwards and pulled right off her feet as Monique launched herself off the jetty and into the boat.

Without her arms to balance or break her fall, the dive instructor landed hard and let out a shrill scream. The boat rocked violently and water fountained into the air.

Jade's own landing was cushioned by Monique, but, even so, the impact was like a body blow. The side of her head cracked against the edge of the boat and her knee struck something rough and solid.

And then Zulu shoved Neil off the edge of the jetty. His arms also bound behind him, he too had no choice but to fall head-first towards them. His shoulder hit Jade in the solar plexus, punching all the breath out of her, and she heard an awful crunch as his face smashed into the bottom of the boat.

The boat rocked again as two of the men climbed down and got in. Not Zulu. He was staying behind.

'Go right out to sea,' he said, untying the mooring rope. 'Remember, the whole of the harbour gets dredged. And as soon as you're done, I want the workers disposed of.'

'No,' Monique began to sob loudly. 'Please.'

Bradley ignored her and started the motor, manoeuvring the craft away from the jetty and out of the harbour into the blackness of the ocean.

In her backward-facing position, Jade could just see over the stern. She watched the shape of the jetty swiftly disappearing into the fog. But when the boat turned to the left, her view was lit up by the bright spotlights that were trained inwards around a large construction zone.

They were sailing past the section of the harbour that had been barricaded off. Now, finally, from her ocean-going vantage point, Jade got a full view of what was inside those tall steel walls.

The barriered-off section contained no contraband goods that she could see. She saw no containers waiting to be filled or emptied before being smuggled in or out of the harbour. No stockpiles of anything illegal at all.

The area surrounded by the high sheet-metal walls was about half the size of a football field. Running down its middle was a wide concrete roadway. It was indisputably a tanker bay, just as she'd been told. And floating low in the water, secured by ropes to the steel mooring points, was a medium-sized oil tanker.

Or, rather, the skeleton of one.

Even with her inexperienced eye, Jade doubted whether the vessel would ever leave the harbour. Its tall sides were mottled and dappled with huge crusts of reddish-black rust.

The ship was giving out a series of eerie-sounding groans and creaks and, as it swayed against its moorings, Jade heard the scream of ancient metal against metal, as if the torque forces of the ropes were enough to tear it apart. It was a dying vessel, surely way past any hope of refurbishment or repair, one that would never embark on a sea voyage again. It reeked of despair, and looking at it made Jade shiver.

A trace of faded, white lettering on its rusted hull caught her eye. Staring hard, Jade could just make out the word '*Karachi.*'

As they passed it, she realised that above the salty smell of the sea she could identify the thick, corrosive smell of old oil.

With a start, Jade remembered the story about an oil tanker she'd seen on Sky News. Perhaps this vessel had also got into trouble during a storm and been abandoned, eventually drifting towards shore, and then towed into Richards Bay to be broken up by a private salvage operator.

Peering into the fog, Jade could see definite signs of activity on the far side of the ship. She caught a glimpse of two black-clad men walking slowly past the vessel, pushing something that looked like a large drum. Off to one side, three freight wagons were being slowly pulled up the hill by an ancient-looking railway engine.

The tanker was being emptied. Whatever cargo it had held in its final journey across the seas was now being offloaded, decanted into drums and taken away for storage or disposal. Perhaps that was why the steel walls were in place—to prevent possible contamination from a toxic load.

Or perhaps not. Maybe it wasn't being emptied at all.

With a start, Jade remembered why Zulu had looked so familiar.

He was none other than Patrick Zulu, CEO of Richards Mining, whose ambitions to strip mine the dunes in the national park had been documented by the journalist, along with his photograph, in the online article she had so recently read.

'If it pays, it stays,' he had been quoted as saying. He'd made it clear that he would go to any lengths to ensure that his plan to expand the company's mining activities was not thwarted by the environmentalists' findings.

By arriving at the harbour that morning, Jade and David had unwittingly presented a threat to those plans, and Zulu had given orders to dispose of them.

As she tugged vainly against the tight bite of the wire binding her wrists, Jade couldn't help but wonder what Monique had done to incur Zulu's wrath.

37

Jade could feel the speedboat's motor throbbing. From the wake she could see streaming out behind them, she guessed it was going at top speed. The boat's prow lurched upwards and dropped downwards as it breasted the waves, now heading straight out to sea. With every movement of the boat, she heard something heavy on the bottom of the boat shifting.

For a while she had thought it was Neil, still unconscious after the hardness of his fall, but she gradually realised that there was something else in the boat that was solid and heavy.

Like bricks, perhaps.

Jade's stomach lurched as she remembered how it had felt to be crushed by tons upon tons of water. The fear she had felt as she kicked her flippers and descended deeper and deeper into the ocean, despite her breathing apparatus and her instructor by her side. She didn't want to think about how that downward rush would feel with heavy bricks attached to her ankles—and the weight of another person behind her.

Monique's sobs had subsided into whimpers. Jade needed her to listen. She had to get the message through to her that they must act, and fast, before the boat reached the spot where their captors planned to put those bricks to use.

They had to act together, because she doubted she would be able to wriggle out of the wire that bound her. It was far too tight. She stretched her thumbs up, trying to find the loose end that had jabbed her earlier.

There it was again. She pushed it with her right thumb and felt it bend round.

But with her hands behind her back, she had no idea whether she was pushing it in the right direction or only succeeding in further tightening the bonds.

'Monique?' Jade whispered, trying to keep her voice as soft as breath.

No response. Jade tried again, a louder hiss this time, turning her head and pressing her cheek against the dive instructor's wavy blonde hair.

The other woman's only response was a sob.

Jade was considering her next option when, to her surprise, the dive instructor took a shuddery breath and whispered back, 'Yes?'

'We're going to have to . . .'

But Jade was interrupted.

'This isn't my fault, you know,' Monique whispered.

'I don't . . .'

'I never blackmailed him.'

'Blackmailed who?' What on earth was she talking about, Jade wondered.

'Him. Bradley.' And now Monique's voice was a hiss.

'So you know him?'

'We dated. A while back. I didn't know when I met him, but he'd just come out of prison.'

Prison?

Questions jostled for position in Jade's mind. So many she wouldn't have known which to ask first, even if there had been time. But there was no time left now. And in any case, Monique was in full conversational flow.

'Jade, he became obsessed with me. Violent. It was horrible. Even when I thought it was over, he still used to phone and SMS me at all hours of the night. I would never have blackmailed him. I was just glad to get away from him.'

'Monique, that's interesting, but . . .'

'Then he started to get weird. He invited me to his flat one day and he . . .'

'Monique, we can talk about this later. Right now we need to . . .'

'This is all so unfair.' Another sob.

If Jade's hands had been free, she would have grabbed the other woman and shaken her in frustration. Here they were, just minutes from certain death and, instead of listening to Jade's escape plan, all Monique could do was whine on about how none of this had been her fault.

'Listen. This is important. We need to go over . . .'

And then, abruptly, the engine cut out and the boat stopped moving forwards. They coasted to a stop, the craft rocking gently on the waves.

If Bradley had reached his intended location, it might already be too late for her plan to work.

'Pull him up.'

Bradley's voice. What was going on? Jade craned her neck, struggling to see. The beam of a flashlight pierced the darkness, momentarily dazzling her, and she heard a dull scraping sound.

Sneaking another look, she saw the guard was gripping the torch in his teeth, holding the unconscious Neil by his shoulders while Bradley worked on his legs, attaching what Jade now saw was a heavy-looking concrete block with a rough hole through its centre.

Go overboard with one of those lashed to your ankles and you would never come up for air again, she thought.

'We have to jump over the side,' Jade whispered. 'It's our only chance. My left, your right. Count of three.'

She felt Monique tense. Then she squeezed Jade's finger in response. Finally, the scuba instructor had listened to her.

Jade breathed in. Deep, fast breaths. Forcing her lungs to take in as much air as they could, then pushing it out again. Oxygenating her blood to give her the best possible chance of survival when they were under the water.

'One.'

Another breath.

'Two.'

Jade eased her legs as far underneath her as they would go.

'Three.'

They struggled to their feet, limbs tangled, fighting for balance on the slippery bottom of the boat. It was not the quick and easy manoeuvre she had hoped for, that was for sure. It was more like a free-for-all.

And then she heard Monique scream. 'Help! Don't!'

The torch beam swung in their direction again and, with a cold rush of terror, Jade knew that they had been too slow.

And then she did it. A desperate sideways lunge took them over the edge of the boat. Jade gulped in as much air as she could as they tipped into the cold, heaving sea.

But as they fell, a gunshot split the air and Jade felt Monique's body convulse.

As they sank deeper under the water, she realised that her worst nightmare had come true. The dive instructor had been shot. She was not moving and her body was slack. And now, whether she lived or died, Jade was joined to her by a tough and unbreakable length of wire.

38

One minute underwater. That was what Jade knew she had left until she could no longer breathe.

She opened her eyes wide, desperate to orient herself. It was a waste of time, because only claustrophobic blackness greeted her. Her fear swelled to scream-inducing terror as she realised she didn't even know which way was up.

A minute was the maximum she had left—and probably less than that, because the adrenaline that was now sluicing through her body was causing her heart to race, gobbling up the oxygen that was a precious and scarce commodity. Very soon she would no longer be able to hold her breath. Monique was either unconscious or dead—she certainly wasn't moving, let alone struggling—and her weight was pulling them down, causing the wire to cut even more deeply into Jade's flesh.

Jade's lungs were burning. She kicked her shoes off with difficulty, because Monique's legs kept on getting in her way. She had to try to get back to the surface. It was impossible. Her feet had no room to move. Instead, they slammed into the drifting body behind her.

Panic overwhelmed her as logical thought fled. All that remained was the imperative to struggle and fight against the dead weight that pulled her back.

And then the loose end of the wire scraped against her wrist again.

Her lungs were throbbing and her diaphragm was starting to hitch with the overwhelming need to breathe. She couldn't help it. She let out some of the only breath she had, the only breath she was going to get. Bubbles swirled around her. The pressure on her lungs eased a little, but the burning need for more air grew worse.

Jade pushed the end of the wire as hard as she could. Now she could reach it with her other thumb. She continued the pressure, pulling the wire round, but she couldn't seem to get it any further and, in despair, she realised that she must have been tightening it instead of helping it to untwist.

And then, suddenly, she felt it. The wire jerked and loosened. It didn't come apart, but the gap pulled open enough for her to wrestle first one wrist and then another out of the steel loop.

Monique was gone.

She was free, but she had no idea how deep she was or how she was going to get back to the surface, wherever it might be. This was it. She just could not hold this breath in any longer.

And then, from the direction that she would have thought was below her, came a loud and heavy splash. Jade sensed, rather than saw, the weighted form travelling swiftly past her, on its way to the depths.

Neil's body.

'Which way is up?'

'Follow the bubbles.'

Her mother's voice, echoing from her dreams.

Jade kicked out in the direction of the splash, fighting the need to gasp in air with every ounce of will that she possessed.

She felt her lungs contract, forcing out the remaining air. She clamped her mouth shut and concentrated on kicking herself upwards.

And then she was bursting out of the water and gulping in the sweetest, deepest breath she had ever taken.

Jade trod water and took in rapid, gasping breaths, quickly feeling the strength flow back into her limbs. Now she needed to find the boat. It must still be nearby, its presence camouflaged by the rolling waves. She couldn't see it; and, in the darkness, its occupants couldn't see her. But if they swept the area with a light, they would easily pick her out. Bradley would have known his shot had hit Monique, but she was sure he would check, for the sake of thoroughness, that neither of them surfaced again.

Sure enough, a bright torch beam cut through the darkness to her right, turning the ocean from black to dull grey-green.

Jade ducked under the water just as the light moved round towards her. Above her she could see the beam's reflection on the water. It moved slowly round, searching, and then headed further and further to her left until it disappeared from view.

Coming up, she could hear them shouting at each other, but couldn't make out their words.

Eventually, the boat's motor started up again. It made a low droning sound as it turned a slow half-circle. The prow lights came on, but they were facing away from her now. Then she heard the throttle increase and saw the boat speed away, leaving her floundering in its turbulent wake.

Kicking herself as far out of the water as she could in an attempt to locate the shore, Jade saw that the harbour was now far off to her left. There were other lights straight ahead of her that signalled a coastline, but they were faint and shimmering; a long way away. How far? She guessed she would find out soon. Either she'd make it or she wouldn't.

She did know, however, that the added weight of her clothes would slow her down and eventually drag her under. With some difficulty, she wriggled out of her cargo pants. Her bare legs felt much lighter. Perhaps she would be able to do this.

Swimming with strong, regular strokes to discourage any sharks that might be on the hunt for easy prey, Jade began the long journey back to shore.

She had no idea how long it took her. Perhaps an hour, perhaps more. In that dark water, time telescoped into infinity and the distance seemed endless. Despite her earlier intentions of show-ing strength, there were times when she flailed in the water, howling as she endured agonising cramp in her feet, and other times when she floated on her back, panting hard, her quivering muscles simply unable to continue without rest.

When she eventually felt sand under her feet, she tried but failed to stand up. Inch by excruciating inch, she managed to drag herself out of the water and onto dry land before she finally passed out.

39

'She's coming round. Theunis, come over here, quick! She's coming round.'

Voices pierced Jade's head, dragging her back to consciousness.

Footsteps, running over the sand towards her.

A man's voice. 'Are you hurt?'

She lifted her head up from the edge of the towel that somebody must have placed underneath it, realising that the rest of the towel was wrapped around her. Her skin felt sandy and her cold, wet hair flopped over her face in thick rats' tails. In the dim light cast by a weak torch, she saw two people squatting in front of her—or rather, two pairs of shoes. They were Crocs. Pink and beige. One pair smaller, one larger.

With arms that felt utterly leaden, she pushed herself a little further up and looked into the concerned faces of her would-be rescuers.

'What happened to you?' the woman asked.

'I fell out of a boat,' Jade said.

'And they didn't stop for you!'

'Are you sure you can move all your limbs? Nothing is broken?' This question from the man.

'Theunis, can't you see she's exhausted? And probably suffering from exposure. She could have drowned out there.' The woman bent down and grasped one of Jade's hands in both of hers. Her skin felt very warm. 'You need to lie down, dear. Just lie there quietly until the ambulance arrives.'

'No, honestly, I'm fine. I don't need an ambulance.' Pulling away from the woman, Jade tried to stand up, but her legs were as limp as soft spaghetti and she would have fallen right back down onto the sand if Theunis hadn't grabbed her first.

'We've already called them. And you do need to go to hospital. Come on. Rest here while you wait.' He lowered her carefully back down and checked his watch, while the lady wrapped the towel around her again. 'Should be here any minute, I think. I'm going to go up to the road and look out for them.'

Jade clutched the towel hard. Under her sodden T-shirt, she was shuddering with cold and her skin was tightly pimpled with gooseflesh.

'I'm so sorry, love, but we didn't have any other clothes in the car. All we had was the towel,' the lady said apologetically.

'That's OK.' She forced the words out through chattering teeth.

'Theunis, look, they're here.'

Bright headlights accompanied by a red flashing light swung off the main road and headed down towards the parking lot, stopping next to the car that Jade guessed belonged to the couple who had found her. Carrying a powerful torch, the paramedic walked briskly down the concrete steps to the beach, with Theunis excitedly explaining how he and his wife had found her.

A minute later, the paramedic was crouched down beside her, placing his kit bag carefully on the sand before balancing the torch on it. 'Hello there. How are you . . .?'

Upon hearing his voice, Jade looked up in surprise. It was the man who'd arrived at the scene after David's shooting; the one who'd told Pillay that she had saved his life.

He recognised her too, and looked her over in blank amazement.

'Are you having a run of bad luck?' he asked after a short pause.

'You could say that,' Jade said.

The paramedic raised an eyebrow, then nodded. 'I could, I suppose.'

'She fell off a boat,' Theunis said, shifting from foot to foot in his khaki Crocs. 'They didn't even stop for her.'

'Fell off a boat,' the paramedic echoed. Jade thought she could detect a hint of irony in his tone.

'Do you need us for anything else?' Theunis asked. 'Because we've got to get back to the children . . .'

'Go right ahead,' the paramedic said. Jade managed to unclench her teeth long enough to utter a heartfelt thanks to the couple who'd found her. Her shivers were starting to reduce as she warmed up. She wriggled off the beach towel, which the paramedic replaced with a blanket, and passed the towel back to her rescuers. Theunis shook the sand off it, and then they turned away and made their way back to their car.

The medic took her pulse, then wrapped a blood pressure cuff around her upper arm, inflated it and peered down at the reading.

'How long were you in the water for?'

'A couple of hours, I think.'

'Do you know how you got this cut on your left wrist?'

'From wire.'

The paramedic's eyebrow arched upwards once more.

'I can walk,' Jade said. 'I'm OK, really. This isn't a medical emergency. I was just exhausted from having to swim so far. I need to rest a bit longer, and I need a sugary drink.'

'Mild exposure would be my guess. But if you can walk, then come up to the ambulance with me.'

Once again, Jade struggled to her feet. Her spaghetti-legs weren't working much better than they had before, but this time at least they felt al dente, rather than completely overcooked. Leaning heavily on the paramedic's arm, she made her way carefully up the beach.

The paramedic opened the door of the ambulance. 'Get in the back.'

'I said I'm fine.'

'Just get in the back and sit on the bench. There's a heater running in there.'

Warm air suffused the small space. Jade climbed in and sat gratefully down on the bench. The paramedic disappeared briefly and returned with a bottle of Energade and a Bar One.

'Emergency medical supplies,' he said, with a smile.

'Thank you.'

'Your friend, the Indian guy, he made it to the hospital. He went straight into surgery. I can't be one hundred per cent sure, but I think he'll come through it OK. He seems like a strong guy.'

'He is. Thanks for getting him there alive.'

Jade downed half the bottle in one go. She bit into the Bar One, feeling thick chocolate crush under her teeth, then softer toffee. Sugar. Energy. Exactly what she needed. Her body screamed for more.

'I don't know what to do with you,' the paramedic said. 'I don't know what you're involved with. I'd ask you, but I guess you won't tell me.'

Her mouth crammed with chocolate, Jade could only shrug in response.

'I'm scared if I let you go, the next call-out I get will be to take you to the morgue.'

Jade blinked, swallowed her mouthful and looked into his concerned brown eyes.

'There won't be another call-out,' she promised.

'You know, for your own sake, I should take you to casualty and book you in. Get them to put you under sedation for the night.'

'You could do that,' Jade agreed. 'But if you do, there's a good chance I won't be alive by morning. And nor will my friend.'

'A hospital is a secure place . . .'

'Are you willing to bet two of your patients' lives on that? Given that we were ambushed earlier today by a man wearing a perfectly authentic Metro Police uniform.'

Sitting in the warmth, Jade was starting to feel strength seeping back into her limbs. She wasn't back to normal, not nearly. But halfway there, perhaps. She took another swig of Energade to try and speed things up.

The paramedic tightened his lips. He glanced down at Jade's bare legs and feet. His gaze moved over the damp T-shirt clinging to her body and her wet, sandy hair, and he sighed.

He climbed out of the rear doors and went round to the front of the ambulance. Jade heard him using the radio to call into headquarters.

'False alarm,' he said. 'The patient didn't need any medical attention after all. I'm going to head back to base now.'

He came back round to where Jade was sitting.

'I'm going back to the hospital to wait for another call-out. If you want to ride along, you can. It's illegal, of course. If anyone asks, I'll deny you were ever in my vehicle.' He spread his arms in a gesture that eloquently conveyed the fact that this wasn't the only illegal activity going on that night in Richards Bay.

'Thanks,' Jade said.

The paramedic didn't reply; he just slammed the back doors. Seconds later, the ambulance started up and drove away.

The journey to the hospital took ten minutes and, by the time they got there, Jade's T-shirt was almost dry and the back of the ambulance was starting to feel like a sauna. She felt the vehicle rock as it negotiated the two speed bumps just before the turn-off to the hospital. A left turn took them through the main gate. A few metres more and then the ambulance stopped.

What to do now?

She didn't want to be seen climbing out of the back of the vehicle, because that would get the paramedic into trouble. But she also didn't want to waste any more time. Another problem was her bare legs. She would have to beg, borrow or steal a pair of trousers, and she was sure she could do that somewhere in Richards Bay General Hospital. The problem would be getting into the hospital looking like she did now.

The rattle of the ambulance's back doors opening made her jump. The paramedic tossed a plastic bag inside.

'This is the best I can do for you,' he said. 'When you hear me knock on the side of the ambulance, it's safe to climb out.'

Jade looked inside the bag and found a pair of black Lycra three-quarter-length gym pants.

'Thanks,' she said, surprised.

'Couldn't find any shoes.'

'No problem. I'll be OK without shoes.'

Last year, Jade had managed to grab a woman in the act of fleeing a crime scene. The lady had been stunned during the struggle, but as an added precaution, Jade had removed her court shoes and thrown them out of reach.

After the incident, Jade had realised that she herself could also have been effectively immobilised that way. It didn't make sense to her, when she thought about it. As tough and fit as she had conditioned herself to be, if you took away her running shoes, she couldn't have outpaced a toddler. This was no good.

So she'd started jogging without shoes. The first few outings had been little more than tentative limps down the rough road from her cottage. Gradually, her feet had toughened up. She wasn't quite at the stage where she could run her full cross-country route barefoot, but she was almost there.

Shoes were not a problem. The lack of a weapon was a more serious issue.

'Do you have a spare knife, by any chance?' she asked the paramedic. She saw him shake his head in reflexive denial.

'Are you sure?' she said again.

This time, he thought about it.

'I can't give you one of my knives,' he said. 'Too risky. It's standard issue from the company I work for. But I can give you something with a blade. It's not much, but better than nothing. Nobody will miss it—it was a freebie. They handed out hundreds of them as gifts, and this one's been lying here for years.'

Leaning into the back of the ambulance, he rummaged around in one of the lockers and then handed Jade a small penknife.

It was so tiny it could have fitted into a Christmas cracker. A miniature oval-shaped handle with a blue and white logo, and a shiny, slender two-and-a-half-inch blade.

It was practically a toy. It couldn't have sliced the tenderest, most perfectly cooked piece of fillet, never mind pierced human skin. It was useless for anything except perhaps cutting through a thin length of fabric.

If Jade was attacked, the best she could hope for would be that her assailant died of laughter when he saw her defence weapon.

'I appreciate it,' she said.

The paramedic closed the ambulance door and Jade wriggled into the Lycra pants. She pushed the knife into the waistband. A while later, she heard a knock on the side of the ambulance.

She scrambled out. The car park was empty and the paramedic was standing a few paces away with his back towards her.

Jade's number one rule for getting anywhere without being stopped was simply to move purposefully. In a business-like, but not aggressive, way; as if she knew exactly where she was going and was in rather a hurry to get there.

That attitude had certainly given her access to quite a few places where she would otherwise have been denied entry. The fast walk also helped, of course.

Taking a deep breath, she lifted her chin and headed into the hospital building. One way or another, she was going to see if she could get to David.

Visiting hours were long over. With a shock, she saw that the clock on the wall was ticking its way towards eleven P.M. Where had the night gone? It was slipping away like sand through her fingers and, with every hour that passed, her chances of catching up with the criminals were growing smaller.

A uniformed receptionist was at the front desk, head bent over a magazine. A nurse was standing beside her, looking through a pile of files. To Jade's surprise, they didn't so much as give her a second glance. It was as if the women hadn't even noticed her at all.

Puzzled, because it wasn't usually so easy, Jade continued through the foyer and into the main corridor of the hospital.

She realised what had caused the foyer staff's inattention when she saw a small group of casually dressed people walking down the corridor in the direction of the exit doors. They were wearing name tags and carrying gift bags with the logo of a drug company emblazoned on the front.

There had been a function or launch of some kind at the hospital, and guests—the last of a larger gathering, perhaps— were now leaving. One or two of them cast curious glances at Jade's bare feet, but most of them had their sights firmly set on getting home.

Glancing at the signs above her, Jade turned in the direction of the ICU. More of the departing crowd passed her. Some casually dressed, some smartly dressed, only a few in uniform.

And then a well-groomed brunette wearing a cream-coloured skirt and jacket called out a name she recognised.

'Dr Abrahams!'

Abrahams?

The hospital chairman; the man who might be able to tell her more about her mother?

Jade stopped and looked.

The brunette click-clacked her way towards a group of business-suited men further down the corridor. She was carrying a briefcase in one hand and, in the other, a white a4-sized envelope with the logo of the same pharmaceutical company on the top right-hand corner.

A drugs rep, then.

And the tall, silver-haired man who stopped, turned and greeted her warmly—he must be the same Dr Abrahams the receptionist had told her about. The retired doctor who was now the chairman of the hospital board, and the person that Mrs Koekemoer had said knew the secret about where her mother was buried.

Although the receptionist had said she would pass on Jade's details to him, the doctor obviously hadn't bothered to contact her and probably never would. This might be the only chance she had to learn more about Elise de Jong.

The rep hadn't lingered. She was already walking away. Dr Abrahams, now holding the envelope she had given him and engrossed in conversation with one of the other suits, was making his way towards the exit.

'Dr Abrahams,' she said quietly, as he reached her.

Once again, the silver-haired man stopped. He didn't look nearly as pleased to see Jade as he had when he saw the drugs rep. He looked down his hooked nose at her, the same way a bird of prey atop a crag might consider a rabbit that it wasn't too interested in eating. His demeanour made Jade remember everything she had ever heard about famous surgeons and their egos.

'Yes?'

'I'm Jade de Jong. I left a message for you a couple of days ago.'

'Jade . . . ' His frown deepened when he noticed her messy

hair and bare feet. Suddenly, Jade wondered whether the receptionist had given him the message at all.

'My mother died in this hospital, a long time ago. I'm down here on holiday and I thought I'd try to find out more about her. I never knew her, you see. I was a baby at the time.'

Now Dr Abrahams was staring at her with an expression on his face that suggested she might benefit from a day or two in the psychiatric ward. A couple of his business-suited colleagues were giving her the same look. She even heard one of them chuckle.

'I'm afraid that really is impossible. Our records don't even go back that far. If she'd died in the last five years or so, we could have pulled something out for you. But beyond that, no. I'm sorry, but you're asking for something that cannot be done.'

The doctor pushed back his jacket sleeve with a neatly manicured finger and checked the time on his gold Rolex, making the gesture sweepingly obvious.

Jade stood her ground.

'Mrs Koekemoer said you would know something.'

'The old maternity ward head? You've spoken to her?'

'Yes. Just this morning, in fact.'

The chairman shook his head. 'I'm sorry. This function ran late and I need to be on my way now. I don't know what information I could provide that Koekemoer couldn't.'

'Nor do I. But she said you'd remember.'

Abrahams gave an impatient sigh.

'What was your mother's name?'

'Elise de Jong.'

As she said the words, the chairman's eyes narrowed and he rubbed his chin thoughtfully. When he spoke again, the impatient tone was gone.

'Well, Mrs Koekemoer was right. That name I do remember.'

'Would you have time to . . . ?'

'Tomorrow morning. I'll be here from nine to ten. Look out for me in reception.'

'I'll be there,' Jade called out to his retreating back.

40

As she left the hospital a while later, Jade heard the clicking of heels and the well-dressed medical rep hurried back down the corridor. She looked tired now. Her mascara was smudged below her eyes, as if she'd been rubbing them, and she was carrying a large and heavy-looking bundle of equipment in her arms.

'Can I help you with that?' Jade asked.

The rep stopped and frowned at her, just as the doctor had done. Looked at her bare feet and her untidy hair.

Then she glanced down at the stuff she was carrying and Jade saw her thinking, as clearly as if she'd said it aloud: This is only a bunch of posters and banners. There's nothing valuable here, so why not?

'If you wouldn't mind,' the rep said aloud. 'I'll go back for the rest of the stuff, then. My car's parked just outside the main entrance. It's a silver Renault.'

Jade took the armful of equipment from the lady and headed out to the car park, where she found the car. The boot was unlocked, although the doors to the car itself were not, and Jade stacked the equipment carefully inside. From the amount of signage, it was clear that this drug company knew how to fight a propaganda war.

The rep had soon returned carrying a large cardboard box in her arms. She pressed the remote control to unlock the doors and stowed it carefully on the back seat of the car.

'Is that everything?' Jade asked.

'Yes, it is.' She looked at Jade, and once again a small frown creased her forehead as if she was wondering who she was and why she had offered to help.

'May I ask a favour in return?'

'What?' the woman responded, in a tone that suggested she would rather have said no.

'Could I borrow your cellphone for five minutes? I need to make an important call. It's local. I won't phone overseas or anything.'

'Well, I . . . yes, I suppose you can.' The rep dug in her hand-bag and produced a BlackBerry. She handed it over reluctantly.

Jade walked a few steps away before dialling.

After the number had rung ten times she thought that no one was going to answer. It was, after all, very late in the evening to be phoning. She decided to give it another five chances. Craig picked up on the third.

'Jade? I thought it might be you, but I didn't recognise the number.'

'I'm borrowing a phone.'

'Can I call you back, then?'

'Yes, please.'

She cut off the call, waited for the phone to ring, and answered immediately.

'Listen, I need your opinion.'

'My opinion? On what?' Now he sounded as if he was smiling, although Jade knew that his good humour would soon disappear when he heard what she had to say.

'Tell me more about used engine oil, Craig. Please tell me exactly what it does to the environment.'

'Do you want the short answer or the long answer?'

Jade glanced over at the medical rep who was now walking back towards the hospital entrance. Perhaps she was giving Jade some privacy. Or maybe she'd remembered there were more banners piled up in the function room.

'The long one,' she said.

'Well, the difference between new and used engine oil is that, during its use, the oil picks up a lot of heavy metals. Arsenic, barium, cadmium, lead and aluminium, among others. They are toxic and are also known carcinogens, as well as being terato-genic, which means they cause a higher risk of birth defects if people—and animals—are exposed to them. But that's not the biggest problem.'

'What is?'

'The biggest problem is the number of PAHs, sorry, polycyclic aromatic hydrocarbons that this oil contains. These hydrocarbons do occur naturally in oil deposits, but they're also formed during combustion in motor engines, so their concentration in used oil is extremely high. Do you want me to explain what they are?'

'Yes, please.'

'Well, they are chemical compounds that basically consist of a number of rings fused together. They're known as aromatics, because their atoms emit a powerful aroma—it's what gives used oil that sharp, almost choking smell. They can be incredibly toxic—far more so than the heavy metals themselves, and they are a lethal organic pollutant.'

Craig took a deep breath before continuing.

'Benzene is the simplest of the aromatic hydrocarbons, and probably the only one most people have heard of, but you won't find it in used engine oil. You'll find the more complex ones there. The more dangerous ones, known as priority pollutants. Naphthalene, pyrene, fluoranthene, phenanthrene, benzanthracene, benzoperylene. And others, too. There are probably more than twenty different PAHs in that oil, including the alkylated phenanthrenes and naphthalenes.'

Jade felt her heart sinking so heavily it was just about down on the tarmac next to her bare feet.

'What do they all do?' she asked.

'Long term, a number of them are known human carcinogens. They're also teratogenic, as well as mutagenic, which means they are capable of changing your DNA. Most commonly, this will increase the incidence of various cancers over time.'

'What about the short-term effects?' she asked.

'Exposure to the fumes can cause nose, throat and skin infections, as well as lung irritation. The eyes can be affected as well.'

Jade could understand that.

'Exposure to the oil itself would cause skin irritation,' Craig continued. 'Allergic contact dermatitis. Itching, sores, swelling, redness. The hydrocarbons can be absorbed through the skin. They are stored in the body's fat cells. People who come into contact with used engine oil have an exceptionally high risk of bladder cancer, because the hydrocarbons are detoxified by the liver, but retoxify in the kidneys as the body tries to excrete them. But we're back to the long-term effects now, because the latent period for disease after exposure can be as long as twenty or twenty-five years.'

'That's the risks for humans?' Jade said.

'For humans, yes.'

'What about animals? Smaller organisms?'

'The smaller the organism, the more serious the effects will be. Just one litre of used engine oil is capable of contaminating a million litres of water. And it ends up in the water. It always does, even if it's spilled on land. Whether it's washed away by rain over time, or seeps down through the soil to the water table, it will cause severe pollution. It will kill off fish, plankton, frogs, anything it comes into contact with. The ones that survive exposure to the oil itself will die later, as a result of disease. A high concentration of used engine oil dumped into a water system could cause an environmental catastrophe.'

Craig cleared his throat softly.

'Why are you asking, Jade?'

'I need you to sketch out a hypothetical scenario for me.'

'Go ahead.'

'I don't know if you remember a news report a while ago, about one of Pakistan's old tankers that was headed for recycling with a load of used oil, and ended up sinking just off the coast of Sri Lanka.'

'Yes, I remember that well. What about it?'

'What would happen if another of those tankers ended up sinking just off the coastline here, and discharging its load of used engine oil into the St Lucia estuary? And what if it happened later tonight, at the peak of the spring tide?'

Silence at the other end. Then, 'Tonight?' Craig repeated.

'Yes.'

The medical rep walked out of the hospital again and headed purposefully towards her car. Jade circled round to stand behind the Renault.

'The oil would flood the estuary. I don't think you could avoid that happening. The problem is that the estuary is a sheltered environ. Now, if you're going to have an oil spill, the two main issues are the time it will take the oil to disperse and the initial biological impacts of the spill.'

'Tell me more.'

'Ideally, you'd pray that it spilled on an exposed, rocky headland, where it would disperse in about six months. Next best would be a coarse-grained, sandy beach, which would be free of oil in about a year. Incidentally, that was what the beach in Sri Lanka was like. But an estuary is extremely vulnerable, because it can retain oil for more than ten years. And, of course, the numbers of species that will be affected by the spill will be extremely high.'

Ten years? Jade swallowed hard.

The sales rep moved closer, eyeing the BlackBerry in a way that told Jade her five minutes were already more than up.

'Carry on,' she said, edging away from the blonde woman. With any luck, she'd be able to keep the car between them for long enough to hear everything Craig had to say.

'The oil would probably reach Lake St Lucia itself, and it would basically annihilate every small organism in its path. We're talking instant and total destruction of everything from plankton to bivalves to the smaller crustaceans and urchins. It would wipe them out. It's difficult to think of a bigger ecological disaster, because more than a hundred species of fish use the estuary as a nursery.'

'What else?'

'The other creatures that would be worst affected would be sea birds, larger fish and crustaceans, and those that survived the oil would no longer have a food supply.'

'If you don't mind . . .' The sales rep's voice was sharp. She headed around the back of the car towards Jade.

'Just one more minute, please,' Jade whispered to her, pressing a hand over the phone's mouthpiece.

'The estuary and the surrounding beach would be a mess, of course. A blackened, stinking, desolate mess. The coral reefs and sponges would be totally contaminated. Boating and all other water activities would be banned until the oil had dispersed. Economically, the tourism industry would collapse. Fishing would no longer be possible. It would be . . .'

Craig paused for a moment. Then he spoke again with a new sharpness in his voice. 'Jade, please tell me this is a hypothetical question. That there's not a tanker drifting towards the shore-line right now. My God, if there was, if that happened—it would destroy everything we've been working so hard to achieve.'

'It's not at sea yet, but it will be soon,' Jade said. 'It will be heading out from Richards Bay harbour in a couple more hours.'

'From the harbour? But why?'

'Because the CEO of Richards Mining, a man called Patrick Zulu, is behind all of this. I think he's been planning it for months, probably ever since he got hold of the report on the other tanker. He's going to engineer an environmental catastrophe that will make it impossible for the government to rule in favour of the environmentalists, and will allow strip mining of the dunes within the nature reserve. Craig, I don't know what you'll be able to do in that time, but you need to do something. Call Pillay. Get him to get hold of the Green Scorpions. They'll have to try and stop that tanker before it gets out into open water. And I have some other instructions for Pillay as well. These are very urgent. Please tell him it's a life or death situation.'

'I will.' Craig's voice sounded firm.

Jade told him, as fast and clearly as possible, what she needed Pillay to do.

'And you need to organise a clean-up crew to get to the harbour as fast as possible.'

'I know. I'll get onto it immediately.'

'Good.'

'But, Jade, what about you?'

'Don't worry about me.'

Jade ended the call and, thanking the medical rep profusely, handed the woman her phone. She was barefoot, wearing borrowed clothing. She had no ID on her and no money, and was armed only with a Christmas-cracker penknife. There was no way she'd get through the harbour gate again, and nothing she could do to stop the tanker from setting sail. But there was somewhere else she needed to go, because if Pillay didn't make it there in time, people were going to die.

41

It was a ten-minute jog from the hospital entrance to the dilapidated block of flats where Jade had first seen Bradley. She ran the last section, praying that she wouldn't land squarely on a piece of glass with her bare feet. She ran past a pub on the corner—or perhaps it was more of a shebeen. At any rate, it was the only sign of activity in the area. A few old cars were parked outside and through the open door she saw the drinkers—all black men—sitting at the bar.

Jade guessed that in this poorer part of town, black and white would still be strictly segregated. This wasn't the well-off middle class with their starched shirts and leather briefcases, the ones that were shown drinking and laughing in the Castle Lager advertisements, all races together in brotherly unity. This was the ragged edge of society and, even though circumstances might force them to live side by side, they remained deeply distrustful of those who were different, the old scars of apartheid still as raw and ugly as they had always been.

Up ahead was the block of flats—number seventeen, where the Zulu mother had been caring for the noisy children. And flat number eighteen. Its windows were unlit.

The street outside the apartment was also quiet. No sign of any police cars, marked or unmarked. But Jade couldn't let herself think about what would happen if Pillay had misunderstood what she wanted him to do. Or underestimated its urgency.

In the darkness, she had to cast around for a while before she found the narrow but well-used pathway she had been down the last time she was there.

Stumbling over roots and branches in what was now almost total darkness, she stopped halfway and listened for any sounds, but there was nothing to be heard.

And then she reached the embankment above the railway track.

Jade half climbed and half slid down the steep slope. Then she sprinted down the centre of the track, her feet barely making a noise on the railway sleepers, to the building she'd seen before. At the time, she had assumed it was occupied by squatters. With a chill, she now realised the truth of what she'd seen, but hadn't understood.

She recalled the old train stood in the dilapidated station, seemingly neglected and forgotten, and those shiny well-used tracks that ran in the direction of the harbour. It was the same train that she'd seen chugging up the hill away from the harbour, as Bradley had taken them out to sea on the speedboat.

Most tellingly of all, she remembered the smell. That choking, filthy stink of used oil. At the time she'd thought it was coming from old machinery, but now she realised it wasn't.

And she remembered the coughing sound she'd heard. A miserable, rough, painful cough, coming from damaged lungs.

Lungs that had, perhaps, been damaged by ongoing exposure to the fumes of used engine oil.

The oil tanker she'd seen was in no way seaworthy. So, if it was going to go out to sea carrying a load of toxic oil, it would have to be refitted first. Welded, patched, its hull repaired in order for the cargo to be loaded. That would have required materials—and also a labour force.

Now that she was closer to the station, the air smelt harsh, bitter, chemical-laced. She breathed in as slowly as possible, because the poisonous fumes were catching in her throat and burning her nose, and it was taking all the effort she possessed not to cough them straight back out again.

She moved closer to the large square entrance. This time, the huge gates were wide open. The interior of the building was dimly lit. She moved off the tracks and approached the entrance cautiously, crouching down before she peered round the edge of the doorway, hoping nobody would be watching the entrance.

The three-wagon train was inside, and the floor of the gloomy-looking station was covered with what looked like thousands of cylindrical objects, each about a metre in length and half as wide. They weren't stacked neatly, but were scattered in higgledy-piggledy groups. Some lay on their sides, others were stacked on their tops in tall piles that reached almost to the ceiling.

Their shape looked familiar, although it took her a moment to realise what they were.

Oil drums.

There was a mass of drums here. The small space was filled with them. The oil smell was so sharp it seemed to cut through the air.

But if these drums represented the *Karachi*'s entire load, it was good news. A full tanker could carry the contents of hundreds of thousands of drums. So perhaps this meant the ship was not sailing with a full load. Perhaps this was all the oil they'd been able to get hold of. In which case, if it sank, the extent of the environmental damage would surely be far less.

Jade couldn't see anybody in the disused station. She waited, listening.

Then, as quietly as she could, she walked across the floor, weaving her way around the piles of empty drums, grimacing as her bare feet encountered viscous and stinking puddles of oil. There must be a way through, an entrance that would lead her to the place where she had heard the man coughing.

A man who was not a vagrant; not a drunk.

A man who was one of those in their twenties and thirties that Pillay had told her had disappeared.

Fixing up a toxic tanker would require a labour force. And what better way to go about getting one than by kidnapping and imprisoning people who would be disposed of once the job was over?

At the far end of the building, she saw a door.

This was it. This was the place she'd heard the coughing.

The door was narrow, made of steel, and it was bolted shut from the outside. Its two giant metal bolts made the ones the handyman had welded to the doors of the chalets at the resort look like toys.

'Hey!' she shouted. She rapped on the door, leaned close and listened. 'Anyone in there? I've come to let you out.'

Nothing but silence.

And then she heard a cough.

A deep, hoarse, rattling cough that immediately made her think of lungs that had been exposed to too many toxic oil fumes.

The men were in there. They were staying quiet, out of suspicion perhaps. They were sick. But at least they were alive.

Jade grabbed the lower bolt and wrestled it open. Then she turned her attention to the top one. This one was more difficult and she found she couldn't budge it. Glancing around for something that could help her, she saw a number of bricks. Big, rough breeze blocks with holes through the middle. The same kind of bricks her captors had tied to Neil's ankles before they had sent him on his final deadly plunge.

Jade picked one of them up. Using this would help her to knock the stubborn bolt open.

But just as she was about to strike the metal, she heard footsteps approaching. The piles of drums had a weird effect on the acoustics of the place. Although there was, logically, only one entrance to the building, Jade wouldn't have been able to tell from which direction the steps were coming, because the sound was bouncing off the rounded surfaces of a thousand drums.

Could this be Pillay?

Jade's heart quickened at the possibility. But if it wasn't, she needed to get out of sight. Taking the brick with her, she squeezed behind one of the big piles of drums.

'. . . How long to go now?' A man's voice, with a strong South African accent. Like the footsteps, the voice seemed to come from everywhere and nowhere at the same time. Jade shrank back behind her makeshift cover.

With a cold feeling, she realised that she was too late. There was no sign of the police, and these men must have come ready to dispose of the workforce.

'They're leaving the harbour now, Kobus.' She recognised Bradley's voice. High and tense. He sounded wired. A torch was turned on and the beam bobbed up and down, casting crazy shadows on the ceiling, giving her a rough idea of where they were standing. 'Another hour and the *Karachi* will be in position.'

'And then you make the call?' Kobus emphasised the word 'you.'

'Then I make the call.'

Both men laughed loudly. Then Kobus groaned. 'I need medication, man. More of those pills. My arm is bloody killing me. That bitch. Drowning was too good for her. You should have let me . . .'

'Hey!' Bradley interrupted him.

'What?'

'The bottom bolt is open.'

'Well, who was the last person to lock it?'

'I was. When I brought the crew back here earlier.'

'You wouldn't forget something like that.'

'No, I wouldn't.'

The torch beam swung to and fro, searching. Jade ducked lower behind her cover.

'Well, with all these drums around, you're not going to find a prowler easily. Why the hell were they all dumped here, anyway?'

'Insurance,' Bradley said. 'I told the bosses we didn't need to top up, that three-quarters of a tanker-load would do the job. But they wanted more oil. They wanted that tanker so full of dirty oil that its pods were bursting. That's what they told me. The heaviest load possible. So I got hold of another few thousand drums from another supplier in Pakistan and managed to ship them over in time. Just to be sure. It's all inside the *Karachi* now.'

Jade bit her lip hard. This was the worst news possible. The tanker was fully loaded and it was going to spew the maximum load of oil into the ocean when it sank. Or, to be more accurate, when it was scuttled.

'What's going to happen to the drums?' Kobus asked.

'They'll stay in here with the bodies. This building's harbour property. It'll be demolished next week. They'll implode it and compact it and lay concrete over it. Quick and easy. It'll hide everything.'

'What about our payment?'

'Your money's in the bag here.'

'Great. I'll leave as soon as we're finished, then.' Jade heard the distinctive sound of a zipper opening.

'Thanks. Hey, man, thank you.' Kobus was clearly impressed by what he saw. 'So—you going to give me the gun, then?'

'What?'

'The gun. Your silenced weapon. I told you, man, I'd do this job. I'd sort out these workers for you. I know you don't like killing, but I'm OK with it.'

'Kobus, I know that. And I tried.' Bradley sounded unexpectedly sad.

'What?'

'I tried for you. I really did. I wanted to give you another chance after you killed the wrong girl at the chalet.'

'What girl? What are you talking about?' Jade heard panic in his voice now.

'The stabbing. Look, boet, I'm sorry. You messed up then, big time. There was no need to do that. It was the dumbest move you could have made, and it could have jeopardised the whole operation. It nearly got me fired, and it alerted the police.'

'The stabbing? What are you talking about? Wait, buddy, remember back in jail we promised . . .'

'I'm sorry. I'm just so sorry.' Bradley sounded as if he was about to cry.

'Shit! Don t . . .'

The air was split by the muted bang of a silenced weapon. Twice in quick succession. Thwack . . . thwack.

Looking round the drums again, she saw Bradley train the torch onto Kobus's prone body. He sniffed and made a sound that Jade could only guess was a sob.

She hunkered down. Didn't even breathe.

Then Bradley bent down and picked up a brick, hefting it the same way Jade had done. He was going to use it to knock back the rusty bolt on the door, and then he was going to murder the occupants of that room in exactly the same way he'd just killed his old cellmate. Except most likely he wouldn't be crying while he did it.

The bolt moved back with a screech.

Bradley swung the door open.

Beyond it, Jade saw the steel bars of a sturdy security gate. Christ, the men were being kept in a cage.

This was going to be like shooting fish in a barrel. He could get to every one of the occupants of that room. They had nowhere to hide and no means of retaliating. She could see their hunched forms and frightened faces as they cowered away from the light of the torch. The beam flickered over clothes and skin stained pitch black with oil.

What should she do now?

She could let this happen and simply stay where she was. There was a good chance he would make a hasty exit after the shooting, and an even better chance that he'd be out of ammo.

Or she could try and stop him before he started shooting.

As Bradley raised his gun, Jade took a deep breath and threw the brick she was holding with all her might.

42

Craig stabbed the disconnect button on his cellphone. Moving over to the window, he stared outside. It was completely dark—there was a new moon—but he could hear the sounds of the sea. Reassuring sounds that had, in various places and at various distances, soothed his mind for most of his life.

He still couldn't believe that this could be the last night that this estuary would remain an unspoilt natural paradise.

Craig kicked out at the sofa in frustration. He'd done all he could. First, he'd contacted Inspector Pillay, who had promised he would notify his superiors and the Green Scorpions straight away, and get a team down to the harbour as soon as possible. Pillay had also said he would do his best to get a clean-up crew on standby, but that this could be tricky as it was usually organised after a catastrophe had taken place.

Craig had made sure he'd given Pillay Jade's specific instructions. Don't go down to the harbour, Jade had said. Go straight to the old station on the corner of Plantation and West streets. Go there with another police officer and have your weapon ready. If you hurry, you'll be in time to save lives.

Craig had then phoned a mate of his who worked in the National Sea Rescue Institute in Richards Bay and asked if he'd be able to help. The buddy had said he doubted he'd be able to do anything at such short notice, but he would try.

And then he'd called another friend, a marine ecologist who owned a boat that was currently moored at one of the resorts in St Lucia. The ecologist hadn't picked up, but Craig had left him an urgent message on his voicemail.

What more could he do? What more?

He'd spent the last ten minutes pacing the room, each time stopping when he reached the window.

Outside, he could hear the waves rushing to shore. The spring tide was coming in, marking the beginning of the end for the estuary and its incredible, unique ecosystem.

Craig had seen the devastation wreaked by oil spills. He'd walked over the sticky, stinking sand and seen the corpses of fish floating white-bellied in the dark and oily shallows. He'd seen birds desperately trying to preen the oil from their saturated feathers, in the process ingesting enough of the toxic substance to kill them. Some died fast, some more slowly. Many starved to death, flapping in blackened, pathetic little heaps on the dirty sand.

He thought of St Lucia's beautiful pink flamingos . . . how many would survive, he wondered?

The worst of it was that, until now, nobody in the world had ever had to deal with a tanker disaster in such a fragile ecosystem involving massive quantities of used oil. Predicting the full effect all the added toxins and the PAHs would have was impossible.

'Are you managing with your phone calls?'

Elsabe's soft voice floated across the room. He turned and saw her standing near her bedroom door, watching him. He never could quite read her expression. Once again, he wondered why she was with him now. She'd made it clear that romantic involvement was out of the question right now. He'd thought she needed time to heal, to recover from her loss, just as he had done. But how much time was enough?

Perhaps she saw him as a sort of big brother—somebody to lean on.

'I'm fine. I just wish there was something I could do.'

Elsabe shrugged. 'You've done all you can. You've made the calls.' She moved over to the fridge, opened it and poured herself a glass of water from the plastic jug inside.

'I have. But standing here isn't going to save the damn estuary.'

'They also serve who only stand and wait,' Elsabe said quietly, and it took Craig a moment to remember the title of the sonnet she was quoting from. It was 'On his Blindness'—they'd studied it in Matric and he'd practically learnt it by heart.

Then she continued, as if she'd thought perhaps he hadn't understood what she was saying, 'You can't always go out there and save the world yourself. Sometimes you have to leave that job to other people.'

'Other people who aren't going to be able to get the damn job done,' Craig muttered.

He wished he could be out there now, fighting the battles himself, defending the coastline he loved. Like Jade was doing. Jade and her cop friend, David. She had said there were irresolvable complications in their relationship, but he thought the two of them were well suited. They were both people who were accustomed to acting, not waiting. To getting out there and doing what needed to be done.

What was he?

Things weren't going to work out with Elsabe. He knew that for a fact. Perhaps he'd known it instinctively the very first time he'd met her, when they had both been standing at the edge of the tarmac and gazing in horror at the wreckage strewn in front of them.

But would he . . . could he be strong enough for Jade?

He had a feeling that her tastes ran towards short-haired, muscular men. Men of action, tough and unsmiling. Men who were familiar with firearms and close-quarter combat.

How on earth could a long-haired, bearded environmentalist compete? He didn't know, but perhaps . . . perhaps he could try.

Elsabe cleared her throat, tearing Craig away from his thoughts.

'I'm going back to Johannesburg tomorrow.'

'Oh. You are?'

She nodded. 'I want you to come and visit me. Soon, because I'm flying to Namibia on Monday morning. Come and stay with me for a night or two. If you're not busy, I'd love you to travel with me as well.'

Craig was stunned. 'You'd like that?'

'I would.' She smiled at him and, for the first time, he thought she was really looking at him. At Craig, the person. Not simply staring out from her own tormented thoughts.

'I'd love to. That would be great. Of course, it depends on what happens here. I might be busy sorting out this disaster. But if I'm not . . . then yes, I'd love to come and stay.'

'I'm sorry.' Elsabe moved closer and touched his arm. It felt electric. 'You've been so patient. You've given me what I needed most. Time. Time to heal. To get over what happened. Craig, I think I'm nearly ready.'

Standing on tiptoe, she brushed her lips against his. Then she turned and walked back to her bedroom, leaving Craig rooted to the spot, in a state of disbelief at what had just happened.

43

Jade didn't throw the heavy brick at Bradley. That would have been pointless. Even if she'd managed to hit him, which was unlikely given the distance and the dim light, it wouldn't have slowed him down for more than a moment.

Instead, she threw it diagonally away from him. She launched the brick at the tallest pile of oil drums she could see. It smashed into them with a deafening clang, and then thudded to the floor, bouncing off a couple more drums on its way. Her aim was true, and the impact rocked the topmost drum sideways. It teetered and fell, banging and bouncing down the pile before clattering to the ground.

The noise was thunderous. Discordant sound filled the covered railway siding, seemingly coming from everywhere and nowhere at once.

Bradley's reaction was swift. He spun away from the locked door, weapon in one hand, torch in the other. Its beam of light danced over the drums and Jade flattened her body against her makeshift cover, smearing herself with oil in the process. Her heart was banging so fast and loud she almost thought he might hear it.

She hadn't saved the men inside the doors. Not yet, anyway. All she had given them was a stay of execution. But she had sent Bradley a message, loud and clear, that there was somebody else in the building.

What was he going to do now?

Jade strained her ears, which were still ringing from the cacophony of the falling drums, but she could hear nothing.

Was he standing and listening too?

What was he doing, dammit?

The silence stretched to breaking point.

And then, suddenly, Jade heard a soft footfall. She couldn't make out the direction from which it was coming, but it sounded close. Too close.

And then the torch beam shone onto the wall above her.

Bradley was checking every possible hiding place, quickly, quietly and methodically. It was just a pity that the drums Jade had chosen to hide behind were the ones nearest the makeshift prison, which was the first place that Bradley would logically look.

The beam's arc grew smaller and brighter as he drew closer.

Jade took a deep breath. Talking wouldn't get her far, but it was her only option now. She didn't know what she should say. Babbling nonsense was probably the best bet. Something unexpected that would surprise him, make him hesitate, if only for a couple of vital seconds. Because, thanks to the example that Kobus had just given her, she knew that begging for her life wasn't going to work.

And then, from the doorway, she saw a second flashlight beam appear and the thick silence in front of her was then broken by a male voice—one she recognised, although it sounded as if its owner had recently inhaled some helium.

'Police! Who's inside there? Come out with your hands in the air!'

It was Inspector Pillay.

Bradley's torch swung away from her hiding place and she heard his sharp intake of breath. Now she knew exactly where he was. He was right opposite her, on the other side of the wall of drums, and now he must be aiming his gun at the approaching detective.

Jade did the only thing she could. She kicked out at the nearest drum and sent it, and the one above it, toppling down and away from her.

Please let it hit him or at least throw him off balance, and give Pillay the chance he needed, she prayed.

Then, even above the clanging of bouncing metal, Jade heard

only too clearly the sound she'd heard three times too many on this holiday so far—the shattering report of a gun being fired.

Chetty had captained a tugboat many times in the past. Sitting in the control-room chair with his hands on the two joystick-like controls in front of him, the sight he saw when he lifted his eyes from the brightly glowing gauges and computer screens to stare up and out of the window was all too familiar. He saw only miles and miles of blackness. Waves lit only by the faintest glimmer of the lights that came from the tugboat itself.

New moon and the harbour was blanketed in darkness.

Zulu was standing at the back of the control room and Chetty heard him catch his breath as he stared out of the rear window at the sight behind them.

A sight that was the polar opposite of usual. Something that Chetty knew he'd never see again.

High above the tugboat towered the steel mass of the ruined tanker, blackened and cancerous with rust. They were anchored right in front of it to allow the two men who were temporarily manning the tanker to winch up a narrow line. This in turn would pull up the towrope—a gigantic braid of Kevlar almost twelve inches in diameter and with a breaking strength of half a million kilograms, which was twice what the loaded tanker weighed.

Once the rope was securely fastened in place, nothing could stop them. Nothing at all.

The *Amandla*, the tug that they were using, was the most powerful of the harbour's fleet. She was one of the new generation of tugboats, a successor to the most famous pair of South African tug legends, the *Wolraad Woltemade* and the *John Ross*.

The *Amandla* was more than capable of handling the heaviest and largest super-tanker all on her own. Towing the smaller *Karachi* thirty-five nautical miles to the St Lucia estuary would take well under an hour.

'It's done.' Zulu's deep voice interrupted Chetty's thoughts.

'Are the men in position?'

'They are.'

The tanker had no working radio communications; in fact,

most of its rotting and rusting deck was impassable, a fact that they had discovered a few months ago when a repair crew member had broken right through a weak spot. The rusted, paper-thin metal had split under his weight and, with a scream that Chetty had yet to erase from his memory, he had tumbled more than thirty metres to his death.

For the voyage out to sea, the two crew members would remain on deck, but in one of the few small areas that, like the tanker's entire hull, had been properly patched and repaired.

The powerful tugboat responded instantly to Chetty's commands. The engines pushed the craft forward, travelling slowly until the slack in the towrope had been taken up. Then he heard the change in their tune; a deeper, growling noise as they took up the immense weight of the tanker and started to move her relentlessly forward.

It would take a while for their speed to build up, but they were now on course. They were moving out of the harbour and nothing, nothing at all, could stop them now.

44

On the other side of the drums, Bradley let out a cry of pain. A thud followed, as if he'd staggered sideways into one of the barrels.

He'd been hit. Shots had been fired and Inspector Pillay's bullet had found its mark.

A moment later, she heard Pillay's rather breathless voice again.

'Drop your weapon and put your hands in the air.'

A whimper from Bradley.

'I can't. I can't do that. My shoulder . . .'

'Drop your weapon now.'

Pillay's command was followed by a clattering sound that could only be Bradley's gun hitting the floor.

Jade stepped out from behind the empty drums.

Bradley was motionless, as if pinned in place against the barrels by the beam of the torch. He was grasping his right shoulder with his now-bloody left hand.

'Jade!' Pillay glanced up at her in surprise before returning his attention to his prisoner. 'Get down on the floor. Down. Flat on your stomach. Put your arms behind your back.'

'My shoulder . . .'

'I don't care about your shoulder.' Pillay stepped closer. 'You should have thought about the consequences before you fired your weapon at a police officer.'

The drum rattled as Bradley lowered himself awkwardly to the floor.

'He wasn't only planning on shooting you,' Jade said. She pointed towards the barred doorway. 'Those missing people you've been looking for—well, they're in there. They were forcibly recruited for the tanker repair job. They're sick from exposure to the oil, and probably from malnutrition as well. The job is finished now and he was going to shoot them all and leave the bodies here.'

'I see.' Pillay briefly knelt down to slip a pair of handcuffs onto the now-prone Bradley's wrists. 'Here. Put your hands in front of you and I'll cuff them that way round.'

Then, keeping his gun trained on Bradley's chest, Pillay dialled a number on his cellphone.

'Moodley?' he asked, and Jade realised he was speaking to his assistant. His voice sounded firm, although his hands were trembling like branches in a high wind. 'Yes, I'm inside already. I came in through the big entrance where the railway tracks run. You can join me, but first call an ambulance. In fact, call three of them. I have one man with a gunshot wound and a number of other people who require immediate medical attention. Oh, and I've got one dead body too.'

He waited, listened, glanced at his phone, and then his expression changed.

'I'll see you soon,' he said. 'I have to go. Captain Macpherson from the Environmental Management Inspectorate is on the line.'

Jade listened to the one-sided conversation as the detective spoke to the official from the highly specialised environmental police unit that was popularly known as the Green Scorpions. Pillay's responses were brief and she saw his hopeful expression change to one of helpless disappointment.

Inside her, the knot of anxiety tightened. They had been in time to save the lives of the workers, but if the entire St Lucia estuary was contaminated, the criminals would have won.

Jade didn't know what could be done out at sea. Perhaps a navy vessel could be dispatched to stop them. Hell, if necessary, perhaps a military helicopter could be used. Surely some contingency plan could be put into place within the limited time.

After the call came to an end, the police officer turned to Jade. 'The EMI crew won't be in time,' he said. 'They're still fifteen minutes away from the harbour and they've learned that the tanker has just left shore. He says there's nothing they can do to stop it. Not at such short notice. The closest navy vessel is in

Durban and they were unable to requisition a helicopter. They will be able to prosecute the offenders, but by then the damage will have been done. The estuary will have been destroyed.'

Ten depressing minutes later, Pillay's assistant arrived.

'Attach a pair of handcuffs to this suspect's ankles, please,' Pillay told him. 'Then go and fetch the first-aid box from the van. We need a dressing and a bandage to protect his bullet wound while we wait for the ambulance to arrive.'

Bradley didn't utter a sound as Moodley fastened a pair of handcuffs around his ankles.

Pillay bent down and unfastened the bunch of keys hanging from Bradley's belt.

'I wonder if any of these open that security door,' he said.

He walked over, stepping carefully over Kobus's body as he called out a sympathetic-sounding greeting to the men locked inside.

'Don't worry,' he said. 'We'll get you out of there as soon as we can and the paramedics are on their way.' He paused, then unclipped a small torch from his belt and shone it into the dingy room. 'Mr Baloyi, is that you over there? I recognise you from your photograph, sir. You've been on our Missing Persons list since August. And Mr Padayachee? You'll be glad to hear that we have already reported your missing truck.'

Sounding as happy as if he'd just arrived at a long-awaited school reunion, Pillay set about unlocking the big steel-barred door.

Jade didn't share his emotions. Perhaps that was because her world was too black and white. You lost or you won and, right now, they had lost and the criminals they'd tried so hard to beat had won.

Frustration boiled inside her as she thought of the tanker, sailing out of the harbour, every minute taking it closer towards its intended destination. It was impossible that it could not be stopped; that the ship could sail freely for another half-hour until it reached its destination.

Dammit, she didn't even want to think about that beautiful blue ocean. Those golden sands. The wealth of ocean life. All soon to be blackened, poisoned, eradicated after the ship was scuttled, which would presumably be done through strategically placed explosives. They would punch through the hull, sinking the ship and sending her lethal load of oil spewing out into the ocean.

Who would press the button? Jade wondered.

And then she remembered what Kobus had said before he died.

'And then you make the call.'

There must be a remote control trigger for the detonator. Nowadays, these devices could easily be set off by making a simple cellphone call.

Then Jade thought about the chunky phone that was around Bradley's neck. He seemed to wear it permanently. In fact, there it was now, lying on the concrete next to him, attached to its owner by a tough-looking lanyard.

Was it possible? Jade wondered.

Was it?

She felt in the waistband of her borrowed Lycra pants and took out the tiny knife that the paramedic had given her. Then she walked over to where Bradley was lying, his eyes closed, having his wounded shoulder bandaged by Pillay's assistant.

'Excuse me,' she said.

She opened the knife, knelt down and, in one swift movement, cut through the lanyard.

The phone felt strangely heavy in her hand.

'What are you doing?' Moodley asked.

At that point, Bradley opened his eyes. When he saw she had his phone he reacted immediately.

'Hey!' he screamed. 'Give that back!'

He started to jackknife like a stranded fish, bucking and writhing in a vain effort to get free of the handcuffs that bound him. Moodley dropped the bandage and sprang to his feet, fumbling for his gun.

'Er . . . Ms De Jong, that phone may contain important evidence. Please don't tamper with it,' Pillay shouted, his voice worried.

Jade ignored him.

Bradley's reaction had told her everything she needed to know. The trigger code for the detonator was right here, hidden in the cellphone's address book. She was sure of it. If she could find and dial the right number in time, the oil would still be spilled, but hopefully the spillage would be confined to the harbour area where it would cause far less damage than if the tanker was scuttled near the estuary.

The question was, which number was it?

She was sure Bradley would have it saved on his phone, ready to dial.

She scrolled through his list of contacts. How would she recognise it? It could be saved under a random name. There was a number for Chetty. Another one there—her heart jumped in surprise—for Monique. More numbers—for steel suppliers, welding equipment rental, harbour security, and a few more names of women.

She couldn't dial each of them in turn. The list was too long. Too many numbers saved on this phone.

And then she saw it.

It was so obvious she could have laughed.

Karachi.

Bradley was still yelling, but his voice was beginning to sound ragged. He was pounding his fists on the concrete in front of him.

Jade had no idea if this would work or not, but she knew she had to try.

She punched the dial button and waited for the call to connect.

45

Zulu stared through the back window of the captain's cabin. Behind him, all he could see was the great bulk of the rusty tanker, so close that it almost seemed as if the ship would run them down. Zulu had little knowledge of ships and sailing, but he'd seen the skill with which Chetty had handled the tug, sending the craft back and forth across the waves with such power and dexterity that the sea underneath them had felt like a hard, rutted dirt road.

He was confident that the *Karachi* would not mow them down.

'Five more minutes and we'll be out of the harbour,' Chetty said.

Zulu didn't want to tempt fate by responding to the comment.

In spite of the impenetrable front he presented, he was still far from confident that this operation would succeed.

The problem was that not everything had gone according to plan. He just hoped that he himself would not be implicated in any way. At least he'd tried to put failsafe plans in place for that.

Chetty had made all the arrangements with Bradley, his second-in-command. The phone calls that Chetty had made to Pakistan and the companies that he had dealt with were all part of Zulu's plan to implicate him as a terrorist sympathiser. He'd made other calls on the man's office line as well, calls that would later be traced to people connected with known terrorist organisations. And while they had been working so closely together, he'd even managed to send a few emails from Chetty's laptop that, in due course, he was sure would be picked up by the police.

As for the money he'd paid him for his role in this project—even those funds had been transferred from a Karachi bank that in turn had obtained it from a shell account whose owner would prove to be untraceable.

Hopefully, when the investigation was completed, it would become clear that Chetty had willingly committed this act of environmental sabotage after being well paid to do so by an extremist group.

'Watch your seas, people of the Western world.' That would be the message that this tanker would send. 'You think you are safe from us now. You believe your airways to be secure. But what about your oceans? We have more oil. We have enough oil, new and used, to destroy every beach from Miami to Chesapeake Bay, from Cornwall to the Gold Reef.'

Zulu hoped that the message, even if unwritten, would be clearly understood once the trail of evidence had been followed.

And, of course, Chetty himself would not be alive to argue the facts, having committed suicide shortly after jettisoning his lethal load.

He was sorry for whoever found his body, because it would not be a pretty sight.

Neither would Bradley's.

Zulu smiled grimly as he thought of his arrangements for disposing of the engineer who'd handled the repair project so efficiently. He had no doubt that this, at least, would succeed.

He himself had arranged for his private helicopter to take him off the tugboat and out of sight. The helicopter was already standing by, and the pilot could definitely be trusted as he was Zulu's eldest son.

It hurt him to admit it, even to himself, but he had made some poor decisions. What had started out as a multi-billion rand business, thriving and cash-rich, had turned into a financial black hole that was devouring all the money he had poured into it. The dunes he currently had permission to mine were now depleted of minerals. He'd used his final chunk of capital in attempting to rehabilitate them—a process that if not correctly followed would lose him the contract he was so desperately hoping for.

The one that would turn his business around, the one that would make him wealthy beyond his wildest dreams—permission to mine the dunes inside the conservation zone.

Though extreme, the damage caused by the capsized tanker would not be irreversible. Given time, Nature would heal herself. The lagoon and beach would eventually be repopulated, although admittedly they would never be the same, as many of the indigenous plants and animals would have been permanently wiped out.

The repopulation, Zulu estimated, would take about ten years. Possibly a little longer.

In the short term, the tourism and fishing industries in the area would collapse. This would cause a massive loss of jobs and bring the property industry to its knees. The local economy would be dealt what was, to all intents and purposes, a death blow.

And, in the light of this environmental catastrophe, the prospect of dune mining in a park that was otherwise a wasteland would suddenly seem a whole lot less important. In fact, it could be seen as a solution to the new—and serious—problems that would beset the area.

Mining would provide jobs that could no longer be offered by tourism. Zulu was certain that in the event of an act of environmental terrorism that put a stop to tourist-related activities in the area, the industrial and mining sectors would, through necessity, be encouraged to grow.

And legislation would be swiftly changed to allow it.

It had all seemed so good on paper, and putting the plan into action with the help of the corrupt harbour master and his Pakistani connections had seemed so surprisingly easy.

Until that damn blackmail attempt. He should have ignored it; told Bradley to pay the woman a couple of grand, which would have kept her quiet for long enough. And he would have, if he hadn't feared that somehow the blackmailer had found out about this operation, that Bradley had let something slip.

After that, everything had started going wrong. That single

decision had precipitated a chain of events that would prove to be as destructive as acid water leaking from a badly drained mine. Starting, of course, with the shocking discovery that the wrong woman had been murdered at the resort where Bradley's blackmailer was working. Why had Kobus done that? Even though he hadn't admitted to it, this error had almost jeopardised the entire operation.

There were still some loose ends to tie up—the policeman in hospital was one that he still had to sort out, and he hoped he would be able to do that discreetly and in time.

Whatever happened next, the *Karachi* would complete its deadly mission, providing the opportunity for Richards Mining to move into the iSimangaliso Wetland Park.

'Almost out of harbour waters,' Chetty said.

And then Zulu was jerked away from his thoughts as, suddenly, the impossible happened.

The tug tilted up like a see-saw, throwing him off his feet and flinging him back against the window he'd so recently been staring out of. The back of his head hit the glass and his vision blurred.

Then the tugboat was hit by a massive shockwave and the sea turned from rippling velvet into a jagged series of peaks and troughs. Huge waves crashed around them, flinging the tug from side to side.

'What the hell?' he heard Chetty cry. The engines accelerated to a scream as the *Amandla* bravely struggled to obey her captain's demands, but, even on maximum power, her efforts had no effect.

Again the deck tilted backwards. Steeper and steeper. Coffee cups, glasses and pieces of equipment tumbled off the shelves and slid around the floor.

Struggling to his feet, Zulu grabbed hold of the wall in front of him, which was now slanted at a forty-five-degree angle. He peered out through the porthole, unable to believe what he was seeing.

The *Karachi* was sinking, and fast. Faster than he had ever believed a ship could go down. Her prow was already fully underwater. As Zulu looked on in horror, a wave hit the glass of the captain's cabin and left behind a streak of oil.

'Hayibo!' he cried in shock. Her hull had been breached and

there was only one way that it could have happened so suddenly and violently. The explosives that had been so carefully placed at strategic points on the newly built hull must have been triggered.

Once the hull was pierced, the rusting vessel would have no integrity against the waves. Water would shoot straight up into her decaying body. Inside, the *Karachi* was like a colander. He remembered Bradley saying that.

Like a colander.

Two hundred tons of colander. Enough to drag the *Amandla* down with her.

'Get the cable undone!' he screamed at Chetty. 'The towrope. Get rid of it! The ship's going to drag us under!'

'The men are gone!' Chetty wailed. 'The men on the *Karachi* must have fallen overboard. They aren't responding to my requests.'

'Don't you have a bloody emergency cut-off mechanism here on this ship? Something that will free the damn line? What the hell good is a tugboat without a contingency plan in place for . . .'

But the tug lurched sideways and Chetty tumbled out of his seat and slid backwards down the near-vertical floor, howling with fear.

Moments later, Zulu felt the inexorable downward pull.

The tanker sank to the ocean floor, dragging the *Amandla* down along with it.

Dark, oily water surged around the tug and there was a sudden smoothness as the choppy surface of the ocean was replaced by still water. The power flickered and then died. The pressure of the water forced open the doors to the steering room and Zulu felt it lift him swiftly up against the canted ceiling. He kicked hard, desperately striving to keep his head above it, but his head banged against the ceiling and then there was no room.

There was no room.

Zulu's last thoughts were strangely comforting.

If Bradley had tried to double-cross them, he would not have lived to see the fruits of his efforts. Just a few moments after the explosives were detonated, he too would have died.

∎

Jade waited for the call to connect. All it took was a couple of seconds, although it felt like half a lifetime, before she heard it ringing

It rang once. Twice.

Then she heard a click and the call was cut off.

Standing in the old station, holding the phone with its broken lanyard in both her hands and looking down at its screen, Jade had absolutely no idea if her hunch had been correct. They were too far away from the sea to hear, or feel, the blast, which would in any case have taken place underwater and been muffled by tons of water.

Had she managed to sink the *Karachi* before it reached open water?

She had no idea.

Perhaps she should redial, to be sure. If it rang again, that would mean that the SIM card at the other end was still in existence and that the explosives hadn't been detonated.

But she didn't.

Jade couldn't have said what made her do what she did next— whether it was just one factor or a combination.

Perhaps it was instinct, perhaps blind luck. Perhaps it was the feeling she had that every loose end in this operation was being cut off with ruthless efficiency.

With a gentle underarm motion, she tossed the heavy phone back to Bradley. It landed on his thigh and slid down onto the floor.

'Oh, no, Ms De Jong, don't give it back to him now,' Pillay warned. 'He'll destroy any evidence on it.'

Eyes bulging, Bradley lunged forward with his handcuffed hands and grabbed hold of the instrument, groaning again as the effort hurt his damaged shoulder. Pulling himself into a kneeling position, he bent over the phone.

'Take it away from him and put it in an evidence—'

In a blinding flash of light, the cellphone that Bradley was clutching exploded.

Jade twisted away from the white-hot fireball, squeezing her eyes shut as she heard Pillay and his assistant shouting in shock. Flying shards stung her back and pricked her arms like miniature daggers.

She looked back and saw that, for Bradley at least, it was over. His hands were gone.

The project manager lifted bloody stumps to a sightless face, a face that was running with blood. His starched shirt and shiny tie looked as if somebody had taken a shredder to them.

He collapsed into a crouch, and then forward onto his head. His choking gasps soon fell silent.

46

David blinked, bright lights piercing his strangely sensitive eyes.

Where was he? Lying face-up on a hard mattress, the muted beeping of machinery all around him and the sweetish smell of disinfectant in his nostrils.

A tube in his wrist that tugged painfully at him when he shifted his arm, and his chest hurt.

Clearly, he was in hospital somewhere, but his befuddled brain refused to tell him where or why.

Memories trickled back, interrupted by periods of drowsiness when he fell asleep again, although whether this was for moments or minutes, he wasn't sure.

He remembered being shot and that Jade had been in the car with him when it happened.

Was she all right? When he tried to recall exactly what had happened in the time after the shooting, the best he could come up with was a confused and painful blur.

She must be alive. She must.

She was. Another memory, this one more puzzling than the others. Jade had been standing by his bed. Her hair was wet and bedraggled—she looked for all the world like she'd just climbed out of the sea.

'You took a bullet for me, David,' she said. 'You should never have done that, but you did. I love you.'

David smiled at the memory. And then he opened his eyes to see her there again, standing at the foot of his bed, watching him.

'Jade,' he said in a voice that was surprisingly hoarse and rusty.

The figure moved closer and David focused on her face.

It wasn't Jade.

It was Naisha. Dark hair tied back in a neatly pinned knot. Wearing a pale-blue maternity blouse over a pair of grey trousers. One hand protectively over her stomach and a look of confusion in her eyes.

'I'm sorry,' David whispered. 'I didn't mean . . .'

She shook her head. 'It's all right,' she said in a small, hurt voice. 'I'll come back later.'

She turned and left his bedside, walking swiftly away.

'Naisha, no!' David's attempt at calling her back didn't work. Shouting made him cough, which sent a lance of agony into his chest and set a machine behind him beeping loudly.

A nurse hurried over and fiddled with his drip.

'No talking,' she reprimanded him. 'Please, Mr Patel. And definitely no shouting.'

The world faded away into a grey blur.

When David woke again, another figure was standing at the top of his bed and staring down at him. Luckily, the identity of this solidly built man was unmistakable.

Moloi.

'Welcome back, Sup,' the black detective said.

'Where the hell am I?' David now found himself able to think more clearly.

Moloi looked pleased with himself. 'Richards Bay General Hospital. I took the early flight to Durban this morning, along with your wife.' He shifted his feet, frowned down at them and winced. 'You know, these new shoes are killing me. I've been standing here in them for about half an hour waiting for you to wake up.'

The black detective looked round for a chair. Spotting one at the other end of the ward, he walked over and fetched it. He lowered himself down into the flimsy plastic seat with a sigh of relief.

'I'm in icu?' David asked.

Moloi nodded.

'How'd you get in here then?'

'It was difficult.' The smug expression on Moloi's face dissolved as the chair let out an ominous cracking sound. Planting his feet more firmly on the floor, he continued. 'They said family only. I said I was family. They didn't believe me. Said if I was family, I'd be an Indian, like you. So I had no choice, Sup. I told them I was your brother-in-law. Do you even have a sister?'

David found, to his cost, that laughing produced the same painful results as coughing.

'Anyway, they let me in.' Moloi continued.

David tried to speak, but choked, each movement of his chest prompting a fresh wave of extreme pain.

'Take it easy, sir.' Moloi had obviously noticed his struggle.

David fell silent for a while. Every fibre in his ruptured, damaged body seemed to be screaming at him. He prayed for it to stop, but it didn't of course.

'I followed up on Themba, your man in Yeoville.' Moloi said.

The chair gave another loud creak and the black detective jumped. He stood up and carried it back to the corner of the ward. Then he returned to David's bedside and stood, shifting his feet uncomfortably.

David was still trying to make sense of his last words.

'Themba who?' he asked.

'Themba Msamaya, according to his lease agreement. The one you asked me to investigate.' Seeing David's blank look, Moloi hastened to explain. 'The postcard in the bedroom of the dead scuba-diving instructor. Something about 813. You said it might have relevance to her murder.'

'Oh, yes. Yes, of course.' The facts surfaced in David's befuddled mind, as did the recollection that something about the postcard had been nagging him. 'So, did you go there? What did you find?' he asked, realising he'd lost his familiar impatient tone, and instead sounded quivery and frail, like he'd suddenly aged by thirty years.

'I did.'

'And?'

'Msamaya wasn't in.'

'What do you mean, wasn't in?'

'I mean he was out. Not at home. His flat was locked.'

'Did you speak to anyone else?'

Moloi nodded. 'I spoke to the landlord, who also happens to be the caretaker. Not that it looks like he's been taking much care of the building.'

'What'd he say?'

'Said Msamaya hadn't caused any problems since he'd moved in, which was about six months ago. Paid his rent on time, lived quietly. The only issue Msamaya had was wanting Internet access, but the landlord couldn't organise a Telkom line so I think he gave up on that and found another way.'

'And the Internet?'

'He was job-searching. Apparently he's unemployed.'

'Oh.'

It all seemed plausible enough.

'The landlord thought I'd come to ask about his neighbour.'

'Msamaya's?'

'Yes. It seems the man who lives next door to him has had a couple of run-ins with the local police. He's suspected of dealing in heroin.'

'Ah.'

'Seems the neighbour is two months behind with his rent. He's been ducking and diving, and the landlord has a feeling that he's going to end up doing a runner. I said I'd go back later this week. I'll see if I can have a chat to Msamaya. Ask him about his neighbour and about the contents of that postcard.'

'Thanks.'

'I'll come and visit you later this afternoon, sir. Oh, and when you're out of ICU, I'll bring you some flowers, like a devoted family member would do.'

This time, David's chest was too sore for him to think about laughing. Besides, Moloi's mention of the word 'family' brought the situation with Naisha to mind, in all its painful clarity.

He groaned.

'I'd better go. Take care.'

David's eyes closed again as Captain Moloi walked out of the ICU.

■

At nine-thirty a.m. Richards Bay General Hospital was busy. Day-shift nurses in fresh-looking uniforms bustled down the corridors between the wards. The distinctive aroma of well-done toast still hung faintly in the air, signalling to Jade that the patients breakfast had been far better than hers.

In fact, Jade hadn't eaten anything at all and, although she was tempted to buy a coffee from the cafeteria she could see across the road from the lobby, she didn't want to risk missing Dr Abrahams.

If, indeed, he was still planning to visit the hospital that morning.

She stood in the corner next to a row of chairs that were all occupied. An elderly man in a wheelchair was parked at the end of the row. Jade waited as minute after minute ticked by, trying to suppress the urge to pace back and forth as David did in times of stress.

She'd decided she was going to drive back to Johannesburg as soon as she'd spoken to Dr Abrahams. The new rental car that she'd picked up earlier that morning was packed with holiday gear—David's as well as her own.

She checked the time on her phone again.

Nine thirty-five.

She could go now, if she wanted to. She didn't have to wait for Dr Abrahams. She could simply walk away with her questions unanswered. It wouldn't be the end of the world. She told herself she'd managed to live quite contentedly for nearly thirty-five years without the answers.

Admittedly though, until recently she hadn't even known that there were questions to ask.

Perhaps that was the problem. Once she had known there were questions, she was compelled to find out the answers.

Why was there no Elise de Jong buried in the Richards Bay cemetery?

Why had Mrs Koekemoer said it was a secret?

Right now, establishing the facts seemed like a good way to occupy her mind. To distract her from the memory of what had happened the night before, from the sound of Bradley's choking gasps and the sight of splintered bone protruding from ragged stumps.

Her arms would have looked like that if she hadn't followed her instincts and thrown the phone away. Her chest would have had a crater-sized hole in it, and her face would have been torn and shredded from the effects of the powerful explosives.

Jade rubbed her forehead to physically clear the thoughts.

Then she allowed herself to smile at the memory of the paramedic's utter confusion when he'd arrived at his latest call-out to find her there, yet again.

'Are you stalking me or something?' he'd asked. 'We can't carry on meeting like this. People will talk!'

Jade gave another private smile as she remembered how she'd waited for a moment when Pillay and his assistant were preoccupied with the forensics crew at the other side of the station. Then she had unzipped the gym bag that Bradley had handed to Kobus just before shooting him, and quietly passed each of the filthy, oil-streaked prisoners a generous wedge of the tightly packed money inside. It was the only way they were going to get any payment, she reasoned. Once the bag reached police headquarters, who knew what would happen to the cash? In any case, they deserved a sizeable bonus as compensation for their imprisonment, their near-starvation and their consequent health problems.

The news of the oil spill had travelled fast. It had been the top story on the radio earlier that morning. Clean-up crews were working hard to contain the oil. Thanks to the fact that the tanker had gone down when it was still in the harbour waters, it appeared that only that area had been contaminated. To Jade's relief, the spill had been successfully contained, and the St Lucia estuary and the surrounding coastline would remain an unspoilt paradise.

The elderly man in the wheelchair next to her began to cough, bringing her attention back to the present. It was a soft, dry cough, but once he had started, he couldn't seem to stop. Hands gripping the arms of his chair, shoulders shuddering, the man hunched over as the coughing overpowered him.

Jade turned away and walked out of the hospital's side entrance and into the cafeteria. The smell of toast was replaced by the aroma of coffee, and once again she was sorely tempted to order herself a mug.

Later, she decided.

She took a small plastic bottle of still water off the shelf, paid for it, and returned to the hospital lobby.

The elderly man was sitting upright again, taking in small, careful sips of air, as if frightened that breathing too deeply would provoke another round of coughing.

'Here you are,' Jade said, loosening the cap and placing the bottle gently in his lap.

'Thank you,' he whispered. 'My throat . . .'

Jade nodded. 'The air is very dry in here.'

He seemed to be breathing more easily now. And if he started coughing again, at least he would have some water to soothe his throat.

Jade turned her attention back to the lobby and saw Dr Abrahams. Or, rather, the back of him. That distinctive silver head of hair atop another dark suit. He was heading down the main corridor, walking briskly.

Today he was alone.

Stepping away from the elderly man in the wheelchair, Jade ran after the doctor, calling his name.

Dr Abrahams didn't look pleased to see her again, although Jade couldn't help wondering if he ever looked pleased about anything.

'You said I should wait for you in the lobby this morning and that you'd tell me about my mother.'

The doctor nodded, pursing his lips as if considering what he should say next.

A nurse holding a clipboard hurried past them, followed by an orderly who was walking more slowly and pushing a large steel trolley piled high with crumb-encrusted plates and dirty cups. The crockery rattled as the trolley bumped over a gap in the linoleum.

Jade wondered if Dr Abrahams would prefer to go somewhere quieter or more private, but he didn't move. After a short pause, he began to talk.

'Your mother was admitted to this hospital after a near-drowning incident when she was pregnant, and again when you were born. Then, a few months later, she came back for the third and last time.'

Jade nodded. Mrs Koekemoer had told her this, too.

'So the third time was after she developed cerebral malaria?' she asked.

With her question, Dr Abrahams's frown deepened. Behind him, another orderly with a loaded trolley approached and Jade stepped closer to the wall to allow him to pass.

'Your mother never had malaria,' he said. 'We tested her for it, of course, when she was admitted. But malaria was not the cause of the kidney failure that led to her death.'

'But . . .' Jade felt her mouth fall open and she made a conscious effort to close it.

But my father told me she died of cerebral malaria.

Or had he?

Had he ever actually said so in so many words? Or had he simply allowed Jade to assume that that was how she had died?

Had he simply presented her with a series of facts that led towards an obvious conclusion that she, as an investigator's daughter, would be drawn to make?

Old, half-remembered fragments of conversation spun through her mind. Her father answering her questions, or so she had thought at the time. Now, she realised, he had not been answering them directly at all.

'How did my mother die?'

'Kidney failure.'

'What caused that?'

'Cerebral malaria causes it sometimes.'

'How did my mother get malaria?'

'There was a very wet summer the year you were born. A lot of mosquitoes around. They can carry it. Richards Bay is a high-risk area for malaria in summer.'

Another realisation hit Jade like a punch in the gut.

In all likelihood, there had been a wet summer the year she was born. But now she remembered that her mother's death certificate had been dated early August. Right at the end of a cool, dry South African winter, a time when the risk of malaria would have been at its lowest.

So her father had gently guided her into believing a blatant untruth.

Jade found this almost impossible to accept. Commissioner De Jong had been a man of great integrity; a follower of the truth at all costs, no matter how long the hunt or how hard the result.

There was only one reason he could possibly have kept the real facts from his only child—he thought they would be too difficult for her to accept.

Jade swallowed hard. She met Dr Abrahams's enquiring gaze and looked directly into his hawk-like eyes.

'So what did cause my mother's kidneys to fail?' she asked.

47

The doctor moved aside, rather impatiently, as two more orderlies pushing wide linen carts approached.

'Perhaps we should talk somewhere else,' he said. 'Come this way.'

The doctor strode off down the corridor and Jade followed, staying behind him, just like his business-suited retinue had done the day before. She guessed that was what Dr Abrahams was used to—what he expected.

Their zigzagging walk through increasingly quieter and newer-looking corridors took a couple of minutes. Then Dr Abrahams stopped in front of a door marked 'Supervisor.' Taking a bunch of keys from his pocket, he quickly selected the right one and opened the door.

The small office was home to a desk, two chairs, piles of cardboard boxes, which Jade assumed from their labels contained spare uniforms and stationery, and shelves upon shelves of ancient-looking files.

There was a window at the back of the office, shaded by off-white blinds. Dr Abrahams walked over to the window and drew them up. Morning sun streamed in, dust motes dancing in its rays. Outside, Jade saw green lawns stretching away to a high, face-brick wall.

They sat down, the doctor on one side of the desk and Jade on the other.

Dr Abrahams cleared his throat.

'Your mother was very ill by the time the ambulance brought her here,' he said. 'When she arrived, she was suffering from hyperpyrexia. That's a dangerously high fever. Hers was one hundred and seven degrees Fahrenheit, and she was semi-conscious. She was also vomiting—and passing—blood. She had a number of other even more unpleasant symptoms. But by then there was very little we could do for her. She was too far gone—she was dying.'

'I see.' Her words came out in a hoarse croak.

'We placed her in isolation immediately and ran a battery of tests. We attempted to get her fever down as a matter of urgency, but it spiked even higher—to one hundred and nine, which is an extremely dangerous level. The human body simply cannot cope with sustained high temperatures like that. The brain swells, causing long-term damage and vital organs to fail. The doctor on duty packed her in ice, but by then she was comatose.'

'Was my father there?'

Abrahams shook his head. 'He was at a police conference in Johannesburg. He returned as soon as we notified him that his wife was ill.'

'Did you . . . did you ever find out what it was?'

Abrahams shook his head.

'We thought at first that it might have been a type of viral haemorrhagic fever similar to Ebola—as you may know, the very first recorded case of the Ebola virus occurred in Zaire at around the same time. There are a number of different strains in existence, all contagious and some up to ninety per cent fatal. They make the news every so often. Most recently, you may have read the news reports about the tourist who died in a hospital in Johannesburg after falling ill in Luanda. A few days later, the paramedic who was with her during the flight became fatally ill, and a nurse at the hospital where she was treated also died. They called that one the Lujo virus, because its only occurrences were in Luanda and Johannesburg. No other cases have been reported before or since.'

'Was my mother's illness never diagnosed, then?'

'No. We still have no idea whether it was an Ebola-type virus or something completely different. Although, according to your father, Elise hadn't travelled outside of South Africa after you were conceived, or, as far as he knew, come into contact with anybody who had visited West Africa. Of course, he had been away from home....' Abrahams inclined his head. 'It was unlikely that she'd gone anywhere, he said, because of course she had a small baby. Although when he arrived at the hospital, he was extremely distraught, because you had disappeared.'

Jade blinked.

'How do you mean?'

'He told us his baby daughter was missing. He didn't know where you were. He visited Elise briefly—she was in complete isolation by then, so he couldn't actually have any direct contact. Then he rushed back home where, I presume, he must have discovered you alive and well.'

Jade stared at him.

Her father had never told her any of this.

What had happened during those few days at their house in Richards Bay? How had her mother fallen so suddenly and seriously ill? And why had she, Jade, been missing when her father arrived back from his conference?

She would have been less than a year old. She'd obviously lived through the experience, although she had no memory of it. Perhaps there had been a simple explanation. Maybe Elise had asked a neighbour to look after her child when she started getting sick.

'How long did she take to die?' Jade asked. The question felt awkward on her lips. She didn't even know why she asked it. Morbid curiosity, perhaps. Or simply not knowing what else to say.

'She was dead within twenty-four hours.'

'Oh.'

Jade was going to ask where she had been buried. Perhaps, due to the mysterious and lethal nature of the illness, her father had not been allowed to bury his wife's body in a public cemetery. But before she could ask this, another thought occurred to her.

'If it had been an Ebola-type virus . . .' she began.

The doctor lifted one bushy eyebrow.

'Yes?'

'You said those viruses are contagious. I remember reading about the paramedic who died after transporting the woman from Luanda. If my mother was the only one who died from this, then surely it couldn't have been?'

Dr Abrahams looked her in the eyes.

'You're wrong,' he said.

'How do you mean?'

'She was not the only one.'

Jade felt cold inside.

'Who . . . ?'

The doctor held his right hand out in front of him with the palm facing Jade, as if he was about to swear an oath.

Then, with his left hand, he counted off the fingers.

'The day after she died, the paramedic who had attended her in the ambulance became critically ill. He subsequently died. The following day, her doctor and two of the triage nurses developed the same symptoms and were dead within thirty-six hours. The doctor's wife and the husband and children of one of the nurses were also fatally infected. Fortunately, by that stage, we already had the families in isolation and the virus was contained.'

Jade nodded wordlessly.

'Eight deaths. That's how many we had, before it ran its course. Eight deaths in less than a week, each one in our newly built isolation ward. By the time the nurse's family was admitted, the ward had been sealed off completely and the team of doctors and nurses were working in full biohazard gear, with oxygen packs strapped to their backs.'

Abrahams pushed back his jacket sleeve and looked at his watch in what was a deliberately obvious gesture.

'What happened afterwards?' she asked.

But the doctor misunderstood her question.

'There wasn't much about it in the news,' he said. 'In those apartheid days, news was censored and the government didn't want this made public. Didn't want to cause a national panic, especially not when they had no idea what the cause was. It was kept entirely under wraps.'

'No. I meant—what happened to the bodies?'

'Ah, I see. We had no say in the matter—the government told us what to do. We were informed that on no account were the bodies to be removed from the hospital premises. Instead, they were to be incinerated on site.'

He paused and turned towards the window, now unwilling to look at Jade while he spoke.

'The bodies in their body bags went in together, in one big load. We needed to get everything done as quickly as possible, because we couldn't risk anybody else falling ill. In the next load, we burnt their clothes, all items that had come with them to the hospital, their bedding, every single used swab and medication. And then the mattresses went into the incinerator. The staff involved wore biohazard suits throughout the process. And then, as ordered, we dug a deep grave and lined it with thick concrete. The boxed ashes were placed at the bottom and covered with one and a half metres of concrete. A wall was built around it, the one you can see over there, in fact. That's where your mother is buried. Under that.'

Jade gazed out of the window at the high brick wall. Now she understood why Dr Abrahams had chosen this room for their meeting.

Her mother's remains were part of a jumbled mass of cremated corpses, clothes and bedding.

As was her ring.

With the urgency of her admission, there would have been no opportunity to remove it. And when Elise de Jong's body had been dumped into the hospital incinerator, her ring would still have been on her finger. Perhaps it had come out the other side as a deformed, half-melted chunk of silver, with the jade stone long since detached, its shiny green surface scorched and blackened.

The ring would have been swept up and interred with the ashes and bone fragments, Jade supposed.

Commissioner De Jong had been a great believer in respect; in doing things the right way. It must have broken his heart to have his wife's body burned side-by-side with the other corpses, her final resting place being somewhere he could never visit, never leave flowers to honour her memory.

'Can I go there?' Jade asked Dr Abrahams.

Both his eyebrows lifted a half-inch.

'Over there?' He turned his head towards the window again.

'Yes.'

'You can go up to the wall, I suppose, as long as you're quick. The exit at the end of this corridor will give you access to those grounds.'

'I'll go in a few minutes, if that's all right with you.'

'I have another meeting now. Good luck for the future, Jade.'

'Thank you very much for telling me about my mother.'

Jade shook Abrahams's hand. His grip was firm. He didn't look at her. He held the door for her while she walked out and, as she made her way back towards the hospital reception area, she could hear the sound of him locking it again.

The little kiosk next to the cafeteria sold flowers. There wasn't much choice to be had. Only some wilted-looking pink rosebuds and some mixed bunches with sunflowers and chrysanthemums and other flowers whose names Jade didn't know. Still, they were colourful and pretty, and cheerful.

And, in any case, by the evening they would be dead.

She paid for the biggest mixed bunch she could find and walked back through the hospital, following the twisting route that Abrahams had taken. She made one wrong turn and had to retrace her steps, but soon she was walking past the door he had so recently locked behind them, and up to the narrow exit door that had an opaque, reinforced glass window. It let light in, but you couldn't see out.

Outside, the lawn was neatly mowed all the way up to the foot of the brick wall. Jade couldn't see over its top, but she walked all the way around it. It didn't take long, because each side was only about ten metres in length.

Jade guessed that the concrete square inside would be dirty, dusty and spattered with bird droppings. She wondered whether a few tenacious grass seeds might have germinated inside the walls and taken hold, sprouting thick yellow-green shoots. She would never know, because there was no way in. The concrete-covered grave inside was barriered off—if not for eternity, then as close to it as the Richards Bay hospital could manage.

She didn't say anything, in the end. No quips about needlework. She just closed her eyes and thought of the photo she now kept in her cottage.

Her mother, looking down at baby Jade in her arms, her eyes filled with love.

Her death had been a mystery, as had her life. A woman who had worked as a killer, an assassin. A woman who had given up her career at some stage, but whether it had been before she had met Jade's father, or whether that meeting had prompted her to turn her back on her old life, Jade would never know.

How had she contracted that strange illness?

She guessed that too would remain a mystery.

Jade opened her eyes again. Then she drew her arm back and flung the bunch of flowers, high and hard, over the wall.

A couple of seconds later, she heard the soft thud as it landed.

She turned away and walked quickly back into the hospital, through the maze of corridors and out of the main entrance. She didn't stop for coffee after all. She just got into her car and drove out of the gates, along the main road and past the town cemetery.

48

To Jade's annoyance, when she drove to the yard where her hired car had been towed, she found that the original of her gun licence was no longer in the glove compartment. The manager of the panel-beating company apologised, rubbing his hands together in a washing motion that Jade thought he might be doing to subconsciously absolve himself of any responsibility.

The car's bloodied seats had already been removed, he said, and the interior thoroughly cleaned and scrubbed down with industrial disinfectant. Many people had been in and out of it. It was impossible to say what could have happened to one folded piece of paper.

Jade had no option but to go home without her gun, apply for a new licence and then see whether her Glock had managed to do the same kind of disappearing act under the guardianship of the bent Metro cop.

As she headed west along the highway, Jade found her thoughts returning, almost obsessively, to the events of the past few days. That wasn't surprising, of course. She'd intended to have a relaxing, peaceful, relationship-nurturing holiday, but in every one of those areas it had been nothing short of a disaster. And her original plan of finding out more about her mother had backfired in a shocking and unexpected way, leaving her with the uneasy knowledge that what had happened to her mother before her death was a mystery that would never be solved.

To top it all, she hadn't even managed to master scuba diving. What a complete waste of a trip to one of the most beautiful coastal areas in South Africa.

Thinking of what might have happened—the worst-case scenario of the scuttled tanker—Jade gripped the wheel harder. In her mind, she replayed the firecracker burst of the exploding cellphone. Wired to kill, just moments after Bradley had dialled the number to detonate the bigger and even more deadly explosion out at sea. Jade wondered whether his employers had actually intended for him to set off the explosives at all. Or whether they would have done it themselves at a time when they were a safe distance from the doomed tanker, and then let Bradley dial the number afterwards.

Both Chetty and Zulu had drowned when they'd gone down with the tugboat. Their bodies had been discovered that morning, together with the bodies of two other men. Harbour workers, the police guessed.

The two bosses had run a tight operation. Without Jade's intervention, every witness would have been disposed of, every loose end tied up.

Except for one.

Over and over again, Jade found her thoughts returning to Amanda Bolton's bloodied body, sprawled on the floor of her chalet. There had been a reason for every other death or attempted murder that had occurred. This was the only one that seemed entirely senseless.

With a stretch of the imagination, Jade could believe that Amanda had been killed in error. Monique, her neighbour, had made an amateur attempt at blackmailing Bradley and he had sent Kobus along to dispose of her. In error, Kobus had murdered the wrong woman.

Jade pulled into the fast lane to pass a slow-moving lorry.

But Kobus had stammered out a denial just before Bradley had shot him.

He hadn't killed Monique. That was what he'd said.

Jade knew only too well that when faced with the business end of a gun, people were not necessarily going to tell the truth. They were far more likely to blurt out exactly what they thought the shooter wanted to hear.

Even so . . .

It didn't make sense to her.

And then, of course, there was the door, with its lock splintered, but not broken. As if Amanda had opened it to somebody she knew.

There must be an explanation for her murder. Of course there must. But pinpointing it was like trying to focus on a dark object at night. Every time you looked directly at it, it disappeared. Only when you stared at a point nearby could you make out its shape.

Jade tried to think about something else, but it was impossible. She turned on the radio and caught the scratchy remains of East Coast Radio playing a song by Freshlyground. Not even the cheerful lyrics of 'Buttercup' managed to distract her from her thoughts, which were churning over and over in her mind, as if on permanent loop.

She stopped at a petrol station just before lunch. After filling up with fuel, she went over to the Steers next-door to the garage shop and ordered a giant-sized coffee and a greasy toasted cheese sandwich with extra chilli sauce. She drank the bitter coffee and ate her sandwich at a window seat and watched motorists coming and going. Most of the cars had GP number plates and were also heading west, holiday over, back to Gauteng. Grim-faced at the prospect of returning to work, with their tank tops and shorts revealing deep sun tans and post-holiday flab. Arms as bloated and brown as cooked sausages, feet slapping along in flip-flop sandals. Kids trailing behind them, bored, restless and yelling.

By the time Jade got back in her car, she'd been sufficiently distracted from her previous thoughts and the next couple of hours passed calmly.

Her pit-bull-like subconscious, however, refused to leave the topic alone. As Jade drove past the rather stark-looking sign notifying her that she was now in Gauteng Province and ordering her to enjoy her stay, the truth hit her like a ten-pound hammer.

She dug in her pocket for her cellphone and, after checking her mirrors for any signs of cruising Metro Police vehicles, pulled it out and made a call.

49

The next morning, back in Johannesburg, Jade got up at dawn and went for a run. Bonnie, the cheeky Jack Russell from down the road, wriggled under the fence and joined her for the last section, bounding alongside her in the middle of the road in a death-defying sprint that led them to Jade's front door.

The sand road felt coarse and scratchy, but not uncomfortable under her bare feet. They were toughening up well. She was going to continue her barefoot running regime, she decided. After all, there were times when it could prove very useful.

Back at her cottage, she had a quick shower, put the kettle on, made herself a coffee and gave Bonnie a bowl of water and a doggie treat. Jade wasn't sure exactly how the packet of bone-shaped biscuit treats had ended up in the cottage. She definitely couldn't have bought them for the dog on one of her infrequent shopping trips. Not when she'd enforced a strict no-feeding rule after Bonnie had worked out how to get through Jade's garden fence and had become a regular visitor.

After breakfast she checked her emails, did a load of washing and hung it out to dry.

And then, finally, it was time to head off to the interview that she'd managed to set up yesterday afternoon.

The secure estate where Larry and the flame-haired Roxanne lived was a twenty-minute drive away, in a suburb called Blue Hills. She arrived there at nine in the morning and, after making a phone call to confirm that she was expected, the guards let her in.

Roxanne's description of their house had been both vague and difficult to hear. When Jade had called her, the signal hadn't been good, but she still had the feeling that Roxanne wouldn't actually mind if she lost her way and never arrived at all. What she had been told to look out for was a newly planted mature olive tree by the gate and a Tuscan-style fountain in the courtyard.

Roxanne, or Roxy, as she preferred to be called, had sounded very proud of those two possessions.

The fountain, when Jade finally saw it, was a monstrosity—a circular concrete pool twenty feet in diameter, with a pinkish, faux-Tuscan finish and a water-spewing, tunic-clad goddess on a pedestal as the centrepiece.

The olive tree didn't look too good either. Set in a raw circle of earth, it was taller than she had expected, but as scrawny as an anorexic teen, and its scanty leaves were dull and drooping.

Jade allowed herself to briefly entertain the appealing possibility that Larry had wasted a large chunk of his money by buying that full-grown tree.

She climbed out of her car and walked over to the front door, where she pressed the door bell.

After a minute, she heard soft footsteps. A key turned in the lock and the door swung open.

The expression on Roxanne's face was a roughly equal blend of resentment and suspicion. She was wearing a turquoise and silver sarong over the now-familiar bikini. The toenails on her bare feet were painted Hummer-orange, to match her hair.

'You found us, then?' she said in a tone that clearly conveyed she wished Jade hadn't. 'I don't have a lot of time. I've got to get ready to go out in a minute. What do you want?'

'I need to ask you some questions.'

'Larry said we should only talk to the detective. He said that's how the police work and that we mustn't discuss it with anyone else.'

Jade bit back the impulse to say that the detective would have found it much easier to talk to Larry if he and Roxanne hadn't left for Jo'burg almost immediately after the murder.

'Is Larry here?' she asked.

A sullen headshake. Orange hair flopped across Roxanne's heavily made-up face. 'He's at work.'

'The questions I want to ask you aren't about the murder. Not directly.'

'What are they about, then?'

Jade looked pointedly past Roxanne's shoulder, across the tiled hallway, where she could see wide glass sliding doors opening onto a massive covered entertainment area. The colour scheme was an uninspired white and blue pinstripe. Bar stools, sofas, wicker armchairs, squashy armchairs. Enough furniture to accommodate the whole of the United Nations.

Roxanne got the message.

'Come through,' she said, entirely without enthusiasm.

Jade settled herself on a white canvas chair opposite the sofa where Roxanne must have been sitting before Jade arrived. There was a *Hello!* magazine lying open on the sofa arm and what looked like iced coffee in a tall glass on the nearby table.

Fat drops of condensation slid lazily down the outside of the glass, reminding Jade of how hot the day was becoming. Roxanne didn't offer her a drink, though. She took a sip of her own, ice clinking.

'What do you want to know?' she asked again.

'Tell me about Monique,' Jade said.

Roxanne blinked, as if puzzled. 'How do you mean?'

Suppressing a sigh, Jade wondered exactly who was supposed to be asking the questions here.

'You spent a lot of time with her out on the boat.'

'Well, not just me. We were all on the boat.' Roxanne sounded defensive, as if Jade was accusing her of something.

'Did she talk much?'

'Oh, ja. She was one of those people who had, like, verbal diarrhoea. She would bang on and on to whoever was willing to listen. Which, unfortunately, turned out to be us. And that other woman, the one who never smiled.'

'What did she bang on about?'

Roxanne paused before continuing. 'Her life. How many tough breaks she'd had. Larry said she was one of those "Poor Me" people who were always on the lookout for money and sympathy. He also reckoned that, given half a chance, she'd be into anything with a dick.' She smiled in a smug way, as if pleased that her man had sussed out the instructor.

'What did she say was wrong with her life?'

'Well, she spoke a lot about some crazy ex who wouldn't leave her alone. She said that was why she was working here now. She said she'd been managing a bigger resort on the other side of the estuary, but after he'd tracked her down, she'd had to leave. You see? "Poor me." Like it was everyone else's fault, not hers.'

'Really?' Jade leaned forward in her seat, hoping her obvious interest would encourage Roxanne to keep talking.

'I mean, half the things she said I don't know if I believed. I thought they were exaggerations. Larry thought they were lies.' Roxanne took another sip of her drink, then put down her glass and examined her orange nails.

'Like what?'

'I can't remember exactly. Something about the guy having been in prison, but getting out early for some reason. Oh, and on that subject, one thing I do remember her saying was that he actually kept her prisoner in his flat. Like literally locked in. She told us that one time he tied her to the bed and didn't let her go for twenty-four hours. He put an adult nappy on her and went out for the day. I nearly hurled when she told me that. I mean, how disgusting!'

'It seems strange that somebody would make that story up,' Jade volunteered.

'Well, maybe she didn't make that part up.'

'Did he know that she was working at Scuba Sands?'

'Oh, no. She was in hiding. Or so she said. But one time, on the way out to sea, he did SMS her. She showed it around. I mean, it might have come from anyone, but it was a bit creepy, all about how much he loved her, that she was just like his dead wife, and that he wanted to be with her all the time when his job was over. I remember she went as white as a sheet when she read it. That's about it, I think.'

At that point, Roxanne folded her arms in a way that very much suggested Jade's time was over.

'You and Larry left without paying. Why?' Jade said.

Roxanne's face shut down like a steel trap. 'What's that got to do with you?'

'Nothing. I was just wondering . . .' Jade let her voice tail off on purpose.

'Look. The resort wasn't well secured,' Roxanne snapped. 'We could all have been killed. Larry said that if people don't provide value for money, he won't pay.'

'Fair enough.'

Roxanne smirked.

'You have a lovely house.'

'Look, don't start insinuating that because we're wealthy people . . .'

'No, no. I wasn't thinking anything of the sort. I meant it's very well kept. Clean and neat. Do you have one maid working here, or more than one?'

'None,' Roxanne said carefully. And then, as if deliberately trying to shock Jade, she added, 'Actually, Larry won't have blacks working in the house. It's one of his rules. So I do the housework. Not that there's much to do. We eat out most of the time. And the washing gets collected and delivered by a laundry service.'

'That's handy,' Jade said, keeping her voice neutral.

'Yes, it is. Is there anything else?'

'Nothing at all. Could I use your bathroom before I go?'

'Down the passage.'

Roxanne glanced in the general direction of the tiled corridor. Then the cellphone on the coffee table started buzzing.

'Hey, girlfriend,' Jade heard her say. 'No, not busy at all. We still on for brunch later? I was thinking the Castle in Kyalami. For the view.' She laughed. 'Yeah, I guess it has to be.'

Halfway down the corridor, an open door led into a palatial bathroom. Sunken bath, gold fittings, twin basins, gilt mirrors.

She glanced back over her shoulder. Roxanne was still talking into her cellphone and fiddling with her hair as she finalised her plans for the morning.

Jade walked on. The open door at the end of the passage led into an even more grandiose master bedroom that had its own lounge suite. Fluffy white floor throws surrounded a monstrous four-poster bed that seemed bigger than Jade's living room.

Swiftly, she slipped inside. The bed wasn't made. Minus one point for Roxy's housekeeping skills. But lying at its foot was a turquoise leather handbag—the same bag that Jade had seen Roxanne carrying around from time to time at the resort.

People generally keep money in three places. In a safe, in bedside or desk drawers, and in their purses or wallets. Jade couldn't access the safe, although she was sure there was one. A quick root through the turquoise bag yielded only a couple of crumpled fifty-rand notes and a fistful of credit cards.

When she opened the bedside drawer on what she guessed was Larry's side of the bed, she struck gold. Inside a half-empty box of men's tissues, she discovered a thick wad of hundred-rand notes held together by a tightly stretched rubber band.

Quickly, Jade removed half of them and stuffed them deep into her jeans pocket. Then she hurried out of the room and back down the passage.

To her relief, Roxanne was still on the phone and still on the couch. As she adjusted her position, Jade caught a glimpse of a small, but unmistakable, roll of fat around her middle. Too many brunches, perhaps. Jade wondered whether Larry was the type of man who would one day trade her in for a younger, trimmer model.

'Yes, exactly. We could go shopping afterwards in Sandton. You think Tanya will also be free? Well, do you want to call her or shall I? Hang on a sec.'

She looked up at Jade, stood up and then walked over to the front door and unlocked it.

Jade stepped out into the stifling morning.

'Thank you,' she said, but Roxanne didn't reply.

'Tell Tanya to meet us at the Castle,' she said to her caller, and slammed the door in Jade's face.

Jade walked over to her car with a victorious smile on her face. She could feel the stack of notes, their edges hard against her thigh. Although Neil was dead and couldn't use the money they owed the resort, Jade had decided she'd see if there was a suitable charity—something run by surfers, perhaps—that she could donate it to.

Failing that, she would give it to the SPCA.

Larry might never notice that half his stash of cash was missing, but if he did, he couldn't blame the domestic worker, because there wasn't one. Jade wouldn't have wanted an innocent person to be fired because of what she had done.

She drove round the gaudy fountain and headed out of the estate, waving a friendly goodbye to the guards as they raised the exit boom to let her leave.

50

Jade's first call on her way back to her cottage was to Inspector Pillay.

'You'll probably get around to investigating Bradley's flat before too long, but I thought I'd give you a heads-up on what you might find there,' she said. 'I think he somehow got hold of the woman— the one who was reported missing on your list. She's being kept prisoner there. Tied up. Perhaps tranquilised or sedated in some way. And it would save her a whole lot of discomfort and potential health complications if you went to fetch her now.'

'Dear God!' Pillay exclaimed. 'We were going to go and search his residence later on today, but I'll send a team there immediately. Thank you. How did you . . .'

'You'd have picked it up in your interviews,' Jade said. 'I've just spoken to Roxanne, the woman who left early and went back to Johannesburg. She told me that he'd done the same thing to Monique.'

Pillay thanked her again. His voice was filled with excite- ment—presumably at the thought of rescuing the imprisoned woman and thus clearing his Missing Persons backlog completely.

Jade drove on, deep in thought.

Her musings were interrupted by the beeping of her phone. Looking down, she saw Craig had sent her a text message.

'hope ur doing well. guess what? am in jo'burg 2day. going 2see elsabe this eve. we're flying2 namibia 2moro 4 a week together! wish me luck. think it's serious this time. thanks 4 everything. all the best, c.'

There it was again, that horrible suspicion her subconscious was still grappling with. It loomed, large and ugly, but dissolved into shadow when she tried to grasp it.

She decided not to go home after all.

Instead, she turned around and drove towards the M1 highway—slowing as she was caught in the last wave of the morning rush-hour traffic—and took the south lane, going towards central Johannesburg.

Back in Johannesburg, Moloi had sat down at his work desk before six A.M., having broken one of his own rules by leaving home before his young daughter had woken up.

He'd gone in to see her, though, and spent a few minutes there with his wife, smiling down at their child's wiry black hair and soft brown skin, half buried under the folds of her pink duvet and clutching the stuffed giraffe of which she was inordinately fond.

Even so, he still felt guilty about being at work and not at home.

But he had too much on his plate today. A suspect in one of his murder cases had been arrested and was in detention at Hillbrow police station. Moloi would be driving there in an hour to question him. Then it would be straight back to the police station and into a meeting with the Hawks—the new elite organised-crime unit—followed by another meeting with somebody else from Organised Crime in the department where David now worked. And then, back to his own department for a lunchtime team briefing, and a phone conference with a pathologist from the Germiston labs after that, assuming that the urgent post-mortem had been completed by then.

And then the rest of the afternoon he planned to devote to tackling the sizeable mound of paperwork that had accumulated on his desk—a programme that would take him well into the evening. Or so he thought.

It didn't work out that way.

While he was interviewing his suspect in Hillbrow—sweating, stammering and, to Moloi's experienced eye, as guilty as sin—he missed five calls on his cellphone, which he'd switched over to silent.

Two of the calls were from the same number—the captain from the Hawks who had requested the urgent case meeting. Listening to the voicemail, Moloi learned that he'd had to fly to Cape Town for another case and wanted to know if their meeting could be rescheduled for tomorrow.

Moloi phoned the captain as he hurried back to his car through the station's ammonia-rich basement car park. Whether this was from human urine or artificial cleaning agent, he couldn't tell. Both were unpleasant, and he stepped carefully to avoid the suspect puddles on the concrete.

He left a message on the captain's voicemail to say that tomorrow would be fine and climbed into his car, slamming the door on the unpleasant stink with a sigh of relief.

It was only when he was driving out of the basement parking that he realised two things.

One, he had an unexpected hour's gap in his schedule.

And two, Dunbar Street, where Themba Msamaya lived, was only five minutes' drive away.

He did have other work demands that could easily have filled the hour, but he owed Patel more than a few favours, and being able to set his former colleague's mind at rest was infinitely more appealing than catching up on his long-overdue filing and form-filling.

The Hillbrow police station was just beyond the crest of the hill on the eastern side of the suburb. Moloi scowled as he noticed the banks of old and rotting litter that were piled up on the sides of the road just outside the exit. Surely the station commander could make a better effort at keeping his precinct and its surrounds in good order, he wondered, as he drove down the hill towards Yeoville.

When he turned into Dunbar Street, Moloi was surprised to see a small group of people standing outside the entrance to Msamaya's building. A couple of cars were parked outside at odd angles, as if the owners had braked to a hurried stop before jumping out of their vehicles.

Moloi parked behind the dented bumper of a Toyota Corolla and climbed out. Before he even began to make his way over to the building's entrance, the caretaker he had spoken to on his previous visit hurried across.

He was gripping a cellphone in his right hand.

'Thank you for getting here so fast, Captain. Thank you so much for coming,' he gabbled. 'It's terrible, just so terrible, what has happened here.'

Moments later, when Moloi heard the blare of approaching sirens, a feeling of impending doom descended on him. He followed the caretaker into the building and up the stairs to the door of the shabby flat that he had knocked on just a couple of days ago.

Now the door was open and several shocked-looking people were gathered on either side. One of them, a woman, was sobbing. A couple had their hands cupped over their eyes as if attempting to block out the reality of what they had just seen.

Moloi could smell the blood before he even reached the flat.

He looked inside; stared at the badly butchered body sprawled on the floor of the cramped bedsit.

He was too late for Themba Msamaya.

51

The block of flats in Dunbar Street was easy for Jade to find—a tumbledown three-floor building just a block away from the crossroads she had driven through.

But as soon as she saw it, she realised that something was wrong.

A cluster of onlookers was gathered outside on the pavement, keeping a respectful distance from the two police cars that were parked near the entrance, their blue lights flashing.

Jade parked nearby and walked towards the main entrance. Litter wafted past her feet, fluttering in the breeze. Empty crisp packets, plastic bags. A torn white envelope addressed to Mr Themba Msamaya caught her eye. She stopped and picked it up, handling it carefully, because it had a dodgy-looking brown stain on it.

It was from an organisation called ATCSA Human Resources, with an address in Kempton Park. Business correspondence, she supposed. Perhaps Msamaya had applied for a job with them. She didn't know, because the envelope was empty.

Jade tossed it into one of the steel bins nearby and, since there were no policemen controlling access to the block of flats, started walking up the stairs only to hear heavy footsteps above her. Just as she reached the first landing, she saw Moloi at the top of the next flight, with a uniformed cop closely behind him. He was on his cellphone, gabbling out instructions.

The policeman was the first to see her.

'Lady, go back downstairs. Out of the building, please.'

Moloi looked up and saw Jade. He paused, turned to his colleague and held up a hand while continuing with his phone conversation.

'Yes. Then get hold of Inspector De Wet from Organised Crime. Tell him I'm going to have to reschedule our meeting.' He paused. 'Yes. Yes, the team briefing is still on. Same time. OK. Thanks.'

He pocketed his phone and walked down the stairs to Jade.

'What are you doing here?' For once, the usual disapproval in his tone was missing.

'I came to talk to Themba Msamaya.'

'Well, you can't, because he's been murdered. Earlier this morning, from the look of it.' The stocky detective turned to the uniformed policeman. 'You go on down. I'll be a while here.'

She took a deep breath. 'What happened?'

'He was stabbed. Twice. First in the stomach, then in the chest. The knife's still in the chest wound.'

Jade's breath caught in her throat. In her mind's eye, she could see the bloody scene where Amanda's body had been found. She had suffered two knife wounds, just like Msamaya. A stomach wound and a fatal chest wound.

'It's a pattern,' she said. 'Amanda Bolton, the scuba instructor who was stabbed to death in Richards Bay, was killed in exactly the same way. The only difference is that the murderer removed the knife.'

Moloi's expression hardened. It wasn't difficult for Jade to guess what he was thinking.

Serial killer. A detective's worst nightmare.

'We need to find the link,' Jade said. 'They know—knew— each other. He sent Amanda a postcard. There is a connection there.'

Moloi nodded, but didn't speak.

'I've been thinking about what happened down at St Lucia,' Jade continued. 'We got caught up in a big crime. Something that had been planned for months beforehand. The people behind it were ruthless and clever, and they were careful. They were so careful, in fact, that we should never have known about it.'

Moloi's face remained expressionless. Jade carried on talking, but she couldn't help wondering what the stocky cop was thinking.

'The only reason the criminals' attention was drawn to our resort was because of a blackmail attempt made on one of them by a mystery person—apparently a woman.'

On hearing this, Moloi's gaze sharpened.

'I don't think it was really blackmail, though,' Jade continued. 'It was purposely done to bring trouble to the resort. Someone knew—or found out—that the other scuba instructor, Monique, had been involved with an ex-convict with a history of violence towards women. I think the blackmail attempt was made in order to deliberately provoke that man and, at the same time, to let him know where his old victim was working.'

'And why would anybody do that?' Moloi's voice was soft.

'Because it provided a very handy smokescreen for Amanda's murder. Monique was terrified of Bradley. She was hiding from him. The killer found that out, and twisted the situation to their advantage. They now had a previous victim—Monique. They had a known criminal who'd done serious jail time—Bradley. They baited the trap by organising the fake blackmail attempt, and then waited for Bradley to walk into it. Knowing, of course, that if the police investigated another murder that had occurred at the same time, he would end up being the first suspect.'

Jade met Moloi's gaze. She had no idea what he was thinking. His face gave nothing away.

'Carry on.' he said.

'This person probably had no idea that Bradley was involved in a massive criminal operation or that the situation would explode the way it did. For them, that was just an extra piece of luck.'

'And what would have happened if Bradley had not taken the bait?' Moloi asked.

Jade shrugged. 'I think Amanda would have been murdered anyway, just like Themba Msamaya was. But by creating that smokescreen, the killer bought some time. More time to commit the next murder, and perhaps more time to make a successful getaway, since no formal suspects have been arrested yet.'

Moloi rubbed his chin with stubby fingers, still listening intently.

'You said the blackmail attempt was made by a woman?'

'According to the criminals, yes. But I don't know who she could be. Excluding me, there were only two other women at the resort, and neither of them had any obvious grudge against Amanda. No motive to murder her, still less to kill Themba Msamaya. So either you'll have to dig deeper into their backgrounds or you'll have to look for somebody else. Perhaps a man did it, and contacted Bradley by email or text message.'

Moloi gave a small, humourless smile in response to her suggestion.

'You made your biggest mistake there, Jade.'

Jade frowned. What was Moloi talking about?

'How do you mean?' she asked.

'You got too clever. Too brazen, as I think the expression is. You left too many clues and you were too obvious.'

Moloi's voice was hard and mocking, but the expression in his eyes told Jade that he was deadly serious. Captain Moloi had come to entirely the wrong conclusion about the identity of Amanda's killer.

'It wasn't me, for God's sake. I liked Amanda. She gave me private lessons. Because I had problems with going deep underwater, I couldn't go out with the rest of the group.'

'Convenient.'

With a sick feeling, Jade realised that yes, it did sound that way now. She had booked the holiday, too. It had all been her idea.

'Look, Moloi, what motive could I possibly have to . . .'

'As both of us know, you don't always need a motive to kill.'

Jade felt her blood rush to her face. She opened her mouth to argue this point, but realised she could find nothing to say in her defence.

'Jade de Jong, I am going to hand you over to the officer in charge of this investigation. You will accompany him to the police station, where in due course I hope you will be formally charged with the murder of Amanda Bolton.'

'No! You can't possibly make an arrest with such flimsy evidence.'

'In this case, I don't have to,' the black detective answered smugly.

'What do you mean?'

'You already have an outstanding arrest warrant in your name. You fled a roadblock in KwaZulu-Natal after being found in possession of an unlicensed firearm.'

'But I didn't . . .' Jade felt her mouth drop open in shock. The bent Metro cop who'd confiscated her gun and alerted the criminals to her whereabouts had actually had the gall to lay charges against her for leaving the roadblock after he'd disappeared.

But how to explain all this to Moloi when he was so firmly convinced of her guilt?

'We were going to send an officer round to your house today to bring you in for that,' the detective told her. 'Thankfully, you've saved us the trouble by turning up here. And by the time your forty-eight-hour custody period is over, I am more than certain that we will indeed have sufficient evidence to charge you with this other, more serious crime.'

Before she knew what was happening, Moloi had reached out and grasped her right arm with his meaty hand and frogmarched her downstairs.

52

Outside, the officer in charge clipped a pair of handcuffs around Jade's wrists. The cold clasp of the metal was uncomfortably tight and, glancing up, Jade was aware that the many bystanders were watching, fascinated, as the scenario played out. She dropped her eyes again, furious and ashamed.

The officer made a show of frisking her for weapons and then opened the van's back door. Moloi, who was still holding her tightly, then picked her up like a kitten by the scruff of its neck and dumped her inside.

The door slammed shut and Jade heard a snicking sound as it was locked behind her. A moment later, the engine started with a rattle and the van lurched into motion.

The floor was made of hard, ribbed metal with a thin layer of rubber matting over it that Jade supposed had been put there for the comfort of the prisoners. It didn't feel very comfortable to her. As the officer drove fast down Yeoville's potholed streets, every bounce and rattle was transferred directly to her spine.

The window separating the driver's cabin from the back of the van was covered with a sturdy sheet of steel mesh, as was the small and grubby window in the van's rear. The interior was gloomy and it smelled strange. Jade thought perhaps it smelled of fear.

She could do nothing to escape. All she could do was to brace her feet against the tyre well and her shoulders against the opposite wall, and try to find the best way of riding out the uncomfortable journey.

Tipping sideways as the van turned a tight corner, Jade felt something hard in her jeans pocket press against her hipbone.

Her cellphone. Although he had frisked her for weapons, the officer hadn't taken away her phone, car keys or wallet. Jade had no doubt that these possessions would be removed as soon as they reached the police station. But for now, if she could get the phone out of her pocket....

With her hands cuffed behind her, it was an almost impossible exercise. Almost. Jade was very flexible and, by stretching her right arm all the way backwards until it felt like her elbow might snap, she was able to get her left hand far enough into her pocket to touch the solid shape of the phone with her fingers.

But then the van swerved. Without her arms to balance her, Jade fell hard onto her side. She didn't care. She had her index and middle finger firmly scissored around the phone. After some painful twisting and tugging, she managed to work it out of her pocket.

She grasped it tightly in her left hand.

There was only one person who could get her out of this situation, and she hoped to hell that he was not medicated, asleep or receiving a bed-bath at that moment.

Twisting her arms round her body as far as they would go, with her muscles and tendons at screaming point, Jade was able to see the bright screen of the phone. She managed to scroll through her recently dialled numbers to find David's. It took three tries for her to press the 'Call' button. Then she placed the phone, screen side up, on the rubber floor of the van, shuffled backwards on bent knees and lay down on her side, balancing herself uncomfortably on her left shoulder and pressing her ear to the phone.

Faintly, above the rattle of the van's transmission, she could hear ringing at the other end. It rang five, six, seven times. To her enormous relief, just as Jade was thinking it was about to go through to voicemail, her call was answered.

'Kevin and I went to visit his cousins last night,' Naisha said chattily.

Lying, propped up on pillows, in the high-care ward, David watched her stroking the dark, shiny hair of the boy by her side—not a young child any longer, he realised with a jolt, but a boy who had started to sprout upwards like a runner bean and was only a couple of years away from being a teenager.

Naisha's other hand rested protectively on the small bump beneath her red blouse. She shifted her feet, as if finding standing uncomfortable.

'Go and get that plastic chair in the corner, please, Kev,' she said.

The boy fetched the chair and placed it carefully next to the bed.

'Watch out,' David warned. His voice was still hoarse and weak, and talking still made his chest hurt. 'Those seats are quite flimsy.'

Naisha lowered herself carefully down onto the seat with a sigh of relief and smothered a yawn.

'Kev wanted to go to the beach for a swim today, but I don't think we'll have time,' she told him. 'We're flying back tomorrow morning, and we have to see Auntie Bhavna and Uncle Sanjay for lunch, and then I said I'd go round to my mother this evening after we've visited you again.' She turned to look at her son. 'Maybe next time, ok?'

'Let him swim,' David croaked, taking in his boy's disappointed face. 'Can't you make time . . . in the afternoon? I'm sure . . . he won't want to spend all day . . . with relatives.'

'Well, it's not often that we get down to KwaZulu-Natal, you know,' Naisha snapped, her tone defiant. 'I have family obligations. And my relatives all live in Durban, which is a long drive from here and it's already half past ten.'

David exchanged a sympathetic glance with Kevin. He remembered visiting Bhavna and Sanjay years ago. They lived in a tiny house in Pinetown. The interior had been hot and airless, stuffed with enough furniture and knick-knacks to stock a fair-sized shop, and overrun by three small, yappy dogs. Framed photographs and artwork covered the walls. For some obscure reason, there was a huge painting, done in garish acrylics, of Christ on the Cross. Pillar-box red blood ran down his face, which had been contorted in a rictus of agony.

After choking down a plateful of Bhavna's extra spicy lamb vindaloo, David understood how he'd felt.

'Maybe Kevin could swim . . . in Durban,' he suggested.

God, the hole in his chest. It hurt so damn much, and he knew that the badly damaged, bruised and swollen flesh would continue to cause him pain for months as it healed.

He closed his eyes for a moment, tuning out Naisha's chatter.

Again, he thought of Jade and the moment when the gunman turned his weapon on them.

Struggling with her seatbelt, she hadn't looked scared. Not Jade. He clearly remembered the expression on her face being one of pure frustration.

He could so easily have ducked down out of harm's way. But the thought had not even occurred to him. He'd simply leaned forward to present himself as a more appealing target for the deeply tanned man.

Why had he done that? He was a married man, soon to become a father of two. What he had done was completely irresponsible.

It had been crazy.

'. . . And you are looking tired. Your face is quite drawn. Do you need more pain medication?'

Naisha's voice intruded once again into his troubling thoughts.

'Think I'm OK, thanks,' he managed.

And then his cellphone started to ring.

He opened his eyes and lifted his right hand—slowly, as if he was moving through glue. The movement caused him to hiss in agony.

'Here, let me. Let me.'

Pushing herself up from her chair, Naisha hurried round the bed to the table where David's phone lay.

She picked it up, glanced down at the screen.

David's stomach clenched in dread as he saw her expression darken.

The police van hit a pothole with a bump that knocked the phone away from Jade's ear and sent it sliding down underneath her chest. She wriggled along the floor, hoping to hell that David wouldn't hang up and force her to repeat the whole painful process again.

'Hello?' she said, squirming to get her ear close enough to the phone. 'Hello? You there, David?'

Jade recoiled as a woman's voice spat down the line at her.

'I cannot believe your cheek. I just cannot believe the cheek of you, Ms Jade de Jong, you inconsiderate floozy. Calling my husband on his cellphone while his family is visiting him in hospital.'

Jade's eyes closed briefly and she suddenly felt sick.

It was Naisha who'd answered and with every word she spoke, Jade felt her hopes of rescue slipping away.

The squeak of shoes moving over linoleum. No doubt, Naisha was walking away from David's bedside to continue the conversation in a more private place so that she could speak her mind freely.

'You are a nuisance,' she heard the other woman announce. 'Nothing but a blasted nuisance, running after my husband like a . . . like a . . .' Clearly unable to find an appropriate simile, Naisha continued, now in full flow, 'Do you know how hurtful it was for me to find out that you invited him on holiday? And all this while I am expecting his child? If he hadn't gone down to St Lucia, he wouldn't have nearly been killed. You do realise that, don't you? Now, do me just one favour, please. Leave our family alone. Do not contact David again. I will be turning his phone off now. He needs to rest. Are you understanding me, girl? Are you?'

Jade took a deep breath. All she could do now was plead.

'Naisha, listen to me, please. I've been wrongfully arrested and I'm being taken to Hillbrow police station. Please, please, let me speak to David, just for a minute. He's the only person who can sort this out. He . . .'

The van rounded another sharp corner and the phone slid away from Jade's ear.

'Wait!' she shouted. 'I'm still here!'

She inched her way over to the phone, but saw that Naisha had ended the call.

After redialling, Jade found herself listening to David's voicemail.

A cold, helpless fury filled her as she realised that Naisha had ignored her desperate request.

Her last hope was gone.

53

The police van made a final turn before jolting to a stop. Jade managed to jam her phone back into her pocket before the back door swung open, letting in the bright morning light, and the police officer helped her out. 'Fresh' was not an adjective Jade would have thought of using to describe Hillbrow's air, but after the rubbery stench in the police van, it smelled wonderful, and she breathed it in with relief. It might be some time before she tasted outside air again.

The officer—not the detective in charge of the Msamaya murder case, but one of his assistants—walked with her, keeping a hold on her handcuffs. They didn't go in through the main entrance, but walked the short distance across the parking lot to a door that Jade assumed led directly to the holding cells.

'What's she in for?' The large lady constable at the desk looked curiously down at the cuffs.

'Escaping a roadblock and possession of an unlicensed firearm.'

'Oh.' The constable yawned hugely, putting her half-finished plate of food aside before reaching under the desk and producing a blurry photocopied form.

Her father would have spontaneously combusted if that slap-dash attitude had been shown in his precinct. The officer who'd brought her in didn't seem too bothered, though. He removed the cuff on her right wrist and clipped it to a sturdy handle set into the wall beside the desk. Then he turned and left.

Nothing like being a flight risk to complicate things, Jade decided.

Flight . . .

And then she thought again of the letters on the crumpled envelope addressed to Themba Msamaya.

ATCSA.

The pieces of the puzzle finally slotted into place. Fitting neatly and well, but fitting together too late.

The meaning of the acronym.

The dark shape she'd been groping for rose to the surface of her mind, its form suddenly solid.

Of course. Why had she been so slow?

In a leisurely fashion, the constable in the chair completed the admission form. If Jade's sense of humour hadn't deserted her, she would have been amused to note that this was done manually, while the screen saver on the computer swirled in the background. As it was, she could barely stop herself from screaming in frustration as she spelled her name out for the constable.

'De Jong. Two words. D-e, then J-o-n-g.

Soon, Jade's pockets were emptied and her cellphone, wallet and car keys were lying in a neat row on the scarred wooden surface. Then she waited for what seemed like hours as the lady constable noted down each and every one of the items.

ATCSA.

There was only one possible organisation it could stand for.

Air Traffic Controllers of South Africa.

At last, she had realised the link. Both Amanda Bolton and Themba Msamaya were air-traffic controllers. Or, to be more specific, ex-air-traffic controllers. Amanda had told Jade she'd left the industry and started working as a scuba-diving instructor six months ago and, from what she had hinted at, Jade had wondered whether there had been some sort of trouble in her past.

The numbers. 813. Could they be part of a flight number?

What had happened to Amanda Bolton and Themba Msamaya that had seen them both unemployed and then murdered in the same brutal way?

And now, here she was cuffed to a bloody metal handle and about to be escorted to the holding cells.

Jade looked over at the policewoman, who had now finished

misspelling the list of her personal items. 'I was told I would be able to phone my lawyer,' she said, trying to keep the urgency out of her voice.

The constable nodded and she raised her index finger.

'One call only,' she said.

'Can I use my own phone?'

The constable's brow furrowed in thought.

'Yes, if you like.'

Quickly, Jade scrolled through her phone's address book. She noticed her left hand was trembling very slightly. She really didn't want to have to make this call, but she was out of options.

Robbie answered after one ring.

'Babe. Is this a yes, then?'

Jade took a deep breath. 'May I please speak to Mr Goldstein?' She paused for a beat. 'You have two people with that name there? I mean Mr Ian Goldstein, the attorney.'

Although Robbie hadn't hung up, he wasn't saying anything either. Just listening.

So was the lady constable.

Jade pretended to listen again, then responded.

'I'll wait. If he's on another call, I'll hold. Please could you tell him it's urgent, though. I'm phoning from the police station.'

Now Robbie spoke, but softly. 'Is this call being recorded?'

'No.'

'You're in trouble, babe?'

'Yes, I am. I've been arrested,' Jade said.

'Need help?'

Jade continued her conversation with the imaginary receptionist.

'I wonder if you could do me a favour in the meantime, while I'm holding.'

'Fire away,' Robbie said.

'Do you have a computer in front of you? I'd like you to look something up on the Internet. If you're allowed to do that for clients, of course.'

'I'll check whatever you want on my BlackBerry, babe.'

'Oh, that's great. If it won't be a problem, could you please do a Google search for flight number 813.'

The constable looked up sharply at those words.

'I'm still holding for my lawyer,' Jade told her quietly, her hand over the phone. 'Just finding something out in the meantime. In connection with a case. I told you I was an investigator, remember? Look at your form. And I'm not fleeing the country, OK?' She rattled the cuffs, as if to emphasise her words.

The constable cupped her chin in her left hand. But she kept watching Jade, and with more suspicion than before.

Robbie's voice. 'Interesting.'

'What?'

'It's been discontinued.'

'What? Why?' Jade's heart began pounding hard.

'Withdrawn from service after an airline disaster, it says. Want the details?'

'Please.'

'August last year. Commercial airline flight Royal African Airlines 313 from Johannesburg to London. Flying via Freedom, Montapana, which is a tiny country on the northwest coast of Africa. The plane crashed on landing at the airport in Freedom. Everyone on board was killed. Is that the info you need? I can find out more for you if you like, but it'll take time.'

The lady constable's patience had run out. She grasped the desk and heaved herself to her feet.

'He's free. Oh, that's great. Please put me straight through,' Jade said hastily.

She waited a couple of seconds, then spoke again.

'Ian, it's Jade de Jong here. I need your help.'

Silence from the other end of the line.

'Yes, it is urgent. I've been arrested on suspicion of murder. I'm at Hillbrow police station.'

'You want out, babe?'

Jade swallowed.

She did want out. She needed to get out urgently. But even assuming that Robbie managed to accomplish the impossible and get her out of the holding cells, she was only too aware that there would be a heavy price to pay later down the line.

Asking Robbie for help felt like selling her soul to the Devil.

But if she didn't, she might not get out of jail in time to do what she needed to.

'You there?'

Decision made, then.

'Yes, that would be great,' she said, trying to maintain the fiction of talking to her lawyer.

'I'll try for you. I've got connections there. It may take a while, though. Maybe even a day.'

'As soon as possible, please.'

'I'll be waiting for you.'

'OK, then. Thank you, Ian. I know I can rely on you.'

Jade hung up and turned off her cellphone. When it was turned back on, it would require a PIN number to be keyed in before it could be used again. She really didn't want the police checking up on the last number she had dialled.

'Thank you so much,' she said to the lady constable. 'He's got meetings after lunch, but he'll come through later.'

The lady constable picked up the phone and called another cop. He stood by the exit door while she unlocked the handcuffs from the steel handle and cuffed Jade's wrists together behind her back. Then, holding the cuffs in the same way that the detective had done, she hustled her out of the door at the far side of the room and along a short passage.

Around the corner at the end was a row of sturdy-looking doors with small, barred windows set into each one at eye-level. The constable opened the door to the second one on the left, unfastened her cuffs and pushed her inside, none too gently. Jade stumbled forward and heard the door slam shut behind her, followed by the sound of a key turning in the lock.

The small cell had three other occupants, all black women. Two were huddled together on the hard-looking wooden bench. They glanced up at her, but didn't speak. The third was sprawled out on a filthy mattress on the floor, sound asleep.

Jade sat down on the small space that remained at the end of the bench and stared at the peeling paint on the opposite wall.

Her mind was still racing after what Robbie had told her.

The number 813 was a flight number that had been withdrawn from service last August after a fatal crash-landing in Freedom, Montapana.

And, just a few days ago, Craig had told her that he and Elsabe had met in August in a northern African city called Freedom, after his father and Elsabe's son had been killed in a horrific crash.

This was no coincidence. Somehow, one or both of them knew more about these killings than they were telling. Worse still, perhaps they were even directly involved.

Craig had told her he was leaving the country tomorrow morning with Elsabe. Flying to Namibia. Once they were out of the country, they could easily disappear into thin air.

Locked in a holding cell with no means of communication with the outside world, Jade could do nothing about it.

54

The holding cells remained quiet, the silence interrupted only by sporadic and muted conversation. Jade had no real idea of the time, but she thought it must have been about five P.M. when a police constable unlocked the hatch in the wall and pushed a tray through.

On it were four large plastic mugs half filled with strong black tea and eight thick slices of roughly cut brown bread smeared with margarine.

The bread was stale and the margarine smelled rancid. Jade knew she should eat; that any food would provide energy, but she couldn't bring herself to force down even one bite of these doorstop-sized hunks. The unappetising food was only part of the reason. Her stomach was in knots. Had she done the right thing by asking Robbie to help her escape? Or would his attempt fail, landing her in even deeper trouble?

She took a mug of tea, but no bread.

'You have it,' she told the other women. 'Whoever wants it, go ahead.'

Jade's offer was gratefully received. She watched one of the women carefully divide Jade's slices into three even portions using her fingers. After a brief conversation in what Jade guessed was Xhosa, one of the other women took a small bag of white sugar and a plastic teaspoon from a hiding place under the bench, and offered it to Jade.

'Thank you,' Jade said. It was a good exchange. She stirred two spoons of sugar into the lukewarm tea and drank it quickly.

A while later, when she heard voices coming from the entrance to the cells, she stiffened. Was something about to happen now?

No. It was only the change of shift. Another cop, an older grey-haired man she hadn't seen before, walked along the passage holding a clipboard and peered briefly into their cell through the large barred window. Once his inspection was over, the lights in their cell were abruptly dimmed.

Night had officially begun.

Her three cellmates took turns sleeping on the mattress, which Jade now realised was actually two thin mattresses, one on top of the other.

She stayed where she was, on the bench, and leaned over her knees and rested her forehead on her folded arms. It was an uncomfortable position, but she thought she must have dozed off eventually, because the next thing she knew, she was jerked wide awake by a commotion outside.

The grey-haired cop was escorting another prisoner to the holding cells. A wild-eyed, dreadlocked woman who was screaming and swearing non-stop. Her bare legs kicked out at the officer behind her and Jade heard him swear as one of the woman's high heels connected with his shin.

Jade glanced around at the other women. They stared at the new arrival with sleep-blurred eyes, but their frightened faces made it clear that this was not somebody with whom they wanted to share a cell. Jade's first thought was that the woman was on a monster drug high.

She actually had foam at the corners of her mouth.

The cell door clanged open.

The others shrank away as the dreadlocked woman lunged through, ripping herself away from the grasp of the cop who held her before he even had a chance to get her cuffs off.

And then she slipped on the concrete floor and fell forward onto the mattress, narrowly missing the woman who had been lying there moments before. To their horror, she let out a horrible, yammering scream. Her eyes rolled back in her head, her back began to arch and her legs kicked out wildly as she went into what was undoubtedly a major convulsion.

Foam drooled from her lips as her head snapped back.

'Call an ambulance!' the grey-haired cop cried, and his partner went sprinting back along the corridor.

Jade was about to grab her by her shoulders and turn her head sideways before she choked on her own frothing saliva, when the grey-haired cop wrenched open the cell door, grabbed the stricken woman's ankles and started trying to pull her out.

But then she realised that this was it. It was surely no coincidence that the woman had suffered a severe fit just as she entered the cell. This had to be the diversion that Robbie had set up for her. She certainly hoped it was.

She knew it was now or never. She had to make a run for it.

Leaping to her feet, Jade jumped over the fallen woman and shoved the crouching officer to the side as she grabbed the doorframe and pulled herself through.

He overbalanced, shouting in protest, but his voice was drowned out by the gleeful cries of her fellow inmates. 'Run fast, sister!' she heard one of them yell. 'Run!'

She was out of the holding cell.

She raced back down the passage that led to the front office. God, who was in on this and who was not, she asked herself. She knew an escaping prisoner could be shot on sight. Where was the cop who'd gone to make the ambulance call? If he was in the front office as she expected him to be, she'd have him to reckon with as well.

To Jade's relief, the front office was empty.

She burst out through the door and into the badly lit and almost empty car park. Just a few paces away, facing the exit gates, was a shiny black BMW, its engine revving.

Jade wrenched open the passenger door and flung herself into the seat.

Robbie was in the driver's seat. He didn't look at her. Before she'd even got the door closed, the big car was on the move. With a screech of rubber, he accelerated out of the car park, turned hard left and began a zigzag route through Hillbrow's back streets. When Robbie had put some distance between them and the police station, he slowed the car, allowing Jade to fasten her seatbelt.

He turned to her and grinned. His eyes gleamed and his lips drew back from his teeth, which looked sharp and predatory in the gloom.

'Welcome back, babe,' he said.

55

'Who was the woman that had the fit?' Jade asked, struggling with her seatbelt as the BMW accelerated round a bend.

Robbie shrugged, turning his attention to the road again.

'Friend of a friend. She's done this before for cash. Knows what to do. What to take to make it look real. She'll escape later, in hospital, when there's less security around. It was the way we had to do it. Otherwise the officers on duty get disciplinaries, you see. They want to help, want to earn a bonsella—a bonus, you know how it is—but they don't want to lose their jobs. This way nobody's to blame. Even so, it took time, because the old guy refused.'

'How did you convince him?' Jade asked.

Robbie's grin widened. 'Upped the payment,' he said.

Was there anybody in the South African police service who didn't have a price, Jade wondered. Her father had been incorruptible. At any rate, his reputation for integrity had been so fearsome that when criminals had needed to get him off a case, they had opted for the riskier, but more certain, route of murder.

There was David, too, she supposed. A man who chose to go back to an unhappy marriage for the sake of an unborn child showed great integrity.

A pity for her.

'So what's on the agenda?' Robbie asked.

He was heading down Louis Botha Avenue, approaching the sharp twist in the double-lane road that was known as Death Bend due to the number of accidents that occurred there. At this hour of the morning—four thirty-five according to the digital clock on the dashboard—there were no other cars on the road and they negotiated it safely, if too fast.

'I need to know about flight 813,' Jade said.

Robbie nodded. 'I found some more info for you. Interesting stuff. I've got it stored here on my BlackBerry.'

Turning left without indicating, he drove through a badly lit entrance into the otherwise-deserted car park of what Jade saw was the Doll's House, a twenty-four hour roadhouse. A sign on the wall read 'No Hooting, Flash Lights for Service.'

'I'll tell you what I know over breakfast,' he said.

The emptiness of the car park made Jade nervous. Parked at an angle in the middle of the worn tarmac, the black BMW was as obvious as a boil on the forehead of a beauty queen.

'Shouldn't we get out of the area altogether? The police are going to be hunting for your car.'

'The Hillbrow cops are on the lookout for a navy-blue Audi,' Robbie said. 'Cape Town registration plates. When I do something, babe, I do it properly. Your file's gone missing, too.'

A sleepy-looking waiter shuffled over and, without consulting Jade, Robbie buzzed the window down and ordered two large coffees and toasted egg and bacon sandwiches.

'Extra chilli sauce with the one,' he said.

When the waiter had shuffled away again, he turned back to her.

'So. Flight 813.'

'Tell me,' Jade said.

Robbie leaned back in his leather driver's seat and laced his fingers behind his head. Jade noticed a new scar on his left wrist. Ridged and inflamed-looking, it writhed its way up his arm like a snake.

A knife wound, she guessed.

'Flight 813 belonged to Royal Africa Airlines. Seems a couple of years back, some tin-pot dictator on the northwest coast of Africa decided to start up a service offering cheap flights to and from Europe.'

Reflected in the BMW's wing mirror, a pair of slow-moving headlights appeared on the road behind them. Jade twisted round to see better, but the car didn't stop.

'So business is good until, six months ago, Flight 813 takes off from Jo'burg with ninety-eight passengers on board. Comes in to refuel at the airport in Freedom, misses the runway, crashes, flips and breaks apart. Everyone was killed instantly. Most of the bodies were ripped to pieces. They had to fly the passengers' relatives in to ID the victims through DNA comparison.'

Jade felt suddenly cold. Her skin started to prickle and she wrapped her arms around herself.

Craig's words ran through her mind. 'My father was killed in a horrific crash, in a town called Freedom in the north of Africa. That's where Elsabe and I met.'

For some reason, Jade had assumed he'd meant a car accident, but he hadn't. It had been an airline disaster.

'Do they know what caused it?' she asked Robbie.

He lowered his hands, glanced down at the scar Jade had noticed earlier, and scratched it with the nails of his right hand.

'The jury's still out on that,' he said. 'They got the black box, but there's no official verdict yet. Seems there were no problems with the plane itself. It was an Airbus, and a fairly new one. Witnesses say it made a normal approach. No engine trouble or other problems. So they're down to two possibilities. Pilot error or an air-traffic control stuff-up. Possibly a combo of both.'

Air-traffic control. The words stabbed into Jade's gut.

'Air-traffic control how? There was no other aircraft involved.'

'Look, this wouldn't happen at Heathrow or JFK or OR Tambo International. It would be an impossibility. But according to a report I read from another pilot who did commercial flights via that airport, things were different up there in Freedom. Seems a culture of laziness had settled in.'

'What do you mean?'

'Apparently, the air-traffic controllers didn't like having to look into the early morning sun. Very bright and glaring, especially after a dust storm, which they get there from time to time. Now, Freedom airport has a number of different runways, some with more advanced navigation gear than others. But for early morning flights coming in, the air-traffic controllers would often direct them to Runway 9, so that the pilots would be arriving from the west and the air-traffic controllers wouldn't have the sun in their eyes.'

'But the pilots would.'

'Exactly. In addition, Runway 9 had older navigational aids, called runway direction beacons. It was one of the more basic runways.'

A knock on the car window made Jade jump. It was the waiter, carrying a tray. When Robbie buzzed the window down, the waiter immediately began attaching the tray to the rim.

'No, no, don't bother,' Robbie told him. 'We're in a hurry. We'll eat off our laps.'

He handed Jade a polystyrene mug of coffee and a paper-wrapped sandwich, and scooped the packets of sugar, salt and chilli off the tray and dumped them in the Beemer's centre console. Then he passed the waiter a hundred-rand note and closed the window.

The smell of bacon filled the car. Robbie opened his sandwich and bit into it with relish.

'Eat,' he ordered Jade, speaking with some difficulty through his own large mouthful.

Jade unwrapped her food and started eating. She kept watching the mirrors, looking out for approaching police cars, knowing that even if she did see one on the hunt for her it would be too late, because there was nowhere for them to go.

But in her mind's eye, what she was visualising was not a dark and silent street, but a sunrise over a stark, dry landscape. Fierce and bright, blazing through a haze of dust.

'So the pilot made his approach at sunrise?' she asked.

Robbie chewed and swallowed. 'Just after. I read a blog written by some aviation professional that said apparently one of the guys who'd landed there earlier that morning had radioed a warning to the Royal Africa Airlines pilot about the poor visibility. There had been a dust storm. He told him to request a different runway.'

'Why didn't he?'

'Who knows? Probably thought it would be OK. In any case, it seems those sort of requests didn't go down well in that cosy little culture. According to this blog I read, what the ATCs in Freedom Airport would do if a pilot started getting picky, was simply tell him to stand by. They could keep the guys doing that for all eternity, it seems.'

'My God,' Jade said.

Robbie nodded and looked down at the second half of his sandwich as if formulating his strategy for attacking it.

'This *is* Africa,' he said.

'And the pilot?'

'He was a good guy, from what I read. Very experienced. People used to want to fly with him.' Robbie shrugged. 'But somewhere between him and the ATC, someone screwed up. Guess it only takes once, in that situation.'

'I guess so.'

'Now the dictator, he didn't wait for the official report. As soon as whispers started about air-traffic control being responsible, he went ballistic. Blamed ATC for everything and fired all the crew who were there that day. Management and general staff. Old and new alike. Even the woman ATC who'd just been hired and was working her first shift that morning.'

Jade wondered if that woman had been Amanda Bolton.

'He made a statement to the press that went something like . . . let me think now, he used big words, so I saved this page on my phone.'

He held up his BlackBerry and scrolled through a number of screens until he reached the one he wanted.

'Here you go. "The reprehensible misconduct of these individuals has caused a tragedy of unforeseen proportions. They are responsible for the crash, the deaths of the passengers, and the destruction of so many lives. If I have my way, they will never work in the industry again."'

'Seems he managed to blacken their names enough to do that,' Jade said. 'Amanda started teaching scuba diving instead. And Themba Msamaya was still jobless six months on. And then both of them were murdered.'

'There was an earlier murder just after the crash, while all of this was going on,' Robbie said.

Jade stared at him.

'How do you mean?'

'A week after it happened. The manager who'd been on duty that day, a local man called Victor Dimishi, was stabbed to death at his home in Freedom. With all the relatives over there to identify the deceased, and all the fuss going on, it was hushed up. Never made big news. But there was a report about it on the Net.'

'Another stabbing?'

Robbie's eyes gleamed as he turned to stare at her. 'You mean there have been more?'

'I really need to see a list of the passengers.'

Robbie passed his phone to Jade.

'Google it,' he said, before stuffing the remainder of his sandwich into his mouth.

While Jade fought with the compact keyboard, squinting down at the tiny screen, Robbie stirred sugar into his coffee.

She raised her head as she heard another noise over the scraping of the plastic spoon against the bottom of his cup.

The noise grew louder. It was one she recognised immediately, approaching fast down Louis Botha Avenue.

Police sirens. Several of them.

'Shit,' Robbie said. He started the car, his head whipping from left to right, as if considering his options for escape.

'They're too close,' Jade said.

'They're after somebody else. Not you. It's a crime-scene call-out, I'm betting you,' Robbie said. 'But all the same, let's not take any chances right now.'

He slammed the Beemer into gear and it shot forward towards the roadhouse, sending steaming coffee splashing over the back of the cup-holder.

'Hang on, babe,' he said.

He whipped the car round in a tight left-hand turn and headed directly for the concrete panels of the roadhouse wall.

'Robbie . . .' Jade braced against the dashboard.

Just before he reached it, he swung right and into a narrow alleyway.

It led into a small backyard. Slamming on the brakes, he narrowly managed to avoid rear-ending the modest little Toyota Corolla in the staff parking space.

On the main road, two sets of sirens wailed past.

'Could be more coming,' Robbie muttered. 'Better to wait.'

Looking back down at the phone's screen, Jade realised that her search had produced results. Clicking on the link, she saw there was, indeed, a list of the passengers who had died in that crash. It was arranged alphabetically, with the age and nationality of each person in brackets after their name.

Jade didn't have to look far. The first South African was second on the list.

Aidan Marais, aged five. And then Matthew Marais, aged forty.

Jade felt the blood drain from her face.

'Elsabe lost her whole family,' she said. 'She lost her son and her husband in the crash. God, that's just so awful.'

Awful enough to push a woman over the edge and into murder? Jade didn't doubt it.

A twisted revenge, where guilty and innocent alike were made to pay the price for what she had perceived to be their wrongdoings.

No wonder she'd taken an instant dislike to Elsabe. Not because she was so different from Jade, but because she was so similar. Instinctively, Jade had sensed a quality in her that she recognised, and hated, in herself.

The ability to kill.

Jade had never used her ability on innocents, though, and Amanda Bolton had been indisputably innocent.

As a third set of sirens screamed past on the main road, Jade scrolled down further, to the surnames beginning with H. And that was where she made her second unwelcome discovery.

Because there was no Mr Hitchens listed.

Craig's father had not been on the plane. Craig had lied.

56

'We'd better get moving now, babe. You got what you need?'

Jade shook her head.

'What?' Robbie's voice was sharper now.

'There's something wrong here.'

'Wrong how?'

'Craig—he's Elsabe's partner now, I guess—he told me he met her at the crash site. That his father died there. But I can't find his father's name on the list at all. It isn't here.'

Jade breathed deeply, trying her best to dispel the icy feeling in her stomach. The suspicion that, all along, she had been lied to.

Had their meeting on the beach really been as coincidental as she had thought?

Or had Craig Hitchens used it—used her—to give himself an alibi for that night? In the predawn gloom, while she was sleeping, had he sneaked out to do what Elsabe had asked him to do? Or more probably, paid him to do.

She would have sworn on any bible you had cared to lay down in front of her that Craig had been genuine. The man had told her he was an environmentalist, for God's sake. She knew that was true, because he'd proved his knowledge to her. He'd described in detail the environmental implications of the oil-tanker disaster.

But that didn't mean he couldn't be a killer as well.

Jade bit her lip hard enough to make herself wince.

Why hadn't she considered this earlier? Had he been too convincing to arouse her suspicions? Or were her own instincts starting to grow dull?

Robbie released the handbrake, reversed back through the alley and pulled onto Louis Botha Avenue, heading in the opposite direction, away from the police cars.

'Where do you want to go, babe?'

'To Jo'burg Central police station. I'll have to sit down with one of the detectives there. Explain everything to him. I don't think they'll charge me if my file's gone missing. And when they hear the full story, they'll have to move fast and send a team to arrest Elsabe, and Craig as well. If they're flying to Namibia later this morning, I suppose they'll be able to apprehend them at the airport.'

Robbie shrugged. 'Your choice. You think any of the detectives will be there so early?'

Jade checked the dashboard clock.

5.10 A.M. It wasn't quite as dark as it had been. A faint shimmer was starting to appear on the horizon. Dawn was on the way.

'Some of them are early birds. Like Moloi.' The last person on earth she wanted to see right now, but still. 'I might have to wait a little while. But he'll be there by daybreak, I should think.'

By daybreak.

For some reason, the words gave Jade an uneasy feeling.

'I'm not going to hang around,' Robbie said. 'I'll just drop you and go, OK? And remember, babe, you owe me one now. I don't know when this other job will happen, but when it does, you're in it with me. Don't forget that.'

'I won't,' Jade said.

She closed her eyes briefly at that thought. It was growing lighter by the minute and, when she opened them again, she could see the surrounding houses, the trees and walls, in sharp relief.

More memories flooded back.

Craig's face, looking down at her, on the single night she'd spent with him. Every detail of his features was etched into her memory. The tenderness of his expression. The green flecks in his golden-brown eyes.

Craig again, talking about her twenty-twenty vision. Perfect eyesight, an attribute she possessed, and one that she shared with his father . . .

Another possibility occurred to Jade. Picking up Robbie's BlackBerry and stabbing the keys as fast as she could, she did another Internet search, only this time she wasn't looking for the passengers on the plane.

And there it was. His name. Mr Anthony Hitchens. Killed in the fatal crash of flight 813 to Freedom.

Adrenaline surged through her as she realised what this discovery implied.

'Robbie, I'm sorry,' she said. 'The plans have changed.'

'Changed? How?'

We need to get to Emmarentia, and we need to do it before the sun is up. If we don't, there's going to be another murder.'

She dialled Craig's number from memory and listened, willing him to pick up, the knot in her stomach pulling tighter and tighter with every ring.

It went through to voicemail, but Jade didn't leave a message. There was no point.

Robbie was driving at top speed, tearing through the empty streets of Houghton as he cut across the city on the route that would take them to the peaceful suburb of Emmarentia.

Christ, she hoped she would be in time to save him.

She needed to get there before dawn; before daybreak, because that was when the killing would take place, just as the others had done.

The plane had crashed at daybreak.

Craig had told her the truth. Now she understood the real reason for the strange and conflicted relationship that Elsabe had maintained with him.

His father hadn't been on the passenger list for a very good and very logical reason. He hadn't been a passenger.

He had been the pilot.

57

You descend, slowly and gradually, from the brightening skies. The air is like a road and, as your plane meets the warmer updrafts, you feel a series of gentle bumps, as if the highway you were travelling on had suddenly become rough and uneven.

Nothing to worry about. Just a little clear-air turbulence.

Except the air is not clear.

Cloudless does not mean clear. Not this morning, when the dust from the storm hangs in the air, as dense as fog, turning your visibility from good to poor.

And then there is the sun.

You arrived at the same time, you and the morning sun. It breaks over the horizon in all its blazing power and magnificence. Moving swiftly from a bright fingernail to become a full, red orb. And then brightening, as red turns to gold and gold to a whitish-yellow, reflecting off all the dust particles and obscuring what lies below.

Still low on the horizon, the sun is now so dazzling that you cannot possibly look into it.

The radio crackles with information and warnings. You hear them, but you do not listen. Perhaps you think you know better. Perhaps you disregard them. You are, after all, an experienced pilot. Runway 9 holds no fear for you. You have landed there after dawn on many other occasions.

But not at that exact time, on that exact date in the calendar, when the rising sun is at the height and angle where it shines directly into the cockpit.

Not on a morning after a dust storm.

You thought you knew better. You thought you knew it all.
You bastard.

You careless, murdering bastard. Your hubris, your misjudgement; the reasons why they died. Why those ninety-eight people died. All of them. Every single one, thanks to you, the killer.

My son, Aidan. My husband, Matthew.

I grieved the most for my boy. His was one of the first bodies found. I was spared the pain of having to go home with a box of bloodied fragments of flesh that only DNA analysis had been able to identify as being what remained of my child. I was spared that, at least.

But the agony of seeing his body. His beautiful face, perfect in death, as it was in life, looking as if he was only sleeping. Not even a scratch, not even a graze.

Below that, carnage. The huge ripping gash through his ribcage, the other through his gut. Two terrible injuries. Who knew what caused them? In all that devastation, it could have been anything. Anything at all. They said he died instantly, but that wasn't quick enough. He was torn, and so was I, never to be whole again.

You murdering bastard.

The Old Testament preaches an eye for an eye. But I will see you that and raise you.

A son for a son.

'We're not going to make it in time,' Jade said. She found herself blinking furiously, her vision suddenly blurred.

'Why do you say that, babe?' With a roar of the engine, Robbie sent the Beemer howling through a traffic light a second after it had turned red. 'We're going as fast as we can. We'll be in time.'

Jade shook her head.

'We won't. Not in time for him. We'll be in time to get her, but not him. The sun is already over the damn horizon, Robbie. It's up.'

'Not necessarily.' His fingers tapped a staccato rhythm on the dashboard as he drove one-handed, tyres squealing as he sped around the tighter bends on the winding roads. 'Depends where you are. This area is very hilly. If the house is west of a hill, it might be another ten minutes till they see the sun.'

'We'll have to get inside. Even if there's tight security, we'll be able to, won't we?'

'Yup. Free-standing house? We'll find a way in. I've got some stuff in the boot of the car that will help us.'

'What am I going to do then, Robbie?'

'You mean, if she's offed him already?'

'Yes.'

'We might be in time to save him. Knife injuries don't always kill instantly.' Robbie glanced down at his arm again.

'If we're not?'

'Make her go away, of course. You can do that. Easy-peasy, for good, no problem at all.'

'And then lose the only surviving witness to the truth?'

'What? You want to do a citizen's arrest?' Robbie frowned, as if struggling with the concept of leaving a victim alive. 'That's not a good idea, babe. Are you getting soft on me? I mean, the police find a man's body at her place, they'll know she's guilty, especially now all the evidence ties up. Family killed in the plane crash, tickets booked to Namibia and all. She disappears before she boards the plane, they'll just think she got the better of them. My feeling is, when you get a crazy like that, you put them down permanently. And fast.'

'Turn right here. This is Mowbray Road. Now we need to look for number sixty-four.'

Jade breathed deeply, preparing herself for what lay ahead. She unfastened her seatbelt and grabbed the door handle, ready for a swift exit.

What was she going to have to do?

She guessed it would depend on what she found.

Early morning, the soft light of daybreak, and the rich aroma of coffee in the air.

Craig stretched and rubbed his eyes, smiling. He realised the sound of his cellphone had woken him, but he didn't feel like rooting through his trouser pockets to find it now.

He climbed out of the tangled sheets and put on a pair of boxer shorts before following the coffee trail to Elsabe's neat and tidy kitchen. Pots and pans in gleaming steel hung from hooks on the wall and one counter was devoted to pristine-looking white and chrome kitchen gadgets, including a coffee grinder that had just been used. Next to the stove were some professional-looking chef's knives, set in a big wooden block.

Elsabe was already dressed. She looked ready to board the plane, pumps on her feet, her hair tied back, even a touch of lipstick.

'Shall we have coffee outside?' she suggested. 'We don't have to leave just yet.'

Craig followed her out to the back stoep, which overlooked the garden. It was neat and well maintained, apart from a deep drainage ditch that, judging from its raw edges, must have been dug quite recently.

His head was still muzzy with sleep and sex. Blurred but happy thoughts did their best to move through his befuddled brain.

'Sit down here and watch the sunrise,' she said. He glanced up at her in surprise, because the request didn't sound like an invitation. In fact, her voice was unexpectedly sharp, as if she was issuing him with an order.

'It's a bit late for that,' he said. 'Sun's just about up. But we can watch it get lighter, I suppose.'

He sat down on one of the chairs and looked across the garden, blinking in the brightening rays, enjoying the sound of birdsong in the trees. Further away, he picked up a faint rattling noise, as if somebody—a neighbour, perhaps—was struggling to get a stubborn gate to open.

He'd expected Elsabe to come and sit beside him, to pick up her coffee mug, but she'd disappeared into the kitchen.

She wasn't gone for long.

A few moments later, he heard her soft footsteps behind him again.

Acknowledgments

Writing a book is definitely a team effort, and my thanks goes to all the experts who generously contributed their time, knowledge and expertise towards answering my questions.

First, thanks to Chris Davies, ecologist, for his specially written 'worst case' report on oil spills. This was hugely helpful and I can't thank you enough for making the time to write it at such a busy point in your life.

Second, thanks to paramedic Mark Stanton who has the amazing ability to get answers back to me in nanoseconds no matter how obscure or difficult the medically related question is. Mark, you are great, and your help is truly invaluable.

Thirdly, thanks to tech/cave/CCR diver John Woods for reading through the relevant sections of the book and making the necessary changes as well as offering many other helpful suggestions to depict Jade's scuba diving experience more accurately.

And finally, I am grateful to the friendly folk on GunSite South Africa for enthusiastically answering all the questions about weaponry and shooting that I—ahem—fired off at them.

Thanks once again to my delightful editor Frances Marks from Forzalibro Designs—who manages to home in, missile-like, on all those 'little' mistakes and repetitions that creep in, and who emails me amusing pictures of miniature hippos to cheer me up when the going gets tough.

I am so grateful to Frederik de Jager, Fourie Botha and Fahiema Hallam at Umuzi for all their support and enthusiasm, to Hannah Ferguson and Camilla Ferrier from the Marsh Agency in London as well as Debbie Gill from Maia Publishing Services for the tireless work they have done on my behalf, and to the awesome team at Soho Press in the USA—Bronwen Hruska, Justin Hargett, Juliet Grames, Ailen Lujo and Mark Doten. I could not ask to be in better hands.

My final and wholehearted thanks goes to my beloved partner Dion. You are my rock and my inspiration, and I feel so blessed to share my life with you.